W9-BVE-737

PRAISE FOR

Dictatorship of the Dress

"Insightful, charming, and romantic." —*Heroes & Heartbreakers*

"Riveting and pitch-perfect . . . with an honesty and charm that is heartwarming and spellbinding. Topper's tale of loss and love is a winner." —*Publishers Weekly*

"Delivering a fresh twist on boy meets girl, *Dictatorship of the Dress* is full of endearing characters, hilarious yet plausible circumstances, and plenty of surprise twists and turns leading to happily ever after." —Tracy Brogan, author of *Crazy Little Thing*

"A stellar new voice in contemporary romance, Jessica Topper weaves the present and the past seamlessly to tell this sexy, funny, and oft times heartbreaking story. I adored this book! Ms. Topper is a must-read author." —Terri Osburn, author of *More to Give*

"Lightning-quick and full of surprising humor . . . refreshingly daring." —*RT Book Reviews*

PRAISE FOR

Louder Than Love

"An emotional ride with a to-die-for hero and with a sparkling ending. Topper is an author to watch!" —Laura Drake, author of *The Reasons to Stay*

continued . . .

"I was absolutely blown away . . . A wonderful story [and] amazing characters."
—*The Book Pushers*

"I can't begin to say all the reasons that I loved this book . . . I just found myself enraptured and so caught up with the story that I was talking to Adrian and hugging Kat in my mind."   —*Nocturne Romance Reads*

"A beautiful and engaging story that will melt your heart . . . Absolutely an emotional whirlwind and well worth the buildup! I don't want to say too much about the story itself because as I've said before, there is such a raw human element to this book that you need to experience it as it happens. My final words would be to read *Louder Than Love*. Allow yourself to be open to a new experience and reap the rewards! You will not be disappointed."   —*Open Book Society*

Courtship *of the* Cake

JESSICA TOPPER

BERKLEY SENSATION, NEW YORK

BERKLEY
SENSATION

An imprint of Penguin Random House LLC
375 Hudson Street, New York, New York 10014

This book is an original publication of Penguin Random House LLC.

Copyright © 2015 by Jessica Topper.
Excerpt from *Dictatorship of the Dress* copyright © 2014 by Jessica Topper.
Penguin supports copyright. Copyright fuels creativity, encourages diverse voices,
promotes free speech, and creates a vibrant culture. Thank you for buying an authorized
edition of this book and for complying with copyright laws by not reproducing, scanning, or
distributing any part of it in any form without permission. You are supporting writers and
allowing Penguin to continue to publish books for every reader.

BERKLEY® and the "B" design are registered trademarks of Penguin Random House LLC.
For more information about the Penguin Group, visit penguin.com.

Library of Congress Cataloging-in-Publication Data

Topper, Jessica.
Courtship of the cake / Jessica Topper.—Berkley Sensation trade paperback edition.
p. cm.
ISBN 978-0-425-27685-3 (alk. paper)
I. Title.
PS3620.O587464C68 2015
813'.6—dc23
2015005179

PUBLISHING HISTORY
Berkley Sensation trade paperback edition / June 2015

PRINTED IN THE UNITED STATES OF AMERICA

10 9 8 7 6 5 4 3 2 1

Cover design by Lesley Worrell.
Cover photo "Woman" by Tassh / Shutterstock.
Interior text design by Laura K. Corless.

This is a work of fiction. Names, characters, places, and incidents either are the product of
the author's imagination or are used fictitiously, and any resemblance to actual persons,
living or dead, business establishments, events, or locales is entirely coincidental.
The publisher does not have any control over and does not assume any responsibility for
author or third-party websites or their content.

Penguin
Random
House

For Amanda
Writer. Chef. Romantic.
Friend.

ACKNOWLEDGMENTS

If gratitude were a cake, this is how I'd slice it:

Laura Drake, Pat O'Dea Rosen, and Kristin Contino—you deserve huge, sweet helpings for keeping your eye on this book as it took shape. Thank you! Amanda Usen—you'd get the piece with "YOU ROCK" written on it in big swirly letters. I'm eternally grateful to you for the handholding, the brainstorming, and for making me your famous "Get Your Groove Back" soup when I needed it the most. Meesha Axelrad—here's your slice, with a big frosting flower on top, for helping me to better understand name signs and deaf culture. Any mistakes I made in describing ASL are completely my own.

I'm saving the frosting-covered corners for my agent, Nalini Akolekar; my editor, Leis Pederson; her assistant, Bethany Blair, and the entire Berkley publishing team. Any way you slice it, I couldn't do it without all of you!

And you, dear reader—every candle on the cake is dedicated to you, with my best wishes. I hope you enjoy this book!

While my characters are fictional, and their band, festival, and business names come from a fun place in my imagination, ankylosing spondylitis is a very real disease. According to the National Institute of Health, AS and other spondyloarthropathies affect 3.5 to 13 per 1,000 people in the United States. Strength, hope, and respect go out to all those fighting this battle, including Mötley Crüe guitarist Mick Mars. To learn more about AS, and how you can help, please visit www.spondylitis.org.

Dani

OVER THE RAINBOW

"Winner, winner, chicken dinner! I don't know how do you do it, Danica James."

"Easy," I replied, handing the garment bag over the counter and into Bree's waiting arms. "I say yes, spend money I don't have on a dress I don't want, sashay down the aisle in it, and then I donate it to you."

"The only hard part for Dani being a bridesmaid," Laney added, "is not showing up the bride. Otherwise, it's a piece o' cake, right, Dani?"

I watched as my best friend selected M&M's from the candy dish Bree kept on the counter, using a vintage pewter salt spoon. Laney was just as picky about the brown M&M's as David Lee Roth backstage at a Van Halen concert.

She had to go and mention cake, didn't she?

I thumbed the tiny silver charm that hung at the hollow of my throat and wondered how the term *cake* came to mean *easy*.

Bree laughed. "See? And the hard part for me is not showing up *as* the bride!" The shop owner held up her hand, fingers splayed to emphasize not only the number, but her latest rock as well. "Let's hope the fifth time's the charm, ladies."

Bree's habit of "falling in marriage" earned her spots on the local news and was the impetus behind the former fashion model falling into Diamonds & Fairy Dust, her bridal attire consignment business. The tiny Cornelia Street store carried everything from your suburban strip mall off-the-rack dress to the custom couture Vera Wang, which hadn't moved in the five years I'd known Bree. But once annually, she initiated Operation Fairy Dust, a dress drive for local high school girls in need, and accepted donations of gently used bridesmaid dresses to give away during prom season.

"It's gorgeous, Dani." She ran her hand over the ruched bodice and sweeping handkerchief skirt of the brilliant green gown. "We've still got a few schools in the area with prom approaching. You are going to make someone's dream come true."

Laney popped an M&M about the same hue as the dress in between my lips. "So what does she win?"

"Whatever it is, it had better be small enough to fit in my backpack. Unless it's a car, which I would totally accept," I laughed.

"According to my little black book of details, you have managed to donate a dress in every color of the rainbow . . ."

"And don't forget the ones she brought in that *weren't* colors found in nature," Laney reminded, turning to me. "Like that Creature from the Seafoam Blue Lagoon dress my mother made you wear at her wedding."

Bree laughed. "Earning the Rainbow Award is no easy feat. For that"—she rummaged under the counter and came up with the fluffiest rainbow Afro wig I had ever laid eyes on—"a picture on my Wall of Fame, if you will."

"You want me to wear *that*? I don't know where that thing's been!" It looked like a relic from New York's Studio 54 disco era.

"Trust me, it's new. No one but you has achieved rainbow status,"

Bree assured with a grin. "You take 'always a bridesmaid' to a whole new level, Dani."

Always a bridesmaid and never a bride worked just fine for me; marriage required commitment. Of course, so did insanity. Coincidence? *I think not.*

Laney just about choked on her last M&M as I stuffed my mass of blond curls under the synthetic skullcap and mugged for Bree's Polaroid. Then she threw on a wig from the nearby display so I wouldn't have to go through the humiliation alone. Laney was good like that.

"How do I look?" she deadpanned. The long, black Cleopatra wig was just shy of covering her poker-straight fiery red bangs.

"Ridiculous and lovely. Like Cher." I plopped a nearby tiara on the crown of her head, and we pressed our cheeks together for one last photo.

"Yeah, you should talk, Rainbow Brite. I think you used to have leg warmers that matched that hair."

Bree waved the developing print. "For your travels." She traded me the photo for the Afro, placing the small square into my hands as the image appeared, eighteen years of best friendship rising to the surface and solidifying like magic.

"I'm going to miss your visits, Dani. This one, though"—she reached to smooth Laney's fake bangs—"I have a feeling she'll be back. Just as soon as that new man of hers proposes."

"Hey, slow down there, Five Time's the Charm." Laney twined her own tresses with the long hanks of synthetic hair until it resembled a red and black candy cane. "Noah just finished paying off his non-wedding." The lovebirds had recently celebrated his near miss with Bridezilla by throwing a huge charity event in place of the already-booked reception, and were still recovering. "We're not in any hurry," she assured, but her mossy eyes blinked bright with the possibility.

Bree winked, more for my benefit. "Have fun. Be safe." Smiling, she moved on to help a customer.

Laney pouted and pulled off the wig. "I can't believe you're leaving, Dani—*again*. Just after I got you back. You tease."

"It's just for the summer, Hudson. Suck it up."

Despite all we had in common, Laney's homebody habits mostly confined her to the tri-state area without complaint. My wanderlust since meeting Mick, on the other hand, had grown insatiable.

As had my sweet tooth.

"For someone who loves to live out of a duffel bag, you certainly held on to that dress from your sister's wedding for a record length of time. I was getting ready to call the *Guinness Book*," Laney ribbed knowingly.

Posy and Patrick were about to celebrate their first anniversary, and I was nowhere closer to figuring out just what the hell had happened to me that night of their wedding in New Orleans. Or why I couldn't let go of its memories . . .

I stole one last look at the dress as Bree hung it in the store window. Its opulently embellished halter and keyhole neckline had been perfect for the discreet touches and stolen kisses Mick had lavished upon me in public; its wisps of tiered chiffon held every whisper leading us out of the reception and back to my room.

"A wise woman once told me never to let a dress rule my life," Laney murmured.

The serene girl who stood before me was a far cry from the hot mess who'd been appointed dress bearer for her mother's cross-country nuptials this past winter. The one who had frantically texted, asking *WWDD—What Would Dani Do?*—every step of the way, until she had found her own footing. With a hand on my back, she pushed me over the threshold and onto the quaint, one-block city street. "What would she tell you right about now?"

"I'm not as well-adjusted as you think I am," I mumbled.

"You are wonderful." Laney dropped a kiss on my cheek and an arm across my shoulder. "And I, for one, will always look up to you from my perch on your invisible psychiatrist's couch. As well as pay you in brunch food. What do you say?" She nodded toward the red-and-white-striped awning of the Cornelia Street Café. I knew tea and sympathy waited inside, as well as a willing ear if I was ready to talk about my rambling feet and broken heart.

"Sorry, girlie." I gave her a squeeze. "I can't stop; I've got to see a man about a car."

I was about to make my biggest commitment yet.

"So. How does zero interest for twelve months sound?"

My laughter reverberated off the chrome, steel, and safety glass surrounding me on the dealership floor. "Sounds a lot like my love life, actually."

I reaped the rewards of my own joke before the cavernous showroom quickly swallowed up the sound. It was fun while it lasted.

Kind of like my love life.

"Oh, please! I don't believe that for a second, heartbreaker." Jax propped his feet up on the prime Manhattan real estate that was his desk and flashed me a grin. "And everyone says used car salesmen are the scammers and con artists?"

Jackson Davenport was not your typical used car salesman, that was for sure. Upper East Side born and summers-in-the-Hamptons bred. Valedictorian of our high school, Ivy League educated, and handsomeness so rugged, you'd think he stepped out of a Patagonia catalog. But he'd swapped his silver spoon for a ballpoint pen long ago, which he was now tapping against his teeth impatiently.

"Are you going to take the car or not, Dani?"

"Hell yeah."

Summer tour was calling, but it wasn't going to come to me.

Jax popped out of his chair. "Good. Then let's get this paperwork signed."

He spread a tree's worth of paper in front of me and pointed at the first X. "So what happened to that last guy, Marcus? He was cool."

"Firefighter Marcus . . ." I signed with a flourish, and relished the memory of those heated discussions we used to have, along with the slow burn of his lips. "He was a nice distraction."

"How about the bartender?" Jax flipped the page. "Here, here, and initial here."

"Sam? Arm candy." I tapped my temple, and then mimed cocking a gun. "Pretty empty upstairs." I lifted my pen to indicate I had signed, signed, and initialed.

"And Noah's friend . . . from Laney's mom's wedding? Soldier Boy?"

Tim had been a perfect partner in crime for the timeless, torturous bouquet and garter toss at the Hudson-Crystal wedding in Hawaii. After our respective best friends had snuck away from the reception together, Tim and I had been just about the only singles left on the dance floor to endure the humiliation. Tall and agile, he had barely needed to raise a hand to catch the lacy bit. And the flowers had landed right in my hands, despite Lady P, one of the many Elvis impersonators on-site, and her valiant attempt to dive for it in her skintight, rhinestone jumpsuit.

I let a wicked smile slip, remembering how Tim had eased that garter belt up my thigh, fingers climbing so high that I had to smack him with the bouquet to make him stop.

"Soldier Boy was fun," I admitted. He and I had both arrived in town last week to attend Laney and Noah's charity soirée for the Kitchen of Hope and had had even more fun. "But now he's back overseas."

"Pity. Mona and I really liked him."

While I had my dalliance du jour, Jax had long-term *relationships*. Mona—or Bitch'n'Mona, as Laney liked to call her—was his latest ladylove. She had appeared on the scene after I'd moved out of state for my last job, so I didn't know her all that well. But if I knew Jax, it was serious . . . until the day it wasn't. My friend was an open-and-shut textbook case of serial monogamy.

Jax leaned over my shoulder and guided me through the last of the forms. His cologne had a hint of chilled cucumber with a citrus bite, and hung from his neck like a scrapbook for my senses. I was seventeen and running along the ocean shore again, not thirty-two and running away from my memories of Mick.

If that was even his real name.

"Tell me you're not still thinking about Mystery Man from a year ago?"

"Yep."

And I was still dreaming about him, too . . . especially on the nights when I ate dessert after eight o'clock. Mick had been just that sweet, just that sinful, and just that much of an indulgent fantasy.

"Lucky is the thief who steals your heart, Dani . . ." Jax murmured.

Yeah, right. Not to mention the twenty thousand dollars in wedding gifts that disappeared that night.

"Please, don't start. Posy has finally agreed to speak to me again." I ran my fingers along the creamy silk ribbon at my throat, avoiding the charm tethered to it, and refrained from saying more.

While I sometimes found it easier to talk about it with Jax than Laney, I still hadn't been completely honest. The past year had hardly been a cakewalk.

Despite what Mick did to my family, I couldn't shake him from my thoughts. "But you were the one who pulled the slutty Cinderella, right? Leaving him with a hard-on and a glass slipper at the end of the night?" Jax shuffled, collated, and stapled my paperwork while wearing a frown that either indicated intense concentration, or massive disapproval.

Swallowing hard, I managed, "I just thought . . . he was different."

"No, you thought he was perfect. And he wasn't. So your playdar wasn't working that night? Time to forgive and forget."

I sighed; during the plane ride home from my sister's wedding in New Orleans, I had managed to work through all five of the Kübler-Ross stages of grief over Mick's deception: denial, anger, bargaining, depression, and acceptance. Forgiving was in there somewhere.

But forgetting? Kind of impossible. Not when those pale blue eyes haunted me every time I closed my own. His were icy like a husky dog's; mine were more of the Fiona Apple variety. Our gazes, made more electric and mysterious from behind the vintage masks Pat and Posy had insisted everyone wear during their reception, had locked in on each other the moment he'd stepped onto the dance floor.

I replayed his every move in stark, cinematic loops. And I heard his soft, sexy voice in stereo surround sound. I rewound my favorite parts and tortured myself by examining them in slow motion. Mick smiling. Tilting his head back in laughter. Touching my chin. Removing his black and gold Scaramouche mask by its long-beaked nose as he moved to kiss me.

"I still can't believe I fell for a wedding crasher."

"You may just have met your match," Jax gently teased. "Funeral crasher."

I blushed at the title, thinking back to the day he and I met. I hadn't meant to attend the solemn graveside service for Jackson's family's patriarch. But if I hadn't, this townie never would've met the teen tycoon turned used-car salesman sitting across from her. Rolling his pen between his fingers in thought and absorbing everything around him, even though his imagination was light-years away.

Jax didn't need the job at the car dealership. But he took any opportunity to study the human condition as fodder to fuel his fiction.

"Maybe you'll write that story into one of your books someday."

"Maybe." Jax came back to earth and smiled at me. "But right now, I want to put you in the driver's seat. You ready?"

He grabbed my hand, and we wound past the Bentleys and Lamborghinis smugly gracing Jax's uncle's showroom floor. The Davenport footprint was stamped all over Eleventh Avenue, where most of Manhattan's elite car dealerships sat. It had also worn a path down to Wall Street and back with its hard work and success.

Back in high school, hitching a ride with Jax meant showing up at the mall in a vintage Porsche Spyder, and posing for prom pictures in front of the Lotus used on the set of a James Bond movie. Until Laney and her high school sweetheart Allen had decided to reenact a Whitesnake video on the hood of Grandmother Davenport's Jaguar, resulting in a ban on young Jackson borrowing the keys to the family cars.

June heat rose from the city concrete and licked at my bare ankles as Jax pushed me gently through the automatic door and we left the air-conditioned building behind. Still, a shiver rode up my spine as smooth, cool hands slid in place to block my vision.

"You ready? No peeking, Danica James."

"How can I peek with your hands over my eyes?"

Jax knew me too well. I reached to pry his fingers apart to sneak a look, just like I'd do when he'd try to protect me from the gory parts in a horror movie.

His hands dropped to my shoulders, mingling with my curls, and we both gazed upon the mustard yellow Volkswagen bus baking in the midmorning sun of the back alley.

"You like?"

"Oh my God. It's perfect." I gave his hands a squeeze, then shot forward to run my own down the VW's flat face. "How on earth did you get it?"

"Mugged a hippie." I threw him a look, and he laughed. "I put my feelers out. Auction in Michigan. It's a 1972 Westfalia. Fully restored, with a pop-up top."

"I see that." Teetering on the tiptoes of my sandals, I scoped out the camper's interior through the long side window. "A sink?"

"Yep, along with a few other upgrades. Built-in closet, icebox. Table folds out. Convertible bed, the works." Jax rocked back on his heels, pleased with himself. "Check out the seats; I think the upholstery is original."

"Avocado green. So sexy!" I reached through the open window and tentatively touched the wide steering wheel. The cogs in my head were already turning. "How many miles does it have on it?"

"Seventy-nine five."

Not bad for a car ten years older than me. But still. I was going the distance. "Will it last me all summer?"

"It's going to get you where you need to go," Jax said.

I grimaced. That wasn't exactly the answer to my question.

"Treat you to lunch?" he asked. "We can hit the Rocking Horse."

"Depends. Where's your evil twin?"

Dexton Davenport hated me with the fiery passion of a thousand suns. And was often Jax's lunchtime companion if he roused himself out of bed early enough.

"Midtown. I think he was hitting Sam Ash and a few other guitar stores today. Come on," he coaxed. "Manhattan's big enough for the both of you."

"Dex despises me."

Jax rolled his eyes. He'd been stuck in the middle of this tug-o'-war between me and his brother for years.

"No, Dex is just in a mood."

"He's been in a mood since your grandfather's funeral."

Jax laughed. It was a fairly accurate observation; what teenager wouldn't be grumpy upon learning of a deathbed confession that rocked his cushy little world, threw his family's inheritance in jeopardy, and forced him to slum it out in the suburbs for the rest of his high school career?

Jackson Davenport, for one. The good twin.

"So . . . carnitas and margaritas?"

His offer was poetic and tempting.

But I really needed to get going while I had the light.

"Rain check," I promised, throwing my arms around my friend. "How can I ever repay you for this?"

"Make good on the loan," he laughed. "Gypsy masseuse heartbreakers carry their checkbooks out on tour, right?"

"Always." My fingers performed a fluttering effleurage down his spine. "And maybe you'll take me up on that offer of a massage someday?"

"Rain check on your magic fingers," he managed, pulling away before he allowed himself to melt into me. "Oh, and I took the liberty . . ." He reached through the passenger window and pulled out a pair of custom vanity plates stamped with WWDD.

"Oh, Jax." Now it was my turn to melt as I watched my friend affix my favorite motto to my ride.

"Listen to that little voice inside your own head for once, will ya? W-W-D-D?"

What Would Dani Do?

The phrase echoed as I navigated Mean Mistress Mustard, my new old van, through the snakes of traffic and into the Lincoln Tunnel with her headlights on.

It was true; my friends always looked to me for that voice of reason. My perfect mixture of level-headedness and levity. *Just walk away*, I had told Laney tenfold, guiding her through the land mines that came with loving a rock star like Allen Burnside. *Live a little*, I had urged her, when I knew all she wanted to do was die a little after losing him to cancer. And *be open to a grand adventure* were my words that helped get her on that plane to her mom's wedding and move her from heartache to happiness with Noah.

I needed to take my own advice, and taking the job as a backstage masseuse for the Minstrels & Mayhem Festival tour was certainly a start.

The tunnel rose, darkness dashed away by the unblinking eye of the summer sun.

And I would forget Mick.

Starting with no dessert after eight o'clock at night.

The Caged Bird Sings

I had plenty of time on my hands while they rested on the wheel, driving four hundred miles from Manhattan to Hampton, Virginia, for the first stop on the tour. Plenty of time to think about everything, and nothing. And I had come to the conclusion that even the most down-to-earth brides are entitled to their one crazy Bridezilla moment.

For my sister, it was the birdcage.

From the minute Posy spied it during a weekend of antiquing in Cold Spring Harbor, she made it her mission to incorporate the Victorian cage into her wedding plans. It didn't concern her that the thing was tetanus-inducing rusty and large enough to house a vulture. She fell in love with its graceful arches and scrollwork, and paid a mint to have it re-enameled before shipping it to the wedding reception in New Orleans.

It became the silver-stamped motif on her one hundred invitations, and graced the thank-you cards for later. And it had sat, stuffed fat with stiff envelopes for the happy couple, on a long table next to her beautiful hummingbird cake during the entire celebration. All evening long, guests came by to admire both, and to slide their own gifts through the thin, curving slats of the cage. I know, because Mick and I had passed the table at least a dozen times as he swept me off my feet, around and around the ballroom floor. I'd watched the pileup inside, a jumble of pastels and pristine white forming the newlyweds' nest egg. Assuring their future together was off to a solid start.

"Tell me you have the cage."

The tremor in Posy's voice was in stark contrast to the melodic laugh that had followed her around like a little fairy bell during her wedding. Just as the morning sky outside my hotel window, gray with the threat of rain, had been a world away from the golden sun that had streamed down on the wedding party the day before.

"You were my maid of honor." Hysteria wavered through the phone line. "I put you in charge of the cage. It's gone, Dani! It's disappeared."

How the hell could someone have walked out the front door with a gaudy two-foot-high birdcage full of gifts, and not one person had noticed?

I clutched the hotel bedsheets to my naked chest; they smelled vaguely of cake and sweet dreams.

They smelled like Mick.

And he had disappeared, too.

The newly blended immediate family had gathered at the police station to wait for any news.

"We've never had anything like this happen before," assured the catering manager. It was unnecessary, as it didn't make us feel special, or any better. "We are cooperating fully with authorities, and they are reviewing our security tapes now. They don't think it was an inside job, but there is a . . . person of interest we recognized in the footage."

"They're looking at all the cameras, honey," my mother stressed, turning toward me. "Including the videographer's and the digital ones from the vendor rentals. Is there anything you'd like to tell us?"

"Yes, how about it, Dani? Starting with the mystery man you were four inches away from fucking in the photo booth!" Posy screeched. Pat steadied her with a hand to her arm, but I saw his fingers shake. His parents discreetly turned their heads from their new daughter-in-law's justifiable rage. Probably wondering about the questionable morals of the family their son had just married into.

My father's face was stone, only his eyebrows giving away the one thought that I knew had crossed his mind many times throughout my adolescence: I wish I'd had sons. My mother's disappointment was mirrored in his. Wondering how my brain and all its bad habits had formed, despite all their careful parenting. And how they could have spawned one child to follow in their sane, staid footsteps, while the other one turned out to be, for lack of a more scientific term, boy crazy.

Remorse had coated the bitter pill of pride I swallowed. "If anything he said can be believed, then he's waiting for me at the Café Du Monde."

I pulled Mean Mistress Mustard into the first rest stop over the Maryland border. Coffee sounded good right now. Wiping my eyes, I sighed. There was no use in rehashing the memories now. Even Posy had advised against it, once she broke her silent treatment. "Abreaction is so nineteenth century," she joked. Psychologist humor. "Stop beating yourself up about it, Dani."

Well, if the current school of practice frowned upon reliving past trauma, then I would take the cognitive therapy route—a hands-on, practical approach to changing behavior—and I'd achieve it one massage client at a time. Working my way upward through my chosen professional path, and keeping my mind off my joke of a personal life.

The Calling

"Will you marry me, luv?"

The most famous man at the festival had an accent that was crisp and delicious, even when muffled by the face cradle of my massage table. "Christ," he moaned.

I laughed and reached for my revitalizing oil. His wasn't the first proposal since the Minstrels & Mayhem tour had started a month ago.

"Somehow I don't think your wife of twenty-two years would approve." Not to mention he was, at sixty-two, twice my age . . . and a grandfather.

It was so much easier to talk to musicians when they were lying prone and pliant under my hands. Especially when they were as famous as the current client in my tent, who went by one name only and probably had more Grammys lined up on his shelf than I had little amber bottles of essential oils.

I chose two—lemon for energy, basil for clarity—and added tiny amounts to the almond oil I had warming beside me. He had mentioned a dull back pain from sleeping awkwardly during his seven-hour flight over, so I knew my custom blend would work wonders before he had to take the main stage that night.

He was the buffest, sexiest rock-and-roll grandfather on the Minstrels & Mayhem tour, that was for sure.

"My wife doesn't have your magic fingers." He shuddered as I worked my way toward the groove between his spine and erector spinae. Using my knuckles, I slid slowly and strongly along the length of the groove, the oil helping me glide with ease as I worked out each knot of tension along the way.

"There you are," I whispered to a particularly stubborn trigger point, which finally gave under my pressure, and the reward was seeing his strong shoulders release. The platinum recording artist was putty in my hands.

"I want to"—he gasped—"pack you in my road case and"—my stripping technique down his back caused his sentence to staccato—"take you on tour. Good God."

It was high praise for this influential artist to want to add me to his daily regimen, along with his yoga and macrobiotic diet. But I couldn't let it go to my head.

"Thank you, sir."

"Now, my dear. I'm not nearly old enough to be a sir. I quite like my title of CBE, and I highly doubt the queen will be knighting me anytime soon."

Earning a playful wink from the Commander of the Order of the British Empire currently lying shirtless on my table made up for the low pay and grueling hours of my dream job. Not to mention the rampant sexist comments, endless "your mama" jokes and insufferable pull-my-finger gags I'd been subjected to since coming to work for the dudefest known as Minstrels & Mayhem.

I loved my work. And getting the chance to massage a legend was the proverbial icing on the . . .

I sighed and dared a glimpse at the clock to the right of my table.

One of these days I'd make it through a few blessed hours without the memory of New Orleans.

We bantered a bit more before finishing his hour-long massage in comfortable silence.

"Bloody amazing," he murmured as my hands finally came to rest, signaling the end of our session. I took my leave outside the tent to give him privacy as he dressed, feeling equally exhilarated.

Stretching my arms toward the sun, I observed the festival grounds waking up around me. From the second stage came the muted thump of sound check. Security was checking wristbands as fans flowed from the lots through the venue gates. One of the younger Marley brothers' brand of reggae jingled cheerily over the PA, a perfect summer soundtrack. Blankets and lawn chairs already dotted the hill where music lovers would spend the day, and evening, watching the rotating lineup of bands.

I smiled and squinted, allowing my eyes to fully adjust. Out of the calm, cool shade of my massage tent, I could tell the day was going to be a scorcher, both musically and meteorologically. Stagehands were already scaling the scaffolding like tanned monkey gods, while others took respite from the sun in bright-striped hammocks swinging beneath the main stage.

Music and massage. This was where my worlds collided.

I had found my calling.

All the kids I knew in young adulthood had had clear visions of what they wanted to be when they grew up, and noticeable talents. Laney was creating her own comic books before I even met her. Allen had never been without a pair of telltale sticks in his back pocket as a teenager, drumming his way through high school marching corps, garage bands, and into the hearts of millions with his group, Three on a Match. Jax could craft paragraphs that produced laughter, tears, and demands for more in the short time it took to ride the Montauk line of the LIRR from his house to mine. And Posy had followed in our parents' footsteps, PhD in hand and on a tenured university track before the age of twenty-five.

Other than providing my friends with my own quirky brand of pop psychology, I hadn't known what my skill sets were. Until the day I walked barefoot across a boyfriend's back on the dusty floor of his college dorm room, and the innate therapist in me was truly born. I had no idea that type of massage had a name (Ashiatsu) and its own equipment (wooden bars installed overhead) and that there were actual schools devoted to the ancient Asian practice. But I knew that I wanted to, and I could, help people both mentally and physically through massage.

"You're a little overqualified for this job, aren't you?" Maxine, who ran artist hospitality for the festival, had frowned at my credentials and glowing recommendations. "I guess doctor of physical therapy wasn't enough for you, then?"

My Ivy League–educated parents weren't about to let me go half-cocked out into the working world, so I came armed with my BA in psychology from Hofstra and my graduate coursework from Columbia. It took me two more years, on top of my original seven, to gain the additional hours of education and hands-on clinical experience required to become a board-certified massage therapist. But being stuck practicing in an office had never been on my agenda.

"Here's what I expect: dependability, respect, and the utmost professionalism while you work with the artists." Maxine had held my Working laminate backstage pass close to her face, forcing me to stare her down while keeping my eye on the prize. "And here's what you *shouldn't* expect: Glitz. Glamour. Tips. An easy ride. Got it? You're not here to get your drugs on, be a groupie, find a husband, land a recording contract, or any of the other rock-and-roll fantasies. You are here to work, is that clear?"

"Crystal," had been my reply.

Now, tilting my face to warm it in the sun, I smiled. I was here to work right through the summer. Music had never failed to help me, heal me, and hold me up over the years, so it was only fair I returned the favor. This was my next big adventure, right here and right now. No looking back, just facing my soul forward, like the lyrics from my favorite Shonnie Phillips song.

Go through it, darlin'. Not around it.

It was the perfect place to lose oneself. And no one was hiding behind pretty masks and false promises here.

"You're wanted."

Riggs Munro was standing in my sunlight.

It was hard to believe this guy was the mover and shaker behind one of the hottest bands in the industry today. The guys in Go Get Her might've been lean, mean, rock-and-roll machines, but their tour manager stalked around the festival grounds half the time like a pissed-off Pillsbury Doughboy.

"Wanted—how?" I asked. "Dead or alive?" Riggs smirked, as if he didn't care either way. "Elaborate."

"You're *needed*. How's that?" His smirk diminished, and I saw the tension he was holding around his eyes soften. I imagined the job of a tour manager was not an easy one, only hard-asses need apply. "He's in a lot of pain, and asking only for you."

I rolled my eyes. There could be only one "he" Riggs was referring to, and it was current "it" guy, Nash Drama. And he and I hadn't exactly gotten off on the right foot. The late-night incident on the Go Get Her tour bus had happened a week ago, and I had been steering clear of backstage during his set times ever since.

"I can't massage on his bus, Riggs. I could get fired. Your star player's going to have to come here."

Riggs turned and nodded politely toward my last client exiting the tent, then did a double take.

"I'm still levitating! Cheers, Dani." The most famous man at the festival flipped down a pair of shades and took off in a slow jog, back toward catering.

"Was that . . . who I think it was?" Riggs was temporarily derailed.

"Yep." I smiled. "Wow, even jaded tour managers get tongue-tied in the presence of true greatness, huh?"

"Holy shit, he looks good for his age. Better than when I saw him perform at Live Aid like, thirty freakin' years ago." He seemed to remember his mission once again, pulling himself up straighter. "Listen. Nash isn't on his bus. He's in a trailer in the artist compound, right over there. Come on. You owe him one."

Maxine's decree echoed in my head: *Dependability, respect, and the utmost professionalism while you work with the artists.*

You're here to work.

I sighed and dipped back into the tent to grab a few essentials. True, I may have owed Nash Drama a favor. But he owed me a major apology for insulting my intelligence.

One for the Road

Of course my van had broken down two weeks into the tour. Mean Mistress Mustard had given a shudder and a sigh as I coaxed her toward a hilly stretch along Route 321 between Boone and Charlotte, North Carolina, as if to say, "Girlfriend, you want me to do *what*? Please, bitch. I'm forty-two years old."

I had stood by her bumper, cursing Jax and his entire unborn line of privileged progeny. And swore at myself for passing up the chance to caravan with my fellow masseuse, Jade, and her family. Her husband Travis was on the tour as well, selling and blowing beautiful glass in vending, while tending to five-year-old Delilah until Jade's massage day ended. We often rode in tandem between shows for safety and for socializing. If Travis couldn't stand one more go-round of "The Wheels on the Bus" in their family Subaru, he would jump into my VW and we'd belt out "100 Bottles of Beer on the Wall" for the next hundred miles. Or Jade would ride with me so we could gossip about our work-day, away from the eagle ears of Maxine.

They had stayed on to camp in the Blue Ridge Mountains for the off day, while I had been more interested in the creature comforts in town. A much-needed night's sleep in a real bed, followed by a bus-man's holiday of a full-body massage and sugar scrub.

"Take the scenic route," the locals at the gas station advised when I'd inquired about the two-hour journey to the next stop on the tour. "The sun will set over the forest and there's so much less traffic than on the interstate."

Yeah, well. No traffic meant broken down and stranded until well after the sun had set. My cell phone dropped two calls to AAA before I was finally told a tow would arrive "within" ninety more minutes.

A bus had wound its way around the curve and had begun to slow. NO ONE YOU KNOW, the destination signage above the windshield proclaimed. I had seen the same bus idling back behind the stage at the last four shows, but wasn't sure which artist occupied it.

Had I known, I might've taken my chances with the side of the road.

The tour bus door had burped open a few yards up from my broken-down van.

"Kylie, get yer ass back up here and let me take a look!" Half a body leaned out the door; I glimpsed a bare foot and long leg, followed by the teased-up hair of a smiling girl, before whoever was fighting for rights to the narrow stairs won out. "You okay?" demanded a hipster with graying muttonchops and an impatient twitch to his right eye.

"Not hurt. Just broken down." Thunder grumbled from somewhere over the treetops. "There's a tow truck coming, supposedly."

He eyed my laminate. "Well, come on then. Unless you want to waste your day off sitting in some Podunk town, waiting for a repair."

Given the age of my vehicle, I had a feeling the fix might take longer than a day. After quickly surveying my options, I grabbed my duffel bag.

"My daddy always says to fly something white from your mirror!" It was the girl again, squeezing past Mr. Twitchy.

I looked back at poor Mean Mistress Mustard, looking dark and dejected by the side of the road. I couldn't even get her flashers to work. And as much as I made fun of Laney for always wearing drab colors, I realized I was no better. What was in my duffel looked a lot like what I currently wore—black tank top and dark jeans. Dark and neutral were a massage therapist's go-to attire, best for not distracting clients or showing stains.

"Here!" The girl peeled off her white lacy camisole and tossed it to me. The bra she revealed was about as minimal as two postage stamps and some Silly String, but she didn't seem to mind. "I'm fixing to get naked anyway."

Wow. So not something I would say within the first three minutes of meeting someone, but to each her own. "Thanks." I dashed back to the car. The wind was picking up in the hills, and the flimsy garment whipped at my face as I went about securing it to my side mirror. The first slashes of hard rain began to fall, just as I hauled myself up the steep steps and onto the climate-controlled quiet of the bus.

"Welcome! I'm Kylie!" The girl threw her arms in the air like she was hosting a surprise party. "We're the Dramettes!"

She hugged me to her almost bare chest, and I knew the saying "give you the shirt off their back" would never be the same for me again. The two other girls lounging on the couch behind her gave bored waves.

"Cool. I'm Dani. I massage, backstage. Are you an all-girl band?"

"They're groupies." The guy made himself heard over their peals of laughter. "Riggs Munro. I tour manage Go Get Her." He turned to the bubbly trio. "Let's not wake the sleeping giant, ladies."

"He's not sleeping," complained one of the girls. "He passed out on me."

"Power nap," Riggs insisted. "He needs one after—and before—drinking."

"My daddy says you should always eat a greasy meal before you go drinking," Kylie informed everyone. "Fatty foods stick to the lining of your tummy." She rubbed her bare, flat abs in thought. "Maybe someone should've given Nash a burger when Go Get Her got offstage."

The band name I certainly recognized, as they were the summer's darlings of the main stage. The festival's four headliners all took turns closing out the shows, and these guys must've hit the road right after their set. I peeked over Riggs's shoulder toward the curtained-off section of the bus, amused to think the rock stars were cradled in there like babies in their bunks while the "grown-ups" up front carried on.

"Kylie, didn't your daddy ever warn you about hanging around backstage doors?" Riggs cracked.

She cocked her head to the side like a bemused poodle. "Come to think of it, that's one bit of advice he never gave me." She shrugged her shoulders happily, like that explained everything. "Oh well!"

"I'd better go check to make sure he's still breathing," Riggs muttered, lurching toward the back of the bus and disappearing behind a door at the end. "They don't pay me nearly enough for this."

Now that the curtain was moved, I could see all the bunks on either side of the aisle, and they were unoccupied.

"Where's the band?" I asked the girls.

"Probably in Charlotte already. They ride separate. We stayed back to party with Nash."

"Why does one guy get his very own bus?"

There was a ruckus coming from the lounge at the back of the coach, and the girls all exchanged glances.

"Because I can?" roared a voice, slurred with alcohol.

"Because he's an asshole?" Riggs chimed in from behind him.

"But admit it, I'm only drunk when I'm an asshole. Right, Riggs?" Six feet, four inches of intoxicated rock star filled the front cabin. He seemed proud of his logic, which probably made more sense to anyone past the legal limit. "Helllllloooo, ladies."

The bus hit a pothole and he lurched to grab hold of something *solid. In this case, it was me, and down we went, into the cozy dinette space. Awfully convenient how his hands pinned themselves between my ass and the cushioned leather bench I landed on. Two packaged condoms fell out of his bowling-style shirt pocket and onto my cleavage.*

"Hot damn, you're gorgeous. All blond and big-eyed, with those pouty blow-me lips . . . just like a little blond china doll. Wanna move this to the back of the bus?" he stage-whispered.

"You need a shower." And a toothbrush.

Not exactly the most memorable first line I'd shared when given airtime with a celebrity. Or the most flattering.

He shook his shaggy blond hair into his eyes with exaggerated effort. "So you wanna do me in the shower, then? Tight quarters, but I'm game."

"I think you mean gamey." I didn't have much range of motion, but was able to fan my face with my hand and pluck his condoms off my skin. "I'm not doing anything, or anyone, on this bus."

He freed one hand to inspect my laminate. "This one you give a pass to, Riggs?" he complained. "And not . . . not . . . whatsherface . . . you know, the chick with the big j—"

"Jailbait," Riggs dismissed.

"I'm not a groupie. No offense," I added, nodding to the girls.

"None taken." Kylie blew me a kiss.

"And just because I am wearing a pass doesn't give you license to touch my ass."

"Oh look, everyone. A poet! So talented. Is that an Artist pass? No? Just the hired help?" He stared me down. "You do know who I am, right?"

"Yep. A drunk asshole with his own tour bus. Color me impressed."

"Let her up, Nash." Riggs sighed, as if this was something he had to remind his charge of daily. "She works hospitality."

"Well, she's not being very hospitable." Emphasis on the spit.

"Still touching my ass."

He slowly slid his hands out from under me, sitting up and holding them, palms out, at his chest with an innocent "who me?" pout. I shimmied up to a seated position, but he still kept me trapped on the wide bench.

"You're awfully touchy for someone who doesn't like to be touched. Whatsyername, China Doll?"

He may have been drunk, but his watery green eyes channeled depths that, on a normal day, I might've taken a plunge into. But it wasn't a normal day; it was almost midnight and I was bone-tired from working, hands-on, for hours straight. And while employed by the same festival, Nash Drama and I lived in very different worlds. He would get his crazy-dollar-amount guarantee, no matter if he crawled onstage and played the same one note for his entire ninety-minute set.

And me? I would get fired if I so much as looked at Maxine or one of the artists the wrong way. Her words of warning boomed louder than a stack of Marshall amps onstage. Dependability, respect, and the utmost professionalism.

"What's . . . your . . . name?" Nash repeated, obnoxiously slow and loud as if I were new to the language, or hearing impaired.

"Dani."

"And how did you end up on my bus in the middle of the night, Dani?"

"My van broke down, and your tour manager was nice enough to stop and give me a ride."

"Pfft. Riggs isn't nice. Is he, girls?" The Dramettes all giggled and flashed their legs and lashes Nash's way, but his eyes stayed on me. "Riggs has to play the bad cop. I get to have all the fun. Now let me show you a real ride." He proffered up the condom packs again, with a crooked grin. "I won't break you, China Doll."

"Go fuck yourself."

So much for respect and professionalism. But at least I still had dependability on my side.

He dropped the grin, and the condoms. "Good thing you"—he took a swipe in my general direction with a pointed finger—"won't remember any of this in the morning," he announced, swaying slightly. Before I could say a word, his head hit my lap, long legs splaying into the aisle. Out like a light . . . and trapping me in the dining booth.

The groupies groaned, any possibility of being his runner-up for the night obliterated. They didn't seem to hold it against me, however, as they said their good-nights and made their way to the empty bunks in the belly of the bus.

Riggs set a pillow on the table in front of me and plumped it with a meaty paw.

"Seriously?"

"You're welcome." Riggs had finally cracked a smile. Kylie grabbed his arm and they jumped over Nash's long limbo-stick legs.

Looked like the bad cop was going to get lucky.

Whether he was recalling the same memory or not, Riggs wasn't smiling now; the tour manager's mouth was a grim, crooked line as he led the way out of the VIP tents on quick, bowed legs. We passed rows of luxury coaches, their generators purring and windows discreetly darkened, until we reached the artist compound. The inner sanctum of the festival was surprisingly vibeless. Its courtyard was a ghost town, fashioned out of single-wides that were way too nice to ever end up in a real trailer park. Riggs muttered his usual mantra as he held open the flimsy door of the hospitality trailer for me.

"They don't pay me nearly enough for this."

Thorn in the Side

A blast of sweet, cool relief hit me. So this was where the promoters were hiding the air-conditioning! Dang. What the trailers lacked in vibe, they certainly made up for in climate control.

The tour's headlining bad boy was on the thin mattress of the hospitality trailer, shirtless and writhing in agony. His hair tufted in peaks that either obscured (or accentuated) the devil horns that were no doubt lurking under there. Despite the comfortable temps, a thin sheen of sweat rode high on his forehead as he rolled his eyes in my direction, then back up at the ceiling.

"What on earth did you do to yourself?"

I set down my massage gear and tried to assess the situation, but it was hard to get a good vantage point, especially with him jerking around. The bed took up the entire back space of the RV, leaving me no choice but to climb on and kneel beside him.

"Didn't you hear?" Riggs spoke for him.

"Sorry, I don't subscribe to the Nash Drama fan club bulletin."

Deciding to keep him supine, I found two pillows in the cabinet above the bed, still in their plastic, and slid them under his knees. The bolster allowed his lower back to imprint against the mattress, and he let out a trembling hiss. Good thing the mattress was still encased in plastic, too; we were gonna get greasy. I grabbed my Biotone gel.

"I slipped last night," he managed through gritted teeth. "Came down on my hip." His right hand fluttered alongside his body, "And shoulder. Spasms from hell."

Riggs added, "It was that damn whipped cream."

I raised a brow. "Let me guess. You slipped on whipped cream and . . . fell into a pit full of bikini-clad Jell-O wrestlers?"

"Very funny, China Doll. I fell onstage." He bit his lip and winced as I slid my hands under his shoulders and went to work on his upper back. "The singer in the time slot before us got a pie in the face. It's a birthday tradition among the band members, apparently."

Riggs was pacing, which wasn't easy to do in the small space of the trailer. "I'm going to hand that crew their asses on a platter. They had ample time to make sure the stage was cleaned up."

"Kill me," Nash moaned. "Fuck me, just kill me now."

"No one is going to kill you, or fuck you, on my watch. Just try to relax." My fingers continued their light stroking. Compared to the loose, drunken puppet I had met parading down the bus aisle, today's Nash was a bundle of tender, tight muscle groups. I gently worked my way along his upper back, from the center and out.

"Does this hurt?"

"Like a bitch."

I was barely applying any friction. Something didn't seem quite right. My hunch wasn't to go deeper.

"Find a focal point," I advised, knowing that it could help take his mind off the pain.

He zeroed in on my chest above him like he wished he had X-ray vision. "I've seen those breasts before," he pronounced confidently. "Cannes, right? We were in a hot tub. On Kid Rock's yacht."

"In your dreams," I muttered.

Although I had to admit, I had always wanted to go to the south of France.

A smile briefly broke through his grimace. "I think you're right."

I kept my pressure steady and my pace slow, watching his face for signs. His jaw was in a permanent jut, as if he was just waiting for me to hit the spot that was going to send him howling toward the ceiling. But little by little, I felt him melt into my touch and his face went slack, eyes fluttering closed.

Riggs was back in the doorway, leaning in to survey the progress. "You know what they call you, right?"

"Who?"

"The chick that runs backstage." He snapped his fingers, trying to recall her name.

"Maxine."

"Yeah. And the others working hospitality. They call you Doc Ivy."

I blushed approximately two shades darker than my coral paisley sundress, according to the mirrored wall across from me. I hardly felt doctor-like, with my skirt and Nash's skull tucked between my knees. Or with my cleavage in his face. But there was no ideal way to work on him in the confined space, unless I had him rotate his body toward the one side of the bed that wasn't flush with the trailer walls. And I really didn't want him moving at all.

"I'm not a doctor," I murmured, crawling off the mattress and positioning myself at Nash's feet. Gripping one of his long, denim-clad legs under the calf, I carefully brought it up and propped his bare foot against my shoulder.

"I'm going to call you Doctor Feelgood anyway." Nash let out a groan, his hands falling useless against his broad chest. "Much better than the pill pushers trying to"—his breath labored as I laced my fingers around his knee—"numb me up and send me back out."

"Pull your knee away from me," I instructed, as I provided the counter-resistance to work his hip flexors. "What kind of drugs? Pull for ten, nine, eight . . ." I kept counting down, but my brain was whirling through the info he huffed out in small doses. A stockpile of narcotics, anti-inflammatories, and analgesics over the years, not just from this incident.

"The last doc he saw told him it was sciatica," Riggs supplied. "Pumped him all full of stuff."

"I don't think he has sciatica."

"Good," Riggs laughed. "That's so not a rock star disease. More like a little old lady disease."

Not exactly accurate, but I let it slide, concentrating on the areas of concern. There were more to them than met the eye, and my experienced touch. After working both left and right sides, I had him switch to pushing against me.

"What the hell are you doing, prepping him for childbirth?" Riggs asked.

"I'm pulling the muscles to let the joint relax," I explained. I turned back to my client. "Push for ten, nine, eight . . ."

"Relax? Nash Drama doesn't relax. He drinks. He passes out. That's his idea of relaxing."

Riggs wasn't helping matters any. The trailer was small enough without him throwing his weight and his two cents around.

"How about some privacy, please? I think he'll relax more without you breathing down his neck."

"Yeah, dude. Her breath smells better than yours any day of the week." Nash sputtered a laugh as Riggs stomped down the stairs, but the teeth embedded in his bottom lip were a dead giveaway to the discomfort he was experiencing.

"Think you can roll over for me?"

"Of course." He winced as he changed position. "I can play dead, too."

At my request, he pulled his knees up to his chest, facedown on the bed, prayer-style. I had spied Nash shirtless and careening around on the stage, but it was a fascinating flip of the coin to witness him at rest. Passed out in my lap on the tour bus hadn't counted. I ran my hand up the column of his spine, letting his body speak to me. His entire dorsum, from broad shoulders to tapered waist, rose and fell under my touch. The lone tattoo that rode high on his shoulder was a bluebird in flight.

"What?" he asked, hearing me suck back a gasp.

"Your bluebird tattoo."

"It's a swallow. What about it?"

"Nothing, I—I've just seen a similar one." So many fine points of my night with Mick in New Orleans were etched deep enough to leave a mark. A sharp memory of my fingers tracing the shape of his tattoo while cradled in his arms as he relayed its meaning rose painfully to the surface. "That's all."

"Spontaneous decision with my best buds. We all got them, one crazy night when they came to see me on my first big tour. It was something to commemorate how far I had gone. You know, like a sailor, when he's sailed ten thousand miles."

"I've heard . . . it was for the hope of a safe return home."

Mick had sounded so wistful that night, yet so full of hope at the prospect. And I had obviously been so caught up in him that I ignored every other warning sign.

"For some? Maybe. Not me." Nash cast a glance at it, frowning. "I should get a matching one; God knows I've logged enough miles to earn a flock of them."

I moved along his strong shoulders, kneading in long, gliding strokes. We settled into a quiet rhythm, while outside the small trailer window, the festival continued on at its own frenetic pace. My mind began to thumb through the pages of my mental textbooks, thinking about various possibilities. "Little old lady diseases" be damned, there were a hell of a lot of debilitating conditions that tended to strike a patient when they were young, bulletproof, and thirty feet tall. Although the right side of Nash's body had taken the brunt in his fall, his entire sacroiliac joint seemed to be a hot spot.

"Does this area always give you problems?" I asked, my fingers barely ghosting over where his spine met his pelvis.

"Stiff as a motherfucker most of the time," he hissed. "Since I was a teen. Some mornings I can barely get out of bed."

I began a series of circle strokes, massaging over the muscles and not the joints. His shoulders relented in small increments, and a sigh of relief pooled from deep within him.

"So," he started, when breath and speech came easier to him. "You got a boyfriend waiting for you back home?"

"Home?" I began, my fingers snaking up to knead the back of his neck. "I left home broken down by the side of the road last week." Mean Mistress Mustard was still out of commission, sitting south of the Mason-Dixon Line. Jade and her family had generously made room in their six-person tent for me, and I was happy to take turns behind the wheel for them when we pulled up stakes after each gig. But I felt bad constantly crashing their family time. I knew one phone call back to Jax would remedy the situation, but I didn't want to have to rely on him to bail me out. "No boyfriend."

"Swinging the other way, then?" He turned his head to one side and I could see the lascivious grin beginning. "I could see you putting the l-l-lick in lipstick lesbian."

"Sounds like you're dreaming again." God, was this guy incapable of sustaining a normal conversation for five minutes? Laney sat like a devil on my shoulder, telling me to give him a good old-fashioned Vulcan nerve pinch. Instead, I worked my fingers up the base of his skull, satisfied when I saw the goose bumps rise on the flesh of his bare arms.

"I've got a guy who could probably fix your van. Gimme a few days, okay?"

I had a feeling Nash Drama was the type to have a person in every port, happy to do or give things to him. I had a feeling he was used to the getting and the doing, too.

"I think you need to get to a doctor," I murmured as my hands came to rest. An hour-long soft tissue massage was a Band-Aid, at best. I could only give him so much.

"I've got you, Doc Ivy. What more in life do I need?"

"You need a rheumatologist. And quitting drinking might be a good idea, too."

He fell silent, and I feared I might have crossed the line. After all, I was—as he had pointed out on his tour bus—the hired help. And the guy had been photographed with a bottle in his hands more often than not, making me wonder if he had an endorsement from the liquor company, rather than the guitar manufacturer.

"That wasn't a judgment," I added quietly. "I'm just thinking if you have an inflammatory issue—"

"You're not the first. To tell me." He slowly came to an upright kneeling position. Resting his chin on his shoulder, he locked his gaze on me.

"And?"

"And I'll consider it."

"Good."

I moved to the tiny kitchen sink of the trailer before realizing there were no hookups; the taps turned uselessly under my greasy grip.

"So, what's the diagnosis?" Riggs wanted to know, barreling back up the metal steps.

Nash shrugged back into a tight black T-shirt. "She wants to play doctor with me."

Cute. "No, I said you need a *real* doctor." I fished into a dish tub on the counter keeping the beer cold for a few pieces of ice to rub my hands clean.

"Then she suggested we get a room."

He grinned, and ducked as I threw an ice cube at him.

"*No,* I suggested you get a rheumatologist. Obviously you require an interpreter as well."

Nash swung his arms back and forth, and swayed from side to side. Hard to do in the narrow confines of the trailer, but apparently easier now that I had warmed and stretched his muscles. "Good *job,* Doc Ivy," he drawled. I just rolled my eyes and shook my head. "I feel like a million bucks. If you show me your G-string under that cute little dress, I'll shove a few dollars in to show my appreciation."

Unbelievable. "Gee, I think I liked you better when you were writhing in pain."

"Kidding!" he yelled after me as I tripped down the steps and stormed toward catering. Thanks to this asshat and his boo-boo, I had missed half my lunch break. "Come see my three o'clock set. I'm dedicating a song to you."

Kid's Play

"Jade, can you cover my three o'clock?"

My fellow therapist reached to check the appointments clipboard hanging from the pole of our massage tent. "No problem. Hot date?"

"Please. Just wanted to catch Go Get Her's day set." I didn't wholeheartedly believe that Nash would dedicate a song to me, and with titles like "Get Me Some," "Head Girl," and "Ex-Sex," I wasn't really sure I wanted him to. But I couldn't deny my curiosity was piqued.

Jade frowned. "Go Get Her doesn't have a day set today." She showed me her phone app with the daily itinerary and sure enough, they weren't on until well after dark.

Liar, Liar, custom-made leather pants on—

"On the Lemonwheel stage?" Jade hooted a laugh. "No way!"

Her finger tapped the time slot and the detail appeared. Nash was appearing solo on the stage in the Kids' Zone at three o'clock for a "family-friendly sing-along," apparently.

"You've got to be kidding me."

Curiosity was for cats, and monkeys named George. I now had to make it my life's mission to get over to that stage by three o'clock. All I could picture was Nash, with his Norse god hair and his leather pants low-slung on his hips, trying to control his potty mouth and win over the sippy-cup club.

"Jade, can I borrow Delilah?"

"Yay, Kids' Zone!" Delilah grabbed my hand and together we skipped halfway across the festival grounds to the bright green-and-yellow-striped tent. A bounce house was rocking sidestage, and Minstrels & Mayhem's youngest attendees were Hula-Hooping, crafting, and hitting bongos under the watchful eyes of their parental figures and the competent Kids' Zone staff.

I felt a little bad using Delilah as my ticket into the twelve-and-under event, but then again, she never missed a chance to play in the Kids' Zone. Or to catch the musicians rotating daily on the Lemon-wheel stage.

Sure enough, Nash was standing on the low platform, checking levels and tuning up. The production was pretty low-fi compared to the main stages, but I still gave the "earplugs in" reminder. At five years old, Jade and Travis's daughter was a veteran festy-goer, and plucked her own brightly colored foam plugs from the kangaroo pocket of her overalls without needing assistance. A small crowd had already gathered to watch, but behind the fencing set up to keep the family-friendly area separate from gen pop, a large group of Go Get Her's faithful following and curious adult fans sans children waited to hear this bonus and obviously rare solo set.

"Who's that pretty lady?" Delilah asked.

Kylie was waving madly at me from behind the fence. Thankfully she had more clothes on this afternoon than she had had on the tour bus that other night. "Just a friend I made here at the festival." I smiled and waved back as Kylie bopped around in anticipation of the music.

Delilah nodded, plopping herself down on the grass cross-legged.

"I've made some friends. They're all kids, though. Daddy tells me not to talk to the adults unless I'm with him or Mommy or you."

"That's very wise," I told her, kneeling to her level and giving her little shoulders a squeeze. I couldn't help but think of Kylie and her "my Daddy always says" words of wisdom from the other night. *Daddies, don't let your babies grow up to be groupies*, popped into my head, to the tune of the old country song about cowboys.

"Howdy, folks!" a bubbly MC in a neon orange Kids' Zone T-shirt boomed into the mic. "We've got a special treat for you today here in the Kids' Zone! Please give it up for Go Get Her's Nash Drama!"

Kids old enough to clap, clapped; those who were too little sat and stared, or their parents pressed their hands together. The crowd behind the fence whooped and cheered, even though they could only see the back of him. Nash gave me a tight smile, making me wonder whether Riggs had lost a bet, or pulled the short end of the stick. But once he adjusted the strap on his sparkly black guitar, he seemed to resign himself to his fate.

"Hey, guys. It's my first appearance on the Lemonwheel stage, so please be kind. And sing along if you know this one." He began to strum lightly and recite the alphabet. "Of course you know this one. I'm just warming up."

He rolled his eyes as if he were bored, but every child in the audience sang, screamed, and laughed along. When he got to Z, he pretended to take a snooze, letting his chin drop to his chest. Delilah giggled next to me.

"What? Huh?" He sat up with a start. "Sorry. I was just catchin' some Z's," he drawled, lazily slapping at the air. "There's some over there." He pointed over our heads, and kids turned to look. "And there! Grab 'em!" Little hands swatted and swiped overhead as Nash kept his guitar strings buzzing like bees. "Got those Z's? Let's shake them around and get them really dizzy." He cupped his hands and shook, and all the kids did the same. "You, too, dude." He gestured to a huge papa bear with a shaved head and tribal tattoos snaking around his huge biceps, sitting with twin boys on his lap. "What, are you too cool for this?" The other parents laughed as the guy gave in, shaking his head first, and then his meaty paws together.

"Good job, guys. We got them so dizzy, they got all turned around. They're backward now." Fingers flying over the frets, he launched into the alphabet backward, twisting the song smoothly from Z to A before jumping off the low stage.

"Not so bad, for a drunk asshole with his own tour bus." His whisper in my ear brought heat to my cheeks.

"You weren't supposed to remember that," I mumbled in amusement.

Next, he launched into a song that anyone who owned a television set in the last four decades would know. All about sunny days and sweet air . . . except Nash forgot the words, and the tune, about halfway through. He clamped his mouth shut before the f-bomb could detonate. Little Delilah did a face palm.

"It's been a while, okay? Haven't had time to watch much TV these days. Gimme a request."

"'Jumpstart My Heart'?" a mom in the crowd yelled hopefully.

"The MILF in the back wants to hear my breakout song," Nash drawled, not looking up from his fingers as they turned the pegs of his guitar. "What do you all think, should I make her beg for it?"

It was my turn to face palm, as a few adults groaned, a few more whistled, and the kids didn't know what the hell was going on.

Go Get Her's biggest hit was stupid-catchy and its lyrics were passably PG-rated and pleasant. So much so, it was hard to believe Nash would own up to writing it. But his one-man version got the kids up twirling and the adults' hands up in the air. I stole a glance toward Kylie, who was banging her pretty blond head and kicking her hooker heels against the fence in time with the music.

Everyone, Nash included, seemed relieved to have blown off some steam as that one came to a close. Cupping her hands to her mouth to be heard above the applause, Delilah yelled, "'Wheels on the Bus'!"

with as much conviction as a drunk in the crowd bellowing for Sky-nyrd's "FREE BIRD!" The kids in the audience clapped their approval.

"Okay, Pigtails. There's something in the entertainment industry called a teleprompter. Do you know what that is?" Delilah shook her pigtails in response. "It's a little TV that sits on the stage where no one can see it, except for the singer who's too stupid or burnt to know the words."

A little boy tugged on Nash's jeans leg. "You shouldn't say the S word," he scolded, his big eyes earnest.

"Right, right. Sorry. How about that S word? Is that one okay?" He didn't wait for confirmation. "So if you want to hear whatchamacallit, 'Wheels on the Bus,' you're gonna have to be my teleprompter."

Delilah hesitated, giving me an uncertain look. "It's okay," I assured her. "You can if you want."

Nash snapped his fingers offstage and the Kids' Zone MC brought another microphone out for Delilah. He let her take his stool while he stood. "I know the tune, but you need to give me the verse, okay?"

She nodded, biting back her grin. "You have to do the hand motions, too," she instructed.

"Hey. They just pay me to play guitar. And I only have two hands."

Delilah rolled her eyes and the audience laughed. I thought to pull out my camera just in time, so I could film her stage debut to show to her parents later. She and Nash went through a call-and-response, going through the traditional verses of the sing-along until he felt comfortable enough to add a few of his own, somewhat questionable, lines. "The towels on the tour bus go stink, stink, stink," got the kids all plugging their noses, and Nash taught them to pump their fists as he sang, "The bunks on the tour bus go rock and roll," all the while with a gleam in his eye that went far above the heads of any of the children. I shook my head and laughed.

"The ladies on the tour bus go . . . 'Hi, Nash!'" He wiggled his fingers flirtingly.

"Hi, Nash!" all the kids (and Kylie) bellowed back at him. Oh, this man was insufferable. His ego was inflated about as big as the bounce house.

". . . aaaaall over the world!" He strummed a crescendo and mugged for a few cameras. Delilah took a bow and brought the house down.

"Last song of the day, people. And I promised I'd dedicate this one," Nash murmured into the mic.

He cranked up the distortion and I thanked the heavens for small earplugs as he began to jam out a punk version of the old Kenny Loggins crooner "Danny's Song" for my benefit. His facial expressions gave some of the lyrics a whole different meaning for me, and I couldn't help but laugh and sing along.

"Do you want to wait for his autograph?" I asked Delilah afterward. She shook her head. "Okay, let me just go throw this in his case and then you can go jump in the bounce house for a bit, okay?"

"Ooh, can I throw it? Pretty please?"

"How can I deny such cuteness? Of course."

"Why a dollar?" she asked, staring at the bill I handed her.

"It's his tip," I explained. "And an inside joke."

And petty and juvenile, but he deserved it, after his G-string comment to me earlier.

"Well, that went over about as well as a pregnant pole-vaulter."

Nash, finally done with autographs and photos, joined me where I waited for Delilah to bounce herself silly.

"Come on. Not bad for your first time," I joked.

"You're the only one who left a tip," he complained. "And don't deny it. I know you sent the kid to do your dirty work."

I laughed. "You ready, Dee-Dee?"

"Ten more bounces," she hollered back.

"She yours?" Nash asked.

"Huh? Oh. No. I borrowed her. From my co-worker."

He turned to watch the mayhem in the bounce house, shading his eyes from the sun. How he wasn't roasting in his second-skin jeans

and that black T-shirt was anyone's guess. I could feel my own sweat
beading at my neck, frizzing my curls, and trickling down my cleavage
and into my sundress.

True to her word, Delilah bounced right out of the house after ten
hops and pushed her feet into her mini-Tevas. "Did you thank him for
your song?" she pecked at me, like a little mother hen.

"No, but thank you for reminding me." I turned to Nash. "And
thank *you*."

He gave a little nod of acknowledgment. No thank-you for the
hands-on healing from earlier, no apology for the dollars in the
G-string comment, but like the swift-moving clouds in the crystal blue
sky overhead, all seemed to have passed over.

"One, two, three, whee?" Delilah asked.

"Oh, I don't know, honey. His back was hurting him earlier." I
turned to Nash. "It's this thing we do. When two of us walk with her,
we hold her hands and swing her up on the count of three."

"Back's fine." He grunted. "Lay it on me, Slick."

Delilah slid her little palm into his hand, and I scooted to her other
side.

"One . . . two . . . three," she drawled as we all took big steps,
"whee!" Up went her feet, and we hauled her into the air and back
down, far from where she started. It was a little Mom trick of Jade's
to efficiently cover ground fast when little legs couldn't keep up. We
made it about five *whees* to where Riggs had just pulled up in his
festival golf cart, no doubt ready to whisk Nash away from the humiliation and back to the safe confines of backstage where he belonged.

"Take a backseat." He thumbed to Riggs. "I'm gonna drive them back."

I stopped in my tracks, surprised, just as Delilah made it to the
count of three on her own and propelled out of our grip, landing in a
cloud of dust in front of the golf cart. "Yay, golf cart!" she crowed.

"I don't think . . . thanks, but—"

"What? You want me to take a Breathalyzer test before you'll ride with me?" He leaned against the metal supports of the cart's roof and gave me a lazy brow arch.

"No. I just figured . . . you had somewhere else to be."

"Nowhere but away from them." He jerked his head in the direction of the eager fans that were still pacing along the fencing, hoping to catch a photo or an autograph as he left the Kids' Zone compound.

Riggs had already moved to the rear-facing jump seat of the small cart, phone to his ear on a call. Delilah scooted into the middle of the front seat and patted the spot next to her. I sat.

Nash climbed in, turned the key no bigger than a windup toy's, and turned to Delilah. "Hang on, kid."

Wind and dust kicked up as he floored it, and the sights of the festival blurred colorfully by us. What would've been easily a ten-minute walk to the backstage area was accomplished in a mere minute or so. Riggs hopped off before the cart came to a full stop, phone never leaving his ear, and loped toward the production office. "Where to, ladies?" Nash asked.

"Home, Jeeves!" Delilah pointed due west.

"Her dad is a glassblower," I explained. "He's set up over by the festival merch." We were off once again, bumping along the gravel path toward vending.

Festivalgoers stopped in their tracks at the sight of one of the head-lining artists blowing past them in a golf cart. Some gave his name a shout-out, others gave chase for a few yards before realizing he wasn't going to stop and chat. The laminate around Nash's neck fanned out behind him in the wind, reminding me of an eager dog with its head out a car window, tongue out and ears flapping, enjoying the breeze. Delilah clutched my knee as we careened down a small hill, her eyes tearing from the wind. "The wheels on the golf cart . . . ?" she prompted.

"Kid, I'll give you your dollar back if we never have to sing that again."

"It wasn't my dollar, it was Dani's," she informed him.

Nash pretended to drive off the path in shock, much to Delilah's delight. Then he pulled a three-sixty, causing even me to squeal and grab hold of the bar alongside the seat. We were off again, in a beeline in the direction of Delilah's pudgy pointed finger.

Travis tried to play it cool as his child was delivered by rock star messenger, but I could tell he was on the brink of losing it, especially when Nash handed Delilah a few of his engraved guitar picks to keep.

"I'd better get back to work or Maxine will have my head," I sighed. Trav and Dee-Dee waved us off, and Nash puttered toward backstage once more. Without Delilah as a buffer between us, I searched for something to say. "You're good with kids," I began.

"I've got one." The words came out slow, as if he was testing them out for the first time.

"Oh? How old?"

Nash squinted, not taking his eyes off the path in front of us. "Older than Delilah. Younger than you."

"Well, I would hope so," I chuckled. Nash couldn't have had more than five years on me, at most. "Do you get to see him much when you're on the road?"

"I've never met him."

Despite the open frame of the golf cart, our conversation felt keenly intimate. I was at a loss for what to say.

"Would you like to, if given the chance?"

"Can we get a 'Fame and Fortune' tonight, Nash?" a guy asked as we slowed to cross the barricade into the backstage area. He had a Press pass on, notepad in hand, and a photographer was trailing behind him. Nash gave him a thumbs-up as we pulled past security. "Is that a yes?" the guy called.

Nash came to an abrupt stop along the edge of the tree line near the artist compound. He pulled the brake and hopped out. The photographer scuttled alongside the reporter to catch the exchange.

"Sometimes," Nash said, and I knew it was more for my benefit than for the reporter's. "I don't get to choose."

Rock and Rote

Go Get Her's front man and I fell into a pattern as our rock-and-roll circus moved from town to town, just as routine as load-in, sound check, and curfew. Nash automatically became my first client of the day, even if his name didn't always make it onto the schedule on the clipboard. I loved a challenge, which made him my ideal client. Whatever ache or pain he had woken up with, I massaged away, while he swore like a sailor being dragged to his watery death by a sultry siren. Our sessions were becoming the stuff of legend among the other therapists and the musicians who frequented the massage tent.

One rainy morning, I received an SOS text from Riggs with a series of cryptic numbers to follow. It was the key code to Nash's tour bus door lock.

"I can't keep coming to you, China Doll," he managed through thin, tight lips between gaps in the pain. Squirming, like the plush sex-den bed at the back of the bus was his personal torture rack. "Not every time."

"Have you seen a doctor yet?" I asked, caught somewhere between my own personal ethics and the Hippocratic oath. He always gave me the same answer: he'd go when the tour was over. It was against my better judgment to keep working on him when I didn't know the root of his problems. But there was no denying I provided the relief that let him perform each night.

"Bringing tears of joy to my eyes, every damn day when I rise," he'd joke, panting at the end of each session like he'd just completed a half marathon. But often before we began, pain robbed him of the ability to speak.

"Everything's going to be all right." It was a mantra that came out of me in a whisper as I smoothed his hair out of his eyes and got down to work.

These private pain parties were invite-only. Sometimes Riggs would oversee, but mainly it was just Nash and me. Never the Dramettes. And certainly never the other members of Go Get Her.

Despite the magic we accomplished each morning, when the tour bus was rocking late into the evening, I never came knocking. Besides, the artists weren't the only ones who knew how to party like rock stars. On the rare off nights when we didn't have to rush to pick up stakes, or had already set up camp somewhere in preparation for the next tour stop, the hospitality crew let its true hair down. Even Maxine would turn a blind eye to our midnight antics, as long as we cleaned up after ourselves and were ready to report to work come morning.

Spin the Bottle Karaoke was a crew favorite. Whoever was pouring the shots got to spin the bottle, and whomever it landed on was forced to sing the spinnee's choice from the eclectic array of CDs we all brought. It often resulted in hilarious pairings, like Jade and Travis doing a death metal duet, or Deuce from catering shaking his massive ass in his striped Zubaz chef pants and channeling his inner Shakira to our screaming Waka Waka chorus.

"You know I got it. These hips don't lie!" our hulk of a chef boomed, and aimed his Jack Daniel's bottle squarely on me. "Let's see if our Blondie has a little Blackheart in her."

"Ha, you're on." Laney and I had caught many a Joan Jett show in our youth, from the Bowery to the Birch Hill. As Deuce cranked up "Bad Reputation" on the boom box, I let Joan's trademark growl rip from my throat as I hopped up on the picnic table beneath the strand lights and did a low-slung air guitar to the opening riff as my colleagues cheered me on. Who needed black leather and eyeliner? I just widened my eyes, snarled my lip, and dove in. Not giving a damn, just like the song said.

What I hadn't noticed was the small entourage that had gathered on the other side of the wire fencing that separated production and hospitality from the talent. Nash stood with a few of the other headlining artists, arms crossed and legs splayed, one heel turning over in his expensive, broken-in rocker boots. Light from the hydraulic towers set up backstage to brighten the night pooled down, setting his blond hair ablaze like a fiery crown. His eyes were trained on me as I kicked my way down the Solo cups littering the picnic table in my ragged cutoff jeans and combat boots. Let him look. I didn't care.

No, no, no . . . not me, me, me.

I head-banged in time to the chorus, wishing I had Joan's pin-straight, black shag that would never frizz in the damp night like my kinky pile of pale curls. Go Get Her's bassist leaned in to commune with Nash's ear. The lead singer's brow lifted as he nodded, and I could only imagine the conversation going on in their Ol' Boys Club. While Joan could strut the strut with her training-bra chest, I was probably channeling sexy lumberjack in my tank top and the half-buttoned flannel I'd donned to get through the unseasonably cool night.

War whoops and fists punched through the midnight air as I scissor-kicked myself over the keg and ended my song. "Spin, spin, spin!" mixed with chants of "Chug, chug, chug!" and the Jack bottle was thrust into my hand.

Nash had leaned an arm forward, his fingers curled in the chain link. Now his other hand grabbed hold, as if he was thinking about scaling the fence. It looked like the VIPs were on the outside looking in, for once. A small smile played on his lips as I made my way over to him.

"What'up, Doc?" he drawled, gaze never leaving my lips as I took a fluid haul from the bottle.

"You lost?" I rasped, the whiskey adding a layer to my usual husky tone. Behind him, laughter and conversation among the other musicians drifted in the smoke-filled air, and I smelled the skunky burn of pot.

"Not all who wander are lost, China Doll." He fingered one of my curls, coaxing a silken spiral through the chain link to his side of the fence. "How about a drink?"

I held the base of the bottle up, and his throat throbbed as he took fluid swallows. Meanwhile, all conversation had stopped on my side of the fence, as my co-workers watched the festival's hottest act drain half a bottle of their hard-earned Jack, its neck propped through the wire fencing.

"You'll never find yourself, if you haven't yet lost yourself."

"Pretty profound," Nash replied, licking his lips.

"Ivy League, remember?" I quirked a brow and took the bottle to my mouth once more.

"You know what I think? I think you're lost, little girl. Or hiding out. Something—or someone—has you spooked."

"I don't care what you think. Or what anyone else thinks."

Nash cocked his hip as he leaned, the chain link bulging toward me with his weight. Even under the too-bright lights, his pupils were dilated, obsidian eclipsing moss.

"If you really didn't give a damn about your reputation, you'd be on my side of the fence right about now." The slight pucker in his smirk could have been a come-on, or a signal for another swig of alcohol.

"Morning will be here soon enough," I said, and left it at that.

Business and pleasure was one cocktail I didn't mix.

Appetite for Destruction

"Don't eat that!" Riggs nearly smacked the chocolaty goodness from my hand. "Never eat anything left on the bus by someone you don't know," he admonished, as if I were five years old and accepting candy from a stranger. "Especially baked goods, unless they are still sealed in their packaging."

"Oh, gimme a break." I tossed the half-devoured cookie into the trash anyway, glaring at him. It had tasted perfectly innocent, but he had ruined the indulgence anyhow. "Whatever. More for you, you greedy bastard."

His laughter followed me down the bus steps and out the door. "Might want to stay close by, girlie. In case you start to trip."

I didn't want to be anywhere in the vicinity of Nash's goon. But sure enough, I had barely made it to the tree line before I started to see jagged trails. Ugh. I'd seen my fair share of festival-goers tripping balls this summer, leaving me with no desire to experience it myself. Not with Maxine constantly nipping at my heels like a police dog. *I need air. And open space. I'm just going to find a nice tree to sit under, close my eyes, and listen to the music.*

The problem was, the music sounded so, so good. Not dancing was impossible. And when I closed my eyes, the beats had a color. When I breathed in, the melody had a taste.

"Dance with us!" It was the trio of painted, airbrushed girls that followed the festival from town to town. The blonde was done up in glittery blues and greens like the cosmos, her every curve a planet, a moon. Her navel was a star. Star Belly. The tall raven beauty was covered head to toe in scales of purple, pink, and yellow like some iridescent fish, winding her way between the blonde and me. Her arms moved languidly in the air, hands slowly twirling. The third girl had only her top painted, like the sheerest, flexible T-shirt. She took my hand. "Can we paint you?"

The airbrush mist had felt like a whisper against my skin. It was hard not to giggle and sigh, but I tried to stay completely still, even though the music had trailed after us, all the way to the body paint artist vendor's tent. The cool lick of a tiny paintbrush kept time with the rhythm of the drums onstage.

"So beautiful," Raven marveled, as Star Belly and the other girl used my body as their canvas, the spray of the paint as cool and refreshing as the slight breeze blowing through the festival grounds.

I had danced my way backstage, my Working laminate the only thing adorning my body besides the evenly distributed paint job and my barely there thong. I marveled at how the natural camouflage of design and color presented itself in such a way that tricked the eye into believing you were covered. I felt fully clothed, although the air temperature told me different.

As did my boss, who took one look at me and fired me on the spot.

Apparently I had collected quite the crowd as I danced my way back to the artist compound.

"I told you this position required a high level of respect and professionalism," Maxine raged, making a holy production out of unclipping the laminate from my lanyard in front of all my colleagues. "Parading around in your altogether? Soliciting musicians, on their buses? That doesn't fly with me, and it certainly won't fly with the promoters. I told you this was a one-strike job. I won't have you jeopardizing our entire team with your antics. This was your last show. Out you go."

"Antics? You can't be serious?" Jade countered. "Who hasn't gone into the crowd to blow off steam, on an off day? Come on. Dani is our best masseuse."

"Correction. Dani is *my* best masseuse."

The crowd parted as Nash stepped forward. His bare chest was slick with sweat and heaving with an exhilaration that could only come from having sex, or having just played to a crowd of twenty thousand.

It had been his music, pouring from the speakers and washing over me on the hill.

Mind. Officially. Blown.

"I wouldn't have let her onto my bus if I had had any doubts as to her respect and professionalism." He took his own Artist laminate that was threaded through the belt loop of his low-slung, tattered jeans and replaced my Working badge. "You've earned this."

Turning to Maxine, he added, "She stays on this tour. With me."

Fool on the Hill

Life didn't change too much on the road as part of Nash's entourage. The cities still blurred as we made our way back up north. Go Get Her continued to draw the faithful thousands each night, and Nash was in his element, holding court after each set like the king of the world. But I felt like a court jester, just along for the ride. I was grateful for the protective bubble my "I'm with the band" status provided, but once the embarrassment of the incident subsided, regret set in. The Artist pass gave me license to bypass Maxine, but I missed the rest of my tour family in hospitality. I was just biding my time as I skirted closer to home and the looming task of figuring out my next big move. Summer tour couldn't last forever.

I hated glossing over my predicament to my parents, whose phone calls always wound their way back to asking when I was going to come back home and to my senses. And to "put that education to good use." Just because I wasn't wearing a white lab coat and appearing on someone's explanation of benefits didn't mean I was working in some back-alley rub-and-tug establishment.

But I wasn't exactly earning a salary or a 401(k), either.

"Nash needs you for a one-off gig," Riggs said one day in catering, fiddling with the creamers on the table. Up they went into a pyramid, before he shuffled them down into a line across the checked tablecloth like little white pawns in chess.

Bands loved the chance to play a one-off. There was no need to carry production or backline, it's all waiting for you there—lights, sound, the works. You just roll into town, bring the party, and get paid handsomely for it. But trying to sneak in a one-off gig while out on a contracted festival tour sounded a little like a guy trying to grab a quickie with another woman while on his honeymoon—way too much of a hassle and a risk.

"When could he possibly fit in a one-off? This tour goes straight through Labor Day, and any show Go Get Her plays around here would break Minstrels' radius clause, wouldn't it?"

Riggs's brow shot up. "You know more about this business than I had you pegged for, girlie. Vying for my job?"

"No thanks." I stabbed at my salad. I had learned about touring through osmosis, feeling every one of Laney's pangs when the road took Allen. Even during their off years, Laney took a vested interest in where he was at any given time, and where he wasn't. And even though I wouldn't admit it, I had gleaned a lot about the business through Nash.

Riggs continued his shell game across from me, moving the creamers with his pinkies. Gold rings graced both of them, and I wondered whether Nash's money had bought him his bling, or if there had been a long line of Nashes before this current one.

"The band has to take a week off tour when the festival moves up through Canada."

"Has to?"

"Nash has a . . . well, let's just say Canada has a tiny issue with him crossing the border."

I practically choked on a chickpea. "Nash has a record?"

"Kid stuff." Riggs shook two creamers like they were tiny liquid maracas. "Even President Bush had a problem crossing the border when he was in office, and he had a DUI from 1976. Anyway, that was way before you were born. The fact is, this presents a lovely opportunity."

"For?"

Up went the creamers into a tower, end to end. "Nash is up for an award."

I laughed, swishing around the last of my lettuce. "What? The douchebag award?"

Down went the creamers, rolling all different directions across the table. "You've got a dirty mouth, Doc Ivy."

"Nowhere near as filthy as Nash's." Logging miles on his tour bus was like sailing unchartered seas aboard a pirate ship. Nash swabbed the deck daily with such slurs and sexual innuendo that I was ready to walk the plank just to get a break from him.

Still chuckling, I gathered up my dishes and deposited them into the dish tubs lined up along the wall. Doubling back, I siphoned out some coffee from the urn into a large glass of ice, dumped in a pack of sugar, and plunked a straw into it. Back at the table, I stole three of Riggs's creamers, ruining his perfect symmetry.

"So what's this got to do with me?"

"It's like you borrowing a kid for the afternoon to go see his Lemonwheel set. Same concept. But for one week. Then you can run back to your fun, little life."

I smarted a little at the "run" comment. As for my fun, little life—I had gotten fired from my summer gig and was currently at loose ends. What the hell was he proposing?

Riggs reached into his pocket and set a black velvet ring box on the table. It looked very formal amid the scattered creamer cups and the cheery red and white checks of the tablecloth.

"Look. It'll be just as easy as a one-off." Elbows on the table, Riggs folded his hands, and together we stared at the box between us. "Nash is being honored in his hometown, and it's a big deal for him. He doesn't want to show up without a lady on his arm."

"Tell me there isn't a ring in there."

"He just needs to come across well."

"Tell me," I repeated slowly for clarity, "there isn't a ring in there, sitting on a table in the middle of fucking catering." Silverware clattered a few tables down, and a fat, bearded roadie gave an impressive burp amid the cheers of his co-workers.

"It's one week, Dani. You show up with Nash, and everything else will be waiting for you there. Luxury hotel suite, wardrobe full of clothes, the works." His chubby fingers wrestled with the box's tight lid. I glanced around, in a total panic.

"Not. Here." My hiss caused Riggs to freeze, think better of opening the box, and push it toward me to do the honors. I let it sit next to my sweating cup of iced coffee.

"Look. Help him out here. He needs some good press. Rumor mill has it that the label might drop Go Get Her if Nash doesn't get his personal act together. And the band . . ." Riggs fiddled nervously with his pinky rings, twirling them simultaneously with his thumbs. "Let's just say he's on pretty thin ice with them as well."

My eyes widened as I sucked coffee through my straw and came up for air. Now *that* surprised me. Go Get Her's sound was like nothing I'd heard before. It had a fiery spirit and an urgency about it that was infectious. Nash added a slithery groove with his voice and guitar playing that begged the body to move, his wordplay and rhythm designed to delight and excite every kind of fan, and convert the unbelievers on the spot. Together, Nash and the band brought the crowd screaming to their knees night after night with their debauched and sensual set. Each song built heat, and it was amazing to watch as they kept the tunes alive, kept them breathing and growing.

"I don't understand. Go Get Her is pure magic with Nash fronting them."

Riggs smirked fondly at me like I was born yesterday. "Labels don't believe in magic anymore. Magic doesn't always equal the Midas touch. Nash's pageantry and penchant for 'drama'"—he air-quoted—"hasn't won him any popularity contests with the suits crunching the bottom-line numbers."

I nodded, thinking about the private tour bus, as well as the extravagant after-parties and trashed backrooms that made headline news. That probably didn't fly with the promoters and execs.

"I can see that, but . . . the band?" They were so good together.

"Ever date someone that you just can't stand . . . but the sex is so damn good, you can't bring yourself to break up with them?" Riggs was saying. "Yeah. That's Go Get Her and Nash. But even they're reaching the tipping point."

I picked up the ring box.

"Pose with him for one week, back in his hometown. Get him some good press and show the world Nash Drama has calmed down. In the end, you'll get a new wardrobe and a diamond ring to keep for your troubles."

Oh, this guy knew dick-squat about my *troubles*.

"You think I need new clothes?" I demanded, scraping the chair back.

"Sorry." Riggs gave a sheepish grin but his teeth were still shark-like. "But your hippie, earth-mother flower-child look isn't going to cut it, Holly Hobbie. Not on Nash's arm."

I made an angry beeline out of the catering hall toward the artist compound. Musicians and their guests loitered about, drinking at the picnic tables and enjoying the sunshine. Marching right up the stairs of the trailer labeled *Go Get Her*, I yanked on the latch and burst in.

Nash was playing house inside with two topless groupies. The lights were dimmed and the air hung heavy with pot smoke. He lounged between them on the couch, wearing a black tee that proclaimed in white writing FUCK YOU, YOU FUCKING FUCK, his long arms thrown over their bare shoulders. Each girl offered a smoldering joint between a thumb and forefinger to his lips, and he'd take turns smoking between them. All the while, he rolled their nipples between his own thumbs and forefingers, and they giggled and squirmed in delight. He'd exhale smoke across a belly and lick the closest breast above it before moving back to their waiting fingers. It was hypnotizing, but I wasn't there to watch their show.

"Tell *Riggs* this is what I think of YOUR proposal!"

I tossed the ring box, which bounced off his shoulder, rolled down his chest, and settled into the creases near his button fly. Slightly to the left of his massive hard-on that was obvious under the straining denim. The girls gasped and their gaze landed on the box. A diamond ring, sitting on the dick of a rock star? For groupies, that was probably as rare a find as a unicorn horn.

"*My* proposal? That was *his* idea. I just said I wouldn't go home empty-handed."

Nash ceased his nipple-toking and cupped his precious junk (ring included) with both hands. "Go. Later."

The girls responded as if he had called them by their names. Go moved to grab her halter. Later extinguished the joints in the ashtray.

He had his harem. What the hell did he need me for? I didn't exactly fit into his collection. Thanks to mainstream media, I knew exactly what he considered women good for. "I'm never going to be a lady on your arm and a whore behind closed doors!" I informed him.

"Gee, quoting my interview articles now?" He leered sarcastically. "And here I thought you said you weren't a member of the Nash Drama fan club."

"I'm not," I muttered, ignoring the girls' titters. "But I read *Rolling Stone* once in a while."

"I have no doubt that you're a wildcat in bed." His heavy-lidded eyes cruised the length of me. "But that's not why I allowed Riggs to ask you," he said to me. "Come on. Let's take a ride."

"No. I'm not going anywhere with you. Not in that asinine T-shirt. You look like an idiot."

"Fine!" Nash stood up, shoved the ring box into his pocket, and stripped off the tee. "No fucking T-shirt." He tossed it onto the couch cushion he had just vacated, and the girls pounced on it as if it were warm meat. They clocked heads in the scrabble to stake a claim on their favorite singer's piece of clothing, and ended up laughing, locking lips, and rubbing boobs together. Perhaps it was a show for Nash, but his eyes never left me. "Happy now?"

His bare chest rose and fell as we stared each other down. It struck me how intimately familiar I was with this stranger's torso before me, from each time he climbed on my massage table during this tour. Trusting me with it. I knew every curve of muscle and every sinew, his thews on display as he twisted to grab his laminate and keys.

"Let's take that ride," he repeated.

I followed him out of the trailer to where his golf cart waited. This time, he bypassed the flat avenue of merch tents and opted to head straight toward the sloping hill that acted as a natural amphitheater for the stage. That day's festival ground was a small ski resort in winter, but come summer, the concerts blazed at the bottom of the mountain while the fans raged at varying heights of the grassy slope.

"Can the cart make it up this terrain?" I hollered as we bumped and careened higher and higher. It was a golf cart, for heaven's sake. Not an ATV.

"Trust me," Nash yelled over the rushing wind, gunning the pedal harder. "I'm a professional." His sarcasm bit as sharp as the wind at my face. We reached one plateau, but not high enough for Nash, or far enough from the crowds that were already clustering around the dark stage, waiting for Go Get Her's set. The band wasn't even scheduled to start for another forty-five minutes.

Finally we reached a summit that satisfied him, and he threw on the brake. We sat down on the long, wild grass. Nash's fingers pried the box from his pocket. He said nothing, just palmed it back and forth between his hands.

"Why'd you send Riggs to ask me?" I finally asked.

"Because I trust him. He's done nothing but spin my antics into gold." He cracked the box open. "And platinum, apparently." Smirking, he handed it over to me. "Riggs has always been good with damage control."

The diamond bore down on me like an all-seeing eye. I quickly snapped the velvet jaws of the box shut. Riggs's recitation of *they don't pay me nearly enough for this* revolved around my mind like a broken record.

Nash pulled at a tuft of grass and let it sift through his fingers.

"So tell me about this award."

"Key to the city?" He smiled into the distance. "It's a promotional tool schemed up by Riggs, no doubt. *I'm* a promotional tool." He grabbed at more grass, ripping it from the hard earth beneath us.

I waited for him to go on, hugging my knees to my chest and staring out at the vista.

"That." He nodded down to the view, the crowd swelling bigger and bigger as the spotlights began to wink and roll on the stage far below, and the guitar tech began the sound check. "That is my key to the city. Unconditional love. Every night."

I could only imagine the feeling. Before Maxine canned me, my role at the festival had been only a microcosm of the entire production, and nothing compared to the magic that happened when the first note was played. But I had liked being a link on the chain, working out the chinks for these talented men and women.

"I'd rather stay on tour than accept some lame-ass, meaningless award. Fucking Canada." A clump of grass went flying over his shoulder, earth still clinging from it.

"Why won't they let you cross the border?"

"Suspected arson." He flattened me with his gaze, daring me to make one of my usual smart-ass retorts. "B and E. All bullshit. I was seventeen. Who doesn't do stupid shit at that age?"

I didn't answer. I had no desire to refute or rebut his statement.

"Anyway. There's another reason I need to go home," Nash admitted, facing straight ahead and not looking my way. "And I can't do it alone, not as the same asshole I've always been. I'm sick, Dani. I've got something. A disease."

I turned to him, wary. If it was communicable . . .

"I'm sure you're thinking it's sexually transmitted and would serve me right, right? But it's not." He pulled a piece of paper out of his wallet. "I can't even pronounce the goddamn thing." He handed me the paper slip.

"Ankylosing spondylitis."

"Just the fact that you can say it makes me think you've heard of it."

"I have." During school, during clinicals. "It's a form of progressive arthritis."

He took custody of the paper again. "I've been carrying this around with me. Diagnosed just before I left for tour. Haven't told Riggs or the guys."

My mind started to race, thinking of all the possible contraindications, and the damage I could have inflicted, simply by massaging someone in his condition without knowing. "I wish you would've told me sooner."

"Sorry to worry your pretty little head, China Doll." His tone was caustic. "You didn't break me. It's all good."

He struggled to his feet and stood stiffly. I recalled the condition was also referred to as "bamboo spine," due to the way it fused the backbone into a rigid stick, pressing on nerves and causing increasing numbness in the lower part of the body. Not good.

Especially not good for a performer who used his body as his livelihood.

"The doc told me I might lose the ability to play . . . even to hold my guitar. Then what?" Nash said quietly.

"Oh, Nash . . ."

He shrugged, gave a defeated little smile, cupped his hands, and bellowed, "THEN WHAT?" at the top of his lungs. A few people down in the crowd below turned; some raised their fists and cheered. At our distance, they couldn't tell if he was a rock god or just a mere mortal like them.

At our height, they couldn't judge whether he was thirty feet tall and bulletproof.

"I'll stiffen up like the Tin Man. The band will kick me out. Or I'll have to quit. Who will love me then? I've never had a heart in me. I've only had my music."

"You're getting way ahead of yourself," I said, although I didn't blame him.

"Am I?" He stalked back over to the cart and pulled his long legs in. "I need to be prepared. For if the day ever comes. I need . . ." His voice dwindled out in the mountain breeze. "I need to get to know my son."

Nash's statement felt loaded with meaning. "AS . . . ," I began, suddenly remembering more about the condition. "There's a genetic marker, isn't there?"

He nodded. "Most people with the disease have it. I do."

I got what he was saying. He wanted to find out if the son he never met was at risk, too. I joined him in the cart.

"There's that normal curiosity, you know?" He gave me a wistful smile. "Like, is he going to look like me? Will he have my smile, my hands?" Nash turned his palms over, displaying his nimble guitar-playing fingers, flat at the tips with calluses as custom made as his signature Les Paul. "Will he hate me? Even before he knows . . . or is old enough to understand?"

I didn't know what to say or do, other than cautiously wrap my arms around him, clasping his bare shoulder with my hands. I had never hugged a client before, but he wasn't on my massage table right now. He was on my imaginary psychiatrist's couch. And he didn't feel like a client, he felt like a friend who had just confided in me.

Nash surprised me by leaning and placing a chaste kiss on my forehead, before turning and staring down the mountain as the sky grew darker and the crowd grew larger.

"Going home isn't going to be easy," he said. "Not with my past track record. I've burned so many bridges there . . . I'm gonna need someone to help me cross the Delaware. My son's mother isn't going to let me near him if I show up without someone next to me to make me look good."

The velvet box was growing sweaty in my grip. I had forgotten I was even holding it. "Why me?" I blurted, setting it in the cup holder of the cart.

Nash had his choice of girls, as evident from Go, Later, Kylie, and the rest of his groupies. Hell, they had named themselves the Dramettes. *We stayed behind to party with Nash,* I recalled their words on the tour bus. Would they truly stay with him, were the party to end? Could they live up to their name, or would the drama become too much?

"Because you, Doc, are the perfect package. Fucking Ivy League," he scoffed, "and you sound smart when you talk. You have more on your mind than sex and money, and these hands . . ." He took both of my hands in his. "These magic mojo hands. I *need* them on me every day. And that is probably the first time Nash Drama has ever said anything and meant it in a totally nonsexual, innocent way. Truth."

I laughed, and so did he.

"You're not totally innocent," I pointed the fact out to him. "You'd be lying to your whole town." *And I would be, too.*

"It wouldn't be the first time." He tossed his hair back, and there was the old bravado I was used to. "Unless you want to really let me make an honest woman out of you? Maybe Riggs had the right idea, after all. You know, Nash Drama doesn't like doing things half-assed, darlin'."

Perhaps this was my next big adventure?

I loved massaging—everything about it, from the atmosphere of the candles to the smell of the oils. Most of all, I loved to help people. But what Nash was asking was way out of my scope of experience.

"Would it be so awful, being married to a guy like me? You wouldn't have dudes pawing at you any longer, not on my watch. No boss bitches pulling rank on you . . ."

Those points were tempting. But just the tip of the iceberg, and it was going to take a lot more to get hell to freeze over and get me to agree to *I do.*

"And the sex—"

"Would be amazing, and whenever you want it." His bare chest puffed with pride.

"It would be nonexistent," I corrected. "Between us, anyway." I waved my arm to indicate my point. "Personal and professional boundaries are high on my code of ethics."

Was I seriously spouting off about ethics, while sitting on a mountaintop with a half-naked rocker? "If you want me to help you, *really* help you, you need to see that anything beyond platonic would seriously muddy the waters under that bridge you need help crossing."

Nash stared at me for a long minute. The sigh he released deflated his chest to normal size. "Makes sense, I guess. In the long run."

The long run. He truly wanted to go the distance.

"And then what?" Echoing his words was deliberate on my part: had he seriously thought all this through?

"You'll help me finish out the tour and decide how I'm going to treat this thing. Then . . . I don't know. Maybe go back out west."

"There are docs in Philly, you know."

"Yeah, but I won't want to overstay my welcome. See my friends, get to know my kid. Take the damn key they're offering me. And should the rock-and-roll dream—and my body—go belly-up, maybe there will be more of a shoulder to lean on, you know? And—hold up . . . how do you know where I'm from?" Nash asked.

He had me there.

"Let's just say . . . maybe a little of the Nash Drama fan club has rubbed off on me." I pinched my thumb and forefinger together. "Just a little."

"So is that a yes?"

Nash pinched his thumb and forefinger together, too—offering up the ring.

Now it was my turn to ask myself *why me?* I knew Nash's reasons for entering into such a thing. But my own? *WWDD?*

Guitar riffs floated up the hill, distant and haunting. A tech tested the Vox organ on stage, coaxing carnival sounds from it. Nash began to hum the opening lines from The Doors' "You're Lost Little Girl" in his dark, throaty timbre. Go Get Her frequently covered the song during their encore, and its meaning wasn't lost on me.

It had been easy to hide behind my smug rhetoric from the other side of the fence.

You'll never find yourself, if you haven't yet lost yourself.

I had caught the bouquet at Laney's mom's wedding. And before that, I had pulled a wedding cake charm from my sister's cake, and let my heart and my mind get away from me. Maybe this was the way it was meant to be. All signs were pointing to commitment, but maybe it wasn't so crazy after all. Especially if it was for a good cause.

I was tired of running, and making excuses to everyone and myself. If I said yes to Nash—for real, and for more than a week—I wouldn't have to think of reasons to say no to everyone else. I wouldn't have to protect my heart, or my dignity, from guys like Mick. I wouldn't be left to make any more wrong choices. And I could truly help this man, who was obviously not used to asking others for help.

All I had to do was say yes.

All we had to do was go through with it.

Go through it.

"You've got one chance to ask me, mister. So you'd better make it right."

Mick

THE HONEYMOON IS OVER

I woke up in a pool of chocolate sauce.

Better that than my own blood.

Dabbing a thumb against my sticky cheek, I licked and sampled the goods. It was a step up from your average household-variety chocolate. But it certainly wasn't the Valrhona I used in my shop. Torani, maybe?

Whose house was this?

Under the crisp sheets, my bare foot made contact with the cool stainless of a whipped cream canister. Oh yes, I remembered going there.

Reaching over, I touched the sticky hip of the woman sleeping with her back to me, and ran my fingertip along the string of her apple-green thong.

Oh, Mick. You motherfucker.

I had worked the Davis-Dixon wedding last night. Party of two hundred. And Jack Daniel's and I had officially crashed it, late night.

"Ms. Davis, the caterers have arrived," called a voice from the other side of the door. A light knocking followed. "Ms. Davis?"

The lady of the house sat bolt upright. Hours of private Pilates lessons had kept her abs tight and her bottom firm, and I admired both from my side of her massive king bed. "Be right there!" she called with false cheer to her housekeeper. "Oh my God, what time is it?"

Her voice wavered as she turned to look over my head at her bedside clock. "Mick, you have to get out of here. Sixty out-of-town guests will be here in a half hour! Shit, shit, shit!"

Even with her eye makeup smudged, and her professionally done hair now a matted mess, the mother of the bride looked delectable. The swell of her breasts had my chocolate fingerprints all over them, and I had a vague recollection of all the places I had garnished and drizzled last night.

"Is there time for a shower?" I had had so much fun getting dirty with her. It would be nice to get clean with her, too. I rolled over, my thigh tacky against hers. She had sprayed a garland of whipped cream down there last night, and had had an all-you-can-eat extravaganza.

Early-fiftysomething babes were the best.

"For me, yes." She rolled off the bed and into her silk robe. "For you . . ." She tossed me my work pants in response. "Take the back stairs, please."

"Yeah, yeah." I knew the drill.

"You were fun, though," she conceded, reaching to button me back into my double-breasted chef's coat and pulling me in for a stale, sugary kiss.

"Be a dear and put these back where you found them, please?"

Be a dear? That sounded like something a grandma would say. Okay, maybe the seventeen-year age gap was a bit of a chasm.

With sneakers in one hand and numerous edible items I had raided from the pantry in pursuit of late-night fun in the other, I crept down to the kitchen. After a night of passionate servicing, I was well aware why I had been relegated to the servants' staircase.

Story of my life.

I loved my freakin' life.

Chocolate and caramel went back into the fridge, honey into the pantry, and what was left of the big bowl of grapes and berries was returned to the mammoth kitchen island. I refilled the ice cube tray with calm and calculated domesticity as the catering crew stepped lively around me.

If it weren't for the honey in my hair and the caramel-streaked scratch marks across the back of my coat, I could totally pass for the man of the house. If there were one. And half the town knew there wasn't.

A familiar, tattooed arm reached past me to light the Sternos under the chafing dishes. "You look a little rough, Spencer. Just punching in?"

Leave it to Jerry Blake to arrive for sloppy seconds. He'd copied off me during our time in culinary school, and now managed one of the trendy catering upstarts in the township. Whose desserts couldn't hold a candle to mine.

"Nope, I'm not working this party. Just did a double." I was officially punching out my time card on the Davis affair.

"You see this morning's front page?" he asked, jutting his chin toward the paper still in its plastic sleeve on the counter. "Big news about your buddy, Nash Drama."

"Thanks," I said, tucking the paper under my arm. When it came to my oldest friend, he lived up to the stage surname he gave himself at age nineteen. No matter what drama was playing out in the news, I wasn't going to give Jerry Blake the satisfaction of watching me go hunt for it. But curiosity got the better of me by the time I reached the front hall.

LOCAL GUITAR HERO TO RECEIVE KEY TO THE CITY

Okay. The world had totally gone mad. In what alternate universe was Nash a "hero"? Hell, calling Nash "local" was a stretch. The guy hadn't been home in ten long years. Still, it was a short enough time for me to still hold a grudge.

Outside, my ride was completely cock-blocked by catering vans and a florist truck parked on both ends of the circular drive. *Great.* I fingered my useless keys to the Night Kitchen van, and flipped them back into my pocket. At least it didn't look out of place. I'd have to come back for it later with Bear.

The thought of my best friend made me pull out my phone and check the time as I began to hoof it toward town. Nine forty-five. "Damn it!"

Like clockwork, and because my aunt Sindy always swore Bear and I shared half a brain, the phone buzzed its retort against my hand.

Quinn on warpath. Logan needs cake.

I had promised Bear's nephew I'd help him bake a cake today. It wasn't just any old day; today was his tenth birthday. I had Spiderman cupcakes back at the shop ready for his party guests later on, but quality time in the kitchen with me had been high on his wish list.

I could just picture Quinn standing in the doorway with a cake server. Ready to scalp me with it. Bear's sister didn't take kindly to people disappointing her kid. Especially in favor of a booty call.

Quinn Bradley was not a fan of the booty call.

Not since she had been one, ten years and roughly nine months ago.

"Where you headed, kid?"

The trucker's shout and idling engine startled me. Second nature had forced my thumb up and my arm out. I had been walking with my back to the west and hadn't even realized it.

"The Half Acre. Just past the 32 curve." I had been hitchhiking my way there since junior high. "You know it?"

"I can't take you over the New Hope–Lambertville Bridge; my rig's over the weight limit. But I can drop you close enough. Hop in."

We were on the Jersey side, but if he got me to the bridge, I could be at the Half Acre on the Pennsylvania side in twenty minutes. I began to sift through my mental recipe box for a quick cake to make with Logan. Two layers max, with seven-minute icing.

"Used to drive these roads all the time," the trucker shared as we bumped along slightly faster than the speed of sloth. "Up Route 32. Didn't they used to call it Heaven's Half Acre?"

"That was a long time ago. It's just the Half Acre now."

I tried to fix my gaze on the road ahead, but the trio of beads swinging from the rearview mirror caught my eye first. They were Mardi Gras colors—green, gold, and purple—with tiny glittering masks that clicked cheaply against one another. With a shaking hand, I reached out to silence them, my thumb rubbing over the tiny hump of the gold mask's nose.

God, I had managed to make it almost a whole morning without thinking about her.

It was hard to forget a girl like Dani.

Not to mention spending the evening with the girl of your dreams and waking up in a Louisiana jail.

"You like those, eh?" The driver leered. "Got 'em down in New Orleans this year. Ever been to Mardi Gras?"

"Yeah. I lived down there. For a time." It felt like a lifetime ago.

"You see a lotta tits when you lived down there?"

"I saw my fair share." Mardi Gras was a season down in New Orleans. But I had seen some in the off-season, too.

"The ladies on Bourbon Street sure love the beads. But I had to keep a few. Beads, I mean." He laughed. "'Course I wouldn't have minded bringing some of them ladies home, neither."

The gold mask continued its hypnotizing sway.

I had come home empty-handed, too.

Gold for power, Dani had said, relinquishing the sequined and feathered mask she hid behind that night. I hadn't known there was significance behind each color until she'd told me. *Green for faith*, she had whispered, allowing my fingers to slowly zip her out of her dress until she'd stood before me in nothing but a lacy thong. *Purple for justice.*

I hadn't known the power she would hold over me.

And I was losing faith in the hope that I would ever find her again.

No justice in this world.

The driver had braked to a stop, and the bridge was in sight.

"End of the line."

"Thanks." I jumped down from the rig, still under the spell of Dani's memory.

She wasn't just the one that got away. She had gotten under my skin, just like I knew she would, the minute she came parading down Royal Street.

"And here comes another one! Those brides from up north sure do love a second-line parade." Derek, *our captain waiter, took a shaky drag off his cigarette, nodding his head to the blare and the beat of the brass band slowly making its way toward us.*

We had just finished service on a wedding for two hundred, and while I couldn't vouch for the rest of the guys, I was bone-achingly tired. Taking both a server job and a pastry apprenticeship at a busy New Orleans hotel kept me hopping from before dawn until well after dusk. And unlike my fellow waitstaff born and raised on the Bayou, my internal thermostat was still having trouble adjusting to the climate difference, despite having left Pennsylvania three years ago. And especially while wearing the penguin suit the caterers insisted upon.

"How do you know they're from up north?" I asked, giving a tug on my bow tie as the happy bride and groom came strutting behind the band with a twirl of a painted parasol and colored cane. Their police escort gave a whirl of his siren and lights, getting into the mood, too.

Derek smiled wide, showing a gold tooth on one side and a gap where its twin was missing on the other. "Oh, you'd know if they was locals. Believe me. Northerners, ain't I right, Eddie?"

"Throw a rock on Royal Street, you'll hit a second line these days." Eddie's shoulders were already rolling to the grooves being laid down. "It's the city's bread-and-butter, not complaining. But that there ain't nothing like a jazz funeral. Now there's a second line!" He took a stealth haul off the flask of Maker's Mark he kept in his jacket pocket

before passing it to me. "I'll show you one of these days, Mick. Just need some old cat like Derek to kick it," he affectionately teased.

Derek and Eddie were third cousins, or maybe it was second cousins, once removed. Something like that. Eddie had told me all about his almost-famous relative the day we both got our jobs. "He's got brass in his blood," were his exact words. And after having the pleasure of seeing old Derek pick up a saxophone in some hole-in-the-wall jazz club last spring, that explained it all. He should've been first in line with the band, not stuck in catering.

We passed the flask and watched as clusters of wedding guests moved past, self-consciously waving handkerchiefs and shuffling. Sure enough, they were wilting in the sultry heat like true Northerners.

Save for one.

She was smack in the middle of the bridal processional, shimmying all the things God gave her. The tumble of wild, white-blond curls caught the late-day sun like a cascading blaze as she twirled in her bridesmaid dress and stepped high to the beat of the big bass drum. She shook her white handkerchief with abandon, one slim arm raised to the sky as the other snaked smoothly out to catch the crooked elbow offered by old Derek. Around and around they went, swinging in a fun and frenzied dance, until she broke off, blowing him a kiss and laughing as she continued down the street.

"Now that you don't see every day." Eddie blew out a breath, hypnotized. Derek was still clapping and laughing, doing a little jig in the street as it emptied.

"Seriously." My bow tie was in my hand. "Cover for me?" In some kind of trance of my own, I also shed my penguin coat, tossing both to Eddie and running to catch up with the parade before I even had time to consider what I was doing.

I had to find out who the girl in the emerald dress was.

Actually, it was more like an absinthe green; I had been mixing icing colors in my aunt and uncle's bakery since the tender age of thirteen and learned there were more hues of color out there in the world than there were moods. I had the feeling that, like the drink, just a taste of that girl would intoxicate me. You could tell her spirit was potent.

"*You got this, my boy!*" *Derek called after me.* "*Jump in the line!*"

Dani

MEET AND GREET

"Can you even see the end of the line? I thought the signing was supposed to end by noon."

I craned my neck and stood on my tiptoes. People snaked through the music section and around the entire first-floor perimeter of Manhattan's flagship mega-book and media store. The guys had been at it since ten o'clock, and there was no way they'd get through all those people on time.

"Relax, Dani." Riggs chomped on the end of a plastic coffee stirrer. "The band's doing great."

Eager fans shuffled forward with CDs in hand as the musicians reached across the table, Sharpies in hand. It was like some weird mating dance, an exchange of commerce and pleasantries. The dreaded in-store meet and greet. Last chance for the band to be promo whores before their weeklong forced hiatus began.

"I'm totally relaxed, Riggs. And it's not the band I'm worried about."

Nash was at the end of the row. The pièce de résistance that everyone clamored toward, the singer they wanted to linger with. It wasn't happening. Fans got a quick hello from their favorite performer, and a riot act from the tour manager: no pictures with him, please; no touching, one item to sign. Then they were handed off to a store employee, who directed them toward the escalator for a nice latte in the café, or a new book to go along with their beating heart and fleeting fantasies.

I sighed, wondering how long they'd let the line get before someone had the sense to cut it off. And I wondered how much work I'd have later on, massaging the cramps from Nash's fingers as he signed his name over and over and over again. He was the only one I was worried about.

It was my new job to worry about him.

Go Get Her's front man slouched in his chair with typical rock star panache, like an exotic creature that didn't necessarily belong under the harsh fluorescent lighting of corporate chain store America, but like he knew he owned the attention. Yet I could see every once in a while, he'd shift his scapulae, shoulder blades sliding up and down his back. Like a powerful, injured bird in captivity, testing the strength of his wingspan and waiting for the right moment to break free.

Noon couldn't come soon enough.

"We're in a bookstore, for fuck's sake." Riggs turned on me, made impatient by my resulting sigh. "You're telling me you can't entertain yourself for another hour?"

Of course I could. I could take a wander through Fiction and Literature to see if anything held a candle to the stacks of paper sitting unpublished on Jax's writing desk. Or through the Psychology and Behavior section, to count the number of times my parents' names appeared on the spines of the tomes there. I'm sure that deep within the indices and tables of contents, my headshrinker parents would have strong opinions about just what the hell I had gotten myself into.

Engaged within two months of meeting him, Dani? *Seriously?*

My mom would probably fall back on alpha males and sexual

selection, being the animal behaviorist she was. My father, a noted psychologist, would skip the Freud-Jung psychosexual stuff and head right for the good ol' Savior Complex.

Jax and Laney would have a complete conniption.

Engaged to Nash Drama? *The* Nash Drama, of Go Get Her fame? My mantra would morph from *WWDD* to *WDDDI*. Friends would no longer police themselves in situations by asking *What Would Dani Do?* They would simply want to know *Why Did Dani Do It?*

Betrothing myself to one of the country's cockiest, rowdiest rock stars was hardly a moral imperative.

And it was the reason I hadn't told anyone I was coming into town.

I had absently wandered down the Wedding Etiquette aisle. The bindings of the books there were thick, the fonts elegant, and their color choices subdued and stylish. There was something there for every situation—from the *Town & Country Insiders' Guide* to the *Total & Complete Idiot's Guide*—that walked you step-by-step through the proposal, planning, and executing stages of the wedding of your dreams. I ran my hand vaguely over them, as if to glean answers via osmosis. The two-carat oval-cut stunner, set in platinum and hanging from my finger, was my invitation to the exclusive club chattered about within the pages.

Or was it?

If there really were something here for every situation, would I find the solutions to mine within the alphabetical index?

I pulled the fattest tome from the shelf and flipped to the back. Nope. Nothing under *Convenience*, as in "Engagement of." Nothing under *Fake*, *Sham* or *Have you lost your flippin' mind, girl?* either.

Sighing, I pulled the slimmest book from the shelf and let it fall open to the middle.

Deciding on a theme first will guide you and your groom in the decisions and selections of the venue, décor, food, and drinks, as

*well as many other critical details to ensure a flawless, fun-filled
day is had by all. Choose a theme which best suits your personali-
ties to help set the tone for your perfect day.*

I chuckled to myself. After spending almost three months traveling
with a major music festival, my only requirement would be a venue
with indoor plumbing. I didn't want to see another Porta-John or rustic
shower for the rest of my life. Nash's idea of "setting the tone" would
probably be choosing Madison Square Garden as the venue and using
scrims, mover lights, and hazers for the décor. Dinner would be self-
serve from chafing dishes left out by catering for a questionable length
of time, and drinks would be on ice in coolers under the tables. Groupies would be in attendance, and clothing would be optional. *It's a
backstage greenroom free-for-all wedding theme!*

I slid the book back into its slot. Posy had done a beautiful job with
her New Orleans wedding. More "concept" than theme, my sister and
her husband Pat's nuptials were the most genuine and personal expression
of love I had ever witnessed. I would've expected nothing less from them.
Part vintage, part vaudeville, wholly authentic to their aesthetic vision.

A second-line parade had led us through the quaint French Quarter from ceremony to reception, where a sign commanding MASKS ON
ushered us past a red velvet curtain. The large space had crumbling
stonework, wrought iron balconies, and a soaring whisper dome. I
remembered the way everything transformed the moment I tied the
ribbon to secure my gold mask with its black feather plumes and
stepped in. The air felt electric.

And it crackled when Mick had walked into the room.

*I noticed the vest right away, its black angles against the stark white
of his dress shirt creating a timeless look and accentuating his well-
defined arms. Many of the guys at the wedding had already stripped*

themselves of their formal jackets, but their ties still held them in a stranglehold, making them look like awkward teens at a school dance. With his collar open, sleeves rolled up, and his hands in his pockets, this guy was coolness personified, as if he had just decided to take a stroll around the dance floor.

While I was positioned at ten o'clock on the perimeter of the large circular space, chatting with Posy's best friend Emma, he was stationed at four o'clock. I moved on to give a hug and a kiss to my new brother-in-law, standing at one o'clock; this guy stepped over to seven, interacting with nobody, his eyes never leaving me. His fluid movements purposely kept him exactly opposite me. I moved in his direction, on to where my cousins were clustered at six o'clock on the dial. He turned on his heel and meandered toward midnight.

His mask of choice had concealed the top half of his face, and its long, hooked nose and slit eyes had a sinister, eerie quality. But the way he bit back a smile from his full lips was utterly disarming, and I liked the way his hair tufted over the top of the mask, almost as dark as the black mask itself, with its gold scrolling detail.

Feeling bold behind the cover of my own disguise, I strode to the center of the floor just to see what he would do. Within seconds, he joined me there.

"Once upon a time, women who wore masks had their reputation questioned, you know."

My cheeks heated beneath my mask, and I dropped my gaze demurely. I had a feeling if I wasn't careful, I would let him ask me just about anything. Those eyes of his were powerful truth serum.

"I was wondering who would end up with that particular mask," I opened with, extending my hand. "I figured the guy who wears that must be very confident with his manhood."

"No doubt there," he said, lacing his fingers through mine and claiming my waist. "Now, if only I was so confident about my dancing skills."

I laughed. "I always get blamed for trying to lead."

Thinking back to prom, when I kept stepping on Jax's shiny black shoes by accident, made me miss my old friend that much more. He was supposed to have come with me that weekend, but pulled out at the last minute. I had no doubt it was girlfriend issues. Pre-Bitch'n'Mona, his latest Little Miss She's the One for Me, for Now, was toeing the line.

My mysterious dance partner gazed down at me. "I would follow you."

His final word was stilted, as if he wanted to add more, but didn't.

We needn't have worried about leading and following; Mazzy Star's "Fade Into You" thrummed through the room, closing the gap between us. I smelled bourbon and brown sugar on his skin, reminiscent of the pralines baking in shops on almost every New Orleans street corner. And we began to move as one, under the whisper dome.

God, I really needed to stop thinking about Mick.

It was time to file him away under "dodged that bullet" and stick that book on the back shelf of my brain. Onward.

"Oh, happy day. Who's the lucky guy?"

I started at the sound of the familiar-yet-foreign voice, my head jerking against the top row of bridal books. His timbre and lanky build were identical to his twin brother's, but his cool stare and the woodsy musk smell of his cologne, so unlike Jax's, tipped me off.

Dex Davenport smirked at my choice of reading material, and locked in on the behemoth diamond. His *Who's the lucky guy?* comment came across more like a smart-ass *Who in their right mind would marry you?* demand.

Over one and a half million people on this island, and on the one day I happen to be in town, this is who I run into?

"No one you know," I replied, although he was clutching a freshly signed Go Get Her CD in his hand. "Promise me you won't tell Jax . . . I want to talk to him myself."

He smiled his evil twin smile. "Of course."

Which could mean, of course he would, of course he wouldn't, or of course I wanted to. With Dex, you never knew how he was going to manipulate your words or your intentions.

"Didn't you sell your soul to Shonnie Phillips and move down to Austin?" Dex squinted and cocked his head, as if he just realized why he hadn't seen me in Manhattan for, say, the last eighteen months. And not like he missed me at all.

"I did. Move, that is." My prior job as personal masseuse to the feminist folksinger had been all consuming, but Shonnie was a sweetheart and I wouldn't have traded the experience for the world. We reluctantly parted ways when she decided to take a yearlong sabbatical from music and the road to spend time with her family, but we still e-mailed each other regularly. It was Shonnie who had recommended me for the job with Minstrels & Mayhem, and Shonnie who gave me the sage advice when I had come back, raw and defeated, from New Orleans last year: *Go through it, darlin'. Not around it.*

I could still hear the twang of her accent, and the tang of bittersweetness that could only come from someone who had been through it herself.

Face your soul forward, just like the words of my favorite Shonnie song.

"I'm between gigs now," I supplied, pulling myself up straighter. "You?"

"My band's got a month-long residency at the Sound Bar." His tone was all closed doors, no red carpet. Fine by me. I would be out of town within the next half hour, anyway.

Nash was taking me home for a week to meet the family.

I rubbed the smooth surface of the diamond with my thumb, envying its strong, unbreakable characteristics. Suddenly, Riggs appeared from around the corner, like a genie being summoned from a lamp. "Time to roll, girlie. Nash is looking for his bride-to-be."

Dex's entire frame took a jolt of electricity at the drop of the lead singer's name. "Drama?"

I had called Dex many choice things over the years. But incredulous was never one of them.

"Please. Just tell Jax I'll call him soon, okay?" I asked, my eyes pleading their case as Riggs hooked my arm.

"Two words: confidentiality agreement," the tour manager hissed a reminder in my ear.

"Two words," I gritted back. "Shut up."

I had enough drama in my life right now without Dex adding to it.

Mick

HOMECOMING

The Half Acre's grandame of a house awaited me in quiet, lacy-curtained disapproval. Even the square, windowed cupola perched atop the flat roof seemed to be giving me the stink eye. The Italianate structure actually reminded me of the wedding cake I had created for last night's nuptials: strong and square, with pillars rising up from the bottom layer to support the supple porch roofs whose white moldings were as thick and smooth as rolled fondant. Swathed in a wash the exact hue of peach buttercream and studded around the edges with ornamental brackets as evenly spaced and precise as the beaded border I had piped, the one-hundred-and-fifty-year-old house was a work of art. It rose tall, proud and unapologetic next to its much smaller, plainer neighbors.

I cut across the lawn and skirted toward the side entrance. Only guests of the Half Acre Bed-and-Breakfast used the front door, its elegant façade warm and welcoming. But those who lived in it knew its perfect appearance was just that: a façade. As shocking as a beautiful fashion model exposing her scarred cheek to the world, the house had a charred, disfigured side where fire had claimed an entire wing.

The old limestone foundation had been filled in and seeded, and grass now grew where ten guest rooms once stood. Luckily, a fire wall placed when Quinn and Bear's father had the addition built spared most of the original landmark, save a bit of smoke damage.

Those who lived here loved it all the same, and accepted its tragic deformity. Bear had done some halfhearted patching to protect the wound from the elements, then gave up and moved on. Quinn, normally a perfectionist when it came to running her family's B and B, was strangely unapologetic when it came to guests who enquired why the inn no longer looked like the photos on the Internet, with "no, this didn't happen since you booked," and "yes, you can still have a room with a Jacuzzi tub."

Logan knew no different, didn't know the loss. It had happened before he was born.

It had happened before Nash left.

And me?

I was used to filling culinary sinkholes with cake scraps and buttercream; this was beyond me.

Logan was at the large kitchen island, shaking dregs of powdery cake mix from a box. It sat like a weird, gray volcano in a mixing bowl that was slightly too small. At the boy's feet sat Bacon, one of our two resident Burmese. Judging from the way the cat was fanatically rubbing his face with his paw, I'd say his whiskers caught some of the fallout.

"Hey, buddy." I reached for the heavy white crockery I preferred to use and tapped him on the shoulder, but too late; Logan had already cracked a thumb through his first egg and let it ooze down the powder volcano like lava.

"Your bowl is too small," I said, trying to catch his eye with my thumb and forefinger to emphasize my point, but he refused to meet my gaze and reached for the oil. I hated to think about ingesting a cake that only required three ingredients: eggs, oil, and water. Whatever the hell was in the powder I didn't consider an ingredient.

Logan used the back of his bony wrist to push his wispy blond bangs from his temple, but still earned an oily cocoa smear in the process.

"Where's your mom?"

He wrinkled his nose at me and looked around for something on the counter.

"Is she in her darkroom? You shouldn't have started without me."

Bear lumbered into the kitchen, carrying a guitar missing half its strings. Leather pants were his Sunday lounging attire, and he was the only guy I knew who could pull it off without looking like a total tool. His tattoos popped brightly in contrast to the faded yellow damask wallpaper in the hallway behind him.

"I'm supervising," Bear said by way of greeting, or explanation. "And yeah, she's in her darkroom. Exposing you for the drunk ass you are." He plunked the guitar onto the small kitchen table and nimbly began to re-string it.

Quinn had worked the Davis-Dixon affair alongside me last night, as the official wedding photographer. I remembered seeing her snapping a gazillion digital shots of the cake before reaching for her old-school Leica camera. She was probably the last photographer in Bucks County to still use film, but she loved shooting her black-and-whites that way. "More dynamic range," she'd say, whether she was shooting the bridge at night, the shoes of a wedding party all in a line, or a raccoon, dead in the orchard. "Infinite shades of gray."

And apparently, infinite ways to prove I was an idiot. Negatives of all my negatives, printed in black-and-white and waved in front of my face. Stacked up to save as ammunition later. No quick delete button of forgiveness when it came to Quinnlyn. No glossing or Photoshopping over my blunders.

I groaned and plucked what Logan had been searching for—a balloon whisk—out of his hands. Small bowl plus balloon whisk would equal my having to clean the eruption from every flat surface of the kitchen.

"Buddy. Let's start again, okay? From scratch."

I ran my fingers up and down his back apologetically, but he ignored me.

"He's giving you the silent treatment."

Bear guffawed at his own joke. His fingers tweaked and tightened the pegs of his Flying V, tuning the guitar by memory rather than by ear first, like some goddamn Jedi master.

"A little help, here. Please?"

Bear abandoned the guitar and approached his nephew. "Logan. Mick says your bowl's too small and he wants to bake a new cake with you. Homemade."

I watched as Bear's fingers flew along with his audio cues. He brought his flat palms close together to show Logan the bowl was dinky. His left hand then went palm down, and he arched his other hand into a claw, bringing it down on top of his flat hand like a cup.

Logan bit his lip and fidgeted with the empty cake mix box.

I clutched my fist to my chest and rolled it emphatically.

Sorry was the one word in sign language I was becoming really good at.

Logan gave me a curt nod and then his fingers began flying. With one palm up, he karate-chopped it with a V-shaped slicing movement. I thought I caught a couple of letters I recognized, but was helpless without Bear to interpret.

"He says he's pretty committed to this super-moist devil's food cake but you can help him make frosting."

"Okay then." If Logan had his heart set on the box cake, we were going to make it the best damn box cake ever. With a little help from an extra egg, milk swapped for water, and a stealth addition of instant pudding.

Three layers, no problem.

Bear went back to his guitar, and Logan and I worked in perfect harmony in the kitchen. The cake pans went into the oven and Logan chose sour cream fudge frosting from the recipes stored on my phone. Luckily, I kept a small store of Perugina dark chocolate on hand in the Half Acre's pantry. I put Logan to work breaking the bars while I yanked down pots from the gleaming rack overhead to start a double boiler. The clanging metal and cloying sweetness of the chocolate were debilitating with my hangover, but I pressed on.

"Double digits, huh?" I formed my words carefully. "The big time."

Logan gave me a broad smile, all teeth. He proudly rocked his fist back and forth, his thumb up. "Ten."

I smiled back. "Happy birthday, buddy."

Logan was profoundly deaf. He knew no different; to him it wasn't a loss. It had happened before he was born.

"No, we don't know what caused his hearing loss," Quinn would sweetly respond to a curious well-wisher's inquiry. "But let's pass the responsibility on to his father, shall we? Give him a little credit in all of this."

I hoped Nash would take a few precious seconds out of his busy rock star schedule to at least call today, and check in on the son he'd left behind.

"Did you see the paper today?" Bear happened to ask, that "share half a brain" thing in full effect.

"Nash getting a key to the city? Yeah. Crazy, right?"

"Totally," Bear agreed. "We don't even live in a city. It's a borough." Bear's mind worked in mysterious ways, and his earnest expression made me laugh.

"It's all symbolic," I assured him. "I hope he knows it won't get him lap dances."

"Or out of parking tickets," Bear joked. "Let's not mention it to She Who Runs the Household. Not today, anyway."

"Agreed." At twenty-nine, Bear's sister was the matriarch of the Bradley family. Not that anyone would ever dare call her matriarch.

"So I heard the wedding was quite a circus." Bear gave each string a good stretch before cutting off the excess with wire cutters. "Or maybe it was a zoo . . ."

Hardy har har. I knew what he was getting at. There were no cougars in the circus.

"Which band are you gigging with tonight?" I asked, changing the subject.

Bear played in at least a dozen cover bands around the Northeast. He called them "tributes," and was able to not only flawlessly re-create the music, but fabricate the look of the lead guitarist responsible for it as well.

"Guess!" He grinned. "We're called No Bone Movies."

The names were almost always references to the most obscure songs in the original band's repertoire, that only the die-hard fans would make sense of. But I recognized the black and white polka-dot V-shaped guitar. "You're Randy Rhoads tonight."

"Yep. Ozzy tribute. You should see the singer, he's got the shakes and everything."

"Nice. I like the paint job."

"Uh-oh, here comes the Mighty Quinn," Bear warned, running through a few power chords that sounded like the theme from *Jaws*, ominous even without amplification.

Her pounding ascent up the porch steps belied the one-hundred-pound, soaking wet weight and petite, slim stature that eventually appeared in the kitchen doorway.

"I started him on the box mix because you were MIA."

My chocolate in the double boiler was silky and smooth. Quinn's voice was anything but. Logan handed me the butter and in it went, melting effortlessly as I stirred.

"A word, Spencer." There was ice in her tone, but she smiled big toward Logan and signed what I could only imagine meant, *Wow, sweetie. Your cake smells heavenly even though the devil incarnate is helping you bake it.*

"Bear, help Logan with the sour cream and Karo? Just whisk it in," I directed, turning off the burner. "It's going to need to stand awhile."

"Seriously, Mick? The one day when I could do with you being present and accounted for?" Quinn had turned her back so Logan couldn't read her lips as she ripped me a new one. And sure enough, she gripped fresh 8x10s in her fist. "It's his goddamn birthday and all he wanted to do was wake up and bake a freakin' cake with you! And you roll in, reeking of whiskey and mother of the bride? For fuck's sake!"

"Body language," I said through gritted teeth, jerking my head toward the dining room. Logan might not have been able to read our lips, but a blind man would've been able to sense the tension.

She stormed ahead of me. On the seldom-used antique oak dining table, where we served the rare, occasional guests their breakfasts, she smacked one photo down after another. There I was in stark, monochromatic clarity. Clutching the neck of a bottle of Jack like it was an extension of my dick. Jeez. The next photo was a bit more benign: the bride, looking lovely, with the ladies of her wedding party. Even though the picture was in black-and-white, I remembered the colors. Her bridesmaids wore navy, while her mother was voluptuous and stunning in periwinkle blue. Not a hair out of place. On to the next shot: me on the dance floor, grabbing a handful of hot, periwinkle mother-of-the-bride ass.

"Mandy Davis, Mick? Seriously?"

"I know, I know. It was just . . . God, she called in a panic saying the caterers were butchering the cake trying to cut it, and I was just around the corner, so I popped in the back and sliced it for her—"

Quinn interrupted with a disgusted click of her tongue. "And then she wanted to repay you so she gave you a bottle from the top shelf and one thing led to another, right? Jeez, Mick. I *recommended* you for the job. What does that make me look like?"

"A pimp?" Bear supplied, loud and clear from the kitchen.

Quinn's eyes widened, infuriated. Their warm brown color always made me think of my first experience tempering chocolate in pastry arts class. When Quinn was calm—or properly tempered—her eyes were shiny, smooth, and creamy pools. When she was angry, they took on a dull, mottled, and waxy look. It took me tons of practice to learn how to temper chocolate correctly. And I still hadn't mastered tempering Quinn.

"I let Bear talk me into allowing you to live here because I thought it would be good to have another guy around, for Logan. And so you could help out on the breakfast side of things with guests. But you've been bedding every skirt that comes your way in, in . . . I don't know, some vain attempt to fuck your misery away after moving back from New Orleans? It's getting really old, Mick." Her voice shook. "I think you need to start looking for a place of your own. You've been back home almost a year now."

"Come on, Quinn. I'm sorry. I *do* help out, I never mind chilling with Logan, and you know I would *never* hook up with a guest, or bring anyone back here . . ." The latter was one of the most appealing things about living at the Half Acre. If I had an itch to scratch, it was separate from my life here, with my friends. It was just an itch. That was it.

"It's only a matter of time." Her words cut deep. "And you are taking up a room I could be renting nightly."

I had been stewing in my wounded pride, letting ego and anger simmer for a while now. But even I had a boiling point.

"Guess what, Quinn? Summer tourist season, if you want to call it that, is over. The phone barely rings. And besides the leaf-peepers who will be here for a week this fall, and the random gay couple escaping Queen Village for some antiquing upstate? Who's coming to book your rooms, huh?" If anything, my monthly rent was helping her keep the damn property in her family. "You're not exactly turning a profit as an innkeeper."

"All the more reason not to mess with my wedding business." Her eyes had tempered to hard and unbreakable.

"We're in the same business," I reminded, my hands outstretched to appease her. "Same mission, Bradley. I'm on your side."

"Well, Mandy Davis is on the chamber of commerce board. And I like my membership there. So keep your dick in your pants and your head in the game."

A blistering guitar solo rattled the stained glass windows of the dining room, and Bacon skidded by, ears back and claws scrambling. Bear had united the rock-and-roll trinity of guitar jack, power cord, and amplifier.

"It's no wonder we have no guests here!" Quinn bellowed loud enough for her brother to hear. "It's a madhouse!"

"No, that's next week," Bear called. "Anthrax tribute."

She gathered up all the photos with a hefty sigh, and I sincerely hoped she was going to make the incriminating ones disappear. "You'll help Bear with the party tent? And the tables? And the piñata?"

"Yes, yes. All of it. I just have to go down to the shop to get the Spidey cupcakes, and meet with one bride. My aunt set up a Sunday consult. I promise it will be quick. Just a meet and greet."

"It had better be."

I gave Quinn my best *trust me, I'm a total professional* look.

She moved to go, but turned back for one last scrutinizing glance.

I thought she was going for the old "what's that on your shirt?" gag we all used to do when we were kids, as she came at me with a pointed finger. Many a nose had been flicked as a result of falling for that bit. But Quinn wasn't in the joking mood. Her curiosity morphed into disgust.

"You've got chocolate syrup in the hollow of your throat."

Dani

WALK THE LINE

"Nash! NASH! I love you!"

"Marry me, Nash!"

"NASH!"

The term "screaming bloody murder" had nothing on the girls gathered who were "screaming bloody matrimony." One well-placed shriek at close range from the sea of groupies made me wish I had thought to grab my earplugs off the tour bus. I barely gave them a second thought at concerts; they were a necessary evil.

The groupies, that is. Earplugs were a godsend.

But we weren't at one of Go Get Her's concerts; we were trying to get a mere twenty feet from door to curb where the limo was waiting. "So much for sneaking out the side door," I hollered at Nash's back. The rest of the band had already been whisked off by the bus, along with a hoodie-and-shades-wearing decoy from the road crew roughly the same height and build as their lead singer, twenty minutes prior. The Nash worshippers were apparently smarter than Riggs gave them credit for.

Their arms undulated like stinging anemone: pretty but painful if they made contact. "Give him room, ladies. Move back!" Riggs barked, his elbow going up to block limbs being thrown in his path as he led us through the melee. With one hand resting on Nash's shoulder and the other at his waist, I brought up the end of our demented little conga line.

A lacquered talon of a nail hooked around one of my curls and yanked. I gasped and reflexively moved my hands to my head, letting go of the back of Nash's shirt. Like predators sensing a weakness in their prey, a few girls pounced at their chance, inserting themselves behind him and shoving me back.

This is crazy, the thought jostled my brain. *Just walk away.*

It would be so easy to slip farther back into the crowd and disappear altogether. But a deal was a deal, and the ring on my finger had been placed there in good faith.

Nash needed someone who wasn't going to blow smoke up his ass.

The girls were mewing and clawing at his backside, jockeying for position behind him. All dead giveaways that Nash had lost me in the shuffle.

I didn't blow smoke up his ass, nor did I kiss said ass, or fondle it.

"Try not to get separated from him, girlie. Not when he's only just proposed to you," Riggs barked, pushing Nash into the plush sanctuary of the limo and pulling me in behind him.

"Speaking of which . . ." Nash poured vodka from the limo bar. "I'm up by three today. Drink."

Riggs shook his head as I downed the shot. "Only you two would make a drinking game out of marriage proposals."

"I'm still winning," I proclaimed, delicately wiping my lips with the back of my hand. "I'm pretty sure the proposal I got from that certain British singer earned bonus points."

"Laugh it up now, buttercup. You can bust my chops all you want behind closed doors, all right? But when we get to New Hope, it's all eyes on me, China Doll. I'm your world. Got it?"

"Yes, Mr. Drama." I made my voice as shimmering and breathy as Marilyn's during her birthday sing-along to President Kennedy. Riggs rolled his eyes, but seemed to relax as the limo provided us a smooth escape from the gawkers and groupies, carrying us down the turnpike toward Newark airport.

"I'm off to L.A. for the week." Riggs pried the empty shot glass from my hand and replaced it with a lengthy, printed list. "I want to see him back in New York at the label headquarters first thing next Monday, after the award ceremony. Big meeting about the next album and tour."

All games were now over, apparently.

"What, have I become his pro bono publicist as well?" I asked, perusing the bullet points meant to get Nash through the week with as much good press as possible. They read about as opportunistic and clichéd as a politician's baby-kissing along the campaign trail.

"Aren't 'better halves' naturally designed to do damage control?" Riggs teased. "Don't throw that out the window," he warned my fiancé. "I'm e-mailing her a copy anyway."

He handed Nash a parking garage ticket. "My Porsche is in P4. Enjoy the wilds of Pennsylvania." To me, he gave a wink. "Don't pick up any hitchhikers."

Mick

CAKE DUMMY

It didn't matter how long I had been gone, or how much our tiny tourist town had changed. The minute I turned off Bridge Street, the aroma of vanilla in the air socked me in a strange place between my gut and my heart. *Wolkoff's Bakery—every batch baked with love!* was the motto of my aunt Sindy and uncle Walt's shop, and as a kid it was my go-to place through every season.

Pennsylvania winters were cold and I was never dressed quite warm enough, but the inside of the bakery was a safe haven of buttery steam, where a cup of hot cocoa was always waiting. Spring was ushered in with samples of Walt's famous wet-bottom shoofly pie, and summer days weren't complete without dipping into one of Sindy's towering icebox cakes. Fall would come and I'd go with my aunt and uncle to Heaven's Half Acre, where the Bradleys would let us pick apples from the orchard to our hearts' content, in exchange for some of the resulting tarts and pies. Their guests gobbled up the apple, the pecan, and the pumpkin delicacies produced from September until it was time to start baking for the Christmas rush. And then the cycle would begin again.

Throughout it all, the wedding cakes in the window were a constant fixation for me. I'd press my nose against the display, just a layer of glass between my tongue and the perfectly iced cake dummies, which I had no idea were fake. The royal icing spread across them like an untouched field of snow. Crispy curled lines along the borders, sugar shells scalloping the corners, star-tipped peaks stiff and glittering—my teeth ached to sample it all. I'd let my eyes drop out of focus, staring at the endless palette of white on white, on top of even more white.

No matter what, those cakes never changed.

They stood the test of time, just like I thought Aunt Sindy and Uncle Walt's bakery would. *Wolkoff's Bakery—every batch baked with love!*

Sometimes even love just wasn't enough to sustain you.

"Hi, Mick."

I turned in the direction of the flirty greeting. A leggy brunette with a yoga bag slung over her shoulder sauntered toward me. It took me a minute to place her.

It always did.

Zuckerman wedding. Naked chocolate cake with raspberry buttercream, twelve layers.

"Hey, how are you?" I flashed a polite but friendly smile. Her strapless lavender silk bridesmaid's gown had been a bitch to get off. *That* I remembered vividly.

"When are you going to start making those white chocolate cheesecakes again? Lizzie brought one to our book club last month and oh my God, I practically had a foodgasm!" She squeezed the strap of her yoga bag and all but moaned at the memory.

"I can let you know when I put them back on the menu."

She fished through the side pocket in her yoga bag, and pressed her business card into my hand. "Definitely do."

Flashing a grin, she sashayed away, Lululemons hugging her firm, ripe bottom like nobody's business. *Heaven help me.*

I peeked at the card as I unlocked the door to the Night Kitchen. *Sarah-with-an-h*. I remembered her saying that now. Grabbing a pen, I flipped the card over, jotting down *w. choc. cheesecake* on the back of it and tacking it on the corkboard near the register.

I really didn't need to write down, or remember, the other stuff.

The Night Kitchen was at its quietest on Sunday morning. Everything scrubbed down and *mise en place* waiting for me to start my weird brand of culinary black magic. *Mick Spencer's sweet voodoo*, one food critic hailed.

When the keys to Wolkoff's were handed down, I turned the tables on the old bakery standard and created a dessert bar that jumped until midnight most weekends. It was a date-night destination with serving sizes made for sharing, a pickup joint with sweet sultry fare, and the place people stopped off at after work for carefully crafted, decadent desserts to bring home. Sindy was a morning person, and I was a night owl. We made a great team, along with our hipster staff of movers and shakers from the local community college culinary program.

And we did wedding cakes, too.

The planner book displayed *1pm— James wedding cake consult* in my aunt's shaky, old lady scrawl, followed by a New York cell number. Sundays were usually our day of rest—for Sindy, it was church day. And for me, usually recovery from whatever sinning I did on Saturday night. I liked to come in around five or six in the evening and start prepping and baking for the week.

"But this couple's from out of town," Sindy had informed me after she took the call. "And the bride sounded so sweet. I made an exception. Promise me you'll be there at one o'clock to meet her?"

"Promises, promises," I muttered, flicking on the lights and making myself an espresso. Logan's Spiderman cupcakes sat undisturbed, right where I had left them upon receiving the frantic cake emergency call from the mother of the bride last night. Pulled sugar was used to create his webbing, and the faces were airbrushed a toxic-looking red. I sincerely hoped Quinn had checked with all the parents about dye allergies.

Tilting my head to the left and right resulted in a much-needed neck crack. I'd showered away the evidence but I still had a sugar hangover, a whiskey headache, and the lingering scent of Mandy Davis's perfume in my nostrils. But it was all fading by the minute.

Soon she'd just be another memory. A vague recollection: Oh yeah. Davis-Dixon wedding. Vanilla champagne cake with peach buttercream. Periwinkle dress.

Story of my life.

I sat at my empty bar, allowing a sigh to escape before downing the shot of espresso.

Who was I kidding? I was still waiting for my life to start.

"At the risk of sounding horribly cliché, where have you been all my life?" Dani had murmured, her lips catching the spot between my jawbone and earlobe. "Please tell me we are not related."

Her words had made me chuckle, although their strength forced me to weigh my own words carefully. "We aren't . . . unless you're talking on a cosmic level." I brought her hand, fingers still laced with mine, up for a lingering kiss. "If so, then yes. Most definitely."

She wore no rings, and I bore no strings—this night could be anything she wanted. I was all consumed, and I was all hers.

We had danced and talked straight through the cocktail hour, shunning any offer of passed hors d'oeuvres, choosing instead to devour each other with our gaze. Now dinner was being served, and I had no desire to let her go.

"So you must be on Pat's side, then?"

Ah yes, this was a wedding, after all. There were mutual friends, but the blending of families was just beginning. If I wasn't on her side,

I must be on Pat's. Now if only I knew whether Pat was the bride or the groom. Damn androgynous nicknames.

"Yep. I'm the black sheep that doesn't quite fit in."

There was a bit of truth to that. From New Hope to New Orleans, I had traveled twelve hundred miles and was still trying to figure out where I belonged.

Dani laughed and turned us toward a large table of well-dressed wedding guests. "I know what you mean. Check it out. Every person sitting over there has a PhD, MD, or PsyD after their name." She reached out and snagged a fizzing champagne flute from a passing tray. "The only PhD I've earned is 'Parents having Doubts' about me. Otherwise known as the 'third degree,' which they put me through every time I come home."

"Funny, my degree is in 'Pathetic hopeless Dreaming.'" I twirled her away from the tables. "You should come see my diploma sometime; I've got it framed on my wall."

My clever retort earned a smile from her that heated up all of New Orleans Parish and sent lust sweeping through me. I wanted to shed the ridiculous masks we were both hiding behind, hating any barrier between us as we swayed, hips locked, across the ballroom floor. But then again, they freed us from convention and heightened our senses. I loved the feel of the feathers mingling with her curls as I ran my hands over her hair, and to watch her long lashes flutter against the cat's-eye holes of her glittering mask. The way she bit her bottom lip, glossed like an all-day sucker, as she ran her thumb along the hard edge framing my cheek was damn hot. The mask might have disguised my appearance, but there was no hiding my desire. She was forcing my nether regions to give my long-beaked disguise a run for its money.

"May I cut in?"

The bride stood before us, radiant from her big day. She toyed with her own mask, a white glittering affair that was perched on the *end of a stick. There was a detached serenity about her that, as a wedding vendor, I'd noticed other newly married women develop as their wedding day wore on.*

"How can I refuse?" Dani said, as I reluctantly released her and bowed deeply to my new dance partner. It was hard to tear my eyes from the vision in green as she wove through the crowds toward the bar.

"Having a good time?" the bride asked, smiling at me. She was pretty in a sharp-boned way, her hazel eyes made more dramatic by her wedding makeup.

"I've been to a lot of weddings," I began, choosing my words carefully. "Yours is by far one of the most . . ." Dani shook back her curls and leaned on the bar, and I almost forgot what I was saying. ". . . breathtaking."

"Thank you." We danced formally, forced to hold each other at arm's length because of her full gown. I saw her take in the occupational hazard of sheet pan burns neatly parading up my forearms. "Everyone told me the day would go by in a blur, and I'd be so distracted I'd forget to even eat, but you know what? I didn't. Now my sister, on the other hand . . ." She turned her regal neck in the direction of Dani, who had downed her champagne and was now talking to the bartender.

"I normally pay no mind to her love life. It's always been easy come, easy go with Dani and I can barely keep track. Plus she takes care of herself. But you . . . you've distracted her. And before you let that go to your head"—she tightened her grip on my hand, the new wedding band grinding against my knuckle—"know that I'm watching you, Bird Boy. I don't know who you are, or where you came from, but you'd better know exactly what you want, and what it's worth to you, okay? I know my sister better than anyone. And to see her so . . ." She shook her head, as if she needed to shake the words into place. "Just consider yourself lucky."

I did feel lucky, among many other things. Dani was more than just a pretty face and a smoking-hot body. She wasn't just another easy lay in the Big Easy. I could see the playful calculation behind that blue velvet stare of hers. She was up for the adventure, but following her own road map when it came to the journey. I was up for whatever ride she wanted to take me on. She had matched me, flirt for flirt, line for line, and challenge for challenge that night.

"I do," I said, realizing the irony of those two specific words being uttered to a bride, on her wedding day. "And thank you."

For not throwing me out on my ass, *I wanted to add.* For giving me a shot—and possibly your blessing—with your maid of honor. *I was a fox in the henhouse, as my friend Nash always liked to say, being called out by the queen of the coop. And she had made it clear. There would be no blood on the feathers during her watch.*

Dani's sister broke contact with me, bringing her mask up to her face as our song ended and another one began. A cluster of women descended, wanting to retro dance with their friend to the nineties Deee-Lite classic pumping from the speakers. Something about those dark eyes flashing from behind all the glittering white conveyed a solemn pact that I couldn't help but enter into. Don't fuck up.

I turned away; my only goal was getting Dani back in my hands. The bar was layered now three rows deep with people, but there she was, grooving to the music and shimmying back into my arms. She slid a shot glass to my lips and threw back her own. Tequila and adrenaline raced like white lightning to my fingertips as I boldly traced the hint of cleavage through the opening in the neck of her bridesmaid dress.

Grabbing my hand, she pulled us across the reception hall to the deserted lobby. There was a photo booth in one corner to capture both a souvenir shot and a duplicate for the guest book. An old-fashioned typewriter sat on a table, along with heavy cardstock in pastels, waiting for guests to pound out their well wishes and pin them to a clothesline draping the walkway. Dani strutted to the table, leaned delectably down, and began to hammer out a message. Then she snagged a clothespin and clipped the card to the black velvet drape of the photo booth curtain.

"It's not seventy-two-point font, but it will do."

"Out of order, huh?" I gave her a wicked smile as she pulled me in. Her stiletto kicked the red-lit button, and the countdown on the screen began.

"Oops, my bad!" she joked, and we mugged stone-faced in our masks for the camera before collapsing into laughter. "I thought it might buy us a few minutes of alone time."

It was actually larger than most rented booths of its type, its red-and-cream-striped sides resembling an old vaudeville tent, and outfitted with a long leather seat and several hooks on the wall for photo props. More masks, as well as feathered boas and strings of beads, hung above us.

"Your sister's really into this whole Mardi Gras look, huh?" I asked as Dani draped herself over me. "The colors, the masks . . ."

"Did you know the Mardi Gras colors have meanings?" she asked, slowly removing her mask and setting it aside. She had the face of an angel, with a devilish look in her eye. "Gold for power," she said softly.

"And?" I prompted, my fingertips rushing to touch the creamy skin unmasked. God, she was gorgeous.

"And . . . I'll get to the rest later. Now, let me get a look at you, mystery man."

I pulled off the black and gold mask by its long-beaked nose. Finally rid of the cumbersome proboscis, I could pull her in close for a kiss on the lips. They were as soft and lush as the blooming buttercream rosettes I spun endlessly in the bakery, and I longed to trace them with my tongue, starting in a tight spiral and moving out.

She sighed and deepened the kiss, the lime and tequila on her tongue intoxicating me as it mixed with the heady scent of almond and lavender on her pulse points. "You smell good enough to eat," I whispered, moving my lips along her wrist and down her forearm as she snaked her fingers through my hair.

Her laugh was breathy. "I massaged the entire bridal party earlier. My wedding gift to Posy and Pat."

She hit that sensitive spot again between my jawbone and ear, causing me to buck up against her, already rock hard and ready.

"You're a good sister." I groaned as she gyrated slowly on top of my lap, gently tugging on my earlobe with her teeth. Cupping her ample breasts, I kissed my way, openmouthed, down the keyhole neckline of her dress, causing her to gasp as I flicked my tongue under the silky fabric.

"I'm the worst maid of honor, though." Her fingers reached down behind her and caressed the hard-on already straining at the seams of my dress pants. "'Cause I'm so ready to bail on all my duties, run off, and have my way with you."

This girl was driving me mad. My knee jerked, hitting the camera button again, and she threw her hair over one bare shoulder, glancing with a sly wink at the screen as the first flash popped.

She knew exactly what she was doing to me.

Well, two could play at this game.

I quickly flipped her on my lap, causing her to squeal in surprise and catch me around the neck. "Don't lose me," she pleaded. The camera captured us tangled and gazing into each other's eyes.

"Never."

I dipped down to drop a kiss on her lips for the final shot, feeling the flash bright behind closed eyelids. There my mouth lingered, gently exploring hers, long after I heard the finished photos drop down into their slot for pickup.

"Will your family miss you?" she asked as we finally came up for air.

I felt a twinge in my chest, caught somewhere between the lie that had brought us together, and the truth that might break us apart. I just wanted—no, I needed—more time. I craved to know her.

"They won't even notice I'm gone."

Hand in hand, we moved toward the exit door.

"Wait! The pictures." I looped us back and palmed the double prints from the slot in the side of the booth, tucking them into my vest pocket just as a hand clapped on the back of my shoulder.

"Hurry," a well-meaning guest urged. His next words caused the baker in me to stop in my tracks. "They're about to cut the cake!"

With shaking fingers, I thumbed to the back of my planner book. Tucked deep in the back pocket of the portfolio were both sets of photographs, the only tangible evidence I had of the girl who tortured my memory. But there was no time to brood over them, not with a bride and groom on their way.

Dani

SOCIAL CALL

"This is silly," I blurted as Nash threw the car into park at the bottom of the hill. "Maybe we should go to Philly and check into the hotel first. Make some calls?"

Prepare your people?

While driving through his small hometown, the enormity of what we were about to do hit me, and I was suddenly nervous to meet his friends. Ten years was a long time to stay scarce, and he hadn't informed anyone of our impending arrival. While the main drag had been lively, this part of New Hope looked half-asleep and all the red carpets were rolled up for the weekend.

"Oh, come on. This'll be fun. It's been forever since I've busted Spencer's chops." He gave my knee a pat, but his attention was on the rearview mirror, running a hand through his haystack of hair and doing a big-smile teeth check. "How do I look?"

"Exactly the same as you did when we left New York."

Something about him did seem different, however, under the quiet canopy of the tree-lined street. I took in his whole ensemble: from snakeskin cowboy boot tip to the four-hundred-dollar aviator sunglasses he pushed over his lank, dark blond locks. I couldn't put my finger on it exactly, other than the fact that he had been surrounded by fans, handlers, wranglers, runners, publicists, ass-kissers, his manager, and countless other musicians since the time I had met him. And now, in this sleepy little town of his birth, he had no one to hide behind.

Except for me.

"You go on inside through the front." He cleared his throat and nodded at the deserted-looking bakery. "I'm gonna sneak through the back door and surprise him."

"You sure your friend still works there? And he's not armed? What are the gun laws in Pennsylvania?"

Nash's laugh followed me out the car door. "He's the owner. And believe me. Spencer is a lover, not a fighter," he called after me.

I hurried across the street, looking both ways as an inherent New Yorker, even though there was only one stoplight, blocks away, and barely any traffic. The handwritten sign hanging on the Night Kitchen's window read *Closed* in curvy, eclectic letters, but the heavy blue-black door yielded under my push.

Inside was nothing like any bakery I had ever seen. Rich marbled walls in a deep golden brown greeted me, rising up to a curved ceiling that was painted the same midnight blue as the front door. Tiny twinkling lights crisscrossed it like stars in the sky. High tables for two dotted the wood-planked floor and faced out for a street view, and a long bar of sleek black granite curved against one wall. But the showstopper was the bakery case that ran along the opposite wall.

Holy Mother of Cakes.

The selection was unreal, and the concoctions looked ethereal.

Every dessert has a story behind it.

The memory of my mystery man's words hit me so hard that I left fingerprints on the glass case just to keep myself upright. It had been Mick who had explained the tradition of the groom's cake, not to be eaten at Posy and Pat's wedding, but rather to be boxed and sent home with the guests. "In days of old, single women would sleep with it under their pillows in hopes of dreaming of their future husbands," he had added with a devilish raise of his brow. I'd already had to endure the cake pull, which was slightly less physical—and pathetic— than having to dive shamelessly for the bouquet. Mick had also shared the significance behind that Victorian practice, which New Orleans had made its own: stuffing little silver charms attached to ribbons between the wedding cake layers, which unmarried women pulled for good luck and fortune.

Why are single women depicted as always having to be plied and consoled with sweets? I had challenged, *and how come you know so much about cakes?*

I like stories, he had replied simply. *Every dessert has a story behind it.*

Somewhere within the bakery, a clock chimed once.

One o'clock, on the dot.

"Dani?"

Mick

CHARMED, I'M SURE

"Mick?"

She had a voice that sounded like she smoked a pack a day, but a body that looked like a temple no one would dare desecrate. Just like I remembered.

I had ruled out hallucination, but there was no scientific proof that the girl I had thought of every goddamn day for the last eleven months was standing in my shop. And wasn't just a figment of my lonely and desperate imagination.

Until her shaking fingers made contact with the silver charm resting at her throat.

She had pulled it from her sister's cake that night, had laughed and swung it seductively from its satin ribbon before turning in my direction and slowly licking the frosting from it with a wink.

You'll be next, Dani! an ancient relative of hers had crowed.

For Dani had pulled a tiny, silver three-tiered wedding cake as her charm.

"How in the—how did you—?"

Her eyes widened, just before mine were clamped into darkness by a pair of mammoth hands. Native fear iced my spine, just as cold as the silver ring crushing my cheekbone. Already hopped up on the adrenaline injection of her presence, I launched into automatic combat mode. My heel kicked back against my attacker's shin as my elbow swung into ribs. Hard.

"Christ, Spencer! I thought you were a lover, not a fighter," gasped a voice that I had only heard via phone lines and the radio airwaves for the better part of ten long years.

Vision unblocked, I spun around. Ready, willing, and able to deliver a knee to the groin of my oldest friend in the world.

"Nash?"

He was doubled over and clutching his torso. Dani materialized at his side, helping him upright.

"What the hell did you do that for?" For a split second, I thought she was yelling at him, but then I realized the venom was directed toward me. "Do you always attack people who come into your shop?"

"Gee, maybe I should've called the cops instead," I snarled, only satisfied when I saw her face grow crimson. Confirming my yearlong suspicions.

The New Orleans gendarmerie had descended upon the Café Du Monde at dawn. I keenly remembered the surreal feeling. Like out of a film noir. Especially with the rain, slicking the dust down from the landmark's awning and leaving it a shiny green and white. It had felt like an out-of-body experience, like I had been watching from high above and not dragged to the curb of Decatur Street like a dog.

My only crime had been believing she could've fallen for a fool like me.

Dani fussed over Nash, but he waved her away. "It's okay, babe. No harm," he labored, "no foul."

I hadn't recovered from my shock of seeing Dani, and couldn't reconcile why my best friend was sneaking through my kitchen and pulling the peekaboo act.

I needed a rewind. A do-over. What the hell was Nash doing here, and—

Wait. *Babe?*

He grabbed me in a tight hug. "Hey now, is that a rolling pin in your front pocket, or are you happy to see me?" He had obviously recovered fast, as his lame baker joke mechanism was intact.

"Offset spatula, actually." I thumped on his back. "Good to see you, man. You scared the daylights outta me." My eyes met Dani's over his shoulder. "Never in a million years . . ." I murmured. The blush that spread across her delicate features turned my heart upside down.

"Ha, gotcha!" He grinned. "Did you meet your one o'clock appointment yet?"

1pm—James wedding cake consult. Her name and number had been living in my appointment book for a week, and I hadn't even known it.

Nash slung his arm around my shoulder and propelled us around to face her. "This is my fiancée, Dani James. Dani, meet the infamous Mick Spencer."

If Dani was doing any recovering of her own, it wasn't apparent from her expression. She swung her curls back off her shoulders and pasted a smile on. "I've heard a lot about you, *Spencer.*" Her hand extended to grasp mine, and I saw the flash of platinum and diamond.

"The man, the myth, the legend," Nash added, for nobody's real benefit.

Fiancée. *Oh, fuck me sideways. Seriously?* Touching just her hand was torture. I wanted to pull it against my heart, to pull *her* out of the shop with me, never to return. But I settled for a quick and meaningful squeeze.

"Please." I reddened. "Call me Mick. Most people do."

"Except for Mandy Davis, who I heard was calling you 'Oh God' last night," Nash laughed, giving my arm a conspiratorial punch. "Bear told me about your hookup. On her daughter's wedding night, no less!"

The bakery was missing a trapdoor. Falling through the floor would've come in handy right about then. Dani's eyes were on the hardwood as well, and I had to wonder if she was wishing for the exact same escape route for herself.

"When did you talk to Bear?"

"Didn't." Nash helped himself to a chocolate chip cookie from under the glass dome next to the register. "He texted me."

Seriously? Bear had nothing better to text our mutual best friend about? He couldn't drop a little hint about something slightly more important? Say, the tenth birthday of the child Nash had never seen?

"Dude, I totally tapped that back when I was in high school!" Nash bellowed. "Could've given you my *crib* notes, if you know what I mean."

It was impossible to not know what he meant. I cringed inwardly.

Dani cleared her throat. Not that I could've ever forgotten that she was there, but Nash apparently had.

"So, Dani . . . is that short for Danielle?" *I searched for you,* I tried to convey with my eyes. *Scoured the Internet for your sister's wedding announcement, knowing you shared a maiden name. Hunted through the White Pages . . .*

"Danica."

Ah, no wonder. I hoped every Danielle James in the tri-state area would forgive me for cyber-stalking them. It hadn't occurred to me there might be a variant.

"So, um . . . how'd you two meet?" *And where? And when?* My brain wanted to scream. And why. *Why, why, why?*

Nash's arm slid around Dani's waist, pulling her against his hip. "We met on tour, if you can believe that. She was a damsel in distress."

Dani gave a cute snort. "You thought I was a groupie in heat."

"My bad." Nash gave a shrug and winked in my direction. "I'll never forget, seeing her out the tour bus window for the first time. She was standing by this old, broken-down van at the side of the road, waving a white lacy thong like a matador—" He butted his forehead against her shoulder, like a big bull come to rut.

"Oh?" I managed, swallowed hard. The espresso I'd had earlier threatened to burn its way back up my throat.

"It wasn't a *thong*, you perv!" Dani gave a tug on his long locks. "It was a camisole. And it was the only thing white I had."

I felt cheated out of my own first glimpse of her, seeing her waving that white kerchief in that New Orleans second line. That was my precious memory, and now Nash had bragging rights to a similar vision? Where was the justice?

While I had had very little growing up, Nash had had even less. Living on a slice of the Half Acre's property in a broken-down trailer with his father, inheriting Bear's hand-me-down clothing. I remember how jealous he had been the year Sindy and Walt bought me a Huffy Green Machine big wheel for my birthday. I was the neighborhood badass on that thing, until Nash knocked me off and bloodied my nose for a turn.

And now he had something that made the eight-year-old green-eyed monster in *me* want to pop him in the face for.

"It was his tour manager who stopped, concerned," Dani supplied, bringing me back to the here and now. "This one?" She thumbed back at Nash, who was still clutching her waist. "He offered me a condom and *a real ride*."

"Hey, that was a compliment, darlin'. There were already three other girls on the bus ahead of you that night, and I only had two condoms with me. You do the math."

"I'm not doing anything or anybody." Dani laughed. "Isn't that what I told you that night?"

She gave him a push away, and went to look at the baked goods at the end of the case.

Nash dropped the rest of the cookie he didn't offer to pay for into his mouth and brushed off his hands. Somewhere deep in the pockets of his designer jeans, his cell phone was ringing. The clown actually had his ringtone set to "Jumpstart My Heart"—who uses their own biggest hit as their ringtone? Someone way too impressed with himself, obviously.

"The hard-to-get act; such a turn-on, right?"

The lopsided grin he flashed me was his liar face. I hadn't seen it in a decade, but it wasn't one I'd forget. He'd gotten out of homework, detention, and speeding tickets with that grin. And he had gotten into plenty of panties with it, too.

I really didn't want to think about Nash being anywhere near the vicinity of Dani's panties. Instead, I joined her at the end of the case as he took his call, and hoped to get a real word in edgewise. Pretending not to know this woman, when every bit of me craved to make up for lost time, was cruel and unusual punishment.

"That is gorgeous," she said softly, her eyes fixated on the sole wedding cake on display. "Is it real?"

I stared down at my creation under glass as well. Sometimes I could barely believe these hands could be capable of something so breathtaking. I baked every cake sample to keep on display when I knew a bride was coming in, and then it became part of our dessert selection. Amazing how many repeat customers came back, just to sample this week's "wedge o' wedding," as I called it. Guys would pull me aside with a wink and a nudge, just to tell me what powerful aphrodisiac effects it had had on their dates.

Gone were the days of Sindy and Walt's unchanging and pristine white displays. I still baked with love, but it was my own brand of love.

Beautiful. Fleeting. And perishable.

"Totally real. The only dummy in my shop is the one you're

marrying," I said, willing her to look at me. Her head jerked up and a pained look lit across her face but only for a second. *Let me in, Dani. It's me, Mick.* We had shared so much that night. Maybe it hadn't been all the right things, or enough. But it had been amazing all the same. Her eyes channeled hurt, followed by anger.

"I'd rather be with a dummy than a thief," she hissed.

Her accusation sent adrenaline on a collision course with my racing thoughts. She had a hell of a lot of nerve coming into *my* establishment and throwing half-baked assumptions in my face. "I might've lost my job that night, but I had nothing to do with that robbery. Turned out I was in the wrong place at the wrong time. With the wrong person, apparently."

Shock and doubt drifted across her delicate face as she absorbed my words, before boomeranging a retort back at me. "Mother of the bride last night, huh? That had to score double points on your Bang the Bridal Party Bingo game." The words were a low blow, but I couldn't deny I deserved them. Dani took a step back from the bakery case. "Sorry you lost your job, but I hope you won at your little game, player."

"Ha, you think *I'm* a player?" It was hard to keep my voice down with Nash pacing thirty feet away from us and yammering away on his cell phone. I leaned in close, relishing the blend of sweet almond and lavender that seemed to be with her always. She was currently the most breathtaking sweet in my shop, and my hands ached to touch her. "Who do you think taught me everything I know?" I whispered against her hair. "You can't marry that guy, Dani. I've known him all my life, and . . . no."

"There's more to the story . . ." She bit her lip, as if she needed reminding to refrain from saying more. "And you can't deny you lied to my face that night."

"There's more to *our* story! You left before I could explain."

I had raced back to her hotel room after the police had released me. Only to find the maids inside, stripping the bed. *Wait!* I had begged, needing to see for myself.

Sure enough, nestled under the pillows had been the small white box holding her slice of groom's cake.

Had she dreamed of me that night?

Without another word, I pulled the Spiderman cupcakes from the case and began to box them for transport in clear, plastic clamshell containers. Feeling Dani so close, knowing she was watching me, gave me the shakes worse than any hangover or sugar high could.

"If every dessert has a story behind it, what's with the dozen Spidermen?"

"Nash's son is turning ten today." I crimped the tops shut and threw a sideways glance her way. "He *did* tell you he has a kid, right?"

"Of course I know about Logan." Dani's shoulders rose defensively. "But . . ."

"But he didn't tell you it was Logan's birthday today. Because I'll bet he doesn't even know."

Nash was off his call now, and back within earshot. I finished my task, and grabbed a loaded fruit tart from the case as well. The kids would have their Spidey cakes, and no doubt would love Logan's lumpy boxed-mix creation. He had only let me help so much, and so its resulting surface was like the craters of the moon. The adult guests would probably appreciate an alternative.

And I had the feeling I had just invited two more.

Quinn was going to string me up in the orchard, pie me with the fruit tart, and let the turkey vultures come peck my eyes out.

"Did you hear that, Nash? What great timing—your off-road time happened to fall during Logan's birthday. How awesome!" Dani enthused, but the look she channeled toward him was anything but awesome. She was clearly embarrassed for him.

Nash had everything now. Hit songs, a huge following, money in the bank. And that was on top of his golden boy looks and what some might call charm. Rock stars of his caliber didn't have to win girls with the pity card.

She couldn't be with him because she felt sorry for him. Could she?

"That's a big reason why we, um . . . we came into town a week early, anyway." Nash was back and fastened at Dani's side again. She winced under his death grip. "To see the kid! And hey, we even brought him a gift. Perfect! When's the party?"

I glanced up at the clock, remembering my words to Quinn earlier. What was supposed to be a quick cake consult had sucked me into a surreal time vacuum. "Pretty much . . . right now."

Dani shifted uncomfortably under the weight of Nash's arm on her shoulder. "Maybe you should call first?" she suggested to him.

"Yeah," I laughed. The memory of almost taking down Nash was chuckle-worthy now. "Too many surprises for one day might be a little hazardous for your health."

Dani raised a brow at me.

"I'll just text Bear." Nash reached for his phone again.

Of course. Leave Bear to do the dirty work. My laugh dried up in my throat. Wasn't that always the case? Nash taking the easy way out. Or Nash just taking, period.

"Well," I said loudly, clapping my palms together. "Sorry we didn't have time for a full cake consult. Next time you're in, *Danica*, we'll do a tasting."

Mmm, there was that blush again. I could mist color across her face just as quick and precise as waving an airbrush across a cake's perfect surface. Nash was too absorbed in his phone to pick up on my double entendre or her reaction to it.

"Not necessary," she stammered.

"I insist. You need a taste before you can really decide."

"No need," she said stubbornly. "I've already made up my mind." Her eyes were cool, shallow pools, forbidding me to dive too deep. But the silver cake charm at her throat shifted as she swallowed hard.

"Bear said he's on his way here," Nash announced, "And something about driving you back to Mandy Davis's for your van? Or maybe you're just going back for another helping of dessert?" He pumped his fists and pivoted his hips to emphasize *helping*.

"This," I said, thrusting the boxed tart toward him, "is dessert. You're better off not showing up at Quinn's empty-handed."

"Please, Spencer. Does it look like I'm ever empty-handed?" He ignored my offering, choosing instead to snake his arms around Dani's slim hips from behind and work his fingers into the tiny slits passing for pockets on her low-slung jeans. "Come on, babe," he murmured against her neck. "Time for you to meet the whole fam-damily."

Dani reached for the box in my hands. "I'll carry it, Mick. And thank you." She snuggled uneasily against him, eyes never leaving me. "Let's get this party started."

Dani

SMALL WORLD

A baker!

A baker had crashed my sister's wedding. A baker, living here in a borough of twenty-five hundred people. A baker, who just happened to be best friends with one of the country's cockiest, rowdiest rock stars . . . aka my fiancé.

Could the odds get any odder?

Nash didn't say another word until we were back in the car. But the second he turned the key in the ignition, he turned on me. "Could you have at least pretended to be attracted to me?"

"Nash, I—"

"You barely touched me. Or laughed at my jokes."

"Oh, was I supposed to giggle and fondle you while you and your buddy compared the notches in your belt?" I smarted, remembering Mick's player comments and who taught whom. "Why didn't you just hire one of your groupies then, if that's what you wanted?"

"You know why!" He slammed his palm on the steering wheel.

Anguish thickened his voice. "You know!" Clearing his throat, he added, "I can't have you getting cold feet right now, Dani."

My feet wanted to burn a trail right back up to the Night Kitchen's door. I wanted to demand more answers. But there was no going back now. I needed to stay in the here and now, and help Nash.

"It's going to get easier," I said resolutely.

"For you, maybe."

I realized too late the folly of my words. Things were going to get worse for Nash before they would get better.

"One down," he muttered. "Too many more to go." His arms folded across the top of the steering wheel, and he dropped his head to rest on them. "Spencer was one of my closest friends. I thought it would be easy with him."

"You're doing great, Nash." I tentatively touched the back of his neck, feeling the tension corded in his muscles.

"How could I have not known it was the kid's birthday?"

"Sweetie, I've only been on tour for one summer, and I can't even keep my days of the week straight. How long have you been at this?"

He slowly sat upright, arching against my hand like a cat. "Ten years," he whispered.

"Well, you know the old saying 'today's the first day of the rest of your life,' right? So let it be the day you start remembering the little things. Like his birthday. And his favorite color. And whether he's afraid of the dark."

"Those are huge things. I've missed out on so much. I never got to . . . sing him to sleep, you know? Didn't get to hear his first words. Hell, I don't even know his middle name. Quinn never even sent me a picture."

"Did you ever ask for one?"

Nash gave me a long look as my answer. Then he swung the car over the double yellow line and gunned it up the hill, down a side

street, and across a small one-lane bridge. I marveled at the fact that
he had probably clocked a hundred thousand miles on the road since
leaving New Hope, and yet he still remembered his way back.

Then again, he had probably memorized his escape route a long
time ago. And coming home was just reversing it.

You've got to go through it, darlin'. Not around it.

Posy and I had a marathon texting session as Nash navigated the back
roads.

> **Did the NOPD rule out an inside job?**

> **Seriously, Dani? Should I start charging you by the hour? If
> you need a good headshrinking, I have plenty of colleagues I
> could recommend.**

> **Just tell me.**

I knew the police had found the birdcage, dented and empty in
the back alley behind the wedding venue. They'd worked the case for
several more months before closing it cold. My phone went dark for a
moment before lighting up with bubble after bubble. The texting
equivalent to Posy's usual mile-a-minute Long Island banter.

> **Every employee on staff that night was questioned and
> released. No one attempted to cash any of the checks; it was
> all just for the cash. A couple was seen in the video leaving
> through the back door, pushing a baby carriage. Since we
> had an adults-only reception, that ruled out any guest
> involvement, too. Coulda been a baby in there. Coulda been
> the birdcage. They probably strolled in off the street and got
> away lucky, Dani. NOPD labeled it a random, unfortunate,
> unsolved incident. So yes. They ruled out inside involvement.**

Which apparently had ruled out Mick, since he had been employed there. I wondered if Posy knew that.

I'm more upset that he played you, honestly, than I am about the money now.

Yep. That answered that.

Just forget him, D! Go party like a rock star! Live!

"So what did you think of Mick?" Nash asked, breaking me out of my mobile revelations.

"Mick seemed . . ." Several words sizzled on my tongue, but I settled. "Nice."

"Oh yeah," Nash snorted. "He's nice. Sugar and spice and anything to get a slice."

"A slice?"

"You know. Of pie. Snatch. 'A piece' doesn't exactly rhyme," he muttered. "I can't believe he hooked up with Mandy Davis." Nash shook his head. "When this cat's away, the mouse must play, I guess."

The box with the fruit tart weighed heavy in my lap for the rest of the short ride.

I remembered how my fingers had grazed Mick's as I had taken the box from his hands, and his thumbs had caressed my palms. One touch from him and my insides turned as gooey as a chocolate lava cake.

Yeah, I bet he heated those to perfection, too.

I could just imagine the line of ladies at the bakeshop door, lured in by Mick's sweetness and lies. Ugh. He probably had a secret back door that led up to some bachelor baker sex den.

So he hadn't ruined my sister's wedding, after all. But Nash Drama's best friend was certainly no angel.

"I thought you said they lived on a half acre?" I exclaimed, marveling at the beautifully manicured expanse of lawn as we crunched up the long, graveled driveway. Even with the mammoth house roosting royally in the center, the property seemed to go on forever. There was a tangle of woods in back, and I could see a swift-moving current at each break in the trees.

"No, it's just called the Half Acre." Nash turned to me. "Look, Dani. There's a lot more that I haven't told you."

Likewise.

"It'll keep," Nash said, reaching for the door handle.

I twisted the ring he'd given me. It was just loose enough to completely rotate, but tight enough not to just slip off. I still wasn't used to its weight, and its brilliance never failed to catch me by surprise. I never wore jewelry when I worked on clients, and even after hours it was an afterthought. Except for the cake charm, of course, which I wore as a reminder that bittersweetness lurked between the layers of lust and love.

As if I needed reminding.

"Can we have all the single ladies out on the dance floor?"

I winced as the DJ repeated his request. Mick's arms were twined around my waist as if he had already memorized every curve of my body.

"You're being paged." His lips and his words teased gently against my skin. "No hurry, I'll be waiting right here."

"Are you still single, dear?" My mother caught my arm as I made my way toward where Posy was standing with her wedding cake. "You wouldn't know it by the way that man has laid claim on you. He's all but shaken out his shiver train."

Leave it to my mother to bring up animal mating rituals in comparison. At least she had gone for the common peacock-feather analogy. Nothing more embarrassing than having your mother wax poetic on the smooth moves of male giraffes (he nudges the female until she pees, then drinks her urine) or the exploding testicles of honeybees.

"Choo-choo," I replied, pumping my fist up and down like a railroad engineer. "I will gladly board that train if it's pulling into the station." I jumped onto the back of the conga line of single women snaking their way toward Posy.

"Nice of you to join us," my sister hollered over the predictable Beyoncé "Single Ladies" soundtrack the DJ had decided fit the mood. "I was beginning to wonder."

"Whether or not I'm still single?" I joked. "You sound like Mom."

"Pat's worst fear." Posy laughed. "No, I thought maybe you already left with Bachelor Number One."

"You mean Only One," I said, turning and blowing a kiss in his direction. He didn't do anything cheesy like try to catch it, or rub his cheek. He just slowly brought two fingers up to his lips, pressed them there, and sent one sailing discreetly back.

"I mean your dance card is usually open-ended, and I want you to be careful." She gave him the once-over once more. "What's up with his arms? Think he's into self-harm?"

"Can we please not psychoanalyze him and just get this cake pull over with?"

In hindsight, maybe it was my head that really needed examining. Jax thought that my player radar, or my "playdar," as he liked to call it, had just temporarily malfunctioned that night. But falling for Mick felt more like a critical error . . . and seeing him today made me realize my system still hadn't recovered.

Mick

SLICE OF LIFE

"Dude. So quiet today," Bear observed as he drove us up to Mandy Davis's house on the hill. "Cougar got your tongue?"

"Jeez. Will you stop with the lame jokes? And for the love of God, don't tell Nash my business, please."

"Come on, Mandy Davis? Total MILF. I gotta live vicariously through you, dude." Bear gave a wistful smile, but I knew his mind was elsewhere. He'd always had a one-track mind when it came to girls, and there was still only one woman in town for him: Ms. Angie Vega. Even during that brief time when she had been Mrs. Angie Alvarez.

"See? And here I'm thinking I need to rip a page out of your playbook," I told him, giving his fist a tap with my own.

"So . . . aren't you going to tell me all about her?"

"Mandy?"

Bear rolled his eyes. "No, Nash's lady friend. Gimme the deets, man! The dirt. What's she like?"

More beautiful than I remembered. Quieter. Wiser. Sexier. More jaded? A total mystery to me.

"She's not what I expected."

She's way too good for him.

Bear just nodded slowly. I seriously considered the notion that we really did share half a brain, after all.

"Thanks for the ride, man." I hopped into my van, sitting lonely now on the circular drive. There had to be hope, I thought, throwing it into drive and heading toward the Half Acre. Yes, she had just walked away from the Night Kitchen with my old best friend's ring on her finger.

But she still had that charm around her neck.

Walking through the French Quarter with Dani had been like a festival in itself. She wanted to dance in front of every bar spilling live music onto the street, and kiss under every street lamp that bore a French name. Which, in the Quarter, was almost every one of them. She'd collected more beads than a Mardi Gras float by the time we reached the iron gates of Jackson Square. All the while, she clutched the small, slim box containing a sliver of the groom's cake, which I'd snagged from the dessert table for her before we ditched the festivities. And that charm, its long length of ribbon wound around her finger like a reminder, swayed tantalizingly.

No matter how I sliced it, no pun intended, my life—and even my love life—seemed to revolve around cake.

"Let's make love in the park," she whispered against my mouth, looping beads around both of our necks as I kissed her under the lamp marking Pere Antoine Alley and Rue de Chartres.

The cool caress of the beads and the touch of her tongue sent a shiver up my spine. Her sense of adventure was a turn-on, but New Orleans at night was a different creature than it was in daylight. The Square was one of my favorite places in the city by day; its low-hanging crooked oak trees reminded me of the Half Acre's orchard back home. But by nightfall, it struck me as a sad and secretive place, best left to itself.

"Let's get you home," I suggested instead. Her hotel was a quaint terraced town house just a few blocks away.

"Where's home for you, Mick?" she asked, tracing the scars up my forearms until she reached the swooping blue bird tattooed there. I had told her earlier why I'd gotten that particular tattoo, following old sailor's lore that when a swallow was spotted at sea, land couldn't be far away. I'd felt lost for so long. Losing hope. Castaway.

Now, with her body pressed tightly to mine, and the ocean of her eyes luring me, I set a course. Straight and narrow, like an arrow to the heart. She felt like home.

"Anywhere you are," I said, voice rough, as I took her in my hands and my mouth right there on the curb of the stone-lined street.

"Then take us both home," she said, soft and serious. Her cavernous eyes gave and took sanctuary. Liberties. Permission.

My mouth moved to kiss her neck, mingling with the beads she wore as I tongued her delicate throat and tasted her salty sweetness. I wanted her, possibly more than I had wanted anything in my entire life.

Definitely more.

I wanted more.

Dani

GRIN AND BEAR IT

A Jeep came barreling up the driveway behind us, spitting gravel as it turned sharply to park on our left. Its soft top was down, exposing just the roll bars. I had always wanted a Jeep like that as a teen, had hung pictures on my walls and begged my dad. But he had questioned its safety and its practicality, right down to its exterior door hinges that would surely rust in our climate. Out jumped a stork of a guy, measuring at least three inches taller than Nash. His hair was a tawny lion's mane, and his grin was little kid in a candy shop, personified. "This must be Bear." I laughed, because nothing about him warranted his grizzly nickname, except maybe his height. "Hi, I'm Dani."

"Bartholomew Bradley, at your service!" The guy took a sweeping bow, quite graceful in his tight leather pants and motorcycle boots. He wore a black short-sleeved work shirt, and sure enough, it had a tiny oval patch that read *Bear* in embroidered cursive over the pocket. Pops of colored tattoos broke up his monochrome look: nautical stars of black and green on each bony elbow and a musical staff wound around his chiseled biceps, red notes dancing along the black lines.

"Dude!" The hero worship in Bear's wide dark eyes was evident as he turned to Nash. The force was strong with this one.

"Can you see," gasped Nash from under the vise grip of his friend, "why we call him Bear?"

"You, too, come on now!" Being hugged by Bear was a full-body, happy experience. He rocked us back and forth. "Home to the Half Acre. I knew you couldn't stay away forever, Nash. And you!" He released me from his squeeze so he could hold me at arm's length. "Check you out. I totally get what Mick was saying."

Just what in green hell did that mean?

Was Mick already telling tales out of school?

Bear held up my hand close to his face so he could inspect the goods. His were workingman's hands: callused and steady. Clean, yet looked as if they'd been recently scrubbed free of grease. "Nice rock, bro. So happy for you guys!" When he brought my hand to his lips, kissed it, and smiled, I knew I had made a friend for life. Despite whatever Mick *was saying*. I couldn't help but smile, too.

"Oops, piñata duty calls!"

"You were right about him," I said, shaking my head and laughing as Bear bounded up the grass like a puppy. Nash had tried to explain Bear on the car ride down from New York, but there was something about him you had to experience for yourself to believe. His unabashed good nature and genuine zeal was infectious.

"He brings my blood pressure down. Like you do."

Nash now had a guitar case in one hand, and my hand clamped in his other as we strode up toward the side yard. Everything looked picture-perfect, like out of a home and garden magazine. A large white tent anchored the festivities, each corner decorated with red and blue balloons and coordinating curling ribbons. Children were squealing and darting in and out, playing some crazy game of freeze tag where the large maple tree was "safe" and everything else was up for grabs. Bear was now hoisting a donkey-shaped piñata high into the tree with a rope as the children used his leather-clad legs as an extension of home base, swinging off him and yelling "SAFE!" at the tops of their lungs.

A rainbow of gift bags and birthday presents overflowed one small table, and abandoned pizza and juice pouches occupied another. Face-painting and temporary tattoos were happening on a picnic blanket where two teenage girls sat, patiently applying magic to the eager faces and arms of kids barely able to contain their excitement.

I thought back to my own birthday parties as a kid; with two worka-holic parents, there was never an "at home" party for Posy or me. Slots were scheduled at a local place, with built-in fun: skating, mini-golf, movie theater, water park. Party "facilitators" were assigned to do every-thing, from games to cake serving to keeping track of your gifts as you opened them. The party started and ended at those places. Not to say our house wasn't fun and loving. But it just wasn't as . . . open-ended.

I heard the whirring of a camera shutter. Our paparazzi had slender tan arms, a floral maxi dress, and a face completely obscured by a professional-looking camera. Between pops of the flash, I caught a glimpse of large hoop earrings and a long, sleek bob of brown hair.

"Quinn," Nash announced in a somewhat resigned tone.

She stayed at a safe distance from us and turned without a word, continuing to document the party through her lens. I couldn't decide if she was rude, shy, or whether she kept herself behind the camera to avoid punching Nash Drama out. Based on just the little history I knew, it was probably the latter.

Her main subject in focus was a little boy with an easy smile and large dark eyes. He stood right in the thick of things, other children tearing around him in tag mode, and dug at the bark of the tree with a stick. The wispy blond hair that kept blowing in his face could only have come from the man standing next to me, who seemed to have lost the ability to speak. My new diamond ring cut into the skin of my other fingers as Nash squeezed and kneaded my hand like a stress ball. I tried to keep it relaxed and malleable for him, but when my eye followed the trail of the moving camera lens, every nerve jumped alive.

Mick was walking up the great lawn toward the party. From the corner of my eye I watched his easy stride, and the way the worn denim of his jeans encased his slim hips. The simple gray T-shirt he wore was made majestic by his strong shoulders and pecs, and its hem hung tantalizingly loose over his flat abs. How could someone work around all that sinful food and stay in shape? The man was either genetically blessed . . . or he had major willpower.

The blond boy whizzed past us, and a half dozen other children followed in his wake yelling "Cupcakes!" at the tops of their lungs. Mick held the treats aloft, grinning as he stepped deftly around the kids who hurled toward him like homing missiles. The Pied Piper act made my ovaries hurt—what the hell was wrong with me?

"Back, back, you little ankle-biters! Except for the birthday boy." A hand came down to tousle the blond locks, and rested easy on the little boy's slight shoulder as they bumped legs and made for the tent.

Nash had barely lifted a snakeskin cowboy boot toward them when a voice stopped him in his tracks.

"You've put it off this long, Nash. Can you at least wait until he's had his cake?"

Her cork wedge sandals gave her a few extra inches, but the mother of Nash's child was still a slight, little thing. Nash made a point of looking right over her head, tilting it left and right as though he didn't see her.

"I hear her, but where is she? Oh, there's Quinn. Up on her high horse," he muttered.

Even if she hadn't had the bulky camera slung from her neck, I got the feeling there'd be no bear hugs from Quinn. She had her brother's cavernous eyes, but all similarities stopped there as she surveyed me with a guarded, cool glance.

My mother suddenly came to mind, and all her endless research

on animal dominance. I knew wolves rolled over to show submission
and baboons presented their buttocks. WWDD? I wasn't about to fall
to the grass or show her my butt, but I wanted her to know I didn't
pose a threat. *Kill her with kindness*, I heard my father say. *Turn
awkward into awesome.*

"Dani, Quinn," Nash blurted. "Quinn, Dani."

Yeah. This wasn't awkward at all.

"Bear tells me congratulations are in order."

Quinn, however, didn't offer up any such thing. She put her hands
on her hips and stared Nash down. Which was kind of funny, since he
towered over her and she had to look up to do it.

"Sis!" Bear yelled from his post. "The natives are getting restless."

Quinn glanced at the tree and labored a dramatic sigh. "All right,
all right. Coming!" I had the feeling she'd rather see Nash strung up
there than the piñata so she could have at him with a big stick. "Welcome to the Half Acre, Dani. We're just one big happy family here."
She offered up a half smile over her shoulder as she moved on. "Don't
say we didn't warn you."

Before I could turn to question Nash, a whirlwind of perfume and
clanking costume jewelry hijacked our attention.

"Stuart Nash! As I live and breathe!" A striking older woman held
her arms out in a *ta-da!* gesture like she was a magician's assistant
waiting for applause.

"You know I don't like to be called that, Sindy," he scolded, but
stooped down so she could drop kisses on both his cheeks.

"That's me," she sassed. "With a capital *S-I-N!*"

"Stuart?" I murmured, amused.

"You didn't think Drama was really his last name, did you?"

Mick was at my side now, cupcake free and fine as hell, sending
my body temp spiking higher than the arches of Sindy's eyebrows. She
had to be well into her seventies, but her voluptuous body, pressed
into a vintage cherry-print swing dress, looked well preserved.

"No, Drama's just his middle name," Sindy answered, before I could think of a clever response to Mick. "I've known this one since he was knee-high to a grasshopper," she cooed, giving Nash's cheek a pat. "You'll always be little Stewie Nash to me!"

"Enough, woman." Nash's voice carried his signature bad boy flirtation, yet was laced with the utmost respect. "Or I'll start calling you by *your* stage name."

"Go right ahead," she dared. "You know I've got nothing to hide." Turning to me, she held out a regal hand. "Sindy Wolkoff."

"Otherwise known as the legendary Sinnamon Sin, Burlington County's most famous burlesque dancer." Nash had outed her, but Sindy just curtsied demurely.

"You see," she added, barely giving me time to introduce myself before clasping my arm conspiratorially. "I grew up in a little Jersey town near here called Cinnaminson, so it was a play on words." She gave a toss of her rockabilly hair and addressed Nash. "And that was a very long time ago, young man. Before you and Mickey were even a thought. Dani, have you met my nephew?"

With a clang of her bangles, she grabbed Mick's arm and fused our hands together.

"Yes," I managed, feeling those husky blue eyes of his roam over me. "At his bakery."

"Oh!" She clapped her hands to her ample chest. "You've been to the Night Kitchen! Come, say hi to Walt!"

"You'll have to forgive my aunt," Mick said, slowly releasing my hand. "She gets a little carried away sometimes."

Sindy was pulling Nash around the perimeter of the tent. He still had that guitar case clutched in his hand and my heart ached for him. He looked so foreign amid the hometown festivities, like mayhem meets Mayberry, USA. There were clusters of adults standing around chatting and laughing, but no one seemed overly taken by the fact there was a rock star in their midst. Perhaps they didn't know? But the way many turned their heads and lifted a hand in greeting, they certainly seemed to know him.

Perhaps they didn't care.

I watched as Nash leaned down to shake the hand of a man sitting under the tent near the gift table. Sindy stepped back and beamed, then motioned madly to us.

"My uncle's in a wheelchair," Mick supplied, as if to prepare me. The tips of his fingers burned through the thin material of my blouse as he guided me around the tree roots and tent stakes with a hand on the small of my back. His assistance was not necessary, but not exactly unwelcome. "His diabetes is pretty bad."

"Neuropathy?" I had seen plenty of diabetic patients when I did my PT clinical rotations.

"Yeah. It got so bad he lost control of the car on his way to work last summer. Crashed right through the bakery window."

"Your bakery?"

"It was his before it was mine. But yeah."

I snuck a glance at Mick; he squinted off into the distance, as if focusing on an earlier point on some invisible timeline somewhere among the trees.

"That's why I left New Orleans," he continued. A conga line of children broke our stride, and gave him a moment to turn and lock his eyes on mine. "Well, one of the reasons. What's yours?"

"You don't know me at all," I whispered. The delicious shiver that left goose bumps despite the blaze of the late-summer sun turned inward with the opposite effect, melting my defenses with the realization that I didn't know Mick at all, either.

"I know enough." His lips brushed against my earlobe. "I know you dreamed of me that night. And I'll do my damnedest to make sure you dream of me again."

His words scorched the frayed edges of my memory. Our evening of dancing, laughing, and stealing kisses in the photo booth had been delicious in its buildup, but my dreams had, indeed, taken things much further than he had dared let things go that night.

When I had told Jax I had been the one to leave Mick high and dry after the wedding, I hadn't exactly been telling the truth.

One night, no strings, with a hot stranger in a sultry town like New Orleans after celebrating all things romance would've been the icing on the cake, so to speak. Had Mick played fair that night.

"I wanted to see you home safe."

"But I still haven't told you about all these colors," I had protested, slowly stripteasing the beads off both of us. Mick felt like everything that was good and safe, and I didn't want him to leave my touch. "Gold was for power, remember?" I whispered, as the last string of beads fell to the floor, and lifted the hair from the back of my neck, turning away from him.

He drew a ragged breath, but hesitated, with his fingertips on the zipper of my dress.

He had all the power. It scared the hell out of me.

"Dani . . ."

"Green," I said, clutching the fabric to my breasts as he slowly eased the zipper down, knuckles caressing, thumb tracing the curve of my spine. "Green for faith."

"Trust me," he breathed. "We should just—"

Just one glance over my shoulder found his eyes locked on me, disarming me with their startling blue and causing me to stumble, falling into him and letting the dress pool to the floor.

"We shouldn't."

I wanted to drown in him. I wished I could stop the dizzying pace in which my head and my heart were racing. I had been drinking, but it wasn't all from the alcohol. He had me churned up and turned on, and this night . . . this thing . . . us. We had to happen.

I stood there, breathing deep, eyes fluttering closed, as his hands found the strings of my panties. "Purple for justice," I panted, victorious. His fingers grazed my belly, then the hem, playing down the lacy dampness to my throbbing core. He let out a strangled groan as if he was the only one being tortured. I wanted to climb on his desire and bring us both crashing down. I wanted to misbehave, and redeem us, for days on end.

"Here's your chance to earn another PhD," I challenged.

"In 'Pinning her Down'?" he growled, hands circling my wrists and bringing them overhead. We knocked back against the exposed brick on my bedroom wall, bumping, nipping, and grinding against each other.

"You could frame me on the wall, right here . . . Passionate, hot . . ." I teased.

"Pounding," he countered, "heaving . . ."

"Dripping." I groaned wickedly, pulling a leg up to wrap around his thighs. He caught it with his hand as I strained to meet him.

"Deep." His lips buzzed against my ear, and I almost creamed myself.

"So deep," I agreed, practically shaking under his touch.

"Drunk," he insisted, gently untangling our hands. His hand gave my thigh one last caress before letting it slide from his grasp.

"Why does it matter?" I was exasperated, and beyond turning back. "We could be so good together—"

"I know," Mick said firmly. "Which is why we wait. And if you're still feeling the same way tomorrow, let me take you out for beignets in the morning. Say you'll meet me at the Café Du Monde."

"But you—" He didn't let me finish, pushing a finger to my lips, then thinking better of it and crushing his lips there, too.

"You don't understand," I said when we came up for a breath. "I haven't asked . . . haven't wanted anyone to stay . . ." Until now, my scaredy-cat brain prompted, but "until morning" came out. Even my looser, drunken mouth wasn't bold enough to say it.

He kissed me gentler then, as if he understood. I let him lead me slowly to the bed with his fingers lingering at my elbows, guiding me with his lips. Softly he set me down, and reached for the piece of groom's cake in its box. I began to protest; I needed nothing sweeter than the whole of him. "No, not for you to eat, silly," he chided me, sliding the box under the mountain of pillows beneath my head. "For you to dream."

Let me take you out for beignets in the morning. His voice had been sticky and hot, as sweet as the offer itself.

That I couldn't refuse.

And so I had awoken that next morning, hungry, happy, and hot and bothered. Sheets twisted and body aching. Victorious; as if some sort of test had been passed. Yet scared as hell.

I had tamped down the dreams for so long, lying to myself and to others about it, and the shame flamed my face, thinking about it now. At a child's birthday party, of all places. But Mick's piercing gaze was forcing the thoughts to rise to the surface, raw and real.

"Too late," I found myself saying. "You had your chance."

Mick

PICK YOUR POISON

It had killed me to walk away from her that night. Now I had to endure not only her walking away, but watching her waltz straight into Nash's arms as he introduced her to my uncle. I was pretty sure I knew how the piñata felt. Every squeeze Nash applied to her skin, every playful glance, every laugh they shared felt like a whack to the gut, the heart, and the head.

"So tell me," my aunt asked, eyes wide. "How did he propose?"

Nash opened his mouth, but Dani beat him to it. "He popped the question on the top of a mountain," she supplied. "It was perfect!"

"How romantic," Sindy sighed. "And was it a total surprise?"

"Nash? Romantic? I'm sure it was a total shock," I couldn't help but interject.

"Like you would know romance if it bit you in the ass, player," Nash shot back.

"Are you kidding?" My aunt felt she had to come to my defense. "Food is love, and this sweetheart knows his way around a kitchen."

Nash turned to Dani. "Yeah. Mick lost his virginity to Mrs.

Butterworth, Aunt Jemima, and Betty Crocker in a hot four-way and never looked back."

I wished I could smack the gloat right off his face, but there were children present.

"There's my boy." Walt turned his chair to greet me. "How was the Davis wedding last night?"

Although out of the business, my uncle still kept tabs on all our orders and events in and around town. He was strictly business about it, however, and didn't seem to know or want to know about the, ah . . . pleasurable added benefits that came from being the only local (and available) baker in town.

I did know a thing or two about romance, contrary to what Nash thought. But usually it was far easier to love 'em and leave 'em . . . before they could leave me first.

"Another satisfied customer," I murmured, ignoring the knuckles Nash held out to bump. He'd probably break my hand with that silver skull ring of his, plus who knew where (or who) those knuckles had been in. I refused to let my brain torture me with images of him with Dani. There had to still be other girls. This was, after all, Nash Drama.

"That's what I like to hear," Walt said approvingly. "Now, if only you'd cut that hair, boy." I ran my hand through my thick locks, which could've probably used a trim but were a perfectly acceptable length. It's not like I was sporting a mop like Bear's, or the sleek style Nash was throwing over a shoulder every chance he got.

"Oh, leave him be, Walt. I like the look myself." Sindy reached up to give me a tousle, and I only tolerated it because I felt Dani's eyes surveying the exchange, amused.

"He's a baker, not a rock star," Walt grumbled.

"Yeah, Baker Boy. This town ain't big enough for the both of us." Nash tipped his shades and peered over them at me in an attempt at clever bravado.

"Are you kidding? This tent isn't big enough for the both of us," I quipped. "Or for me and your ego, anyway."

"Hey, now. Don't hate the player. Hate the game."

Sindy clapped her hands, causing the bows in her hair to bounce like a delighted child's. "I love when all my boys are together," she confided to Dani. "It's like the Three Musketeers."

"More like a three-ring circus," Walt corrected.

"Oh, shush, you big wet blanket. Go mingle, won't you?"

My uncle made his escape, probably more intent to run down partygoers with his chair than to mix and mingle in between them.

"You hear that, Mick? The circus is in town. So why don't you go pitch your pup tent over with Bear and I'll hang here under the big top?" Nash smugly slung one arm over Dani's shoulder and one over Sindy's. "With the ladies."

Oh, it's on. Like a big pot of neck bones, as Aunt Sindy loved to say. I regretted not having employed that knee to the groin back at the bakery when I had the chance. "Okay, I'll leave you *ladies* to the wedding talk, then."

I turned on my heel and smiled as Sindy began yammering a mile a minute about every wedding she had had the pleasure of working on, hint, hint, and scoped the crowd for Logan. He was admiring the cupcakes, set out on display next to his box cake creation and the fruit tart I had given to Dani. Instinctively, I reached for the small flip notepad I kept in my back pocket. It had its own small pen, which stored perfectly in its spiral binding.

Your cake turned out great, buddy. Sorry I was late this A.M.

I set the pad next to the Spiderman cakes, and watched him smile as he read it. We had been exchanging notes this way for the better part of a year, out of sight of Quinn. It saved on a lot of time, frustration, and confusion. Outside of a bit of finger spelling, I wasn't even up to snuff with what Quinn called pidgin sign.

Logan pressed the pad back into my hand.

That's OK. I just hate when my mom gets sad at you.

I wrinkled my brow. Cupping the tiny book in my hand, I quickly fired off: *You mean "mad," right?*

No. She was SAD at you. I saw her crying earlier.

I glanced over at Quinn, who was instructing good battering technique to the next kid about to take a crack at the piñata. There was patience and humor in her tone and stance. So different from the bashing she had given me earlier. I had totally deserved it.

Looking down at Logan, I saw he was still scrawling.

Good thing you bake like a boss.

His eyes danced, watching me read it, and smiled big as I laughed and nodded.

I promise not to upset her anymore, I wrote.

"Mick! Logan's up next!" Bear hollered.

I mimicked swinging the bat and rained my fingers down to indicate the candy bounty that awaited him. He eagerly nodded and ran in the direction of the tree, so my poor attempt at homemade pidgin sign evidently worked.

"Nice work, Mick."

My uncle was at my side, a cupcake shaking between his pudgy thumb and forefinger so he could have a better look at my sugar work.

"What are your numbers?" I asked, knowing his tremors got worse as his blood sugar dropped.

"My numbers are fine," he insisted, resenting being asked. "But they'd be better if you let me eat one of these." He gave me a resigned smile, knowing full well the combination of main ingredients—flour and sugar—was just as dangerous a cocktail to a diabetic as a speedball of cocaine and heroin was to the average human. "It's hard to stay away from such sweet poison, Mick."

"Yeah," I commiserated, my eyes on Dani. "You got that right."

She and Sindy were deep in conversation, and Nash was nowhere to be found. Perhaps he ran to the hills at the first drop of the W word.

I should be so lucky.

Weddings were my world; I lived and breathed their details every day. I fulfilled dreams. There was an entire back wall of the bakery dedicated to thank-you cards from happy brides and grooms, gushing poetic in their perfect post-honeymoon handwriting. All about going above and beyond, of exceeding their expectations. Of saving the day.

Baking was my business *and* my pleasure. All the other stuff, the women and the antics, fell into my lap. And now I let it all fall away. It was, and it always had been, about making people happy with the best possible cake I could serve. *Mick Spencer's sweet voodoo.*

What did Nash do? He plugged an amp cord into a guitar jack and made static and noise. He was chauffeured from town to town, told when to go onstage and who to give lip service to. Promoters, sponsors, record labels. He delivered a one-size-fits-all rock-and-roll dream to fans and was gone by morning, before they even woke up.

And before he did that, he stole. And he lied. And he made promises he didn't keep.

Relieving my uncle of the cupcake, I placed it back with the others and searched Quinn's nearby "party box" for candles. She had thought of everything: Knife in a safety sheath, should it fall into the wrong hands; paper towels to wipe said knife and any sticky fingers. Cake server, plates, forks, napkins. Even hand sanitizer for the little monsters.

Quinn lived by boxes and compartments. And by the motto of always being prepared. Which often made me wonder how Logan happened. Well, maybe not so much the *how* but the *why*. Now that he was here, though, it was hard to remember a time without him. Logan was what Aunt Sindy called "an old soul."

"Need any help?" Dani asked. Just having her close and hearing that husky voice of hers revved me up. *Jeez, Mick. You lightweight.*

It's not like she's hanging from a stripper pole or anything. Although her hand was resting sort of provocatively on the tent pole between us.

"Well, I'm going to go make like a leaf and mingle," said my uncle, God bless him. Walt loved to mangle jokes, and he provided such a dry delivery, people usually didn't get it the first time around. But Dani cracked up instantly, causing Walt to practically pop a wheelie with delight on his way out of the tent.

"Your aunt and uncle are adorable."

"So are you," I said, grabbing the tent pole just below her hand and winding myself alongside her so my arm was practically around her waist. "Wanna make like a tree and leaf with me?" She groaned at my more accurate but nonetheless cheesy pun. "No? How about just making out with me behind the trees then?"

"Smooth," Dani said drily. "You should try frosting a cake with those moves."

"I do. Every day. And I can't wait to frost yours."

"Not going to happen." Her cheeks reddened as deep as the Spidey cupcakes. "The 'cake consult'"—she air-quoted—"was Nash's idea of a joke. He just wanted to bust your balls when he got to town, Mick."

"Oh, so you two are *not* in need of a wedding cake, then?"

"I didn't say that," she stammered.

"Then I do need your help." Reaching into my back pocket, I slid out the pair of photo booth strips I had taken out of my bakery appointment book. Her copies had been keeping mine company since New Orleans. She'd played her hand that night just as well as I'd played mine, and it was now time to return these to their rightful owner.

"I'm looking for this girl I've lost. Have you seen her?" I placed them in her hands.

Dani had been working to keep her shoulders held so defiantly, but at the photographic proof of our chemistry, I watched them drop in surrender.

"Yeah, I know her." Her voice was whisper soft. "Used to, anyway. Heard she got herself engaged to another guy."

"Because she plans on loving, honoring, and cherishing him? And vice versa? Until death parts them, and all that jazz?"

Because I didn't believe that for a second.

Dani's eyes widened, and her delicate nostrils flared. But she remained mute, leaving my challenge un-refuted. She moved to give the photos back, but I shoved my hands in my pockets and refused to take them. *Not gonna happen.*

And this wedding wasn't going to happen, not if I had anything to say or do about it. And suddenly I knew exactly what I was going to do.

I was going to go above and beyond. I was going to exceed expectations.

I was going to ruin their day.

Nash would not be having his cake and eating it, too. Not this time.

"You deserve a beautiful cake," I said, gauging her reaction. "I insist. It'll be my wedding gift to you and Nash."

Dani's lips parted and puffed a surprised sigh at my three-hundred-sixty-degree turn. "Seriously?"

"You heard Nash. I'm a lover, not a fighter. Who am I to stand in the way of . . ." I couldn't bring myself to say it, just gestured with my hand.

"Of what Nash and I have?" she tested. Or perhaps she was having trouble buying into the words, too. Was that too much to wish for? The twist of her smile made me want to kick down the tent pole, pull up the stakes, and trap her under the tarp. Just the two of us . . . and the cupcakes. That's all we'd need.

"Exactly."

"And I don't want to come in between whatever it is you and he have," she said softly. "You guys have known each other your whole lives."

"Nash was the closest thing I ever had to a brother," I admitted.

"I love him dearly. But sometimes . . . sometimes I'm allowed to hate him fiercely."

Dani nodded; she had a sister, so I was sure she knew the delicate balance I was referring to. The blink of her long lashes flashed a wicked game of Truth or Dare. "He's probably going to want you to be his best man, you know."

"I know."

And may the best man win.

"Where is he, anyway?" I thought to ask.

"He went to help Bear with the piñata."

"Jeez, one of them just needs to put that thing out of its misery."

We turned to watch Logan take another swing, full of ecstatic fury, only to sideswipe the thing and send it ricocheting off the tree.

"Why isn't he blindfolded?" Dani asked.

"Oh believe me," I laughed. "Logan blindfolded with a stick in his hand would strike terror in the hearts of both man and beast."

"Why would you say that? He seems like such a sweet and mellow kid." She was genuinely perplexed, and the realization hit me just as Bear took charge and delivered the fatal blow to the piñata. Candy poured out of its cracked belly amid shrieks and squeals.

She had no clue.

"Dani, Logan's deaf."

The look on her face told me Nash didn't know, either.

"Nash . . . wait!" Dani threaded her way through the guests and I followed, hot on her heels.

Nash had crouched down, bracing himself with hands on the neck of the guitar case, as Logan came bounding toward him with a goody bag full of his ground score.

"Hey, dude. You've got a good swing."

Logan grinned and offered up a Tootsie Pop to the stranger in his path. He had seen Nash speaking with all the important adults in his life earlier, which apparently meant they had reached candy-sharing status. I made a mental note to have a chat with him in the notepad about stranger-danger and candy sharing not always being a two-way street.

"Honey, I think you need to—," Dani began.

Nash dismissed her with a wave behind him; a nonverbal *back off* that stopped her in her tracks.

"Hey, I've got a gift for you, too." Nash tilted the guitar case toward Logan, but the boy was too busy unwrapping his own Tootsie Pop to pay any mind. "My old man got me a guitar when I was your age. So now I'm . . . now you've got one, too."

The emotion that laced those last words went unnoticed by not only Logan, but by Quinn as well. She appeared on the scene, a tub of ice cream in each hand, just as Logan blew past Nash to show her his treats.

"Didn't I tell you to wait?" Quinn demanded, shooting daggers toward Nash over their son's head.

"What's his problem? You could teach the kid some basic manners, you know."

"Problem? *Problem?*" Quinn sidestepped her son with an absent touch to his head. She unloaded the cold tubs onto my arms, but their cold sting was nothing compared to the frostbite in her tone as she bore down on Nash. "*You're* the problem!"

Bear stepped into the fray, pulling his sister back by both shoulders. Nash caught a camera lens to the lip as the strap around Quinn's neck swung in response to the inertia Bear forced upon her. Dani was instantly at Nash's side, not unlike that moment at the bakery. Sindy came running as well, pulling a vintage embroidered handkerchief from her cleavage to apply to Nash's lip as Dani helped him to a bench.

"Homecoming . . . who would've thought it would be more danger-ous than jumping into the mosh pit?" His laugh sputtered bloodstains into the white linen.

The party had fallen silent except for the occasional rustle of a candy wrapper. Most of the children stared, as parents broke from their little klatches to hover near their offspring and eavesdrop.

Logan sucked on his Tootsie Pop and looked at me with all kinds of questions in his eyes. Even without the aid of our shared notepad, I had a hunch what he would write.

Is he my dad?

"Ask him," I mouthed, slow and clear.

Logan shuffled shyly toward Nash, who had stopped blotting his lip for the time being. For someone who was used to being in the public eye, Nash had the gaze of a wounded animal, his own eyes darting everywhere but on the boy who was solemnly approaching. Dani placed her hands on Nash's shoulders from behind, and his tension visibly eased.

The lollipop stick rolled from side to side in Logan's mouth as he contemplated Nash. Then he slowly brought a hand up, all five fingers wide, and touched his thumb to his forehead. It was similar to a sign I recognized, although I had never seen it go higher than the chin. Quinn used the lower sign when she introduced herself as Logan's mother. I watched her now, as she lifted her chin high and proud, and gave the boy confirmation when he turned to her: her thumb tapped her own forehead, fingers splayed. Logan whipped his head back to face Nash.

Using a sign language of her own, Dani gave Nash's shoulders a quick squeeze. It prompted him to slowly lift his own thumb up to his forehead and copy their movements, with one large hand spread so wide his pinky practically touched Logan's nose.

The boy grinned and caught Nash in a hug around the neck. I watched my childhood friend's hands, normally so capable of limber movement up and down the frets of his guitar. They hovered useless and foreign for a moment, before coming to rest tentatively on Logan's scrawny back. Dani stepped back, letting father and son have a moment. Her gaze caught mine, and she bit back a small smile before focusing on Nash and Logan.

A few people clapped, and there was a release of nervous laughter throughout the tent.

"Come on, the ice cream's melting," Quinn said, reaching for the tubs, but I held them fast. Time froze as we stared each other down.

"You never told him?"

Quinn kept her eyes on the cartons of ice cream. "I told him there was the possibility. Back when the doctors were testing."

"That was over nine years ago, Quinn. Jesus."

"He never called back," she said softly. "So I figured he didn't want to know."

"No, you didn't think he deserved to know, did you?"

"You spoke to him more than I did, Mick! Did he ever ask you about Logan? Even once? No. Did you ever bring Logan's name up, or was it always 'don't ask, don't tell'? Denial has always run as strong as that current back there"—she gestured toward the river, beyond the trees—"here on the Half Acre. Isn't that why *you* came back?"

The cartons were getting soggy, and she snatched them from my grasp. "Time to do cake and candles!" she hollered brightly. But for my ears only, she added with a defeated sigh, "Logan's been making the same damn wish for the last nine years. It's about time it came true."

Dani

MAKE A WISH

"I have to get out of here," Nash hissed in my ear, "or I am going to totally lose it."

"No," I said. "No way. That would be the worst thing you could do right now. Let's go sing, have cake, and make this about Logan today, okay?"

"I never should've come back here."

"Your *son*"—I stressed the word—"is very happy you came back here."

"He's deaf, Dani. Deaf! And mute. What the hell am I supposed to do with that?" For the second time that day, his voice cracked with emotion, and he had to clear his throat. This was a guy whose voice was an instrument, a tool of his trade that paid his bills and had, along with the sounds that sprang from his guitar, proved him a desirable commodity out there in the world.

And the only person he wanted to win over could never be swayed by it.

"Do *not* walk away."

He glared at me. I stared pointedly back. The words hung between us. If anyone were to glance over at this moment in time, they might've thought we were having a lover's quarrel. Except we weren't lovers. And it was less a quarrel and more a job requirement.

I couldn't walk away, either. Or run.

Damn Maxine and her "dependability, respect, and the utmost professionalism while you work with the artists."

Logan came running and tugged a shell-shocked Nash by the hand toward the tent where the desserts were waiting. Bear had already poked ten candles around a very homemade cake that read:

HAPPY BIRT
HDAY LOGAN!

in wavy letters. Something told me Mick hadn't baked that particular cake, but he smiled down at it as he reached around Bear and stuck in one last candle "for luck."

"I forgot the matches," Quinn muttered, rummaging through her box of supplies. "Damn it. Bear, could you run to the house—"

"I've got it."

There was a flash and a whiff of lighter fluid as Nash flipped the top on his old vintage Zippo. A hush fell over the group; even Sindy was quiet. I caught Bear and Mick exchanging a guarded look. Quinn bit her lip and looked away as Nash moved the flame over each wick. She held Logan to her with one hand across his heaving chest.

I had seen Nash whip out that lighter on many occasions over the last few months: to spark up the occasional joint in social situations, to satisfy some random girl's flirty request for a light, to activate the tiki torches back in the artist compound after a heavy rain doused them. Even to show respect for his fellow musicians from sidestage, as fans raised their Bics, glowsticks, and iPhone virtual flame apps during a particularly moving encore. But never had I witnessed such a solemn look as he completed the ritual for his son. It was all consuming and hypnotizing, as if answers to some ancient mystery were locked deep in the blue-black center of each flame.

The birthday boy grinned at everyone over the blazing candles, then he lifted his index fingers as if ready to conduct an orchestra. The children all began to sing and sign at the same time, four simple signs that carried just as much joy and enthusiasm as the traditional vocals. Some of the adults knew the signs as well, others tried to fake it, and some didn't attempt it at all. As we collectively warbled toward the finish, one voice rose above the others, strong and steady. Nash was doing the one thing he felt comfortable with, that he knew he was good at. He held that last note longer than everyone, adding a bit of melodic vocal range to the end. Nash could've held that note long after the candles had burned down to waxy puddles across the frosting, but Logan didn't give him a chance. With eyes squeezed shut and a whoosh of breath, he blew out every last candle as the crowd clapped and waved jazz hands in the air.

"Why do we wish over cake with our eyes closed?" Mick was behind me, leaning close. "Is it the same reason why we kiss with our eyes closed?"

His close proximity and his question raised goose bumps on my arms and other questions in my head. Was the thought of what we dared to hope for so fragile that opening our eyes would shatter the magic of it?

As the guests drifted away and parents tugged on their children's arms and collars to round them up and offer thanks to their hosts, I walked the perimeter, collecting stray juice pouches and candy wrappers. Nash was by the tree, tossing the disembodied piñata head back and forth between his hands and staring out at the river.

"Hey." I stashed the trash into a garbage bag tied to one of the slats of the picnic table and joined him.

"When I was . . . I don't know, maybe eight or so, I came here for

Bear's birthday party. His parents had hired a magician, I remember. And there was a cotton candy machine, like at the fair. And the biggest piñata I had ever seen." He continued tossing the colorful crepe-covered skull from hand to hand. "We all took a crack at it. Mick, Bear, even little Quinnie. She was a couple years younger than us but had a wicked swing." He smirked. "Still does. But none of us could break that thing. Mrs. Bradley came out with her broom and poked and prodded a weak spot on its belly, until it was nice and tender, and then we all took another turn at it. Bear was our Little League champion; he finally made the swing that cracked it in half."

Nash glanced up at the tree with a slight smile, as if replaying a movie of the day. "I couldn't believe the amount of candy that came pouring out. And plastic jewelry, and toys. Little army men, rubber snakes, every kid's dream. It didn't seem like it would ever stop." He cleared his throat. "All the other kids swarmed under it, pushing and grabbing. I was kind of paralyzed, watching it all. Then I noticed the piñata head, it had rolled over there." He nodded his head toward the base of the large maple. "I remember racing over to it, and claiming it all for myself."

He placed the donkey head into my hands, and I turned it over. The cavity was stuffed with wadded-up newspaper.

"I didn't know they only filled the body with the treats. By the time I realized, all the stuff was gone from the ground. Every child had armloads of booty, and I was left with this." He took back possession of the head and poked at the paper inside.

"Mr. Bradley walked past me to gather up all the garbage, and I'll never forget it. He saw me standing there with the head and he said, 'That's what you get for being so greedy.' And he kept on walking."

"Oh my freakin' God. What a horrible thing to say to a child." That had to rate a good ten hours on the therapy clock, for sure.

Nash shrugged and gave a bitter laugh. "Well, he was right. I remember thinking, 'Why bother with fighting for a few handfuls on the ground when I can have the entire head to myself?' I had taken the easy way out."

"Nash. You were eight years old. Lots of kids would've done the exact same thing."

"Then why did they have all the candy, and I had nothing?" he asked. He turned to face me. "Obey the rules, and you get rewarded. Be a sheep. Follow the herd."

"That doesn't mean you were wrong. You were being smart, and creative."

"I *was* being greedy. I did want it all to myself. Was that so wrong?" His voice began to rise. "And I didn't want to be like all of them!" He did a dropkick and booted the head down the embankment, where it rolled out of sight. We heard a watery *ker-plop*. "Who was I kidding? I couldn't be like the Bradleys no matter how hard I tried. They had a big, beautiful house that people would drive miles to see just for the Christmas lights. I lived in a trailer. My dad would turn off the lights on Halloween because we couldn't afford to give out candy."

I wrapped my arms around him and he buried his face in my hair.

"Can you see why I don't belong here?"

Mick

LOYALTY LIES

I made myself useful, far away from the kitchen window so I didn't have to look out on Dani and Nash's PDA under the old maple tree. Quinn worked silently beside me, sorting trash from the recycling.

"I can't believe Nash is back," Bear murmured from the breakfast nook. He licked the frosting from the bottom of a birthday candle, lost in thought.

I glanced at Quinn from my station at the sink. Her eyes and hands were darting back and forth, focused on their task. Compartmentalizing, like she always did.

"Dani seems nice," Bear continued, absently sticking another candle in his mouth. "Good for him."

"Yes. Hurray for Nash. Let's throw him a party next," Quinn grumbled, yanking the trash bag from the receptacle so hard, the plastic drawstring snapped. She glared at her brother as if it was his fault.

"I meant she seems *good* for him." He sucked the candle clean of frosting and slowly pulled it from between his lips. "For his psyche."

Quinn hauled the bag over to the table where Bear was supposed to be wrapping the leftover desserts. "He has a lot of nerve," was all she said as she swept the nine remaining candles into the bag before Bear could leave his DNA on them. Knotting the frayed drawstring, she made for the side door.

I had a fleeting memory of my mother, carefully washing and drying the candles from my fifth birthday cake to stow in the drawer next to the sink. *We can reuse them for your next birthday, Mickey. Once they're lit, no one will know. Our little secret.* She'd winked.

My mom had had all sorts of little secrets. She was gone before my sixth birthday, so saving the candles hadn't mattered in the long run. The screen door slammed and the memory flickered out.

"Think fast!" Nash tossed something shiny toward Bear, who wasn't necessarily the world's fastest thinker. But his lightning-fast reflexes made up for it. He opened his large palm and inspected the keys that'd landed there. "It'll be in your shop tomorrow."

Bear grinned like Christmas had come early. He rubbed his thumb over the raised VW insignia on the metal. "An old soul. Nice."

"So when did her van break down?" I thought to ask, recalling Nash's story of how he and Dani had met.

"Six weeks ago. It's been to four different garages along the eastern seaboard since, but no one was up to the challenge," Nash scoffed, but Bear needed no buttering up. He was always an eager beaver when it came to helping someone out.

Six weeks! I had royal icing in my shop with a longer shelf life. With a smirk, I took scissors to the mountain of cardboard Quinn had left for recycling. While I would never use the term *love at first sight*, Dani had made me into a believer of "goner at first glance." Yet I found it hard to believe she would rush into engagement after a mere six weeks in the company of a guy like Nash. She didn't seem the type to be swayed by money or fame. And Nash could barely commit to a hairstyle, let alone a lasting relationship. Something just wasn't adding up.

"What are you grinning at, Spencer?"

"Nothing that amounts to much," I murmured, pushing the blades along the seam of the box the juice pouches came in.

"Joke's always on me, right?" Nash began to pace.

"Not everything is always about just you." I kept my eyes on my task, crisply cutting out square after square from the top of each box.

"What the hell are you doing?"

"Box Tops loyalty program," I explained, holding up a colorful cardboard square. "Logan's school collects them, and they earn money for turning them in."

"Well, so much for loyalty here on the Half Acre," Nash blurted. "My kid's uncle has been holding out on me. And you, little Suzy Fucking Homemaker"—he gave my shoulder a shove—"I bet you laughed your ass off, watching me give a guitar to a deaf kid."

"Hey!" I pointed the scissors at him. "It wasn't our place to tell. You could've made a point to come home once in the last ten years, Nash. Instead of holding court in whatever little backstage greenroom you consider worthier than your own stomping grounds."

"Oh, so you didn't like having those VIP All Access passes hanging from your neck? Hated the attention you got from the girls at the after-parties? All those free shows I invited you to? I never showed you a good time at all, did I?"

"You showed us the rock-and-roll fantasy, sure. Very cool. But there was never time for one-on-one. Never time to sit down and really talk."

Nash was shaking his head, an obtuse smile gracing his lips the entire time. "You talk about home like it's some fucking mecca. Maybe it is for you, Spence. But for me . . ." He gazed out the kitchen window. The late summer sky had morphed to blue-black, and the canopy of leaves from the mature trees on the property obscured the moon, making it impossible to spot the old trailer where it sat on the far end of the property. But I could tell his eyes had strayed there. "You talk of home. I didn't exactly have one to come back to."

"So what the hell are you doing here?" I slammed down the scissors and faced him. My earlier hope of Nash taking a few precious seconds out of his day to check in on Logan seemed like a lifetime ago. Since he had arrived in town with Dani, time had slowed to an agonizing crawl. What had I been thinking? *God works in mysterious ways*, my aunt loved to remind me.

Well, I knew how Nash operated as well. Someone was going to get hurt before this visit was through.

Nash stared me down, slowly turning his head to one side. The road life had worn lines around his eyes that deepened as he scrutinized me.

"I could ask you the same thing, Mick."

"He feels music," Bear suddenly blurted. I'd forgotten he was even in the room. "And each sound feels different." Nash winced, taken aback. "It's true. He puts his hands on my amps all the time. I'll show you, tomorrow."

"Show who *what* tomorrow?" Quinn was back, hands on hips.

"I was thinking we could jam," Bear said simply. "It's been a long time, hasn't it?"

Nash just jammed his hands in his pockets in response.

Quinn snorted; she knew and I knew there was nothing simple about it. If Bear wasn't able to get angry, we would just have to get angry enough for him.

"Too good to collaborate with your old bandmate? After all he's done for you?" Quinn wanted to know.

"It's been a day," Nash replied, his voice flat. "Let's see what tomorrow brings."

Quinn turned on her heel. "Dani and Logan are out by the fire pit." She unlatched a cupboard door and pulled a few items. "Make yourself useful, Spencer?" A bag of marshmallows hit my open hands.

Dani's and Logan's fingers danced in the light of the fire pit, set way back on a concrete pad on the property.

"Hey, you sign?"

"I finger spell," Dani corrected me. "And I know a few signs. Yeah." She didn't elaborate.

"That's great. I'm not nearly as fast or as confident." Handing Logan chocolate, I mimed breaking the bars to him, and he began his task. "When I sign, I mean."

"You guys seem to do well together, though. Sometimes you don't need words."

"But sometimes you do." I handed her a box of graham crackers.

The screen door slammed, and Nash's hulking figure paused on the dimly lit steps of the porch. I saw his head turn toward the darkness once more, searching out a memory, before he strode purposefully toward us.

"It's late. We should get going."

"Are you kidding me?" Dani laughed. "I haven't had a s'more in years. Come're." She patted the bench between her and Logan. "Sit."

To my amazement, he sat. Logan smiled at him and handed him a square of chocolate. Dani handed him two squares of graham crackers. They both turned to me.

"Well," Nash drawled. "Lay one on me, Slick."

I popped the bag of marshmallows, and their sweet scent sifted into the air, mixing with the smoke. I tossed one to Nash, who caught it between nimble fingers. I wondered when the last time the bad boy of rock and roll had had his hands on an old-school, fat campfire marshmallow. We hadn't exactly been Boy Scouts growing up.

We sat in silence, save for the crickets and pops of the flames. All the ingredients were there, but without the tools, they were useless.

Quinn came marching out of the house. With metal marshmallow skewers in hand, she reminded me of those army goons the Wicked Witch had in *The Wizard of Oz*. I could practically hear that chorus of "*O-ee-O, whoa, O*" and expected flying monkeys any moment. Or the witch, with her stubby broom.

"One," she signed to her son as she handled him a skewer. "Then bed." Logan screwed his brow up, clearly insulted that turning double digits didn't earn him more fire pit time with the adults. I loaded two marshmallows onto his skewer with a wink, to make up for it.

Quinn doled out the rest of the skewers. "Sorry," she muttered. "I only knew where four were. I had to hunt down the others."

Dani shifted uncomfortably, and Nash speared Quinn with a look that read, *Cool it*. I knew it was just Quinn's way. She was a creature of habit. Marshmallow roasting was a nightly ritual on the Half Acre all summer. Four skewers were all that was necessary, on the nights I didn't work and Bear didn't gig. Otherwise, all she needed were two.

Quinn and Logan were used to just two.

I held out the bag to her and she retrieved her own marshmallow. "Where's Bear?"

"He'll be here in a minute. He's putting his guitar in his Jeep."

Nash and Logan were already twirling their sticks into the flames. Dani had edged away from father and son, to either give them some privacy or to move out of the smoke's current path. She stood there, empty skewer in hand.

"You didn't think I would forget about you, did you?" I asked, soft enough for her ears only.

"It's okay if you did," she came right back with. "I gave up desserts after dark anyhow."

My back was to the fire, but the heat I felt between us had it totally beat. In the firelight, her blond hair haloed her face like a blazing ring. She plucked a powdery puff from the bag that hung from my finger and impaled it on my skewer, her eyes never leaving my face.

"Well, for old times' sake, then." I pushed one slowly onto the tip of hers, before dragging my eyes off her.

Bear was bouncing around, like a Native American performing a fire dance. "Got a show tonight," he whooped. A black leather vest had been added to his ensemble, over his skinny bare chest.

"One of your cover bands?" Nash asked.

"*Tributes*, man. It's all about the tribute." He held up the marshmallow-topped skewer his sister had prepared for him in reverence. "Tonight it's Ozzy." With his free hand, he finger spelled O-Z-Z-Y for Logan's benefit, then stuck out his tongue, Gene Simmons–style, and substituted index finger for thumb to change his Y into the universal sign for metal: the devil horns. Logan threw back his head in silent laughter. "Are you guys coming down to the gig?"

"It's been a long day, Bear. Maybe next time," Nash said slowly. Dani smiled apologetically from behind a yawn.

"Next's gig's Tuesday. Empty Garden . . . it's an Elton John tribute."

"Oh. Jeez. Maybe the time *after* that." Nash gave a laugh. "Promise." Bear turned to me.

"Sorry, man. I gotta get back to the Night Kitchen and get a few things done." Birthday festivities aside, my normal Sunday work schedule had taken a backseat the minute Dani walked into my shop.

"I'm not even going to ask *you*." Bear dismissed his sister. "You never want to go anywhere."

"Hello? Got a kid, remember?" Quinn said. "Speaking of which . . ."

Logan was sneaking more chocolate and crackers, eating them sans marshmallow middle. The excitement of the day had worn him down; he wasn't even trying to read lips and keep up with the conversation. Like any other ten-year-old, he was just trying to catch that last sugar high before crashing.

"Go brush your teeth extra-well," Quinn signed and spoke aloud to her son. "I'll be there in a minute."

Logan made his way around the campfire, doling out knuckle bumps to everyone. I caught the signs he and Bear had used that morning for "cake," right before Logan double fist-bumped me in thanks. "You're welcome, buddy. My pleasure."

He turned to his mother. Fingers slashed through the air and elbows jabbed. Logan stole a glance at Nash, and Quinn gave him a Mom look that clearly meant *we'll talk about it in the morning.* Logan's shoulders slumped, and he gave a tired wave to everyone before trudging toward the house.

Bear grinned. "See?" he said to Nash. "He totally likes his gift. He wanted you to teach him a few chords before bedtime."

"Classic stall move." Quinn thrust her skewer into the fire, like a champion fencer going for the winning point with her foil.

"If it wasn't so late," Nash said hastily. "We still have to drive to Philly. We haven't even checked into our hotel yet."

"Hotel, schmotel. You should totally stay here," Bear suggested.

Holy hell.

Dani's marshmallow caught fire.

Dani

GUEST BEHAVIOR

"Bear?" Quinn managed through gritted teeth. "A family consult first would be nice."

Embarrassment flamed my face and I felt about as crispy as my burnt marshmallow. I knew Bear meant well, but Jesus H. Christ on a Popsicle stick, he was clueless. Quinn had all but rolled up the welcome mat when we arrived.

Bear waved off his sister's drama like he had heard it all before. "We've got tons of room here and this way, Logan can get to know his dad better. And vice versa. Isn't that why he's here?"

Quinn narrowed her eyes and focused in on Nash. She had no camera to hide behind this time. "Is that why you're here?"

"He's my kid. Yes. Dani and I . . ." Nash paused, and that was my cue to take up his hand. "We want to be a part of his life, and him to be a part of ours. Summer's almost over and . . . I want to show him stuff. Like fishing and guitar . . . and maybe take him places, like the Philadelphia Zoo."

"Are you crazy? I don't care that your girlfriend knows her ABC's.

You don't speak his language. You haven't given a rat's ass to get to know anything about him for the last ten years! I wouldn't let you cross the street with him, let alone the county line!"

Bear laid a hand on his sister's arm. "My point exactly. Why should Nash and Dani spend money on a hotel all the way in the city and keep driving back and forth?"

"Why shouldn't he?" she sputtered. "He's got tons of money to go blow on a beautiful suite at the Four Seasons." Her finger jutted in the darkness toward the driveway. "He's got a goddamn Porsche!"

The Porsche belonged to Riggs, but neither of us commented. For all I knew, the guy I showed up with could have a garage full of them back home in L.A.

Nash jutted his chin out. "That's right. We *are* booked at the Four Seasons. It's not like I counted on anyone keeping a light on for me in these parts."

I watched his eyes trail to the dark edges of the property, and wondered if it was the spot where his dad's trailer had stood. Sure enough, he turned on Quinn. "I'll bet you tore it down, didn't you? Got rid of the old white trash eyesore?"

"No," Quinn said, but didn't elaborate.

"I converted it. It's her darkroom," Bear informed him. "She didn't want all the chemicals in the house."

Nash laughed like it was the funniest thing he'd heard in weeks. "Perfect, Quinn! So perfect. Shut everything off and leave everyone in the dark, right?"

Quinn ignored him, focusing on her brother instead. "I'm trying to run a business here, Bear." Exasperation laced her voice. "Not a home for your wayward friends." She waved her skewer toward Nash and Mick.

Mick lived here, too? One glance in his direction, and I felt like someone had pulled my charred, brittle shell away, leaving nothing but that melted, sticky center. The vivid visions I'd had of his sex-den bachelor pad faded until they were as sheer as the lace curtains hanging in the Half Acre's upstairs windows. Surely he did not entertain his women here?

He stood, keeping his eyes on the fire. "I was just leaving."

"You've been saying that since you ran away from New Orleans, Mick," Quinn accused. Hearing his name, and that city, dropping from someone else's lips had a surreal feeling to it. "Yet here you are! At least you cook a decent breakfast. Which, by the way, Dani, is served from eight until ten."

She stomped off toward the house.

"In case you didn't know it, that was a yes," Bear said with a grin. "I knew she'd cave." He fished into his pocket and tossed something to Nash. "Back atcha, man." Two keys clinked together. "Number twelve. Best room in the house."

Mick

ALL-NIGHTER

Holy hell. They always say "what doesn't kill you makes you stronger," but I knew my willpower had no chance against that woman staying under the same roof as me.

And knowing she was behind closed doors with Nash would surely kill me.

I eased the Night Kitchen van through the still, dark New Hope night. Most people were probably home, vegging out in front of the TV or in bed by now. Or out on the make in bars. Or in bars trying to make something of themselves, like Bear. Passing the tavern where his band would soon take the stage was like having a car speed past you with its radio blaring. The noise level rose, but only for an instant before I glided down the silent hill toward the bakery.

The lights were on at the Night Kitchen. My team. They had started without me. I pushed open the door, the din shattering my thoughts about Nash and Dani. Soundgarden blared from the sound system, and trays banged in the back. Tom, my right-hand man, gave a wave from behind the huge mixer, which sounded like it was prepping cement rather than cake batter. The interior was the antithesis of night: fluorescent lighting, gleaming countertops, flour and sugar blinding white in shiny steel bowls.

Sheena was the crumb-coat queen, only taking a break from prepping cakes to chug the iced coffee sweating on the counter beside her. Doris, a holdover from Sindy and Walt's reign, was my supplier of Monday morning breakfast-to-go items: six kinds of croissants and muffins would be tucked into baskets, along with cinnamon buns cooling on the counter, by the time she left to curl up with her husband Ivan, who worked an overnight warehouse shift. And my aunt would be in bright and early to sample one of the goods before she hustled them into bags for her commuter crowd.

But the night was still young, and it was mine. I *was* a rock star, and this was my arena. I wove through my team, who were all moving from one task to another without even asking me what I wanted them to do next. It was a seamless, relentless business, and we all loved it. I hauled a sack of flour in, contemplating what I would make Dani for breakfast.

Dani

INNER SANCTUM

The room was charming, less stuffy Victorian and more rustic English cottage. Its walls were washed in a soothing pale gray, and the iron and brass king bed beckoned invitingly with its crisp linens of white and pale blue. I breathed a sigh of relief. Not a hint of chintz or a tassel to be found. The only throwback appeared to be a well-worn vintage velvet chesterfield sofa in an amazing olive green, nestled next to the fireplace. I ran my hands over its rolled arms, relishing each deep-buttoned tuft. Laney always joked about lying on my invisible psychiatrist's couch, and this specimen appeared to have been plucked from her imagination and made to order.

Nash kicked off his snakeskin boots and collapsed on the bed. "The inner sanctum," he announced to the ceiling. Propping himself up on an elbow, he added for my benefit, "First time I've been allowed past the first floor."

"Are you okay with this?"

"I should be asking you that."

I thought about the suite at the Four Seasons, sitting untouched, un-checked-in. With my own bedroom and turndown service. And the closet full of new-with-tags clothing from the finest stores in Rittenhouse Square, wifey-wear all purchased by Riggs's assistant to prime me for this visit. Along with the spa appointments booked for my downtime, for when I wasn't on the clock. Here I would have to be on the clock, keeping up appearances, at all times.

Maybe that wasn't such a bad thing, considering the fact that Mick Spencer had a bed under the same roof, somewhere within this grand old mansion.

"How many rooms do you think they have here?" I asked.

"It doesn't matter. Asking for separate rooms would raise a major flag."

"It's fine. I'll take the couch."

"Why?" Nash stretched his arms out like an eagle about to take flight. "More room on this king bed together than separately in the bunks on the bus."

He had a point. And had his mission been to take advantage of me, he'd had plenty of nights on the road in which to probably do that. The bed rustled invitingly as Nash nestled his head into the pillow and yawned.

"You're not going to sleep with your clothes on, are you?" I asked him.

He lazily worked at the button fly of his jeans and wriggled until there was a pile of denim and balled-up socks on the floor. Guys. Even the high-maintenance types were slobs.

My jeans were sticky with marshmallow goo, and the fire pit had infused my sheer blouse with its smoky smell. I made my way across the room and pawed through my backpack for a clean T-shirt to wear. "All right. Turn around."

"Oh please. You've seen—and touched—every part of *my* body, except for my junk."

True, I had massaged the buttocks of a rock star. I had pinched the man's earlobes, for God's sake. And dragged my fingers between each of his toes. Still, I shot him a pointed look.

"Like I haven't seen you naked before," Nash scoffed.

"Um, it's a little different when you're covered in glitter and air-brush paint," I mumbled, modestly holding my nightshirt to my chest and blushing at the memory.

"Funny, it takes the power of destiny and fate to bring some people together." He grinned, pushing his hands behind his head, elbows out. "All we needed was a really strong ganja goo ball."

"That was *not* a goo ball." I would've recognized it right away if it had been, and would not have touched its sticky-ass poison with a ten-foot pole. No, this was a huge, blue-ribbon-prize-at-the-fair-winning chewy cookie, sparkling with sugar and studded with luscious chocolate chunks. It looked like it had been baked with loving care by someone's gingham-apron-wearing grandmother. Not by some junkie scientist, clarifying butter for baking with the strongest strain of cannabis on the planet and leaving it on a tour bus. When I saw the plate of them on the narrow counter of Nash's bus that day, covered with plastic wrap and topped with a bow, for God's sake, I couldn't resist. I had been so good about sticking to my rule of no sweets after dark. What harm could come from eating this glorious cookie in the middle of broad daylight?

I should've known. All baked goods were dangerous.

Nash shifted to lay like Tut in the tomb, his arms tight across his chest and his hands clenched. I thought of all those CDs he'd signed earlier, his autograph spreading joy to hundreds who believed in his music like a newfound religion.

I lowered myself gently on the bed next to him and ran my fingers between the grooves of his knuckles on one tight fist. He sighed, allowing me to take his forearm and lift it away from his chest. I stud-ied the veins and tendons with a light touch, reading the guitarist's arm like a road map, tuning in to subtle pulls and twists.

In a gentle squeezing motion, I worked my hand down his arm, pulling as I went. It was a slow process, but my reward was the therapeutic pulse of heat as the tissue gave in to me. His hand went slack, and I began to milk his fingers, grasping, locking, and pulling down on each one. He gave a groan as I stretched his thumb, locking his elbow. I braced it and eased his pinky back to finish his left hand.

"Thank you, China Doll." His breathy praise was better than any tips in the jar. I smiled, cradling his head and massaging his neck before moving to his opposite side to begin the process all over.

Nash was at his truest state when he was at his most vulnerable.

Lemon and maple sifted into my dreams. I snuggled into the stockpile of crisp pillows, relishing the rarity of waking up in a real bed after months on the road. Now *this* was hospitality. Despite Quinn's chilly reception, her qualities as an innkeeper were top-notch. I gathered the Swiss-dot duvet closer to my chin, its just-off-the-clothesline fresh scent enveloping me. The silence was almost loud, with no sound of crew calls or load-ins. Threads of long, flaxen hair covered Nash's face, and he was snoring lightly, his lips pursed like it was finally his turn to make wishes over birthday candles.

I hoped he was being careful what he wished for.

I propped myself on an elbow to study him. Headlining artists hit the stage after dark, so Nash had a moonlight tan at best. His bare shoulder looked pale against sheets of robin's-egg blue. Maybe he'd get a little color while we were here for the week. I set a little reminder to have him show me around the grounds, and around town.

As I arched into a delicious stretch, the press of Mick's fingers at the small of my back, guiding me through the party tent, came to mind so vividly that I gasped.

This town ain't big enough for the both of us.

Nash's challenge to his old friend had been an innocent joke yesterday. But if he knew my and Mick's not-so-innocent history together . . .

It's all eyes on me, China Doll. I'm your world. Got it?

I moved to push the hair off his forehead, but paused, thumb in the spot where his own hand rested during the party. Fingers splayed wide. *Father.*

Nash was a dad.

His son was adorable.

We're just one big happy family here, were Quinn's words. *Don't say we didn't warn you.* Quinn was going to be a challenge.

As was Mick.

I sighed and looked at the bedside table clock. It was eight o'clock on the nose. What I considered "sleeping in" was what Laney called "an ungodly hour" or, more aptly, "ass o'clock in the morning." Sharing an apartment with me and my up-and-at-'em habits must have been cruel and unusual punishment for her back in the day.

Well, at least I wasn't the only early riser in this house. Someone was whipping up something amazing in the kitchen. I doubted it was Mick, as I had heard his van crunch up the gravel and his tender footfalls in the hall as he passed by my door at about two A.M.

Not that I had been listening for them or anything.

The room transformed as daylight sifted through the casement windows. Last night it had been a cozy nook; now it was bursting with light and I could see it was actually quite large, taking up a corner of the house, with windows on two walls. We had a beautiful claw-foot tub in the bathroom that overlooked the orchard, and a skylight above it.

I couldn't help but wonder if Bear had given us the honeymoon suite.

After ensconcing myself into a jog bra, I pulled my T-shirt back on, knotted it at the waist, and threw on a pair of running shorts. I could see paths snaking through the orchard that were perfect for a morning mile. Maybe Nash would be up by the time I got back, so I wouldn't have to face the breakfast crowd alone.

Bed-and-breakfast etiquette had always stymied me; were we really supposed to sit at a communal table and break bread with total strangers? I guess we did a similar thing with each new tour, but . . . that was tour. Crew usually sat with crew, security with security, and the talent held court with their entourage. Taking sustenance before a long, hard day of work was essential, not like exchanging pleasantries over French toast with couples on their weekend getaway without the rug rats.

I tiptoed down the hallway, counting the closed doors as I passed. Number six had a sign hanging from it that looked as if it had been made with a kids' wood-burning craft kit. *Don't wake the sleeping Bear*, it warned, complete with a growling grizzly face to accompany it. I smiled, running the tip of my finger over the indentations.

"Oh, hello." A caramel cat trotted toward me, tail straight up, and headbutted my ankle. "Where'd you come from?" I whispered. He repeatedly rubbed his cheek against the raised panels on the wainscoting lining the hall, with muted thumps.

I followed the cat down the L-shaped hall to a set of stairs, but I noted it wasn't the beautiful curved staircase Nash and I had used last night. Down was down, so I took them anyway, and found myself right in the middle of the kitchen.

Talk about your frying pan, into the fire. I had jumped in, feetfirst.

Mick was standing at the stove, legs splayed in faded jeans. He was effortlessly flipping the fattest pancakes I had ever seen onto a platter. I watched his handiwork: dusting the tops with powdered sugar, dribbling fresh blueberries from his fingers. Bacon was crackling in another pan, coffee was gurgling from the machine on the counter, and the cook was whistling the White Stripes' "Seven Nation Army" as he worked. He was in his element, and I had fallen down the rabbit hole, watching him. *Now what, Dani?* I had lingered too long to try to sneak back up the stairs and find an alternate way. And to get out the side door, I'd have to walk right past him. Indecision paralyzed me.

"Women who walk into my kitchen are in danger of being put to work, you know."

His back was still to me, but I pictured him biting back a smile from those full lips. I crept in closer, taking in the full Victorian kitchen. Elegant crown molding and antique white cabinetry smartly met with a white subway tile backsplash and updated black granite countertops. I admired the open shelves lining one wall, marveling at what had to be a matched service for fifty people. Everything was neat as a pin and white, with pops of rose color here or there that hinted at its former era. It was stark and romantic at the same time.

As was the shirtless, aproned guy in front of me, sporting a wicked case of bed-head and hands full of breakfast food.

"When do you ever sleep?" I stammered.

He grinned, dragging the plate tantalizingly under my nose as he turned to set it on the huge kitchen island next to me. "I catnap. Hi, Bacon."

"Do you always talk to your breakfast meats?" I asked, amused.

"No, but I talk to the cats here." He ducked his head to gesture at the furry friend who had escorted me down the stairs, currently weaving between his denim-clad legs and staring up at him expectantly.

"There's more than one?"

"Oh, you won't see Olive anytime soon. She's shy." He pushed an oven mitt onto one hand and waved it. "Hi to you, too."

"Good morning. Smells amazing in here," I murmured. In addition to the steaming-hot pancakes and the bacon he was hustling off the stove, I spied fresh fruit, croissants oozing with rich chocolate, and a loaf of bread, baked to cracked perfection and studded with sunflower seeds.

I swear the almond extract he used in the bakery must have permeated his skin, as it was ever present and mingled with notes of coffee and cinnamon as he brushed past me.

"Grab that platter, will you?"

He carried the plate of baked goods on one palm and the bacon, still sizzling in the cast iron, in his mitted hand. I followed him into the dining room to the large table, which was elegantly set. "That's all Quinn's doing," he said, referring to the cut crystal water glasses and multitude of cutlery. "Normally we all eat, hunkered over the kitchen island, when there are no guests."

"How many guests are here today?"

"Counting you and Nash?" He set his bounty down and stepped back to admire it. "Two."

The room suddenly shrunk to doll-sized small, as I realized Nash was upstairs, dead to the world, and all this food and fuss—and all eyes—were focused on me.

"I . . . I was just going out for a jog."

He plucked a fork from the table and pushed its side through a wedge of pillowy pancake on the platter I was still holding.

"I have to warn you. You're going to need to run a marathon to work off these bad boys." He twirled the fork teasingly close.

"Hey! Are you implying I need to lose weight?"

"Nope." He grinned. "I'm saying my lemon ricotta soufflé pancakes are amazing."

Rich cheese and ripe citrus exploded across my taste buds as the airy griddlecake melted on my tongue. *Mother mercy.* My knees practically buckled. *Lemon for energy*, I reminded myself, hoping I could muster enough to step away from He Who Had the Power of the Pancake in his grasp. "I'll have you know, I was going to run first. Then eat."

"Oh you were, were you?" The second triangle of pancake still lodged on the fork tines disappeared as he slid it into his own mouth.

I swallowed hard. "Yes. With Nash."

Mick laughed. "Nash doesn't run unless the cops are chasing him."

"I meant eat. With Nash."

"Ah. I see." He took the only thing keeping space between us from my hands and set it on the table. My eyes trailed after the plate, avoiding his gaze. "More for me then," he said, sitting at the head of the table and reaching for the bacon tongs.

I burst onto the porch, screen door slamming behind me. Cool morning air hit my throat, its dew the perfect quencher. The French were spot-on with their culinary term *amuse-bouche*, as that bite with Mick had certainly been a mouth amuser. A torturous, delicious way to keep my mouth, and my imagination, amused.

Run. Cold shower. Repeat if necessary.

Curse that man and his inflated flapjacks. And his sexy apron. Cooking shirtless and barefoot in the kitchen had to violate some kind of innkeeper's health code, didn't it? Let alone allowing cats in the kitchen?

Then again, there were no other guests at the B and B. Did old friends and their fiancées even count?

The Half Acre was more like a "big house with benefits" than a lodging establishment. What had Nash and I gotten ourselves into?

Mick

TABLE MANNERS

"Are you sure he's my kid?" Nash regarded Logan suspiciously from across the large dining table. "I love brunch. How can he not like one single breakfast item?"

Logan was happily munching on a peanut butter and jelly sandwich while his father and his uncle polished off the second wave of my lemon ricotta pancakes and about a pound of applewood-smoked bacon.

"Well, when they invent a pancake paternity test, you'll know for sure. Until then, why don't you just trust good old DNA?" I delivered my suggestion and freshly toasted sunflower bread to the table.

"Yo, dude. You know I like it buttered in the back." Nash gave a wave of his hand, silver rings and mala-bead bracelets jangling.

"Sorry, Your Majesty. I thought maybe you had learned to take care of your own toast during the ten years you were gone."

"Tastes better when you do it," I heard him call. *Yeah, yeah.* I contemplated letting Bacon give his toast a lick, but realized that would just punish Dani the next time she kissed him.

Thinking about Dani kissing Nash was enough to make the lemon and ricotta curdle in my full belly.

Quinn blew in the side door, bringing with her that familiar, vinegary smell of the stop bath. I had a feeling that in situations like this, the darkroom was her place to process, literally. Not just her photographs, but her thoughts as well.

To my knowledge, though . . . we had never had a situation quite like this.

"Get some good shots yesterday?"

"Tons. They're drying." She leaned to kiss the top of her son's head before washing her hands and pulling up a chair. "Where's your bride?"

She didn't look at Nash when she uttered the words, and they left her mouth stiff and stilted, as if she were learning a new language.

"Shower," Nash managed through a mouthful. "She told me not to wait for her. Damn, Spencer. We need someone like you to cook all this shit on tour."

"Can we refrain from the potty talk at the breakfast table, please?"

"Jeez, Quinn. It's not like he—"

Quinn gripped a serrated grapefruit spoon and glared at Nash like she wanted to scoop out his vocal cords. "No, he cannot hear them, but four-letter words are a highly desirable addition to any ten-year-old's vocabulary, no matter the format."

I set down a third platter. Some people stress-eat. Me, I can arousal-eat like nobody's business. After that banter with Dani and watching her stretch out on the lawn before her run, I'd plowed through more than my fair share of pancakes and bacon.

I should've waited for her.

If I were Nash, I would've waited for her.

"Someone's here." Bear peered out the window. "It's a hotel shuttle."

"Oh, yeah. I arranged with the concierge to have some stuff that was delivered to the Four Seasons brought here."

"*Some* stuff?" Quinn stood as the driver wheeled a luggage cart loaded with hanging items and suitcases down the ramp of his van. "Did she buy out the King of Prussia Mall?"

Nash chuckled. "It's not all Dani's. I needed something to wear to this shindig this weekend. Didn't think my stage attire would quite cut it."

"Yeah, ass-less leather chaps and studded collars are so last season," I laughed.

Bear guffawed heartily, then gave pause. "Wait. Aren't all chaps ass-less?"

Quinn screwed up her face, like she'd been squirted in the eye by her grapefruit.

Logan left his crusts in a neat square on his plate and got up to grab a suitcase. It was one of his favorite jobs to help with at the Half Acre, and his rewards were golf-ball-sized biceps that bulged from his lanky arms.

"Thanks, man." Nash palmed a crisp bill into the driver's hand, in exchange for a thin, white box. "You went above and beyond."

Dani appeared in the entryway. Her shapely arms were tan in contrast to her pale yellow sundress, and her ringlets damp from the shower. "Oh, goodness! Thank you," she said, as Bear hauled an armload of clothes past her with a grin. To Logan, she pressed her fingers to her chin and then moved them out. Desire rose and flipped in my gut like one of those soufflé pancakes as she directed a smile toward him with those candy-pink lips.

"You flirting with my kid?" Nash wisecracked. "He's a bit young for you."

"*No.* I was thanking him," Dani said. "It's a little like blowing a kiss, without the pucker. There's a difference." She demonstrated pointedly in my direction. "And thank you, Mick. For the amazing breakfast."

There was a difference, all right. And indifference shone in her eyes, so unlike the night she launched a kiss at me from the center of the dance floor.

"Yeah. Without Mick, this place would just be . . . bed," Bear joked, back to grab the last suitcase. "Or bed-and-make-your-own-damn-toast."

"Just earning my keep," I said modestly, sliding the last pancake, hot off the griddle, onto Dani's plate. "Right, Quinn?"

Quinn tore off tiny pieces of her croissant and changed the subject. "Dani, you are officially invited to my Boo-hoo Breakfast tomorrow. I hold it every year," she added proudly.

"Thanks, Quinn." Dani's smile was a cautious one. "But . . . what's a Boo-hoo Breakfast?"

"It's for the moms in the area, on the first day of school."

Nash's brows went up. "The kid is going back to school already?"

"Yes, Nash. Convenient you showed up to get to know him . . . on Labor Day weekend." Quinn rolled her eyes. "Sort of like how you pulled up in your two-seater sports car. All for show?"

"Hey, I can't help when I'm on tour," Nash protested, before adding glumly, "or when I'm off it. Plus Bear's gonna fix her van." He jerked his head in Dani's direction.

"True, Quinn. Does Logan stay at one school all day? There's plenty of room in my van if you need help carpooling this week, once it's fixed. The lap belts in the back were converted to shoulder belts a while back."

If Nash had a knack for putting his foot in his mouth, Dani appeared to have the prescription for removing it. Quinn's shoulders gave an inch, and I recognized approval in her eyes. Safety was high on her priorities, so the fact Dani mentioned the seat belts scored big brownie points in the Book of Quinn.

"He's mainstreamed, yes. But he does get pulled out for therapy, and for the itinerant program offered by our county. He's kept busy, as are we." Quinn pulled a list out of her pocket and smoothed it down in front of Nash. "You can make up for your lost dad time starting here."

"You're sending me to the office supply store?"

"I haven't had time to get him all his school supplies yet, let alone the luxury of taking him to the zoo this summer. Parenting isn't all glitz and glamour, you know." She turned to Dani.

"I'm sure all the Boo-hoo ladies will want to hear about the wedding. When is it, by the way?" Nash and Dani shared a look, prompting Quinn to add, "Oh, come on. Half the town criers were at the birthday party yesterday. Including Mick's aunt. I'm sure your news has spread."

"Winter," Dani started, right as Nash mumbled something about next summer. "I mean, ah . . . I'd love a winter wedding, but Nash thinks they're tacky. So next summer, it is!"

Nash having an opinion on anything wedding related surprised me. "Are you thinking big or small?" I asked. Number of servings was always at the top of a baker's mind.

Nash cupped his hands and bobbed them in front of him, either indicating a woman with very large breasts, or a huge affair. Everything about Nash Drama was over the top. "Hundreds," he bragged.

"Pretty intimate, I'd imagine," Dani said simultaneously, in contrast. Her baby blues widened about as big as the Wedgwood saucer in front of her, and I swear I saw Nash wince in pain. Had she kicked him under the table?

Quinn looked amused. "Tell us more. Rustic? Modern?"

"We haven't . . . decided one hundred percent." Dani gave a sweet smile toward Nash. "But half the fun is planning, right?"

"If you say so, babe." Nash reached down to rub his shin. "I'm sure those chicks at your sexist breakfast will give you all sorts of ideas."

"So what's in the box?" Dani asked him. The haste in her voice led me to think she was eager to change the subject.

"Oh, yeah. That." He placed the sleek iPad box next to Logan's abandoned crusts. "I decided this was a better gift than a guitar."

Quinn's croissant hit the plate. "You decided? Without discussing it with me first? Eighteen hours under the same roof and you think you know what's best for him?"

Time for the hired help to hightail it to the kitchen. I tried to catch Dani's eye, but she stubbornly stayed put. Was she really into this whole "for better or for worse thing" with Nash? Because I had the feeling shit was about the hit the fan and get a whole lot worse. I began clearing dishes in order to make my escape.

"Hey. You've been making parental decisions for the past ten years. I should be able to make some, too!" Nash countered. "Besides, how different is texting from that little notebook he and Mick pass back and forth?"

Quinn flatlined me with her gaze as I stacked dirty plates. *Great. He's home eighteen hours and I'm getting dragged into their reindeer games.* Quinn and Nash had been butting heads since junior high.

"Lots of kids his age have phones and iPads," Nash continued. "This is a texting generation."

"I won't have him turn into some . . . some mush-for-brains zombie just so he can be like other kids. He's *not* like other kids!"

"If you gave him the chance, he could be," Nash grumbled.

"Take. That. Back," Quinn warned. Whether she meant the expensive gift or the low blow Nash had just dealt, it was unclear.

Dani laid her hand on his arm. "She's right, Nash. Big-ticket electronic items should be discussed."

"Okay, then." Nash made a production of pulling out his own fancy handheld device and swiping at the screen. "Let's discuss . . . *the cochlear implant.* 'A cochlear implant is a surgically implanted *electronic device* that provides a sense of sound to a person who is profoundly deaf or severely hard of hearing . . .'"

"Nash!" Dani looked horrified.

Quinn plucked her napkin from her lap and threw it on her plate. The glassware rattled as her chair crashed to the floor in her hasty departure, and she pushed past me.

"It's been ten years," Nash called after her. "Nothing's going to bring her back, Quinn."

A door slammed.

Dani

DOOR EXPLORATION

"Fuck this noise," Nash announced, pacing the floor of our room. "This is more trouble than it's worth."

I could tell he wanted to break stuff; he wanted to trash things, rock star–style. But we weren't in some generic hotel. Quinn's family heirlooms surrounded us.

"We've been here one day. You need to chill out."

"Did you hear her? She's impossible. Always has been. God. What made me think—?" The clock in the hall downstairs struck ten. Breakfast service was officially over, and all we had were a bunch of hurt feelings to show for it. "Whatever. Never mind."

"That was kind of a low blow you dealt her," I said quietly, even though I didn't quite understand the half of it.

Nash sputtered a laugh. "Believe me, she's going to react far worse when she finds out what's swimming in my gene pool."

"Maybe I can talk to her. Girl to girl," I said.

"Quinn's never been a *girl*." Nash smirked. "She's been Queen Quinn her whole life and she's always done whatever she pleases. And you heard her last night. She won't even let me cross the street with Logan. This is going to take more than a week."

"So we stay longer," I said, although the thought of lingering around Mick for longer gave me the sweats. "Start right here." I pointed to the corner of the room where Nash's own favorite Gibson sat, delivered with the rest of our things.

"What. You want me to serenade her?"

"No. Show Logan how you play. Show him how *to* play."

"I don't know if I can," he admitted, defeat cluttering his voice.

"I've seen you perform for kids."

"Yes, but not for *my* kid. And the stakes are higher," he reminded me.

It was true; but he had nothing to lose and everything to gain by trying.

"Quinn?" I knocked on the door downstairs. "Can we talk?" No answer. I gently rattled the knob.

"You won't find her in there." Even with his towering frame and motorcycle boots, Bear was just as stealth as Bacon the cat. "That's the owner's closet."

"The what?" I turned back to the door, certain it had been the one she'd used. Then again, the old house had a lot of them.

"Owner's closet. All inns have them. See?" He pointed higher than my line of vision. "Dead bolt on the outside. It's where proprietors keep personal stuff they don't want guests to see."

"Oh. Right."

"Growing up in a bed-and-breakfast, you get used to lots of closed doors. As kids, Quinn and I would play hide-and-seek, slamming the doors on empty rooms to throw each other off our trail." Bear leaned against the door, casually crossing his arms as if he was just chatting about the weather. "But my mother always kept the owner's closet locked. Although she did open it for me once."

"Yeah?"

"It was all just a jumble of stuff. You know. Quinn's report cards, my trophies. Stuff like that. Normal people stuff." Bear's dark, wise eyes belied his earnest, simple tone. I understood what he was getting at.

"Too precious to part with, I guess?"

"And too personal to be out for show." He cleared his throat. "Give Quinn some time. She's not used to letting anyone in."

"Can I ask you a question, Bear?"

"Sure."

"It's about Logan's . . ." I drifted off, not sure to refer to it as "hearing" or "deafness." I didn't want to come across as nosy, or offensive. But it was clear both Nash and Quinn needed a liaison. "Can anything more be done to help?"

"He wasn't an ideal candidate for cochlear implants. He was born with very little auditory nerve on one side and none on the other side. And even if he had been?" Bear gave a shrug and a little smile, as if it were anyone's guess.

"Think he can learn to play that guitar?"

Bear rolled the question over in his mind. "It's not a matter of if he *can*. It's whether he would want to. Would a blind person necessarily want to paint a picture, if he could never see it?"

The thought had never occurred to me. "Maybe if he wanted to show others the beauty he created?"

Bear grinned. "Then I think Logan's been waiting to show his dad all kinds of stuff."

I marched back upstairs to room twelve, half expecting to find it empty. Or Nash, packing up his stuff. Instead, he was sitting on the bed, gazing out the window with the Gibson on his lap.

"I've got a favor to ask, China Doll."

"What's that?"

"I need you to teach me how to sign some letters." He threw the guitar strap over his shoulder and met my gaze.

"The alphabet?" I asked.

"No. Just *E*, *A*, *D*, *G*, and *B*. For now."

"Sure." I smiled. "And Nash?"

He raised his brows my way.

"I'll go get the school supplies. And how about you leave the wedding details to me, okay?"

"Gladly. Thanks."

"Just earning my keep," I said, before realizing I had echoed Mick's very words from breakfast. Luckily, Nash had turned back to the guitar and didn't see the blush creep over my cheeks. I thought of the look on Mick's face at the party yesterday when Sindy asked me how Nash had proposed. While it hadn't exactly been a lie, our arrangement was growing teeth by the minute, and I hoped it didn't come back to bite us in the ass.

Mick

SIN AFTER SIN

Even the usual bakery hustle couldn't keep my mind off Dani. I managed to burn the fuck out of myself with a carelessly pulled pan, earning yet another scar to add to the collection. This one, ironically, right above my burnt heart.

Every time one of my staff slid the cases shut up front, a dull thump would echo in my chest. Not even the roar of the commercial coffee grinder drowned out my thoughts of her, as Sindy brewed pot after pot and dished out her gossip with the locals.

Everyone wanted to hear about Nash Drama, back in town to claim his key to the city. My aunt, of course, was more interested in talking about his bride-to-be.

"You know what they say!" My aunt winked to every woman who walked in. "Behind every successful man . . ."

"Is a burlesque dancing queen, stealing the show?" I asked, kissing her cheek. "Get back in the kitchen, will you?" She shimmied back, but not before dropping the hint that she would love to bake that cake when the time came, and had told Dani to come drop in "anytime."

The thought of Dani in my bakery, eyeing my goods, left me with such an aching hard-on, I had no choice but to relegate myself to doing inventory all day, safely out of the public eye. Christ. She had been in town for one day and everything was in an upheaval.

You can play games with the people you love. But don't play games with their heads, Mickey. Or their hearts. My mother's words came sifting down from the pantry shelves, as if they had been hiding up there behind the big tins of baking powder. Sindy might say I was too young to remember her words, but I could hear them, spoken in her tender voice, just as clearly as I could hear her reciting lines from my favorite children's book, over and over again.

What about my head? And what about my heart?

People assumed I was a playboy, but I was only protecting what had been left behind.

Don't hate the player, Nash had bragged. *Hate the game.*

For years I had resented Nash for up and leaving Quinn like he did. And for leaving Bear. And me. And this town. But now that he was back, and now that he had Dani . . .

I needed to jump into the game. The only way I knew how.

"Judas Priest, where's my pocketbook?" Sindy grumbled. "I told Walt I'd stop by the Super Fresh on my way home but I'll be danged. Where is the darn thing?"

A text from my uncle popped up on my phone. *Tell your aunt to make like a goose and get the flock outta there. I'm starving!*

She's asking Judas the whereabouts of her pocketbook, I thumbed back. Sindy pawed through the pantry like a hungry raccoon, the rings of mascara around her eyes widening and narrowing in frustration.

Tell your aunt her pocketbook is on the bed where she left it this morning because she was too busy gabbing about the Nash boy's wedding, the next text read, followed by what looked like a grocery list of contraband, dietician-forbidden foods.

"Tell me what you need, and I'll do the shopping," I told my aunt. "Go on home to Uncle Walt."

Armed with a shopping list from Sindy that was slightly more PC for a diabetic, I left the shop. I was grateful to get away from those four walls and my thoughts, despite the rush-hour-like clog down the main drag. As I drove at a slow crawl past Jenkins Auto Body, I saw Bear directing a flatbed tow and grinning like he had won the lottery.

Dani's van had arrived.

"Kale, salmon, walnuts . . . let me guess. You're baking an omega-three fatty acid cake?" Dani peered down the conveyor belt as the items from my aunt's grocery list sailed by.

"With goldfish cracker sprinkles." The garnish was the one item from my uncle's list. I figured he deserved a little treat after all the superfoods my aunt forced him to eat. He liked a snack that could smile back at him. "Top-secret baking ingredients."

"I'll take them to my grave," Dani solemnly swore, plopping the plastic divider down between my groceries and hers. It was an everyday, innocent gesture . . . made ludicrous by the fact that we had mingled a lot more than just our sundry items in the past.

She looked smoking in a slim black skirt, sling-back sandals, and a pale blue shirt that hugged her voluptuous curves and nipped in at her tiny waist. A world different from the running shorts and T-shirt combo earlier, and the flowing sun-goddess dress from breakfast. She was like the array of glittering impulse items decorating the shelf above the conveyor belt: so tempting. I gritted my teeth and swallowed hard. Was it wrong to want to bite those pearl buttons right off her blouse? Those lucky, lucky buttons.

"And I see you're on the fad diet of pencil shavings?"

"You know it. If I get hungry in between meals, I just huff a little of that rubber cement, and I'm good to go." She laughed, gesturing at the meager amount of school supplies she had scavenged. "Shelves were pretty bare at the office supply store, so I came down here. The town must be preparing for the academic apocalypse."

I glanced at the list, for no better excuse than to lean in close. There were still many items yet to be crossed off. "Tissues, Ziplocs, and Purell? Is this for a classroom or an episode of *Dexter*?" My joke earned me a jostle and an amused batting of those ocean-sized blue eyes and their long lashes. "Pretty sure there's a black market for your plastic folders with prongs and pockets."

"Seriously? 'Cause I found plastic folders with pockets, and plastic folders with prongs, but none with both. Maddening."

"Yeah. We're gonna have to cross state lines for those." I would gladly go on the lam with her, leaving a trail of loose-leaf paper behind us, and erasers to throw everyone off our scent. "Don't forget to label everything after. Double points for that."

"I think this was Quinn's way of testing me . . . I mean, us. Me and Nash," she added quickly. "Initiation by fire."

Her last comment gave me the feeling her groom-to-be hadn't exactly told her the history of the Half Acre.

"Paper or plastic, Mick?" An everyday, innocent question . . . but the flirty tease in the cashier's voice made it as bold as *your place or mine?*

Christ. *Miller wedding. Salted caramel cupcake tower. Black mini-dress. Pearl necklace.*

No forgetting that pearl necklace.

"Amber." I read her nametag aloud. "Hi. Plastic is fine."

She scanned and bagged my items with lightning speed. "George and Holly are back from their honeymoon in Maui. We should totally all go out sometime."

I gave a noncommittal nod, keeping my eyes on the register display so Dani wouldn't think I was trying to take "checkout" to the next level.

"Oh, look at that. Sixty-nine cents is your change." Amber practically poured the coins into my hands with a giggle. "My favorite number."

"Oh, hey, Mick. Are you shopping for my foodgasm?" Sarah-with-an-H had parked her cart behind Dani. Fabulous. All the ghosts of my one-night stands past were piling up on lane nine. With Dani trapped in the middle.

"I made some white chocolate cheesecakes this morning," I said. I hadn't called her about them. But I wished I had, to save myself from this public conversation. "Back on the menu."

"Mmm," Sarah enthused. "I'll be sure to come in"—she checked her watch—"in an hour or so."

"Keep the change, Amber," Dani said crisply, and gave my ankles a nudge with her shopping cart.

"That wasn't what it looked like," I supplied, following her out to the parking lot.

"No? Looked to me like you put the 'fresh' in Super Fresh." Dani hauled the bags from her cart and dropped them into the passenger seat of the Porsche.

"She's just interested in my cakes," I insisted, blocking her between my body and the open passenger door.

"You sure about that, Mick? Because she was basically counting down the minutes to orgasm."

"Foodgasm," I corrected. She'd have to lean into my arms if she wanted to close the door. Or climb over the gearshift in her short skirt. It was a winning proposition for me, either way.

"Whatever lets you sleep at night," she said. "Move, please."

"And if I don't?"

She placed her thumb on the panic button of the key fob and raised her eyebrows.

"I meant I don't sleep at night. Not since New Orleans." Fuck it. Not exactly the conversation I wanted to have in the Super Fresh parking lot. But at least we were alone. "Not well, anyway."

"Well, I no longer dream," she stated. "Not since New Orleans. Guess we're even."

Dani

SPIN DOCTOR

I had left the Half Acre to get Mick out of my mind, and I wasn't even safe at the supermarket, for God's sake. Those women were practically throwing themselves at his feet, yet he had the nerve to pull the whole innocent act.

Music met my ears as I pushed through the front door. Logan and Nash were sitting in the front room, on the curved window seat in the turret. They had a notebook between them, and guitars on their laps. Logan's facial expressions were changing with each note Nash demonstrated, his mouth moving along with the cues.

"C . . . yeah, you got it, kid. Now G." Nash tapped the letter in the notebook, and Logan lifted his hand just long enough to demonstrate the letter before moving it back to tackle the guitar neck. His hand was small for the frets, but his fingers were long and promising. Just like his father's.

"Check you out." Nash grinned, licking his lips. "Very sexy secretary."

I grimaced, smoothing down the pencil skirt I had changed into before leaving for the store. "I prefer my own clothes, but a deal is a deal." Riggs didn't want it to look as if Nash had pulled me right off the festy circuit. But his assistant must've been channeling some eighties MTV fantasy, as every outfit that had been delivered was a cross between Van Halen's "Hot for Teacher" and the sexy librarian gone wild from Adam Ant's "Goody Two Shoes" video.

Mick had certainly done a double take in the checkout aisle. The thought of his eyes roaming approvingly gave me a one-two punch of excitement and guilt in my gut.

I wondered if he noticed I had chosen my blouse to match his eyes.

I spread my bounty of school supplies out on the Persian rug and went to work labeling each piece, as Mick had suggested. If Sharpie-markering Logan's name twenty times on quarter-inch #2 pencils scored points with Quinn, I would gladly take one for the team and huff the fumes.

I remembered my excitement with the start of every school year on Long Island. The nip in the air come nightfall, and the leaves performing their annual drop-and-clog ritual into the swimming pool. I loved pulling out cozy warmer clothes and debating with Laney what we'd wear that first day of school. She'd left me a voice mail that morning, but I hadn't gotten back to her yet. Jax had been uncharacteristically quiet, considering he usually texted me daily.

"One, two. One, two," Nash conducted in time, and Logan proudly strummed two simple chords. Hugging the body of the acoustic against his tummy, he practically thrummed along with it. The excitement was palpable.

I smiled and resumed my labeling, remembering the thrill of cracking into blank notebooks. Relishing the idea of a fresh start, the endless possibilities to do well.

Nash began to accompany him, taking it above and beyond with a melody to his son's simple backbone. I noticed Quinn standing in the doorway, watching, as Nash's nimble fingers tackled the frets and he began to sing, barely moving his mouth, brow creasing as he held the last word of each line.

> *Wasting away*
> *Waiting to be found*
> *Hard to find the words*
> *When I can't hear a sound*
> *Lost in the fray*
> *Stumble to the ground*
> *Cannot be heard*
> *When you're not around*

Logan hit an off note, and Nash winced. I glanced back toward the doorway, but Quinn was gone.

"Rome," I murmured. "It wasn't built in a day."

This was certainly a start.

I spent the afternoon reading up on Nash's condition, and ironically, ankylosing spondylitis tended to worsen during periods of inactivity. So much for Riggs's bright idea of taking Nash off the road to calm him down. He needed exercise and movement, and luckily, we had an eager ten-year-old ready to test out his father's running legs. After dinner, Logan, Nash, Mick, and Bear played Frisbee and horseshoes out on the lawn, under the watchful eye of Quinn. Sindy came and joined us at the fire pit later; the consummate guest, she had even brought her own skewer.

"Dani, you've given those boys a great gift," she said, blowing gently on her smoldering marshmallow to keep it burning. The four were still whooping it up and rolling around on the grass, with Quinn refereeing. "The gift of time. I really don't think Nash would've come home, had it not been for you."

Affection for the woman surged through me; next to Bear, she had been the most straightforward and kindest of them all since we had arrived.

"Darling, speaking of time . . . I hope you'll consider holding the wedding here. Soon. Lord knows this place could use some joyful memories."

The guys were descending, sweaty and hungry, and Sindy made quick business of shoving more marshmallows on skewers.

"Going for a water run," Quinn called, making toward the house.

My heart began to speed up at the thought of things going any faster than they already were. Arriving in town and discovering Mick had thrown me for a loop. I had been evading the eventual questions that I knew were bound to come, and excuses came natural for me. "Well, you know. We haven't even considered who will officiate—"

Sindy waved a hand. "We do it differently here in Pennsylvania. You and Nash can go get yourself a Quaker license. It only takes three days, and it's self-uniting."

Three days? As in, before the week is up?

"Just you, your vows, and two witnesses. Isn't that romantic? Hell, if I could do it all over again with Walt that way, I would," Sindy was saying.

"Do what?" Nash asked, wiping his face with his shirt. He looked exhausted but happy.

"Get hitched right here at the Half Acre." Sindy smiled and presented Logan with a marshmallow-topped skewer and a curtsy, like he was king of the world. I felt Mick's presence behind me, heard his labored breathing, and smelled clean sweat as he reached around me and thrust a skewer into the blaze.

"That's a great idea," Bear said, before anyone else could react. "Right here!"

"At the fire pit?" I laughed, poking the flames with my own stick.

Bear gave a small smile, and pointed up.

I hadn't noticed it before, but the concrete pad we were sitting on rested under a regal metal archway. It wasn't enclosed, and we could see countless stars overhead on the clear night.

"It's an open-air chapel," Bear explained. "We used to have weddings here all the time."

"It will be perfect." Sindy sighed. "Let us help plan the wedding of your dreams."

Mick's gaze met mine as I came back down to earth. Smoldering. The sweets we held between us turning to forgotten ash.

I don't sleep anymore, he had said. *Not since New Orleans.*

I no longer dream.

I turned to catch Nash's reaction, but his eyes were roaming elsewhere. Focused on the dark corners of the property, his mind somewhere in the past.

"I need you. Baby. Please."

There's that weird spot between awake and sleeping, where you can't remember whether you're dreaming, yet everything feels good and right in the world. And you're happy and your mind's at peace, for no real reason.

That's where I was when Nash reached for me.

"Where?" I kicked the covers off of both of us.

"Lower back," he gasped. "Maybe I overdid it today."

"Pain scale?" I plugged in the heating pad I had bought for him, which would help with the inflammation.

"Getting worse by the second." He groaned loudly as I eased him over onto it.

"Relax," I whispered, stroking his hair back as he winced and sighed.

"Christ, I am so tired of this pain. When's it going to go away?"

"Shhh . . ." I began to stroke and knead the tense muscles in his thighs while the heat loosened his back. "You're tired because your body is fighting a war."

Deep down, I knew he was terrified of the pain truly going away . . . because that was the true sign that the scarring had fused the spine, leaving him with limited mobility and balance.

"Can you—" I worked my way to his hips and he moaned in grateful relief as I helped him flex them. "That's the fucking spot, girl. Yeah."

"Deep breaths," I reminded, as I leaned over him.

He ran his hand over mine, breathing hard. "Oh God. Spasm. Need to turn."

It was better for him to lie facedown, but getting there was torture. He muffled his groans and curses in the pillow as I gently massaged the hot spots where his flare-ups tended to occur.

Gradually, his breathing became slower, shallower. "Yes . . . much better. Thank you," he mumbled, wiping the tears and sweat with the back of his hand. His eyelids gave over to the heaviness and fatigue that often followed such an episode, and he was back to sleep within minutes.

I slowly lay back down, willing my heart rate to return to normal. Coaxing my body back toward sleep, I remembered my dream. So much for the lie I had spun in the supermarket parking lot. There were many dreams. And they were always about Mick. This one had me in his arms, on a blanket under the stars by the fire pit. No s'mores, just the sweet and sticky sin of his fingers slipping toward the hottest part of me. I closed my eyes, but was having a hard time finding my way back there. Nash began snoring next to me. The ache for release grew, and my only recourse was to take matters into my own hands. Quiet, gentle and quick, I opened myself to the fantasy. Mick's fingers, not mine, eased the ache and brought sweet sleep.

Mick

HAPPINESS SOLD SEPARATELY

The walls were way too thin at the Half Acre.

Room twelve wasn't far enough away from mine to pretend I wasn't hearing what I thought I was hearing, as I tossed and turned.

Nash led a charmed life, apparently. As evident from his grunts, groans, and "yeah babies," followed by soft whispers, sighs, and creaks of the bed.

Sweet nothings that weren't exactly nothing, I thought bitterly.

The idea of Dani working him into such a state sent me out of my mind, and downstairs to watch some mindless television.

Quiet footfalls on the staircase turned my head. Quinn, freshly showered and wearing one of the inn's signature thick waffle-weave spa bathrobes, padded in. I smirked, remembering she made me relinquish the one in my room when I established residence.

"And I thought those fancy robes were just for guests?"

"Jesus, Mick!" Quinn's fist clutched the collar of her robe. "You scared the piss out of me."

"Sorry. Couldn't sleep."

She gave a snort. "With all their carrying on up there, I'm not surprised."

Good to know I wasn't the only one.

"I came down to watch TV. Do you know why there are no batteries in the remote?" I gave it a shake.

"Why would I know?" she snapped, jamming her hands into the pockets of her robe and glaring at me.

"Because you always watch those ridiculous cooking shows after Logan goes to sleep. Don't bite my head off, kid."

She reddened. "Maybe Bear used them for his guitar pedals. I don't know." She shrugged and turned on her bare heel. "I'm making tea. You want a cup?"

"Nah," I said, but followed her into the kitchen anyway. "Double-A batteries to power his rock? Doubtful, honey."

"Well, look in the junk drawer." She gestured toward the kitchen island. "I'm sure there are some lying around."

"Nope. Already checked. None." I leaned against the counter while she fussed with her tea bag.

"Okay. So maybe Logan's remote-control race car needed batteries."

Her attempt to sound casual was just about as lame as that excuse. Logan got a billion new toys for his birthday, and that old car had been sitting in the shed since July.

"Or maybe," I drawled, smiling wickedly, "Queen Quinnlyn's got herself a battery-operated friend upstairs."

"Oh, shut up," she muttered, yanking the steaming kettle off the stove. I knew I had her.

"Hey, hey, nothing to be ashamed about." The batteries she pulled from her robe's pocket and whipped at me plink-plunked against my laughing chest. I stooped to retrieve them; they were still warm. "We've all been there, Quinn."

"I don't want to know about *anywhere* you've been, Mick Spencer."

She plunged her tea bag into the steaming cup and dunked it merci-lessly. "End of story."

Still chuckling, I placed the double-A's into the remote and clicked the back shut. "The end, all good," I said emphatically, but couldn't help but add, "a good, happy ending. That's all anyone ever needs, right?"

"Get out of my kitchen."

"Come watch TV with me. I'll even let you choose the show."

"Gee, thanks."

We settled into opposite ends of the couch. Quinn blew across the top of her mug while I thumbed through the channels. A nudge of her bare foot to my femur bone indicated her program preference, some celebrity cake competition. Not my idea of relaxing entertainment, but it beat listening to whatever show was still going on up in room number twelve.

Bacon lap-tested Quinn's waffle-weave before clambering over to poke holes in my sweatpants with his claws, kneading and turning until he flopped to rest across my knee.

"That guy reminds me of you." Quinn jutted her chin toward the screen.

"Because he's short, stocky, bald, and looks absolutely nothing like me?" I joked, studying her profile. Cool, blue light flickered down her cute, upturned nose and dotted her cheeks before she answered.

"Because he gets absolutely lost in the joy of doing what he loves to do."

We watched in silence for a while.

"Are you thinking what I'm thinking?" I asked.

"About strangling Bear for inviting them to stay here? Yes."

I laughed. "So what are we going to do about it?"

"The hell if I know. Nash is up to something. I can feel it." She dropped her head on my shoulder, and I pulled her close. "I just wish I knew what it was, so I could head it off at the motherfucking pass."

An idea struck. "You know that old saying about keeping your friends close?" I asked her.

"But your enemies even closer?" Quinn finished.

What about your enemy's fiancée?

"I think we should all go out this week. On a double date. You and me. Nash and Dani."

Quinn smiled for the first time that evening. Or at least, since she left the privacy of her own room.

Dani

GOSSIP GIRLS

"Nash." I gave his shoulder a gentle squeeze. "Nash, time to get up. First day of school." I'd already been downstairs and Logan was a fireball of energy, excited to start fourth grade. Quinn was flitting back and forth like a bird building a nest as she simultaneously packed a brown-bag lunch for him and set the table for the Boo-hoo Breakfast. Mick was readying food for half a dozen women, and Bear was serenading everyone with Elton John songs in preparation for his Elton "tribute" that night.

My job was to rouse the sleeping giant. I gave Nash's shoulder a gentle kneading

He started, then rolled over. "Mmm-hmm."

"Come on. You don't want to miss the bus."

No answer.

"Nash."

His lips communed with the pillow. "You go. I'm not invited to the Boob Breakfast, remember?"

"It's Boo-hoo. And I know. But you could come see your son off on the first day of school."

Nash sat straight up in bed like a horror flick zombie. He tamped down his rumpled hair with shaky fingers. "How late were we up last night?"

"I don't know. Maybe two o'clock?" He'd reached for me in the small hours, which was often when the pain decided to make its presence known.

"Sorry," he mumbled. "Fucking flare-up."

"It's okay. That's what I'm here for." I opened the curtains to let in the eastern light, and Nash hissed like a vampire being disturbed in his crypt. "I hope that's not the beginnings of iritis," I said, running a gentle hand over his brow and inspecting his reddened eyes.

"Eye-right-huh? What the fuck is that?"

"Severe sensitivity to light." I handed him his sunglasses from the bedside table. "It often comes and goes with the AS flare-ups."

"Gee," he said sarcastically, cramming a ball cap on his bed-head as well. "This condition is the gift that keeps on giving, isn't it?"

"Well, well. Look who decided to grace us with his presence," Quinn said, hand on the front doorknob, as we descended the grand staircase. Logan gave a grin and two thumbs up, which caused a shift in his center of gravity due to his enormous backpack. He almost went over like a turtle on his shell. Bear began strumming and singing "I'm Still Standing."

Nash ignored her comment, choosing to smile at Logan instead. I'd reminded him of the importance of facial expressions, especially since he couldn't sign. Yet. "How about I walk him down to the bus stop, Quinn?"

"How about we both do?" she said through gritted teeth. "Seeing as I haven't missed doing it once these last five years." She bared her fist, which held a camera.

"Ah yes. Another Kodak moment." Nash bent down next to Logan and they both mugged for the camera, leaving Quinn no choice but to snap a few shots of them.

"A disguise, really? The ball cap and the shades are probably going to attract more attention than your rock star self. Who are you afraid of?" She rolled her eyes. "Groupie bus drivers?"

"Let's rock and roll, kid."

Logan waved back to Mick and me before turning to march proudly between both his parents down the long walkway. Bear trailed behind them with his acoustic, crooning "Goodbye Yellow Brick Road."

Mick laughed and shook his head. "Now *that's* a Kodak moment. How'd you manage to get him out of bed before eight?"

"My powers of persuasion, I guess," I said, suddenly very aware that he and I were alone in a very, very large house. With a lot of rooms to get lost in.

He shot me a look that sent my mind reeling back to my fantasies of him last night. God. Any alone time with Mick was just fueling my pathetic imagination.

"Need help in the kitchen?" I mumbled.

"I've got it under control," he said, resting a hand on the curved banister.

If I took one more step down, I'd be in his arms. If I hightailed it up the stairs, he might give chase. The thought of that practically buckled my knees.

"Are you staying through the breakfast?" I asked.

Mick laughed. "That's one wall I have no desire to be a fly on. Besides, I have to get down to the bakery. Which reminds me . . . we need to set a date. For you and Nash to come in and choose a cake. You are going to take me up on my offer, right?"

Dessert wasn't the only offer I wanted to take Mick up on. But with Nash's ring on my finger and his well-being on my mind, any indulgence on my part was severely restricted.

For all intents and purposes, you're off the market.

Mick's off the menu.

His hand slid up the banister, on a dangerous crash collision course toward mine, but I stood my ground and refused to meet his eyes. It wasn't fair for him to do this, not when the rest of the inn's residents were just a few steps down the walkway.

"Why are you torturing me?" I said softly.

"Girl, you don't know what torture is. Last night—"

"Enough, Bear!" Quinn marched through the front door and straight into the kitchen to ready herself for the women about to descend. Her brother busted in next, singing "I Guess That's Why They Call It the Blues" in his smooth baritone. His fingers changed chords easily as he made his way up the stairs past us with a grin.

I swept my hand over Mick's as I descended to meet Nash at the door. It had been an innocent-looking move, but I hope it sent him the message loud and clear that I was moving past him, moving on.

I needed to.

Now if only I could convince myself of that. The thought made me want to weep.

I was going to fit right in at that Boo-hoo Breakfast.

The delicious scents emanating from the breakfast room competed against the bevy of women arriving in a cloud of perfume, waving their hands and air-kissing each other hello. Quinn let her best friend Lizzie, a cute cheerleader type with an upturned nose and sweet voice, introduce me to the rest of the gang, whose names I promptly forgot.

"See, we used to get together and cry, back when all our kids started kindergarten. Now," a buxom redhead said, reaching for the pitcher of mimosas Mick had prepared earlier. "We send them off and it's like 'There's the sweet sound of the school bus! Time to pour me a drink!'"

"I'm an honorary Boo-hoo," hollered Lizzie, who was single but invited every year due to her BFF status, "but for the rest of you ladies' sanity, I'll drink to that!"

The other ladies all laughed and clinked their glasses. "None for me," called the blonde with the baby attached on her hip. "Still breast-feeding this little guy."

"Quinn, sit," I said as she whirled by me like the Tasmanian Devil character in the old cartoons. "Visit with your friends. Let me serve."

"Everything's all set," Quinn said breathlessly. "Mick set things up buffet-style before he and Nash hightailed it out of here to keep their manhood intact."

The thought of Mick and Nash out together threw me, but I shook off the uneasy feeling. They had been friends much longer than I had been in the picture for either of them. And like I had conveyed to Mick at Logan's party, I didn't want to make any waves.

Now if only Mick would quit rocking the damn boat.

The women dug into Mick's feast like they hadn't eaten all summer, oohing and aahing over his culinary prowess. I had no doubt it was the kind of praise he ate up with a spoon, so to speak.

"Those cupcakes for Logan's party looked ah-MAY-zing!" Lizzie singsonged. "I can't wait to see what Mick comes up with for Zena's bridal shower."

"Maybe we'll get lucky and he'll pop out of her cake," drawled the redhead, a wicked smile teasing her lips. "Oh come on," she countered the clucks and groans from her gaggle of friends with a shrug of her bony shoulders. "Like none of you have fantasized about that? I guess I'm the only one brave enough to say it."

"I'm still fantasizing about that naked cake Mick made for Jessie Zuckerman's wedding . . . remember, with the raspberry buttercream?" The blonde named Beth rearranged her drape with a sigh and shifted her baby underneath from Boob A to Boob B.

"Please." Lizzie fanned herself. "Don't mention 'Mick' and 'naked' in the same sentence! Mylanta, that man can clog my arteries any day of the week!"

The walls reverberated with another round of their squeals.

"You know Sarah sampled the goods that night, right?" I couldn't decide which woman I hated more right now, the faceless Sarah, or the gloating redhead who was gossiping about her.

"Julia!" scolded the blonde, frowning over the downy head of her breastfeeding baby. "Don't kiss and tell for someone else." Turning to me, she said, "Dani, don't let us scare you off. We're horrible when we all get together."

"Please, Beth. She's engaged to Nash. I don't think she scares easily." Lizzie gave me a conspiratorial wink, and I decided I liked her.

Julia's lips curled as her eyes drifted coolly over me, coming to rest on the rock on my finger. Something told me she might have been guilty of sampling the goods of the musician who had put it there.

"I can't believe Nash decided to settle . . ." Her voice dwindled to a bitter finish. ". . . down."

Kindness. Kill 'em with kindness. And small talk.

"So, Julia. How long have you been married?" I asked, resting my chin in my hand and making sure my ring was in full view. If I tilted it just right and caught the sunlight, maybe I would blind her.

"A year next month," she said haughtily. "Jimmy's my second husband. We're still in the"—she air-quoted and rolled her eyes—"'honeymoon phase.' Please. I just wanted a guy who could snake my drain and de-clutter my gutters." All the women tittered. "Luckily, all it usually takes is a six-pack and the shooting range to keep him satisfied when I don't feel in the mood."

"No new babies for you two?" Beth asked, moving her little one up to her shoulder and patting a healthy burp out of him.

"No way. Gloria's almost a teen, and she was handful enough. Keep your diapers, thank you."

"How about you, Dani?" Lizzie asked. "Think you and Nash will start a family?"

I just about choked on my mimosa. Out of all the wacky scenarios that had paraded through my brain since this charade began, I hadn't dreamed up the event where I might need a party line for such a question. "Well, he . . . we . . . are just getting to know Logan, who is so amazing. I think he wants to make up for a bit of lost time there . . . plus all the touring." *And the drinking and the boning on the side,* I thought, but refrained from voicing it. "We are just having fun planning the wedding."

"I've totally planned mine; it's all up on Pinterest," Lizzie sighed. "Now I just gotta find me a groom." That got a howl from the other girls.

"Well, the cake's a no-brainer," Julia said. "You just sit back and let that fine man down at the Night Kitchen do all the work." She sat back and rubbed her Spanx-smooth tummy, then leaned forward and said conspiratorially, "Here's the thing about Mick. He asks you what you'd like, he listens to your wishes, and then he fulfills your wildest dreams. How many men actually *do* that in real life?" She gave a wink all around. "Given the chance, I'd like to do—"

"Do what?" Quinn asked, finally plopping down with a cup of tea in her hand. "Please tell me you're not drooling over Mick Spencer." She shook her head. "Ever since he came back from New Orleans, he's been on a tear."

"Melly down at the Curl Up and Dye said she heard he'd shacked up down there with a regular witch. She was trying some voodoo spells to get him to marry her but it didn't work. And she kicked him out and had him arrested or some crazy thing." Beth covered her baby's ears, as if she didn't want him to hear his mother spreading the evil seed of gossip.

My ears had certainly pricked up. And my mimosa burned going down as I tried to swallow and act politely disinterested. Judging from their surprised exclamations, I gathered Mick had a blemish-free record before New Orleans. As for Nash? The ladies made it sound like his mug shot could've been used for his senior yearbook picture and no one would've been shocked in the least.

Lizzie made a razzing sound. "Voodoo spells! I wouldn't trust Melly with a pair of scissors, let alone believe a word that comes out of her mouth!"

Quinn shrugged. "She does color Mick's aunt's hair once a month. Well, whatever. I don't know what, or who, happened to him down there, but I'd say he got hurt pretty bad. He's been acting like the biggest pig in Bucks County. Crazy."

"Well, sign me up for the bacon craze, then." Julia smirked and cracked down on a particularly crispy piece from her plate. "I hear he's even better when he's chocolate-covered."

Dani

DAY TRIPPING

When Bear wasn't practicing or gigging with his tributes, he spent every waking minute at the auto body shop. By Thursday, I was convinced he was either having a torrid affair with Mean Mistress Mustard or he had hacked her up to sell her body parts overseas. I decided to go downtown and investigate.

"Give it to me straight. Will she ever drive again?"

Bear grinned at me as he walked from the garage to the office like a surgeon coming out of an operating room. "Good news first, or bad news?"

"Just lay it on me."

Bear wiped his hands on an old red rag. "I'll give you the amazing news first. Come with me."

He led me back to inspect Mean Mistress Mustard's back end, where she housed her engine. "I have never seen such a beautifully restored Wasserboxer engine in my life. The previous owner must've been a purist. Souped her up real good, gave her better horsepower than the original." Bear pointed out all that he loved about the junk in her trunk, his finger stained darker around his knuckles where the grease and oil had collected.

"The bad news is, the more you tweak these pancake engines, the less reliable they become. And finding replacement parts is an expensive scavenger hunt." He gave me a sympathetic frown, which was more than I got from the last two garages. I guess they weren't into the hippie thing.

"Please tell me you can fix it."

"Even better. I can swap it out for a four-cylinder, two-point-five-liter Subaru engine. They make a perfect conversion, and I can have you putting out one hundred and eighty horsepower in this sweet baby." He sounded proud. "Come up front and we'll crunch some numbers."

The place looked like someone had given up decorating—and dusting—it in the 1970s. Everything in the office looked dated, from the metal desk to the clock on the wall, wire-caged so no one could attempt to alter time further. The only modern piece in the room was the Swimsuit Girl calendar, which was surprisingly up to date.

Almost everything above eye level had a layer of grease and was made monochromatic with a furry coating of dust, except for the yellowing pages ripped from a child's picture book and hanging over the desk. Those were brightly colored, and signed in crayon, *TO UNCLE BEAR, LOVE LOGAN.*

I smiled up at the drawings, thinking of the scene I had walked into the night before. Mick and Logan sprawled in front of the fireplace, surrounded by colored pencils and a big roll of parchment from the bakery. I'd watched as Mick patiently showed Logan how to use the opaque paper to trace his favorite comic book heroes, while Bacon stalked a wayward pencil down the length of it, making a crazy crunching sound with his paws. After three straight evenings of domestic docility and playing parlor games, Nash had earned a kitchen pass to check out Bear's tribute band du jour. Quinn had a PTA meeting, so it was just the three of us.

"He doesn't have a sign name for you?" I'd asked, after noticing Logan finger spelling *M-I-C-K* and tugging on his drawing instructor's shirt sleeve several times. I knew a passable amount about deaf culture, and how the unique names were presented by members to those in and out of the deaf community.

"Not yet," Mick had said, a wistful tinge in his voice. "Takes time, I guess. He was pretty young when I left town, and I've barely been back a year." He smiled, leaning toward his young charge and passing him the coveted red pencil, already worked down to a nub.

It made me realize just how pathetically short a week's time was.

"Hungry?" Bear asked, offering up a box of cookies.

"After Mick's usual morning feast? I couldn't possibly. But thanks."

"More good news," he reported between bites, tapping away on the old IBM. White powdered sugar now dusted the grimy keyboard. "Old Man Jenkins has a two-point-five on his property with just fifty thousand miles on it that needs a home. Like an organ donor, waiting to save a life."

I laughed. "Of course this town would have an Old Man Jenkins. With a perfect motor just lying around."

"He owns this shop," Bear explained, turning and pointing to the back of his jumpsuit, which did indeed read, JENKINS AUTO BODY.

"The old man retired about five years ago. But he still collects." Bear had introduced me earlier to the younger Jenkins on the premises, a doughy guy whose eyes practically bugged out at the sight of me in his shop, like one of his calendar girls come to life.

"Now, more bad news. We're talking about forty hours of work. But hey, at least there's no wait time for the engine. Sometimes that takes a good three weeks to a month to hunt down."

My heart sank. Even if Bear worked on my van like a nine-to-five day job, it still wouldn't be ready for a week. "How much would a used engine cost?"

Bear held up a finger while he finished munching a second cookie.

Swallowing, he announced, "Street value would be around five thousand. I'll see what the old man wants for it."

I let out a low, long whistle. Jax had landed me a sweet deal on the van to begin with, but adding five thousand to that?

"Come on. Nash won't blink an eye. How much do you think he laid out for that knuckleduster you're wearing?" He grabbed my hand to inspect it once again. "Thirty, forty K?"

Nash *had* offered to take care of it, as part of our original "deal." I thought back to the day Riggs set the ring in front of me on the catering table, like he was passing me the saltshaker. And how I had thrown it back at Nash's chest. We had come a long way since then. Looking down at our fingers, I realized it had more value than I had given it credit for. Still. I hated to rely on Nash—or anyone, for that matter.

"I really want it back on the road. Let's do it."

Bear grinned and bumped a fist to mine. "Excellent."

Maybe because my livelihood also depended on my hands, I was fixated on watching other people's tools of trade. And I found guys who worked with their hands very sexy. Like Mick's hands, Bear's had tiny nicks and cuts from his trade, but his fingertips also bore the smooth, hard calluses like Nash's, from years of pushing guitar strings. Funny how all three friends worked with their hands. And Bear, unlike the other two, was fluent in talking with them, too.

"How long have you been signing, Bear? You're very good at it."

"Dunno," Bear said, a smile stealing across his face. "Since before I can remember. My mom was deaf."

"Oh!" I started, Nash's words to Quinn our first morning there finally jelling with me.

Nothing's going to bring her back.

Bear rubbed his neck in thought, and as he pushed back his mane of hair, I spotted another tattoo.

Like Nash and Mick, he had a blue-winged bird, but his was on his neck and impaled by a knife.

"I know that bird," I blurted.

He ducked down to grab another cookie from the box. "It's a swallow. Did you know they mate for life?"

"I didn't know that. Why does it have a dagger through its breast?"

"To honor a loved one, lost at sea." Bear's smile didn't waver, but I could tell he wasn't interested in talking about it anymore. "I'll see you back at the Half Acre tonight, Dani."

I hadn't been to the Night Kitchen since that first day in town, but since half the borough seemed to be taking a vested interest in my impending nuptials, I decided to take a gander after leaving Bear and Mistress Mustard. At least I knew its proprietor wasn't on-site today.

"Think you can amuse yourself for the day?" Nash had asked me that morning. "Mick and I are going down to Atlantic City to play some poker."

"No problem," I'd replied from behind a bridal magazine. I'd picked one up, just for show, during a trip to the grocery store with Quinn and Logan the other day. After that morning with the Boo-hoo girls, I figured I should bone up on my wedding vocabulary. But page after page of luscious cakes had left me thinking about Mick and his offer. What was the harm in peeking at his cakes? Especially if the cook had left the kitchen for the day. Sindy had agreed to drop anything and meet me anytime. *Especially Thursdays,* she had stressed to me with a wink. *Always a slow day in the shop, and I can lavish my favorite customers with attention.*

"Can I help you?" A tall chick with a tiny nose ring was bouncing from table to table, replenishing the napkins. I could see how some of Mick's towering desserts could rate as a multi-napkin affair.

God, I could see getting into some sweet and sticky sin with him myself.

Danica James, you should be ashamed of yourself.

"I'm here to see Sindy," I said brightly. "Danica James."

"Let me go find her. If you want to have a seat." She gestured to a table off to the side, devoid of napkins but stacked with scrapbooks, no doubt filled to the brim with his handiwork.

"Thanks."

"Coffee? Tea? Orange-basil-infused water?"

"That's, um . . . specific," I said. "Sure, I'll try the water."

Her eyes widened and the tiny diamond in her nostril flared. "It's the bomb, you'll love it!" she declared. "We make a different fruit-soaked water combo every day. But that one's my favorite." She spun on her heel and happily scampered behind the counter.

I settled into a chair and glanced around. The shop was bustling and I was grateful to channel some of my nervous energy toward people-watching. What was with the facial piercings? A guy with an eyebrow ring waited on an elderly woman and chatted about his trip to Machu Picchu.

Besides the curved refrigerated case for the cakes and pies, there were long counters stained in deep rich wood with tilted glass rising up on a slant in wooden frames, displaying delicate cookies of all shapes and flavors on pedestals and tiered plate towers. A revolving line of customers came and went, coming close to peer through the glass displays like they were admiring fine art in a gallery, although you could see their appetites increasing as they stared, with wide, dancing eyes, at the delectable choices.

Two girls deliberated over crusty macarons stacked in colorful pastel rainbows like they were a hot-button issue: green pistachio or lavender taro? "They're too pretty to eat!" They giggled when Brow Ring Guy surveyed them.

I turned my attention to the daunting books in front of me. All right. I could do this. *Open the damn book, nothing is going to jump out and bite you.* The first one I chose unleashed a flurry of loose pictures into my lap. *Figures.* Many had the small watermark across the bottom that I had noticed on the photos in the rooms at the Half Acre. Quinn's logo. *Jeez, were they all in cahoots?* I leaned to scoop up the few strays that had sifted onto the floor.

"I could see you going with lace. Very delicate. Ultra-feminine."

Mick stood in front of me, water glass in his hand and a smirk on his face.

"More and more brides are going with lace designs on their cakes these days." He set the glass down and knelt with me, taking the photos from my hand. "All that is hand-piped. I can duplicate your dress pattern, or . . . make something up from my imagination."

Those striking blue eyes roamed over mine, lighting a flame in me. I had no doubt I had left little to the imagination, bending over in the low, scooped tank top, which was another item from the hot-wifey dress-up box.

But the frilly push-up bra beneath it was all mine.

"Of course, if that is too much lace for you, you can just slide a layer in between. I'm a fan of layers," he said, practically undressing me with his eyes.

I readjusted my top and recovered, taking a sip of the infused water he'd delivered. *Basil for clarity*, I recited to myself, as if choosing the best essential oil for a massage client. *Don't play his mind-in-the-gutter games.* Where the hell was Sindy, anyway? His wasn't the attention I had expected to be lavished with today.

"Sorry, these were supposed to be filed into a new photo album." He bent close to retrieve the last rogue picture from between the rungs of my chair. "I usually go with a computer slideshow, but Sindy's still pretty old school."

"Is she here? She told me to drop in today."

"She wasn't feeling well, so I sent her home early. I guess you're stuck with me."

"I thought you . . . Nash said—" I clamped my mouth shut.

"What's that?" He gazed up at me expectantly.

"Nothing. I just . . . I didn't expect to see you here."

He stood to full height. "Oh, it's something. It's always something with Nash. Let me guess." He narrowed his eyes knowingly. "Did your fiancé use me as his alibi?"

My face must've given away my shock. "Come on," he said softly, pulling a chair close to mine. "Takes a player to know a player, right?"

I ignored his comment and shook out my curls. "Nash said he didn't care what kind of cake I chose," I lied, directing my gaze toward the albums and brochures so he wouldn't see my cheeks betray me. "What happened to that gorgeous cake you had on display the other day?"

"It satisfied approximately eighteen to twenty people," Mick murmured, crossing his arms and rocking back on his heels, eyes never leaving me. "Although, I saved one piece of it. For you. Care to try?"

And be just another number to *ooh* and *aah* over his edibles? Approximately number nineteen to twenty-one? I'm sure he had given up keeping track of whom he satisfied.

"No, thank you. I just came to look today, that's all."

"*Hola*, Mick!" a melodic voice rang out, competing with the tinkling of the bells on the door. A smiling Latina sidled up to the counter and drummed her long fingernails on the glass expectantly.

"No harm in just looking," he murmured in my ear, before turning his attention to this latest customer. "Hey, Angie. Your order's all set. Let me just go box them up."

"You know they won't stay in the box for long," she called after him in a teasing tone. Her huge doe eyes roamed the front of the bakery case while she waited. "*¡Por Dios!*" Flashing me a smile, she added, "It all looks so good, right?"

"I don't know how anyone can choose just one thing," I agreed, gesturing toward all the brochures around me.

"It doesn't matter what I pick," she groaned. "It all goes right here." She smacked her curvaceous hips. "I wish some of it would go right here," she gestured to her more than ample chest pushing out the ruffles on her tight black top. "Or here." She smacked her butt, which was perfectly adorable, encased in blue jeans. "But no! Mick, he ruins me." She grinned, and one dimple appeared on her right cheek.

"Yeah, keep telling yourself that." Mick was back, pushing a large white box into a plastic bag for her.

"You rock, lover." Her dark eyes batted long lashes in thanks. "See you next week."

"One of your regulars?" I asked, after the door slammed shut.

"Yep," he said, busying himself behind the counter and avoiding my eyes. "Standing order every week."

Ah, so that was why no money exchanged hands. Although I wouldn't put it past the guy to trade favors for . . . favors.

"Gorgeous," I murmured, picking up yet another cake picture and studying it.

"Angie Vega? Smoking hot, if you like that type." He dropped down into the chair next to me again with a grin too wicked to be trusted.

"I meant this one," I said, smacking the picture against the back of his hand. "Not the girl." *Yeah, keep telling yourself that*, my own conscience chided me.

"Ah, yes, the chevron pattern. A very hot style right now." He traced the bold zigzags gracing the cake in the photo with his pinky, right off the edge of the page and up my wrist. "Or maybe you want something a little more timeless," he suggested, tracing circles on the thin skin there. A bold feeling of longing shot through me.

"Maybe I want what Angie Vega is having. Which is . . . ?"

The arch of his brow sent me circling down to Dante's second level of hell, lust sweeping through me like a hot, dusty storm. I longed to be doused with kisses from that mouth, imagining the rough press of his chef's coat against my bare skin as he delivered them.

I had always been a sucker for a guy in any kind of uniform.

"*Polvorones*." The word rolled deliciously off his tongue. "For her parents' restaurant. From my mother's favorite recipe. They're also called Mexican wedding cakes. Even though they are cookies."

He pushed up his sleeves, suddenly all business. "Dot patterns are very popular as well."

It took me a moment to recover and focus back on the picture he held up for me. He was changing the subject. Confusion swept through me, followed by shame. Flirting came so easy with him, yet his three-hundred-sixty-degree change in manner threw me.

"I . . . I need to give this way more thought. I had no idea there were so many choices," I said, feeling stupid.

"Why don't you do a little online research, print out a few pictures you like, and next time we'll take it from there?" He was already up and out of his chair, moving behind the counter to help Nose Ring Girl with a large sheet cake for a customer.

Suddenly I felt silly for coming in, for wasting his time. All flirting aside, the man was trying to run a business, for God's sake. And here I was, playing dress-up and imaginary bridal games.

"We'd get through this little arrangement of ours better if you didn't lie to me, Nash."

"Christ, Dani. I needed to get out of town for a few hours today, okay? Quinn's got me running so many chores in her mom-wagon, I can feel my balls shrinking in daily increments. So I went to get a little girlie-action. So what? That was never verboten in our agreement. Unless you want to amend your anti-sex-with-me stance?"

I glared at him, not appreciating his suggestion, or the fact that he used Mick as an excuse for girlie-action-getting.

"Fine!" He held up his hands in surrender. "I went with Sindy, if you must know."

"To pick up girls in Atlantic City?"

"No." He hung his head in shame. "It was a little pony-action. She likes the horse races, okay? It's just a little embarrassing to say I drove an old lady down there."

I planted my hands on my hips.

"Okay, so she drove! I hate the traffic on the turnpike."

I thought about Sindy, dealing out the sick card to Mick's sympathetic hand at the bakery today. Yet hadn't she said specifically today would be the best day for me to visit? I wondered if Sinnamon Sin, the burlesque dancer turned Sunday churchgoer, still had some aces up her sleeve. Then again, she was an old lady, perhaps a tad forgetful?

"You saw Mick today?"

"That I did."

And it was getting harder to pretend to forget what had happened between us.

With nothing better to do that evening, I contemplated the bookshelves lining the wall, the well-worn spines of worlds waiting, beckoning. A small set of pastel-bound books along the top shelf caught my eye. Each had a year embossed in gold, but my fingers instantly fell upon 1998. That date clanged my memory bells; the year I'd met Jax. And Dex. *Funeral crasher.*

"Allen is gonna freak, we are so beyond late!" Laney picked at the hole in her fishnet stockings that peeked from below the hem of her black miniskirt, and used her tiny Doc Martens–clad foot to pound an imaginary pedal to the metal of the floorboard of my dad's Volvo. *"Step on it, sister!"*

"Talk to the hand, Laney Jane!" I said, although both of mine were planted firmly at ten and two. *Long Island wasn't easy to navigate under normal circumstances . . . much less in the pouring rain and*

only three weeks after receiving my unrestricted driver's license. Months of driver's ed classes and supervised driving hours had prepared me for road hazards, but nothing had prepared me for the vortex of stress riding shotgun and worried about missing her favorite band.

"Maynard James Keenan!" Laney gripped the strap above the door and screeched the way some people took the Lord's name in vain. *"If I miss Tool, I'm going to kill you."*

"They are headlining; we've got hours of time," I assured, gripping the wheel tighter so I wouldn't grab the Sailor Moon metal lunchbox she used as a purse and clock her in the face with it.

"But you just missed the entrance for the L.I.E."

Shit. *"That's okay, we can take the Southern State, too."*

"The expressway's faster. Pull a U-ie. Flip a bitch!" Laney tugged on the Jesus strap in desperation.

"Shut up! Shut up! There's another chance, I just gotta get over." Traffic was crawling in the downpour and bumper-to-bumper on my right. *"Come on, people. Let a girl in, will you?"*

"Just start cutting over and they'll have to. Be aggressive."

I had seen drivers do it all the time, but I didn't want to be that kind of driver. Ugh. My blinker singsonged, Lo-ser, Lo-ser, Lo-ser, *as I cut the wheel and tried to break through the centipede of slow cars, all going way under the speed limit. At least they had their hazards on; so many slowpokes on the road found it perfectly acceptable to go thirty in a forty-five with no apologies whatsoever.*

"Um, Dani—"

"I know, I just gotta—" I had accomplished my mission, but something had raised a red flag.

Literally.

All the cars, both in front of me and behind, had little red flags on top of their hoods, and now that I was in their lane, I saw the whirling lights of a cop car leading the pack.

"Holy shit. Laney . . . we're in a funeral procession!"

"Ugh, summer people," Laney spat, pointing at the license plate tags emblazoned with the logo of a fancy Manhattan car dealership. "It's bad enough they buy up all our beachfront. They have to take up prime real estate when they're dead, too?"

My dad's little Volvo was now sandwiched between two limos in a long line of limos.

I thought I'd be breezing past them once I got through the merge, but once on the highway, another police escort came cruising up alongside the line. We were being forced off at the next exit, onto the service road.

"Flick your brights! Beep your horn!"

"There's a hearse in front of us. I am not beeping."

"You are way too polite." Laney clicked her tongue and scrunched down in her seat, embarrassed to know me. "It's not like you'll wake up the body in the back of it."

"Let me handle this, okay? As soon as I can, I will break away." The rain had let up a bit, at least, but the windows were fogging from the July heat. I cracked mine down and caught a whiff of that strange, clean, earthy smell that only happened when raindrops hit dry concrete after a long dry spell.

Inhaling deeply, I suddenly felt a sense of belonging. If not in this particular procession, at least in this human race. It felt as if it were our duty to stay the solemn course, to pay respects before moving on. We could be two mourners in a long line of mourners, not just two silly girls lost on their way to a rock concert.

Who just so happened to be wearing all black . . .

If I hadn't crashed the Davenport funeral that day, would I have met Jax? I thought of him at seventeen, surrounded by family but still so utterly alone, staring at the tombstones in his family plot. An uneasy, nagging feeling nipped at my heels as I stood on my tiptoes to pull the journal off the shelf.

He had called twice since we had arrived in New Hope, and I had ignored the blinking message lights blowing up my phone. I also hadn't responded to his *U OK?* text, uncharacteristically short for the wordsmith he usually was. No doubt his brother had gotten to him before I had. Sighing, I slid onto the psychiatrist's couch and cracked the binding of the book to break the spell of my 1998, and enter the inn's version of the year.

Page after page of praise, all in different handwriting, with consecutive dates gracing the corners, awaited me. People apparently loved the "homey touches," and the "scrumptious fare," amazed at how their hosts had "thought of everything."

Bill and Tina are by far the most gracious innkeepers we've ever met.

Bill's bananas Foster French toast is to die for!

The owners went above and beyond . . .

It's clear to see Bill and Tina's love for each other, their two children, and for this beautiful gem of an inn. We will certainly be back to Heaven's Half Acre!

I wondered if the "two children" mentioned were Bear and Quinn. And if Bill of the bananas Foster French toast fame was the same guy who scolded a young boy for being greedy.

The books lining the shelf were evidence of a very popular and successful establishment since the year 1986. At least until the year 2002, the last book on the shelf. Curious, I pulled it down and settled back onto the couch with it.

The dated entries were fewer and farther between, as if long spells of time went by with the room unoccupied. I wondered if the inn had fallen into hard times. The hospitality industry had been hard-hit after 9/11. The final entry of the book was the only summer entry.

We had such a quiet, restful stay. It felt like we had the inn all to ourselves!

Perhaps they had.

Nash padded out of the bathroom in a cloud of steam.

"Let's do you on the chair," I murmured absently, searching the shelves for more journals, but all I found were old U.S. inn directories and Bucks County history and guidebooks.

What had happened over the last ten years? And where were Bill and Tina now?

"I love it when you talk dirty to me." Nash's sarcastic quip pulled me out of my reverie. He was sitting backward in the desk chair, arms hanging over the wooden cane back. Droplets from his freshly washed hair darkened the distress marks of his designer jeans.

"Sorry. My portable massage table is still in my van."

The cherry desk behind him held a small brass lamp, a paperweight shaped like an apple, and a desk blotter. And a small notebook. No date on the spine, just a pretty marbled design.

No entries inside.

Defeated, I rested my fingertips on his bare back.

"Nash? Did something happen here?" I felt his shoulders tense under my hands. "When we'd arrived, you said there was a lot you hadn't told me."

"Yeah."

I lightly placed my palms on the thickest part of the trapezius muscle, at the top of his shoulders. Closing my eyes, I listened to his breath with my hands, lightening my contact with each inhalation, and adding pressure when he exhaled. Noticing and following natural respiratory rhythms was a technique I'd learned in my training, said to build deep trust and empathy. A way for him to know, albeit unconsciously, that I was listening and paying close attention to him.

"There was a fire."

I kept my own breathing full and deep, encouraging him to relax. "Was it . . . ? On the mountain that day, you—"

"It had nothing to do with me." He shrugged my hands off and grabbed his shirt. "Whatever you do, don't ask Quinn about it. Or Bear. He won't talk about it."

Our session was obviously over. And I was no closer to understanding what had happened.

Nash wouldn't tell me, and I couldn't ask Quinn or Bear about it.

That left a ten-year-old boy whose language I barely spoke.

And Mick.

Mick

BLACK HOLES AND REVELATIONS

"I'm in hell," Nash said, slapping down Friday's morning newspaper. All week long, the press had been posting snippets about him "returning to his childhood home" and "reuniting with his family," and all week long, Bear and I had taken turns stashing the papers in the recycling bin before Quinn could blow a gasket.

I caught a glance at what had made big news that day. KEY-BESTOWING CEREMONY POSTPONED AS SECOND-OLDEST RESIDENT FALLS ILL.

"Second-oldest living resident?" Dani asked. "What happened to the first?"

"Oh, she's still around." Sindy, who had stopped by with some of Walt's famous shoofly pie that morning, waved her hand. "That old bat is too mean to die. But she got the award, oh . . . I don't know, maybe five years ago? Boys, you should go pay a visit to Mr. Woolhouse. Take him some of those flowers you've been delivering all over town, Nash."

Nash shot Dani a look. Apparently part of his PR team's "making the bad boy look good" to-do list consisted of him supplying the town park where the key ceremony was to take place with a new garden. And a new garden, according to Nash, had been hiring a lawn service to get the job done. What Sindy was suggesting was pretty old school: a house call.

"I think that's a great idea," Dani said, and Nash gave a defeated sigh. It was about time he did a little more around town than put his money where his mouth, and his heart, should be.

"I've got his bakery delivery to take over there anyway." I shrugged. "How about it, hotshot?"

Mr. Woolhouse lived in a Tudor that was built at the same time as the Half Acre, and had the same low bedrock wall placed in front to prove it. While the Half Acre sprawled, the old man's house rose up, up, up, narrow and high. As kids, we used to scale the wall on Halloween and egg old Woolhouse's house. We had him pegged as a child molester/serial killer, with bodies under the stairs and blood in the ice cube trays. No one ever seemed to visit, and no one ever came out.

It turned out he was a writer and the unofficial town historian, married to a Frenchwoman he met during his service in World War II. She'd had MS, and they had had most of their groceries delivered.

Nash knocked impatiently on the front door.

"Who's there?" a shaky voice called.

"Nash Drama."

"Jehovahs? Not interested."

"Drama! Nash Dra . . ." Nash rolled his eyes. "It's Stuart Nash."

Bleary eyes peeked through the half-moon window on the door. "You and Mickey come to egg my house again, Stewie?"

"Again?" Nash mouthed in disbelief. I stifled a laugh; it had been a good twenty years since we raised an egg or any kind of hell together. I was surprised Woolhouse remembered.

"No. He brought some mums," I called. "And I've got your meringues."

A series of locks clicked from within, and the door creaked open. "Like munching on a cloud," Woolhouse sighed, a gnarled hand snaking out to grab one of the cookies. While we had been egging his house all those years ago, his wife was pulling herself up from her chair to make her husband his favorite treat. After she passed last spring, I began making and bringing them to him each month. He would eat one, get teary eyed, and then he would eat another and talk about his darling wife. He would offer me a bite and I'd refuse, and then he would shake my hand and we'd repeat the process all over again the next month.

"You back in town to make an honest woman out of that Bradley girl?" He shook his cane at Nash's nether regions. "Or to make *her* a mum again?"

Nash gave him a dark look.

"How are you feeling, Mr. Woolhouse? We heard you were sick," I said.

"Yeah, what's wrong?" Nash asked, a bit less sympathetic in tone.

"At my age, what isn't wrong with me?" He waved a hand. "Eh. It'll pass. Nothing to worry about."

"Nothing?" Nash said. "They postponed my key ceremony tomorrow for nothing?"

"What's your hurry, boy? I've got less time than you, you know."

"Who's to say? I could be a ticking time bomb, for all you know," Nash argued.

The old man leaned on his cane. "Maybe you should stop rushing and smell the roses . . . and plant those mums while you're at it."

Nash cursed under his breath and went to the shed to fetch a shovel. I hoped the key ceremony would get here soon, too . . . so I could lodge it up his ass. Or crank open his chest with it, to see if my best friend truly had no heart.

New Hope's local guitar hero toiled in the early-fall sun, coaxing holes out of the hard ground, as its second-oldest resident directed him on placement and soil irrigation.

"It's like a kiss from my dear Margaret, every time." Woolhouse placed a wispy meringue on his tongue and let it dissolve there. There were the tears, but they didn't seem to be unhappy ones. "Thank you, Mick."

"You're welcome," singsonged Nash, sweating his ass off in the side yard.

"Who's the hot dish I've seen walking with your aunt in town?" Woolhouse held up a third meringue in offering, and I prepared to make my monthly refusal.

"Nash's fiancée. Danica," I informed Woolhouse, since Nash had fallen into silent mode.

"Think she's got a friend for me?" the old man asked, making a pointed wink at me. "I sure could do with a lady on my arm for the ceremony next week."

"Gee, wouldn't it be great if we could all have a woman who can be a lady on your arm . . . and a whore behind closed doors." Nash hacked the soil into place around the mums with the back of the shovel. "I think every guy should have a chick like Dani."

Whether Nash had been trying to shock the nonagenarian or whether he truly felt that way, I didn't care. Just the fact that he uttered the words with such pleasure made me want to tackle him in the dirt.

Down we went, tumbling and swearing. Nash had always been bigger than me, but I had always been faster. His large hand spanned my face, forcing my head to the earth, but I knocked him at the elbow, then flipped, gaining the advantage.

"Take it back," I ground out. *Let her go.*

"Don't you get it?" he rasped. "Don't you know me at all, Mick?" His bitter laugh blew at the dirt. "My drummer uttered that infamous gem during an interview, yet it got mistakenly credited to me. I thought if I became famous, people would stop assuming bad shit about me. But it's only made it worse."

I let his words sink in, and let my guard down. He leveled me with his weight, just like he used to during our fake WWE matches as kids. I knew all his moves, yet I always fell for them anyway.

"So I can't take it back," he said quietly, nose to nose with me. "If I retracted or redacted shit I never said or did, I'd disappear entirely."

"Don't make me get the garden hose!" Woolhouse threatened, like we were violent dogs that needed breaking up. Suddenly, I couldn't help but laugh. And once it started, it wouldn't cease, even after I started hiccupping, a tight stitch in my side. Nash had tears rolling down his dirt-streaked face, gasping and shaking with laughter.

"Crazy kids." Woolhouse had had enough of us, apparently. He slammed the door behind him, taking his meringues with him.

Nash and I walked, stiff limbed, toward the Porsche. "You okay, man?" I asked, throwing out a dirty hand toward his shoulder. He was holding his hip, and favoring one leg.

"I'm fine," he managed, out of breath. "For a goddamn Tin Man."

Mick

A DATE WITH DRAMA

Standing in the foyer with Nash waiting for our dates to appear, I realized my idea was possibly the most disastrous one yet. Dani was perfection in a short, midnight blue dress, with halter-style straps that crossed in an X above her cleavage before tying in the back. It was reminiscent of the keyhole neck of the bridesmaid's dress I'd peeled off her once upon a time, no doubt to torture me with memories the entire night. Two rhinestone clips swept her unbelievable blond hair back at her temples, but the rest fell in a cascade of loose ringlets. She paused on the second-to-last step, eyes sweeping over me. In her silver heels, she met my burning gaze. "You clean up nice, Mick."

That's right; as far as everyone else was concerned, we hadn't cleaned up—or gotten down and dirty—in each other's presence.

"Take a picture, Spencer. It lasts longer," Nash joked, taking Dani's arm as she maneuvered the last stair in those goddess heels. He wound a finger through one of those ringlets and gave it a playful tug.

"I wish we did have a photo . . . booth," I murmured, just to see the blush spread across the prime real estate of Dani's face. Two could play at the torture game.

"Hey, that's my job," we heard Quinn say. She made her way down the winding stairs, although she didn't have the usual camera strap hanging like an albatross around her neck. Instead, she wore a shimmering silver top that fell off her shoulders, and a black miniskirt that showed off her petite curves. Tasteful black boots rose to her knees, and she clutched a small sparkling purse in her hand, along with her phone. Typical Quinn, she managed to blind us with the flash as she snapped pictures of our surprised expressions.

"You're a girl," I joked, as she linked arms with me. She had pulled her hair back and up into one of those messy buns, and I marveled at her neck. I had never noticed it before, since she was usually wound up so tight.

She smacked me with her clamshell purse, and it felt like a kettle-bell to the chest.

Nash, meanwhile, had fallen very quiet in her presence. Maybe this plan of mine wasn't so bad after all. "Thank you," I mouthed to Quinn. She gave me a puzzled look. "For agreeing to this."

Bear and Logan came to the door to see us off.

"Don't eat a ton of junk food and stay up too late," Quinn warned her brother.

"No chance. We are heading over to Palomar for dinner. Two-for-One Taco Night!" Bear grinned. Logan confirmed their dinner choice with a C-shaped hand turned up like a taco shell, and "filled" it using the sweeping motion of a T with his other hand.

"Angie Vega must be working," Quinn said with a smirk. "You sure Logan won't cramp your style, Slick?"

"You kidding? The kid's a chica magnet." He turned to Nash. "Hey, since you aren't using your Porsche tonight—?"

"Height/weight restriction." Quinn cut him off before Nash could respond, and Bear cursed halfheartedly in defeat.

"The front seat of my luxury performance vehicle is probably safer than the backseat of that death trap he drives," Nash said defensively.

"Fine. He can take my Volvo. We'll drive his Jeep."

"*I'll* drive the Jeep," I corrected. It was a step up from being chauffeured by Quinn in her mom-mobile, but not by much.

"I call shotgun!" Nash said immediately.

"What are you, twelve? Fine," Quinn said. She gave Dani a look that could only mean, *Boys: can't live with them, can't shoot them,* and shook her head.

Nope, I was correct with my first assumption. The date was a fucking disaster. Nash flirted with the hostess the minute we arrived, and promptly began drinking upon being seated. In fact, he couldn't seem to look at Quinn without taking a swig of whatever overpriced straight-up liquor he had ordered. He was drunk and brooding by the time the salads were served. Dani tried to keep up the small talk, telling funny stories from the summer festival and asking Quinn questions about New Hope, photography, anything surface and safe that kept her from engaging with me.

She kept toying with the cake charm at her throat, absently playing with it. Each time her fingers lingered tantalizingly at her neck, it made me want to run my tongue under the ribbon. I could barely focus, much less concentrate on anything Quinn said to me, trying to bring me into the conversation.

The women had ordered a carafe of wine to share, but Dani had barely picked up her glass through the awkward meal. When I reached for my own drink, I realized Nash had drained mine as well as his. And he was tapping on the empty glass like he was going to propose a toast. *Oh, for fuck's sake.*

"My chick looks foxy tonight, don't she?" He looked up at the waitress, as she rushed over to make sure everything was all right. We had landed a coveted reservation at one of Philadelphia's hottest upscale eateries due to Nash's status, but I had a feeling they weren't versed in dealing with drunken rockers using their crystal like it was a dinner bell.

"Nash," Dani hissed a warning.

"You wanna three-way?" he asked the waitress, who was at least ten years younger than us, probably paying her way through college. "You, me, and my fine-ass foxy fiancée?"

"I'll take the check," I said to her, and she gratefully nodded and rushed off.

Nash held up his empty glass and made a hollow toast. "Mick. My best fucking friend in the world. A toast to you, man. And to our ladies." *Okay, that wasn't so bad.* I raised my own empty glass to humor him. Quinn held up her wineglass, filled to the brim, with a smile pasted to her face, and I realized she had just about polished off the carafe herself.

Dani wasn't smiling, or toasting. She glared at Nash like she knew what was coming next.

"May they always be ladies on our arms," he boomed, "and . . ."

So help me God, I would've decked him, if he hadn't already fallen off the fucking chair.

"Come on," he appealed from the floor. "Can't I get some unconditional love?"

"Pull the Jeep around," I said to Quinn, holding out the keys to her. "I'll pay the bill and let's get the fuck out of here."

My partner in crime stared at the keys like she didn't know what to do with them.

"Give me those," Dani snapped. She swiped Bear's keys from me. "She's in no condition to drive."

She had the Jeep outside and running by the time I tipped and managed to get both Nash's and Quinn's drunk asses out onto the street.

"Get in," I ordered Nash, who was making a big production of pulling out his wallet.

Dani helped buckle Quinn in, who smiled happily that someone had remembered seat belt safety. Then she handed me back my keys.

Road rage took on a whole other meaning as I drove. I was pissed at myself for dreaming up this ridiculous idea. To think that by some miracle, maybe Nash and Quinn would rekindle whatever fucking spark had clicked once between them, leaving me and Dani to . . . what? Now we were driving in silence, Dani staring out the window and me staring at the road ahead. Trying to pretend there wasn't a weepy girl and a clueless bastard in the back.

"I owe you, man," Nash kept saying, leaning into the front seat space and polluting it with his drunk banter.

"Dinner's on me," I said, shifting and roaring up the highway ramp.

"No, man. You earned your two-fiddy." He tossed a hundred-dollar bill onto my lap, followed by another one, and then a Ulysses S. Grant fluttered over Dani's cleavage. "We made a bet, remember? Fair and square. Last player standing. I got engaged. You win! Everybody's happy. Everybody is. Fucking. Ecstatic."

He dropped back into the seat next to Quinn, who had passed out.

Dani's controlled breathing told me to not dare try explaining right now.

In the back, Quinn's cell phone began to ring.

"I hope that's not Bear," I muttered, more to myself than to anyone else. He was a capable babysitter, and a phone call might mean something was up with Logan at home.

Dani mumbled something.

I pulled my eyes off the road momentarily. "What was that?"

"I said, he's calling her," Dani reiterated. "That's what he does. When he's had a few."

The ringing stopped. I glanced back to catch Nash with his phone up to his ear. Sure enough, he began to mumble what sounded like sweet nothings to someone—or onto someone's voice mail.

"Are you kidding me?" I sputtered a laugh. "Are you fucking kidding me?"

"Nice of you to join the party, Captain Clueless," Dani muttered.

"He calls her . . . and you are okay with this?"

"I'm not okay with any of this, all right? Including you and your . . ." She reached between my legs and tossed the crumbled hundred-dollar bills in the air. "Your games and bets when people's fucking emotions are on the line!"

"Christ, Nash and I were teenagers when we made that bet. I hadn't even remembered it until he brought it up!"

"I'm not talking about just that!" Dani hollered back, "I'm talking about New Orleans!"

Dani

DASHBOARD CONFESSIONAL

I was out of the car before he even had a chance to throw it into park.

"Dani!" He slammed the door shut and followed me, leaving our drunken dates to sleep it off in the Jeep. "What do you want me to say?"

"How about starting with the truth?" I hissed. "Like why you crashed my sister's wedding and turned my life upside down."

I whipped around to make my grand exit . . . and tripped on the old limestone foundation and right into Mick's arms.

"Look. I'm a baker. I spend half my life at weddings. The last thing I ever thought I would do was crash one. But I had to. I had to take that chance, after I saw you on Royal Street. I couldn't just let you dance away. And I'm sorry . . ."

"For lying to me?"

"That, yes. And for letting that evening end! I was trying to be a gentleman that night."

"And it looks like you've been trying to make up for *that* ever since."

"What the hell does that mean?"

"You wouldn't stoop to having sex with a drunk girl that night because of your so-called 'scruples'"—I air-quoted—"and now I think the challenge of trying to sleep with me when I'm sober is too tempting of a prospect for you. Isn't that what all this cake courting is about?"

"No. It's about getting to know you. And you, getting to know me. No masks. No charade," Mick said quietly. "Don't we deserve a second chance?"

He loosened his grip on me, so he could look me in the eye.

"For what it's worth, I think we deserve the truth," I said, meeting his gaze.

Mick

CAKE AND A PROMISE

You'd better know exactly what you want, and what it's worth to you,
I heard her sister warn.

"Is it true you were living with a girl?" Dani now asked, quiet in
my arms.

"A woman," I corrected. "Much older than me. That would've been
Rebekkah. She made your sister's cake."

In fact, she made all the wedding cakes needed for that establishment, and most for the nearby catering venue. She had taken me in
when I moved to New Orleans, and I had been working with her for
the better part of two years, waiting for the day when she'd allow me
to bake one. I had been relegated to king cakes like I was some supermarket employee, churning out the oval-shaped pastries New Orleans
was famous for, day after day and double the amount during Mardi
Gras. Stuffing baby after baby into the box beside the cinnamon-
flavored ring gaudily sprinkled with gold, green, and purple sugar.

Yes, every cake does indeed have a story. And king cakes were
famous for having a tiny plastic baby trinket hidden inside. Old legend

had it that he who found the baby would have to buy the next king cake, but it also had symbolism dating back to 1800s France and represented baby Jesus. Our clients wanted them for the kitsch and tradition, and the more modern fortune of finding a baby in their slice: luck and prosperity.

I had never found a baby in any slice I'd ever eaten. And at the bakery, we were instructed to serve up the baby on the side for the customers to place themselves, lest any liability arise. Rebekkah had been riding me all that day of Posy's destination wedding, ever since a phone call came in from a customer complaining no baby had accompanied his cake. Apparently I hadn't put one inside the box.

It was a sore topic with Rebekkah. She had been waiting for years for someone to put a baby inside her, and I refused to be the guy to do it. And she'd been holding my promotion hostage in her twisted quest for intimacy. I could've used her to climb into the cutthroat culinary pocket of the French Quarter, but I wanted, I deserved more. It wasn't until I met Dani that I realized what it was. And I knew I had to set things to rights.

Rebekkah had already taken matters into her own hands.

After leaving Dani at her hotel that night, I found my clothes strewn on the brick sidewalk in front of Rebekkah's Dauphine Street residence, and spilling into the narrow road. "Fuck you and the suitcase you rode in on!" she raged from her balcony, before slamming the French doors on me and on the better (or worse) part of two years. I'd had no power in that relationship, she had had no faith, and in the end, I guess we were both justified.

I'd packed my belongings in the case she had upended and headed straight for Café Du Monde. It was open twenty-four hours, and I would wait all night and day for Dani if I had to. "Just keep pouring me coffee every hour," I'd instructed the waiter, and put my head down on the table.

I should've given Dani my last name, I thought. I should've given her my number. I shouldn't have left her but if I hadn't . . . story of my life.

"Why are you telling me all this?" Dani asked, shaking her head as I finished my tale. Sadness laced her voice as she turned back to the Jeep to help rouse our drunken dates. "It doesn't matter now."

"You wanted the truth. And sometimes the truth is messy, inconvenient and fucked up, and no one's fault."

We both regarded the couple passed out in the backseat. While they kept themselves at arms' length in their sober, awake hours, Nash and Quinn were intimately wound together now, under the cover of the night and the guise of alcohol. Her head was nestled on his shoulder, where it fit perfectly. He had one arm wound protectively around her, and his other hand, palm up, in her lap.

"Sometimes," I added in a whisper, "it's better to let sleeping dogs lie."

Dani's sigh wasn't one of defeat; it was one of agreement. "It's warm enough out here, right? To leave them?"

I reached into the front seat for my keys. Nash's bet money was still on the seat. I swept it up and deposited it back into his upturned hand. I had no desire to see his bet, raise his bet, or drag his drunk ass into the house.

Dani kissed my cheek at room number twelve. "Thanks for the double date . . ."

"From hell?" I joked. "Anytime. Think someday we might be destined for a do-over?"

Dani

TRUTH TAKES A TOLL

I woke up before everybody. Or perhaps I never really went to sleep. It was early, even for an early bird like me.

Slipping out the front door, I stretched my hamstrings on the old limestone foundation I had tripped over the night before. A burning desire for new scenery propelled my feet forward, not slowing until I crossed 32 and skirted the old New Hope cemetery. Like massage, jogging provided me time and space for my mind to wander. Thinking about all that Mick had said about truth and trust, and about letting sleeping dogs lie. And recalling memories that lingered long before that. Taking advantage of a drunk girl may have been against Mick's principles, but not all guys were that noble.

"This is crazy," Laney grumbled, tripping over a low gravestone in her Docs. "We are crashing a fucking funeral because you glimpsed a hottie out the car window?"

"*You know you love the macabre; just play along. Consider it comic book research.*"

"*Like* Tales from the Crypt," *Laney whispered as we approached the open earth and people gathered there. "Cool.*"

I couldn't take my eyes off the young guy standing to the side. He stood stoic and sad, legs splayed in what looked like expensively tailored dress pants. His tie matched my eyes, and the sky that was just starting to brighten. His cheeks were high and round, blotched red with emotion. "Like a Botticelli cherub," my nana would've said. And he was holding the hand of a woman who might have been his own grandmother, a regal-looking woman dressed impeccably.

In fact, the entire funeral procession had an air of expensive grief, in tailor-made black with a snaking line of imported cars parked along the cemetery road. Beside me, Laney tugged uncomfortably at her miniskirt, trying to cover up the hole in her stocking.

I shivered in the aftermath of the summer rain, wearing a tiny cap-sleeved white tee under my nineties black bib-overall minidress. All the cool girls had been wearing them that year, like me, with thigh-high black stockings and black chunky-heeled Mary Janes.

I must've looked like the sluttiest funeral-goer ever, but the guy's tear-filled eyes seemed to lighten as he caught sight of my approach. The woman he stood with had moved forward, clutching a handkerchief, to the cluster of her supporters near the fresh-dug earth, leaving him on his own.

"I'm sorry for your loss," I said firmly, reaching for his hand. And I was. I had lost my grandfather that past winter, and the loss was still keen and sharp within me. What had hurt most of all was watching those left behind, like my nana, who seemed incapable of speaking, seeing, or hearing that day. And my dad, a man who never cried, but whose

face profoundly displayed his grief as people from his past, whom I had never seen in my life, moved to embrace him, one after another.

"Thank you." There was no trace of accent in his voice, like most of the boys we knew on the island. Having spent my younger years in New Jersey, I would've been able to pick out that subtle difference, too. Nor did he have the telltale Staten Island twang, or a hint of the other outlying boroughs. No doubt "summer people," as Laney would spit as we walked past their fancy hulking mansions shadowing our beach. "It was nice of you to come all this way," he added.

"Jackson. Come here, my dear boy." The grandmother had an aristocratic accent that sounded like she had been bred in a boarding school, neither American nor British, but somewhere in between the two. Like an old Hollywood actress. She gestured, a small shovel in her hand, and the boy gently squeezed my fingers before dropping them and proceeding up to perform the grim and traditional task of spreading dirt on the casket that had been lowered into the earth.

"Did you get his number?" Laney asked in a loud whisper. "Can we go now?"

"Shhh." I stood up straighter as the clergyman, who looked older than the dirt itself, began to speak of the Davenport legacy. Raised by headshrinker parents, I was probably more attuned to family dynamics than the average teen, and this family seemed to be aligned in two different camps: those who appeared to be rallied around the family matriarch, and those who had turned their backs, literally, on her as they fixed their gaze on the ground before them.

"You know I would follow you anywhere, but this is just weird." Laney's hushed breath brushed my curls against my cheek, and I was surprised to feel them wet with my tears. "We don't know these people at all."

The guy, Jackson, shook back his thick, sandy hair and solidly met my eyes.

"Not true," I murmured to Laney. I felt I knew him, that I had always known him.

"I want to go."

"Fine, go." I slipped her my keys. "Take my car and leave it at Allen's. I'll find my way there and meet you at the show."

"Are you crazy?"

The guy had skirted back toward us, fumbling with two rocks he must've picked up in the dirt. I just motioned for her to go. She gave me a long "have it your way" look, and scuttled off.

He stood stock-still beside me, until the two divided sides at the gravesite began to give way and quietly disperse. Then he threw down one rock. And then the other.

"Are you okay?" I asked.

"What's it to you?" His tone was venomous, and took me by total surprise. "Our grandmother's dirty little secret changed the will and has totally fucked my family in the process. Yeah, I'm fine."

He glared at me with eyes that weren't the same. And there was nothing cherubic, or charitable, about him anymore. His cheeks weren't even red . . . but his tie was.

"Dex. It's not her fault." Jackson stepped up. "The New England cousins aren't in on this fight."

Twins! They were twins. And they thought I was some distant cousin in their soap opera.

"I'm not your cousin," I blurted, just as a thin, blond woman approached and overheard our exchange.

"Boys, this must be the nanny for Aunt Camilla's three. She does have a striking resemblance to cousin Beth, though, doesn't she? Darling, you were supposed to meet Camilla at the house; she was frantic when you didn't arrive. No matter, she left the children with the maids. You'll ride there with us."

I had gone from stranger to family to hired help, before the body was even cold in the ground.

"The house" turned out to be one of Montauk's grandest mansions, bustling with activity. Whatever children I was mistakenly told to *nanny were off somewhere, probably playing hide-and-seek in the rambling house.*

"I'm Jax, by the way." The guy smiled as we followed the crowd into the house.

"Dani. Hi."

"You're not really a nanny, are you?" The one Jax had called Dex was coldly regarding me, and I fessed up and told them everything.

"Whatever, that's cool. Come hang for a while, before you have to leave for your concert," Jax said. "Sweet game room upstairs."

Uniformed servants scurried around the kitchen, preparing food for the bereaved more elaborate than a wedding. His brother grabbed a bottle of rum and jerked his head toward the back service stairs. "What are you guys waiting for?"

The trees of the Half Acre rustled above me, shaking the last of their summer leaves as the long-ago memory faded. I had looped all the way back without even realizing it. I willed my feet to stop running, practically tripping over them as they slowed while the rest of me kept hurtling. Hands out, I used the big maple to break my fall, my lungs burning and heaving. *Darlin'.* I could practically hear the cluck of Shonnie's tongue and see the shake of her head. *Where's the fire?* My former boss and favorite singer always called me out on my on-the-run personality, and blamed it on my New York upbringing.

I had tried to leave New York, and so many of its memories, behind. Pushing blindly forward. Making myself useful everywhere else, trying to help. Trying to please. Doing what I do best.

My breathing and heart rate returned to normal, and I popped in my earbuds, drowning out my own inner voice with Shonnie's as I continued to walk it off. Letting her tell me to face my soul forward, because it was easier to hear it from someone else sometimes, than from yourself.

Mick

LOVE STINKS

Not surprisingly, breakfast was lightly attended the next morning. The Jeep had been emptied of its drunken cargo, I observed out the window. I wondered who had come to their senses first.

Logan was the first one down, soon followed by Bear and his acoustic guitar. Yawning, I worked on autopilot. PB&J for Logan, a quick scrambled mess for Bear and me, and a hearty spinach and cheese egg strata that could withstand sitting around waiting for the others.

"So. No key ceremony today, huh?" Bear strummed the strings absently with his thumbnail.

"No key ceremony." I sipped my coffee.

"Bummer. Think they'll stick around?"

"Dunno."

Bear began to strum and tap, striking up a familiar beat. "Got a tribute tonight. Freeze Frame." He smiled expectantly, waiting for me to guess. When I didn't, he started to sing.

Mick wants Dani
Nash wants Quinn
Bear wants Angie,
We just can't win.

"Dude!" I silenced the strings with a grip to the guitar neck. "Not cool." *Was it that obvious?*

"I'm just messing. And hey, it rhymed." He turned to Logan and signed as he said, "Mom wanted me to remind you, you have Randy Jenkins's birthday party at Sky's the Limit Trampoline Park today. Go shower the stink off you, kid."

Logan grimaced, clearly insulted. His fingers poked and jabbed at the air as he skipped out of the kitchen. Bear just laughed.

"What did he say?"

"He said *I* stink, like Angie's tacos." Bear bit his lip. "Damn straight. Her two-for-one tacos are the bomb diggity."

I put my hand over my eyes, took another sip of coffee, and shook my head.

"So it's the J. Geils tribute tonight. You coming?" Bear began strumming again, singing the "yeah, yeah" chorus of "Love Stinks," one of the band's two hit songs.

"Maybe." I figured with only two hits, it was bound to be an early night. "Gotta get to work now."

I was a little disappointed Dani hadn't shown her face. I figured the other two needed to sleep it off, but she was probably avoiding me. I left her a note under the coffee mug she liked to use.

1pm— James wedding cake consult
I hoped she'd get the hint.

Dani

REVEL AND REVEAL

My heart played Nok Hockey in my chest as the bells above the midnight blue door of Mick's bakery greeted me. *Great, Dani. Way to salivate, like one of Pavlov's dogs, at the mere thought of him.* And that was even before checking out his cake samples.

"Tell him I said *gracias!*" Angie Vega bustled by me with a bag and a wink. No doubt Mick's "standing order" for her had stood to its full attention when she was in the room. She was all curves and smoky softness, from the makeup rimming her dark eyes to the tanned cleavage, riding high. I pushed a hand through my curls, thinking they must look like the fuzz on a newborn chick compared to Angie's voluptuous waves of thick, raven hair.

"Hey! Dani, right?" It was the hipster with the brow ring.

"Yes . . . I've got"—*a date*—"an appointment with"—*destiny*—"Mick." I swallowed hard.

Oh, for God's sake, Dani. It's just cake.

I got a grin in return. "He said to send you on back."

I followed his long, outstretched arm in the direction he was pointing, and wound my way past tall, intimidating baking racks and stainless steel ovens. Mick's team of worker bees were turning out muffins, cranking out cupcakes, and touching down torches to the tops of crème brûlée.

Mick was standing in the middle of all the chaos, a pastry bag gripped in one hand, twirling out fat lilac flowers across the top of a small round cake. It was hypnotizing to watch as he steadily worked from the innermost petal out to create rose after rose in perfect bloom. The tip of his tongue poked through his lips in concentration, and his legs splayed as he leaned to finish off the entire cake, sides and all in the lush, decadent design. Something about a guy like Mick turning out an ultra-feminine work of art was beyond hot. I thought back to our banter about his phallic-looking mask; it was no wonder he was confident in his manhood.

I waited until he stepped back to inspect his work before commenting, not wanting to startle him.

"Does it taste as pretty as it looks?"

He glanced up, tongue still peeking out. "I was just thinking the same thing." He frowned in the direction of one particular flower, and gave it a final touch-up with the star tip. "Sadly, I wasn't invited to the party to find out. It's for a bridal shower tomorrow."

"Zena's?" I asked, remembering the girls gossiping at the Boo-hoo Breakfast.

"Yeah." He sounded surprised. "Have you met her?"

"No, but . . ." Julia's comment about Mick popping out of the cake came to mind, and I giggled. "You know women when they get together. They talk."

His brows went up, and I felt heat creep up my spine, which had nothing to do with the temperature of the commercial ovens cranking behind me. "They're brutal, I'm sure. Don't believe a word they say. Especially if it's about me."

"Didn't you feel your ears burning?" I teased.

"Not half as hot as your cheeks must be right now." He moved past me toward the sink, but not before dotting one with a squirt from the tip of the pastry bag.

"Hey!"

Before I could wipe it off, he leaned in for a quick kiss on my cheek. To the rest of his staff bustling by, it probably looked like an innocent greeting.

"Yep." He licked his lips and grinned. "Tastes as pretty as it looks."

"Cheeky bastard."

"That's one thing you can call me." He looked down at the computer printouts I had clutched in my hand. "Oh, good. You brought some ideas with you. Come back here and sit; we'll have a look."

He tossed the spent pastry bag into the sink, and I followed him to a table set up in the back. A laptop running a continuous slideshow of cakes sat in the center, but he quickly shut it. "Let's see what you brought, and then I can pull up some recent similar examples."

I slid in beside him, our knees bumping under the small space. "It's a little less chaotic back here," he explained. "If I'm out front, well . . ."

"Everybody wants a piece of you?"

"Yeah. Something like that." He smiled, and picked up my first sheet. I had hastily clicked around on a few websites this morning, just so I wouldn't show up empty-handed. Now I was embarrassed, as his eyes glossed over the run-of-the-mill, safe, and staid choices I had made. Especially after seeing the labor he had just poured over the petal-covered cake. I glanced back at it. What I had brought in was an insult to his imagination.

"I think of your lips every time I twirl out a rose like that," he said nonchalantly, as if he were talking about the price of butter these days. "Every time, ever since." He set down the sheets. "You've no idea how the mind tends to wander, when you do a job that keeps the hands busy."

"You're wrong," was all I could manage to muster. So many times, I hadn't even realized an hour massage had passed, because I'd been so fixated on the past. That one night with Mick had expanded me, exposed me, to so many possibilities and missed opportunities. But I couldn't give this guy the satisfaction of knowing. WWDD? In the past, Dani would do what she does best: let them walk away without a fight so they can see their folly later. Or do the walking herself. Until now. What was it about Mick Spencer that made me want to change my tune, and sing a sweet song of surrender?

"Sorry to interrupt, but there's a lady out front." Saved by the Brow Ring. "And she doesn't want to speak to anyone but you."

"Is she a regular customer?"

Mick's employee shook his head. "I don't recognize her. But she's—" He laced his hands and arced them over his torso until they met the waistband of his stovepipe jeans.

"With child?" Mick ventured a guess.

"Very."

I turned my eyes back to the cake images I had printed out. This was either business, or it was . . . personal. Very personal. Either way, I was here to look at cakes. Wedding cakes. I needed to start acting more like a blushing bride and less like a jealous lover.

"Thanks, Tom. Tell her I'll be right there."

Mick scraped his chair back, and I felt the loss as his knee moved away from mine. "Never a dull moment," he murmured apologetically.

I fixated on a scrumptious four-tiered creation, its squares stacked asymmetrically, until my eyes watered. "I'll bet." *Pull it together, Danica*, I warned myself. I felt as off center as the cake in the photo.

"Come with me." His voice was barely above a hush, and when I glanced up at him, he was smiling. "I'll bet it's a gender reveal."

"A what?" I asked, following him to the front of the shop. I expected to see someone standing in nothing but a trench coat, waiting to flash us. But instead, an elegant and very pregnant woman waited, wearing a tailored pinstripe maternity dress and fidgeting nervously with an envelope in her hand.

"It's okay," she addressed Tom, "if he's with another client, I—"

The woman broke into a relieved smile when she saw Mick. "Oh my God. You haven't changed a bit, Mick Spencer!"

There was that bashful half smirk I was growing addicted to. "Well, I sure as hell can't say the same for you, Jenna," he joked. "No more homecoming queen banner."

She rolled her eyes skyward. "Please. My mother still has my room set up as a high school shrine. It's all there. Were you in the middle of something?" she ventured, casting a curious glance at me. "I'm sorry for barging in."

"Oh, my appointment can totally wait," I assured her. Judging from the mound straining at the sash of her stylish dress, I had a feeling she didn't have much longer to go.

"Dani James, Jenna Humphreys."

"It's Humphreys-Blair now. We hyphenated. What a beautiful ring, congratulations!" She looked wistful as she half shook, half inspected my hand. "I can't even wear mine, my hands are so swollen." Turning back to Mick, she pleaded, "My mom's hell-bent on throwing me a huge, tacky baby shower here in town, now that I'm in my eighth month. But Vince—my husband—and I really wanted an intimate reveal party in the city. So . . ." She anxiously tapped the envelope against her hand. "We compromised. I told her we'd do it small and in her backyard, but only if you would do the cake and surprise us."

"I would be honored."

Mick grabbed an order sheet and took down all of her details for when, where, and how many servings needed as I looked on. "Whatever style you decide is best," Jenna said, then glanced at me with a smile. "He was my lab partner in high school. I totally trust him."

I grinned at the image of Mick in a white lab coat and safety goggles, and decided he looked hotter in the white chef's coat. Way hotter.

"I was in charge of lighting the Bunsen burner and I never once caught her hair on fire," Mick joked. "And her hair was huge back then, so not an easy feat."

"You wouldn't know it now, would you?" Jenna patted her sleek chignon and laughed. "You were also my hero when it came to frog dissecting, yuck."

She pressed the envelope to her enormous belly for a moment, then with a big breath, handed it over. "Just you and the doc will know. And the little sweet pea him- or herself, of course."

"I'll guard the secret with my life." He put a hand over his heart. "Lions' honor."

"Go, Lions," she laughed, shaking an imaginary pom-pom on her way out the door. "Rah-rah! Thanks, Mick. Nice to meet you, Dani."

"Best of luck," I called.

Mick turned the sign on the door from Open to Closed and tucked the envelope into his pocket.

"What are you doing?"

"We close for a couple hours in the afternoon on Saturday," he explained. "Day shift left, night shift hasn't come in yet. Tom, my manager, went to lunch. Now, where were we? Oh yeah, styles." He led the way back to where we had been sitting. I stared at him. "What?" he asked.

"Aren't you curious at all? About what's in the envelope?"

"Of course. But right now I'm more curious about you. Am I really supposed to believe"—he shuffled my printouts around on the table—"these generic, impersonal examples you brought today are what you want?"

Busted.

"You can believe anything you want," I mumbled. "It's just a party. It's just a cake. Isn't it the 'ever after' part that really counts? Why place such significance on one day?"

"Because sometimes all it takes is one day," he said quietly. "Or in some cases, one amazing evening."

Mick

BEST INTENTIONS

Dani wouldn't confirm or deny what I had said. She also wouldn't meet my gaze. We stood side by side, going over the different cake designs until she was fidgeting right out of her cute, curly-headed little mind.

"You must have incredible willpower," she laughed. "How can you stand to be in the same room with that envelope and not open it?"

"I'm sleeping under the same roof as you . . . same principle," I teased. Minus the cold showers, of course. "I'm going to let you do the honors."

Dani's fingers flew to her lips. "Do you think Jenna will mind?"

"I hereby deem you," I pronounced, allowing my hands to fall on her shoulders as if I were dubbing a knight, "my pastry sous chef today. I trust you, and she trusts me. I think we're good."

Dani let out an excited yelp and reached into the pocket of my chef's coat. "So official," she said, turning over the sealed envelope printed with the medical group's logo. "How many of these have you done?"

"Maybe a half dozen or so." I thought back. "Never for anyone I knew. Not that I really know Jenna all that well. Haven't seen her since high school, actually."

"Oh, so you didn't . . ." Dani slid the envelope down the slanted buttons of my coat. "Date the homecoming queen, then? Player?"

"Nope."

"Lions' honor?" she toyed. "No sexy experiments in the science lab?"

"Trust me, nothing sexy about formaldehyde and a dissecting probe. Open it, or I will."

Biting her lip, she slid her fingernail under the flap and it gave way. She turned her back and I heard the rustle of paper.

"So what are we baking?" I asked, stroking back her curls from her cheek and leaning over her shoulder.

Dani melted against me. "A pink cake," she said softly. "It's a girl."

"Yay for Jenna," I said, my hand stroking over hers so I could get a glimpse of the sonogram report, too. "I can totally see her spoiling a little princess rotten."

"So now what?" She turned to me, tucking the results back into the envelope and handing it over.

"I'm thinking pink ombré, four layers. Starting very pale and ending in a brilliant, no-mistaking-it, girlie-girl pink." I reached for a pencil and began to sketch on the back of the envelope. "White chocolate buttercream between the layers. And covered in ruffles of white fondant." It would be elegant and classy, like Jenna in her lawyerly pinstripes.

Dani made a face. "I am not fond of fondant. Not that I'll be eating her cake, but . . ."

"You've never had my fondant," I bragged. "Besides, I want absolutely no chance of color showing through. Even the thickest slather of frosting can"—I dredged a fork over Tom's freshly iced cake, revealing ruby red beneath—"betray your best intentions."

Dani's eyes never left mine as I brought the fork to her lips.

"By the way, if you go with the red velvet for your wedding cake, this is the icing I use. It's made with flour. No cream cheese touches this cake."

"Incredible." Dani swooned. "I feel like I'm learning all your bakery secrets today."

"Not all of them," I assured her with a wink. "Gotta keep you coming back for more, right?" Dani licked a fleck of icing off the bowed V of her top lip in response. Good God, how could one miniscule move from her make me want to move mountains? I pulled a spatula from my tool kit and smoothed it over Tom's cake, covering my tracks and preventing me from doing something totally rash and stupid. "Next time, we taste."

Dani

LOVE IS LIKE A SOLDIER

After the date from hell, Quinn yielded a little. She finally let us cross the street with Logan on Sunday, and even take him to the town playground.

My cell phone rang, just as we arrived at the park. Laney. I hadn't responded to her texts last week and never called her back the night we got into town. Time for damage control.

"Hey, hi!" I plugged my free ear with a finger to cut out the noise of the playground.

"It's about damn time you answered. What the hell?"

"Sorry, sorry." I pinched the phone between my cheek and shoulder so I could use both hands to steady the tire swing for Logan. "It's been hella crazy on tour."

Laney was quiet on the other end of the call. I gave up a silent prayer that she'd take all the background shrieking to be festival din.

"I can't chat long, Laney. I've got a client waiting for a four o'clock Reiki appointment."

"So help me, Danica. I'm going to Reiki you over the coals if you don't tell me what's going on." Laney was on a tear. "And where the hell you are."

"I told you, I'm with a client. Nash Drama, as a matter of fact."

"Yeah? Put him on the line, then."

"You don't believe me? Fine. Here he is." I held the phone out to him. "It's my best friend, Laney. Making sure I'm not being held against my will," I muttered.

"So, what are you wearing, Laney?" Nash immediately asked in his panty-dropping sex god voice. I gave his shoulder a shove, but he didn't budge. "Yes, Dani's with me and she's perfectly safe." He listened while Laney no doubt unloaded a slew of unsolicited advice about his music, judging from the look of indignation on his face. "Fair point. Gonna hand you back now."

Laney was already addressing me by the time I took the phone back. "I asked him why he hadn't released anything half as good as 'Jumpstart My Heart' in the last ten years, and told him he'd be in for a world of pain if he so much as harms one curl upon your head."

"Ah." Payback, I supposed, for the heart-to-heart call I had had with Noah, sight unseen, when they'd first met. "Everything's fine. I am all right."

"But you are not on tour." Laney's screech vibrated through the phone.

"How do you know that?"

"My best-friend-superpowered Spidey sense," she said. "That, and remember Anita?"

"The flight attendant?" Only Laney would become besties at thirty-five thousand feet with the stewardess on her plane.

"Yeah. She told me her husband's band, the Scary Marionettes, joined Minstrels & Mayhem on the Canadian leg of the tour. And Scary apparently requested you for a massage on my recommendation, and was told you had been let go. What the fucking fuck, girl? Way to leave a friend hanging! I want the dirt. Especially now that I know you are still with Nash, even though Go Get Her is off the bill."

"They're not 'off the bill,' Laney. Just the Canadian dates."

"Huh. Anita made it sound like Scary would be headlining until the end of September."

I glanced at Nash, wondering when was the last time he had checked in with Riggs. Or vice versa.

"Well," Laney was saying. "I expect to hear more when you come up here and help me pick out a wedding dress . . ." she toyed.

Now my shrieks were louder than the playground full of children. "Tell me everything!"

"No. See how it feels? *Ha!*" God, Laney could be so stubborn sometimes. But I knew that news like this would burst her if she didn't spill the beans. "Would you believe me if I told you he donned *Dreamer Deceiver* cosplay and got down on one knee at Comic Con?"

"That was one of my ideas," Noah's voice poured onto the line. "I also thought about hacking into her favorite video game and popping the question at the end. But I would've had to dump the ROM, hex edit the file, flash it to a new ROM chip, and solder it all back together."

"Congrats, Noah." I laughed at his fluid tech-speak. He'd lost me at ROM. "So tell me what really happened."

"He got a hold of my Magic 8 Ball." Laney gave a dreamy sigh.

Noah added, "I found a kit that let me create my own text for the twenty, um . . . triangular faces, and—"

"You can call it an icosahedron, honey." Laney loved to tease Noah over his knowledge of big words. "Dani has the smarts, like you."

"Oh my God, he proposed on the Magic 8 Ball? That is amazing!" I was so happy for them that I could hardly keep my feet on the ground. Good thing the playground had a rubber bounce-back safety surface as I hopped around.

"And my reply was uh-huh, yeppers, most definitely, you know it and hell yes!" Laney crowed. "Now, when can you get up here and help me shop?"

Just like that, my bubble burst. Technically, I, too, had news. Of an engagement that needed continual perpetuating so long as Nash wanted to continue getting to know his son. Things with Nash and Logan were going so well, Quinn seemed to be thawing, and Mick and I had at least cleared the air. So why did I feel so empty?

For the girl who had wanderlust in her blood, I suddenly felt incredibly homesick. "Hang on a sec." I covered the mouthpiece. "Hey, Boss. When can I get a day off to go up to the city?"

"I've got that label meeting Monday, remember? We can drive up together." Nash had Logan whizzing by in a huge, spinning arc. The boy's eyes were closed, but he sported a full-on grin, so all was good.

Laney and I set a meeting time, and she finally let me off the line with my solemn promise that I would tell her the truth, the whole truth, and nothing but the truth.

God help me.

"Remember, Quinn said not to get him too dizzy, he might hurl." Nash and Logan had been at it a good fifteen minutes.

"He's fine. Quinn is such a helicopter parent." Nash scoffed at himself for the trendy term that had just come out of his mouth. But he did grab the chain to slow it down.

I maneuvered far in front of Logan and carefully signed. With a nod and a grin, he jumped off and trotted to the jungle gym.

"What was that all about?" Nash wanted to know.

"I told him you'd race him down the slides later if he gave me a turn on the tire."

"Selling me out, huh?"

"You could use a little more playtime in your life while you are off the road."

It was a joke, but as I remembered what Laney had said about Go Get Her, I couldn't help but wonder about Nash and the band's status

on the festival tour. I supposed we'd learn just what the deal was on
Monday in New York. Riggs's radio silence troubled me.

"You know more signs than you let on," he said, impressed. "Who
taught you?"

"I know thirty-two. And would you believe me if I told you a chim-
panzee?" I laughed and climbed on top of the tire swing, almost falling
off twice in the process.

"No. Did he teach you to climb, too, Derpy Dani?" Nash asked.

"She. And shut up!" I squealed and clutched the chain rope with
both hands as he gave the tire a good heave-ho.

"I'm listening," he prompted, as the swing whooshed by his head
and he reached to give it another push.

"My mom? Totally married to her work. She was involved in a
research experiment on animal language acquisition, to see if animals,
communicating through sign, showed evidence of things like we
humans experience, like self-awareness, identity crises . . . stuff like
that. So when I was little, she studied these chimps, sometimes
hands-on but mainly on video. And what do parents do with their own
kids when they need to be entertained?"

"They'd stick them in front of a video."

I leaned back, the soles of my sandals facing the sky, and looked
at him. My smile probably looked like a frown, upside down. "Bingo."

"What a cop-out," Nash said, stepping back and allowing the swing
to slow.

"No, it was an opportunity for mother-daughter bonding. But I was
obsessed with Bingo. That was her name, by the way. She was so cute!
And way more fun than my older sister. Bingo liked to play with dolls,
just like me." I remembered how we'd visit her in the summer, in a
place we called camp, close to the university where she lived most of
the year. "Bingo was my girl. She taught me thirty-two signs. Well,
really it was my mother teaching the both of us. But sometimes Bingo
had more patience for me than my mother did." I laughed at the

memory. "Probably the most undivided attention I ever got from my mother was during that summer, actually," I added with a murmur.

Nash placed a foot in the hole of the tire swing and stepped up. His hands grasped the chain above my head, and he swung his whole frame to the left, sending us careening out over the riverbank.

"Nash! Is this thing going to hold both of us?"

"I won't let you break, China Doll."

He let centripetal force do the work, and we swung in lazy circles, the cicadas madly singing their vibrato chorus over our heads.

"My mom paid too much attention to the bottle. Drank herself into a nursing home by the time I was ten." He gave a wave to Logan, who was next in line for the big slide. "His age."

"Then it was just you and your dad?"

"Yep. Me and Nutso Nash. That's what everyone called him, after he came back from the Gulf War. He and my mom were high school sweethearts. She couldn't handle his mood swings. She loved him, but she had to escape."

"I don't get how people can leave behind the ones they love," I blurted.

"Love is like a soldier, Dani. Even if it comes back, it's never the same."

Tears sprang to my eyes, and I turned away. I didn't want to hear that. I didn't want to know that.

I couldn't bring myself to believe it.

Nash's foot dropped like an anchor, raising dust and bringing us to a halt.

"So, whatever happened with Bingo?" he asked.

"I discovered boys that next school year. And so by summer, Bingo blew past me with like a hundred more words, and I was lost. So I never learned any more signs."

"I'll bet you probably learned to be a better kisser than Bingo, though."

"You'd probably win that bet," I said with a grin. It was a pity our best moments of true intimacy seemed to always happen when no one was around to see.

"Would you teach me the signs you know?"

"Nash. Of course."

He kissed my cheek in thanks, and helped me off the swing.

My phone line buzzed like it was Old Home Days, with Laney's news. Even my mother wanted the scoop, with her usual ulterior motive of telling me how well some of her friends' children were doing in their more respectable professions.

"Sheila Blakesberg's daughter is making eighty-seven thousand as a PT in Northport, Danica. Did you know that the average salary for massage therapists is *half* that on the island?"

"Well, good thing I'm not taking a job on the island with an annual salary." I rolled my eyes.

"I know, darling. You love your 'gig.'" I could practically hear her air-quoting. "But you should know your options." The festival life made no sense to her. My mother didn't like the idea of me handling strange, tattooed men under what she called a sideshow tent, and brushing my teeth in the woods using bottled water.

"That's Posy on the other line." I was grateful at that moment for my sister clicking in.

"Go, dear . . . and will you *please* tell your sister I'm sorry again for the frozen monkey brain? She's threatening to join PETA."

"Frozen what?" I asked, but she had already disconnected. I had no choice but to click over and get an earful from Posy.

"This is worse than the time Dad conducted that double-blind 'controlled tickling' experiment on us to see if children would still laugh in the face of danger!"

"What did they do now?" I asked, not sure I really wanted to know. Although I remembered making double my allowance money just for wearing a killer clown mask and being told to tickle my sister mercilessly, she had never quite recovered.

"I was planning on surprising Pat this weekend with reservations at Jezebel," she explained, "that new upscale Cajun place in Williamsburg. You know, for our anniversary."

Oh, I knew. The year marker of meeting Mick didn't have a chance of slipping my mind, not when he kept slipping me hints of how great a reenactment would be since I had arrived in town.

"And then I was going to do the whole sexy candles, blindfolds and dessert thing, and serve him a piece of our wedding cake. Remember, from the top tier I had painstakingly arranged to have transported from New Orleans and back to Mom and Dad's freezer while Pat and I were on our honeymoon?"

Uh-oh. I think this was where the frozen monkey brain came in. "What happened?"

Posy let out a dramatic sigh. "Hurricane Sandy happened, that's what. Causing power outages and mandatory evacuation of their neighborhood, so she loaded stuff from the deep freeze into a cooler and brought it to work, where there was dry ice to be had. Then power went out at work; everyone was scrambling to save lab work and specimens. And remember, Mom had been part of that team brought in to measure the social behavior of amygdala-lesioned rhesus monkeys?"

"Um, if you say so."

Posy and my parents could discuss their peer-reviewed JAMA papers until they were blue in the face, but all I heard was the sound of adults speaking to Charlie Brown and the other Peanuts kid characters: *Mah-wah, mah-wah, mah-wah.*

"Well, coolers got confused, the monkey project got scrapped due to compromised data of the specimens, Mom restocked her freezer once the power came back on and *voila!* The big foil-wrapped object that I picked up yesterday to thaw out for my darling husband turned out to be one hundred percent genuine *Macaca mulatta* brain."

"She threw out your cake?" I bit the back of my hand to keep from laughing.

"Yes, Einstein. And no bakery worth its salt around here is going to be able to bake a replica with this short notice."

"Maybe no bakery around you . . . ," I said.

"I just have to stop at my sister's," I told Nash, the bakery box resting carefully on my knees. "Then you can drop me in the Village."

"I'm not coming in," Nash warned. "Not quite up to twenty questions from the in-laws just yet."

"Oh, but I can meet your whole fam-damily?" I challenged. "That was hardly a walk in the park. Don't worry. It's a doorman building. I can drop it at the desk."

"Doorman building, eh? Fancy."

"Says the man driving the eighty-five-thousand-dollar Cayman."

There was no need to page Posy at the front desk; she was waiting by the concierge and practically jumped on me the minute I walked in the door.

"You got it?" She waved her hands out frantically like I was a drug runner, delivering the goods.

"Exact replica." I cracked open the box so she could take a peek, and the aroma of bananas, coconut, pineapple, and pecans was enough to leave us both breathless.

Mick had remembered the exact type of cake Posy had ordered with the automatic accuracy of a savant. "Hummingbird cake," he had recalled. "Three tiers . . . garnished with dried pineapple flowers."

"Yes."

And ribboned charms. The words were traded, unspoken, between our gaze.

"Rebekkah played it safe with just a sweet cream cheese frosting. But I would've used a pineapple almond butter cream cheese instead."

"Go for it now," I'd told him. "Posy and Pat will love it."

It was an exact visual replica, down to the lone, paper-thin and fluttery pineapple flower on top . . . but I had no doubt it would taste even better than the original recipe, because Mick had made it. As a favor to me.

"Thank you!" My sister threw a quick hug my way, careful not to upset the cake in my hands. "And you . . . you're doing okay?" She peered over my shoulder at the sleek Porsche sitting at the curb. "Anybody you want to tell me about?"

Anybody. Not anything. Fancy PhDs aside, my sister was a smart cookie.

"He sends his regards." I smiled, relinquishing my hold on the box. "And he hopes you enjoy his cake."

"A baker? And with a car like that? You didn't tell me you were dating Jacques Torres!" she called after me as I breezed out the lobby. "Wait, is that a *ring* on your finger?"

Dani

VERA CAUSA

"Holy huge rock, Batman." Laney breathed hard enough to fog the two-carat diamond in its prongs.

"It's not like I need a magnifying glass to find the one Noah laid on you," I said, pulling my hand away and cramming it in my pocket. Today was all about Laney. I hated the thought of my drama with Nash Drama taking any of the spotlight—or the heat—off of her.

I had recounted the last few months' surreal circumstances as we walked arm in arm through our old neighborhood. To hell with Riggs's confidentiality agreement. What had started out as a one-week charade had grown to biblical proportions, as Nash's family and friends pushed us closer to the altar with every well-intentioned piece of advice. I needed to bend my best friend's ear. She responded with typical Laney zaniness and zeal. "Out of all the scenarios I've imagined *WWDD* . . . this one takes the cake!" She threw her black nail-polished hand over her mouth to suppress her chuckle. "Sorry, I couldn't resist."

"All right, enough. You've got me for two hours. Where to, Superbride?"

"Well . . . a dress of some sort is in order." She shuddered with horror and happiness, if ever such a thing were possible. "And I'm sure as hell not going through this alone. Say you'll play dress-up with me?"

With Mick's offer of cake tasting a constant temptation, and Sindy's daily pressure of setting a date ASAP for the big day, the least I could do was attempt to be in the market for a dress. "All right, all right."

"Excellent! Now, pick up the pace . . . we're gonna go see our fairy gothmother."

Bree welcomed us with open arms. "My girls! You're back! And what's this?" She pounced, pulling our left hands toward her in some sort of sixth sense. "The both of you? Oh, honeys!" Her eyelashes, all fattened up with mascara, flashed up and down like dancing girls in a kick line. "Wait. Not to each other, right?"

We both just laughed and shook our heads.

"Okay, honeys. Just making sure! But I do have two matching gowns that would've been fabulous. Sweetheart necklines, chapel trains . . ."

Laney snorted.

"Keep in mind, Bree," I said, thumbing at Laney. "You're talking to the girl who played dress-up in her mother's wedding dress and Converse high-top sneakers . . . at the age of thirty-one."

"And Rainbow Brite." Laney was quick to remind her of my Afro-wig award. "Maybe you can bleach one of Dani's old bridesmaid dresses and pass it off for bridal white. But for me? I'm talking black. Short. With a corset. And a fascinator for my head. No feathers. Noah is allergic."

Bree's lashes quivered as she took a moment to let Laney's demands sink in. "Okay. If I don't have anything in stock, I'll make some calls. What about you, Dani?" She turned to me, desperate for the voice of reason.

"I want to try on the Vera."

"Oh, sweetie. I don't think that's a good idea." She quickly changed the subject, grabbing my hand to inspect Nash's ring. "That's quite a rock! You got yourself a sugar lovah, sweetheart," she said, with a conspiratorial wink.

An image of Mick came to mind, back in the bakery with gum paste up to his elbows.

"Will you look at her?" Bree crowed. "You're blushing like a bride!"

"And you're changing the subject. Why can't I try the Vera? You always say it's a gorgeous specimen."

"Oh, it is. It is. But for someone else. Not for you."

How about for someone who needs to look like she's planning the wedding of the century to marry into rock royalty? I needed an impressive dress in hand. I had Nash's credit card and his blessing. And judging from the stack of bills lining Bree's counter, I bet she could use the sale.

"Look at it. It's perfect. You said it's never been worn, right?"

"Well, not exactly," Bree hedged. "The bride never wore it."

Laney's eyes narrowed. "What happened to her?"

"It's more a case of what happened to the dress," Bree replied, and bustled off to the front of the shop. Laney and I exchanged glances. A mystery. Color us intrigued.

"What size is it?" I asked, stalking Bree from behind a rack of ready-to-wear. "I'll bet it's my size."

She sighed. "Its label says eight. But its street size is a six."

"Dani's a six." Laney butted right into the conversation, pushing between two hangers. "Except in the boobs." I flicked the dresses back in place, shutting the gap on her.

"It retailed for ten thousand dollars."

"And now it's a bargain at five. What is the harm in letting me try it?"

"Because," Bree sighed, pulling a mermaid-style gown and a corseted black dress from the New Arrivals rack. "You are going to fall in love with it."

"And?"

And I promise you, I won't. The dress would be a prop, just like the ring. And the king bed that Nash and I shared at the Half Acre.

"It's cursed," Bree announced. "There. I said it!"

"What the whaaa?" Laney actually stepped through the gap in the rack of clothes. Bree made a beeline toward the dressing room, and we gave chase.

"In you go. I want you to try these on. And then I will tell you the story. Lemme just go lock the shop door."

Laney and I exchanged another look. In the five years we'd known her, Bree was like the mailman. She didn't close due to rain, sleet, snow or even when there was a gas leak in the building behind her. Her business was everything. Yet . . .

"She must really mean business," Laney whispered, and shoved the fishtail gown toward me. "I believe this one's for you."

I shed my sundress, while Laney shucked her jeans, hoodie and tank top. "Here, zip me. Watch the hair." I held my curls off my neck and she eased the zipper up.

"Well?"

I turned to her. The black was striking against her creamy skin and russet hair. It didn't scream wedding, but it certainly screamed Laney.

"Your mother is going to sit shivah for you if you wear that as your wedding dress."

"True." She swished the skirt and pouted. "I guess it would probably violate our latest peace treaty. I can hear her now." Screwing up her mouth, she did a dead-accurate impression of her mother's heavy Long Island accent, "'What kind of *verkackte* dress is that?'"

I wanted to laugh, but the dress I'd tried on was so tight, I was afraid I'd break a rib if I tried.

"How do I look?"

"Like a mermaid porn star."

We both cracked up at my reflection. The dress was a shimmering beauty, but I was spilling out the top of it. "I wonder if Bree sells seashell pasties. I'd be all set."

There was a knock. "Are you ready?" Bree called.

We opened the door, ready to hear the story of the cursed Vera. Not so ready to say yes to the dresses we had tried on.

Bree stood there, with the Vera in her arms, shaking her head. "Silly girls. Those dresses were both for Laney. I would never size you that wrong."

"Oh, good. Because I think I punctured a lung in this thing." Laney unzipped me and I hightailed it back into the room. Without a word, Bree hooked the Vera onto the back of my door and closed me in with it.

"Laney. Into the room next to her." I heard a door click shut. "Dani. Hand over the fishtail dress." I did as I was told.

"But I said black!" Laney protested.

"I know."

"And short."

"Mmm-hmm."

"So, do we get to hear the story of the Vera now?" I asked, tentatively touching its lacy edges. I stood in my red lace bra and panties, admiring it. The dress was a feat of technical engineering, its many drapes and layers so frothy and artfully arranged, it reminded me of a wedding cake. Which of course, reminded me of—

"The curse!" Bree boomed, loud enough for us to hear her through the door. "It may be an urban legend, but a woman came into the shop, dressed in a maid's uniform. Her English wasn't very good, but she relayed she had been sent by the lady of the house. The lady's daughter was all set to marry the man of her dreams. The haute couture dress, the Sylvia Weinstock cake, the fancy Park Avenue venue . . . every little detail was set. But the night before the wedding, the bride-to-be went out with her girlfriends."

"And she was never seen again?" Laney interjected.

"Shush! No! Listen," Bree hissed. "So after she left, the groom called a buddy or two to come hang out. You know. Guy stuff. Watch some football, play some poker, drink some beer. His bride-to-be specifically told him no bachelor party, no strippers."

"Sounds like your typical Bridezilla," Laney groaned.

"Well, his friends decided to surprise him. Body shots, lap dances, the whole nine yards. And when the bride-to-be arrived home that night, she found her husband passed out drunk. And the stripper . . ."

"No!" Laney and I both cried out in unison.

"Yes. The stripper was in the couture gown. Dancing and grinding on him, while the buddies cheered her on."

"Tell me she didn't marry the asshat after that?" Laney said.

"Oh no. She went ahead and she married him," Bree replied breezily. "But the dress was ruined for her. She ran out and bought a new gown the next morning."

"Ugh, rich people," Laney muttered. "What a waste."

I laughed. "Come on. Seriously? I call bullshit."

"Like I said, could be urban legend," Bree said. "But for five years, that dress has hung in my shop, untouched."

"Um, maybe that's because it's the most expensive thing in your shop?" Laney ventured. "It should be in a bulletproof case for that price. Hell, the price tag itself should be locked behind glass!"

I opened the dressing room door.

"Oh, Dani!" The owner of Diamonds & Fairy Dust clasped her hand to her heart. "Will you look at that? No more 'always a bridesmaid' for you!" She fussed with the hems. With one tiny tug, she covered just a hint of my red bra peeking out, just as expertly as Mick had repaired the white icing on his red velvet cake the other day. "Vera is a master. That is Chantilly under here, layered with esprit lace. Feel this? That's horsehair; it gives it that lift. God, look at the way the light and the shadows play when the skirt moves; it's light as a feather, isn't it? And speaking of feathers . . ."

Laney pushed open her dressing room door. "No feathers. No

black. Long, not short! Bree, it's perfect." And it truly was. Laney looked divine. Her body fit like the dress had been molded to her exact measurements. The fitted bodice accented her small hips, and the top that had betrayed my assets tastefully enhanced hers. "Look. It's got a corset." She twirled, and I spied her phoenix wing tribal tattoo in all its fiery glory.

"Oh, Hudson. That is it," I breathed.

Bree nodded sagely. "Now, that's a Badgley Mischka. Last season, but nothing to sneeze at."

"I love it." Laney hugged herself. "I love it more than Mary Jane Watson's dress on the cover of the giant-sized annual, #22, of *The Amazing Spider-Man* when she married Peter Parker." Giving the size and seriousness of her comic book collection, I knew that was Laney's weird way of giving high praise.

Bree clipped a white fascinator with a birdcage veil on Laney and stepped back. "Perfect." She shook her head and smiled. "Why don't we find you some shoes up front?"

"No, no, all set. I'm wearing Chucks. Red." Laney smiled at her reflection in the mirror, relishing the memory. "So is Noah."

Bree collapsed on the plump, white pouf in the corner by our dressing rooms, exhausted by the effort of transforming Laney, one bridal accessory at a time. "Perhaps another day." She waved her hand in defeat.

"Inside joke," I assured her. "I guess we had to be there." No one had been there, save for Laney and Noah. And he had saved her from frostbite by lending her his sneakers during the Chicago blizzard that had grounded their flights, when all she had were flip-flops. "He warmed her toes, and her heart."

Laney's dress needed to stay behind for some minor alternations, but since the Vera had fit like a charm, I was good to go. Except Bree wouldn't accept Nash's card. "Save your sugar lovah's money. Borrow the dress, and bring it back," she pressed. "Our little secret."

"But Bree," I protested. "Look at all those bills. This sale could help."

"These?" She waved her hand at them. "Please. *My* sugar lovah pays those for me."

"Wait, is that—?" The rock on her hand seemed to have increased in size. "What happened to Mr. Five Time's the Charm?"

"Eh, you know. Easy come, easy go. But number six? He's the one!"

After leaving Diamonds & Fairy Dust, I messaged Jax and cashed in my rain check for carnitas and margaritas at the Rocking Horse. Like Laney, my other best friend had big news to celebrate—Jax had sold his first novel to one of the Big New York Five. I was over-the-moon happy for him. It was like I had never left, howling with laughter at our favorite corner table as he regaled me with his latest plot ideas, and I shared my craziest tour stories from the road, including my first night on Nash's tour bus.

"I don't know how you do it, Heartbreaker." He shook his head. "Curious to see how you're going to get out of this one."

"Maybe I'm not going to," I said, toying with the ring around my finger. "Maybe it really is What Dani Would Do, you know?"

Jax set his margarita glass down a little too hard. "To trap yourself in a loveless marriage? To be safe?" He stabbed his straw at the ice in his glass, refusing to look at me.

My mouth suddenly went very dry. "Oh, and you're not 'Mister Safe,' the king of serial monogamy? Before Mona, it was one 'sure thing' after another." I licked my lips, tasting salt, and Jax winced like I was rubbing his wounds with it.

"Mona and I broke up."

"What? Jax! When? Why didn't you tell me?"

"A month ago . . . after you said you'd call, but never did."

Fair point.

"I . . . I don't know what to say, Jax. Other than I'm sorry."

He drained the margarita dregs from the heavy stemless glass, and shrugged. "Did you know that tequila is produced by removing the heart of the agave plant?" he said suddenly. Without waiting for me to answer, he added, "In its twelfth year."

"That's a long time to wait."

"Yes, it is."

His writer brain loved to dig up research; no doubt this was another one of his Jax Facts, as Laney like to call them. Some poetic metaphor for something going on between us, no doubt.

"Only the heart is split open and used. The *piña*," he enunciated. "The rest is discarded."

My cell phone lit up across the table. Neither of us looked at it.

"How long have we known each other, Dani?" he murmured.

I needed no time to add digits or calculate. "Fifteen years."

Jax leaned slowly back in his chair. "Ah. That's a long time."

For what? To wait? I didn't know what he was getting at, or where he was going with it.

My phone brightened again, and I broke eye contact to glance down at it.

Nash.

Parking, his first text said. Then, *Be there in 2.* I'd told him to swing by to meet my friends after his meeting, not realizing Laney wouldn't be joining us. Or that Jax would be putting me under some sort of matrimonial microscope.

"Is that him? Paging you to go out to him like . . . like some call girl?"

"No, he was coming in. But on second thought," I grumbled, "I think I'm outta here."

"Wait, don't." He grabbed my hand as I tried to gather my things. "You don't need to go with him, Dani. Or with any of the scammers or con artists out there. You deserve better. You deserve one hundred percent interest for the rest of your life."

"Jax!" My entire body flashed hot, then drained cold. I needed to nip this in the bud, and fast. Before our entire friendship blew up in our faces. "I can't get into this right now. I have to go."

He rose to meet me at eye level, trapping me with his intensity. "You walk away from everything and everyone! And you think it means you're strong?" His laugh was a bitter bark. "All your love 'em and leave 'em bravado . . . more like fuck and forget. What the hell are you so afraid of?"

I was afraid of losing our friendship. Of losing him.

"I'm afraid of making the wrong choice!" I hollered, pushing my chair back. "Like I always do!"

"Like choosing Dex over me? That day of the funeral?"

The look on his face was a strange mix of tortured release. As if, like me, he had been wrestling with some unspoken secret since the day we met.

Maybe he had.

I had lost my virginity to Dex that day. Along with every bit of faith in myself.

"Did you honestly think he could resist telling me all about it?" Jax shook his head, his lips thin as he pressed them into the saddest smile. "It never mattered to me that you hooked up with my brother, never."

I had always been Jax's rock, and he mine. But with the mere mention of his brother's name, it was like he had turned over a part of me, exposing something I had been hiding, dank and grubby, in the dark for so long.

And it didn't matter?

I turned to leave, smacking right into all six feet, four inches of Nash. Relief hit me back, and I realized that while our engagement arrangement had focused on me being exclusively there for him, I had come to rely on Nash as well. Whatever fucked-up journey of discovery we were on, we had been on it together since the first night we met.

"Hey," I said angrily. "I'm about to be up one on you. Think fast."

He got the reference. "Drinks are on me."

Shots of Patrón were on the bar in no time, and in a blur of stinging swallows and salty tears, I was sucking a lime out of my fiancé's mouth.

Nash responded, capturing my lips, taking my tongue hungrily against his. But there was a detached air, an absence. I don't think either of our hearts were really in it.

"Hey." I finally took the plunge into the jaded green depths of his eyes. "I thought Nash Drama doesn't like doing things half-assed."

Nash accepted my breathy challenge for what it was, fingers snaking down the crack of my bottom, grabbing bunches of my thin cotton dress as he pulled me against his frame.

Money smacked down on the bar next to me, and I sensed a hint of chilled cucumber with a citrus bite breeze past as Jax stormed out.

"What the fuck was that?" Nash broke away, skipping the lime and salt this time, and went straight for the shot.

"That was me, burning the last bridge I ever dreamed I'd burn."

Had my fear of losing Jax become a self-fulfilling prophesy, the minute I realized my fears had been unfounded, all this time? Shock and shame replaced any other emotions I was feeling. The tequila didn't exactly hurt, either.

I had had to protect my heart, after the rest of me was discarded by Dex, all those years ago.

Nash didn't press me. He just passed me another round.

"It's over, China Doll."

"What is?"

"Everything." He waved his hand. "The tour. The band dropped off it. Cutting their losses. Oh, and they kicked me out. I'm too much of a liability, apparently."

"What? Can they do that? What about contracts?"

"I wasn't a founding member and I was dragging them down. So . . ."

"No!" I was outraged. "You do better when you are active. Getting you back on the road would be a win-win. I'll call Riggs—"

His hand fell heavily on mine. "No."

"Then what?" I asked, echoing our strange question from the mountaintop.

Nash gave a tired smile. The rock-and-roll dream had gone belly-up, as he had feared. With me by his side this past week, he had seen his friends, had gotten to know his kid. As he had intended. I guessed it was now time for him to cash in on that shoulder to lean on. If the rocker needed a rock, it might as well be me. It's what I did best.

In some sort of unspoken agreement, we both threw back our final shots in the marriage-proposal drinking game.

Game on.

"Thank you, China Doll."

Nash grabbed the Vera and my hand, led me to the Porsche and back out of town.

I had the ring and the dress. All there was left to do was choose a cake . . . and finally lose any dreams left lingering of Mick.

Dani

HEAVEN'S HALF ACRE

New York seemed to bring a cloud of bad moods back on the Half Acre. There were so few topics acceptable to talk about without arguments or slammed doors. Nash and I were at loose ends. He was pulling away from me, and lashing out at everyone else.

"Don't worry," Nash lobbed to Quinn. "As soon as I accept my key to the city—"

"It's a borough," Bear interjected.

"Whatever. As soon as I accept it, I'm out of here."

"Nice to know where your priorities *lie*, Dad," Quinn seethed as she spooned fruit onto Logan's plate. "You care more about that ornamental key than your flesh and blood! I'll bet it's plastic, and it's not going to magically open any doors around here for you! One freakin' night out of the year. You can't spare that?" She stabbed chunks of watermelon, Logan's favorite fruit, with a huge serving fork and practically flung them onto his plate.

"Then Dani should go, too," Nash argued.

"Go where?" I asked warily. I'd been upstairs and had missed out on the bulk of the conversation.

"Open School Night this week," Bear supplied. "First public appearance together since—"

Nash threw his own fork down with a clang. "Jesus Christ, Bear."

Logan had been moving a hand over his fist as his mother had absently pushed more food on him, but now he was bringing the back of his hand up under his chin.

"Enough." I blurted out the word, loud enough for Quinn and Nash to pause for a second. "Listen to your son."

"You're full, honey?" Quinn asked, looking down at his plate.

Logan made the same gesture, his young face full of fury. That's all it took to change the meaning of his sign for having had enough to eat, to having had it up to "here" with the lot of them. He pushed back his chair, and stomped to his room. Soon we could hear him crunching out frustrated bar chords on the guitar.

"He's had enough of the fighting." I placed a hand on Nash's shoulder. "Remember what Sindy said. This is a gift of time."

Quinn rubbed her temple. "God, could you at least tune that goddamn guitar for him? I wish you'd never brought it for him in the first place."

"Is that really what you want to waste your wish on, Quinn?"

Nash was up and stomping the stairs before she could respond. Quinn just put her head in her hands.

"I'll talk to him about Open School Night," I said to her. "I think it is important for the both of you to go." She didn't protest, but she didn't say thank you, either.

Mick appeared in the doorway then, but he wasn't alone. Two young guys, probably in their twenties, stood there, fidgeting nervously. "Quinn." There was a trace of cautious amusement in his tone. "You have some customers."

Quinn bolted up in her seat, blinking rapidly. "Welcome to the Half Acre. You're looking for a room?"

The guys glanced, horrified, at each other. "Two," the taller one said hastily. "We're not together, together. We're just . . . traveling together."

"Yeah, we heard—" The shorter guy got a bony elbow in the ribs, but ignored it. "Is this where Nash Drama is staying?"

"We don't want to stalk him or anything," the taller guy quickly assured. "We're just . . ." He smiled and appealed to all of us with his hands. ". . . huge, huge music fans, we're totally chill, and we were on a road trip. Once Go Get Her dropped off the tour, we've been . . ." He glanced at his friend, a little embarrassed. "We've been visiting rock-and-roll meccas, you know . . . and birthplaces of our favorite musicians and stuff." He had a slight drawl, as if he might hail from a southern state.

Bear stood up proudly. "Welcome to the Half Acre, and New Hope. This is where Nash Drama grew up." The guys threw triumphant glances at each other. "I can't guarantee you'll get a glimpse of him while you're here, but I can totally show you around. Where he went to high school, where we used to jam—"

"You played with him?" The shorter guy had worship in his eyes.

Bear nodded the affirmative. "I've even got a VHS of us performing for the Battle of the Bands. Totally won that year."

I recognized the Holy Grail moment in Tall Guy's eyes, as he forked his credit card over to Quinn. "I'm Justin," he said. "And this is Rob. We'd like to stay a week."

"Bear," Quinn said, amazement in her voice. "Can you show Justin and Rob to rooms two and four?"

"Those can wait," Mick said to me, nodding at the dirty plates I had stacked by the sink. "And you're a guest, you don't have to—"

"Please." I gave him a look. By now Nash and I had moved beyond guest status. To what, I didn't know. Freak show? Tourist attraction? I hope he chilled out before making any sort of public appearance.

"Let's take a walk." Mick tossed down the dish towel he was holding. He had on a pair of battered suede Vans on his normally bare feet. And a shirt.

"You don't have to get to the shop?"

"The shop can wait."

Small, hard apples had begun to form on the trees of the orchard. Mick scooped up a couple from the ground and tossed them between his hands in a halfhearted juggle as we wound our way through the trees toward the river.

"Ever wonder what it's like to be famous?" he asked.

I shrugged. "I grew up with a guy who ended up making it really big with his band. Sorta saw what he went through." I didn't mention who it was—Allen Burnside—or how fame, and cancer, had abbreviated his life spent with Laney. "Plus I've always worked around famous people. So, yeah. I guess the thought's occurred to me."

Mick threw one of the apples, with a side flick of his wrist, and it skipped like a stone across the water. "Growing up, we used to debate. Would we rather be rich, or famous? Money sounded pretty good to me. But Nash. He always picked fame."

He handed me the other apple to throw, but I held on to it instead. We kept walking along the river, the trees to our right. I rubbed its smooth, hard surface like a worry stone.

"Famous means people thinking they deserve to know your business. That doesn't really appeal to me at all." He turned to me suddenly. "Does Nash put butter or jam on his toast?"

"Excuse me?"

Butter or jam . . . I wondered if this was another test, like the strange wedding-induced "Coke or Pepsi" game everyone insisted on playing with us around the fire pit, ever since Nash and I first opened our mouths with conflicting information about our plans. They thought it was funny we couldn't agree . . . and seemed to have a vested interest in our "Big Day."

"Come on. How does Nash like his toast?" Mick insisted.

"Burnt?" I joked. "He puts butter on it, I guess."

"Nope. If he orders breakfast and the toast arrives dry, he sends it back to be buttered. Buttered in the back."

"Your point?" I asked.

"I don't think you know much about Nash at all," he said. "Probably not any more than those fans in the B and B think they do."

"Don't tell me what I—"

"I'm not saying it's your fault, Dani." He pushed a hand through his hair. "And that's not a reflection on you."

"What do you have against Nash?" I demanded.

"Besides the fact that it's his ring on your finger?" Mick lobbed back at me instantly. "Besides the fact that he has never come by anything honestly in his entire life?"

He grabbed my arm and turned me toward the house. "You haven't watched Logan grow up, peering out those windows and waiting for the day his father shows up. I was that kid, Dani." Mick took a tortured breath. "And that day never came for me."

I sagged against him, a little bit of the fight gone out of me. I wanted to hold him, but our history had woven a complicated tapestry that threatened to ensnare more emotions if I let it. Like with my clients, I stayed silent and allowed him to reach for his own peace and release.

"I don't know what's worse: having him and losing him again, or never having him at all. I don't want to see Logan get hurt. It was harder than you realize for Nash to come here. And I can tell he's thinking about taking off again." He avoided my eyes and added, "As much as it kills me to have you stay here with him indefinitely, I'd rather suffer through that than watch Logan lose you both."

We had arrived at an old garden gate. It was half off its hinges, as if it had been beaten down by someone, or something. I had glimpsed it in passing, on the way back to the fire pit, but had never really noticed its detail. Now I saw it had a design or lettering. Wrought of forged iron and surrounded by blooming flowers, swooping curlicues, and bells read the words *Welcome to Heaven's Half Acre*. Time and the elements had eaten away at the words, leaving them rusty and weak.

"Heaven?" I asked Mick. I hadn't heard the property called by that name in the time that I'd been here. But I remembered reading it in the old guest books. "I wonder how old this is?"

"No one's called it that since the night of the fire," Mick explained. He tentatively touched the curve of the V and it flaked off flecks of rust at our feet.

"Dani. Nash's dad made this sign, many years ago. He was the caretaker here. And everyone thought he and Nash started the fire that killed Quinn and Bear's mom."

Dani

LOVE IN SPADES

Time spent at the inn, with all its unspoken secrets, began to close in on me, so for a change of scenery, I decided a nice long run off-property after breakfast was in order. Lost in my own thoughts, I managed to make it all the way over to Bridge Street before realizing where I was.

I ran into just about my favorite person in New Hope: Mick's aunt. She was sitting on a bench down the road from the bakery.

"Look at you, off for a jog. Meanwhile, I'm *shvitzing* like a hooker in church!" Sindy fanned her face.

"Lunch break?" I smiled, stretching out my hamstring.

"No, I went to deliver Mick's meringues to Mr. Woolhouse. Poor thing is in the hospital; they think it's pneumonia." Sindy shook her head sadly.

Nash had chalked up the second-oldest citizen's ailments and begging off on the key ceremony as hypochondria and stage fright . . . but even he had been out to visit the man regularly in the week since.

"Tell me, dear. How are things out at the Half Acre?"

I tilted my head and regarded her. "Let me put it this way: Quinn still wants me to use the front door."

Sindy nodded wisely. "That girl is one for keeping up appearances." She sighed. "Damn shame, everything."

"Can you tell me what 'everything' is, because people"—*including your nephew*, I wanted to add, but didn't—"are pretty close-lipped up there."

"Oh, me?" Sindy whipped out a hanky and dabbed at her face with it. "I can't get through the whole thing without crying. Come. The town library is a much better resource."

She marched us down the street, into the cool, hushed building, and right over to the microfilm machine.

"Can I help you find something?" a librarian asked. Sindy waved him away and pulled a box from a long file drawer. She slid out the reel, popped it on the machine, and sent it rolling in a blur of days and months.

"Ah, here it is."

It was hard to believe such a story; so many secrets and such pain were encapsulated in one microscopic square of film that would survive five hundred years, if stored properly.

HISTORIC INN BURNS, ONE DEAD, ANOTHER MISSING read the main headline. Below it, in smaller font: GROUNDSKEEPER AND SON QUESTIONED.

"Oh my God," I breathed. The headlines were so primetime surreal, the kind of train wrecks you just couldn't turn away from when you saw them on the news, or on the front page. But when connected to lives of people who you knew . . . Sindy's running commentary in her stage whisper kept it in perspective.

"Quinn was off at college, Bear was out on the road with one of his bands. Tina . . . their mom . . . she was supposed to be visiting her sister in Maryland. But she wasn't feeling well and had turned back for home. Nothing a little chicken soup and good night's sleep wouldn't fix. She'd gone to bed in one of the rooms in the new wing." Sindy shook her head slowly. "Bill hadn't known . . . he'd just assumed the place was empty and it was the perfect time. Nash's father said he heard screaming."

"But . . . but their mom . . . ?"

"Yes. Deaf people have vocal cords, too. They can make sounds perfectly or awfully. They're human beings, nothing more or less."

CO-WORKERS, FRIENDS PAINT A DARK, TROUBLED PATH FOR NEW HOPE PROPRIETOR.

"Bear and Quinn's father did it . . . for the insurance?" I asked, a queer, tight feeling rising in my chest. I felt rage toward the man who supposedly made delicious bananas Foster French toast. How dare he do this to his family?

"The stock market had crashed, and the tourist industry took a hit after 9/11. I guess the poor guy saw loss coming from all directions. Figured insurance from a total loss was the only way. But I don't think he ever meant to harm anyone. Sure, they had issues. What family doesn't?" Her voice dropped even lower. "At first, everyone was quick to blame the Nash boys. Oh, your sweetie was a wild and troubled one, hon. And his dad, Scott 'Nutso' Nash, crazy in the head since Desert Storm. Sole witness, and what with his lighter found on the property."

I remembered everyone's reaction when Nash pulled his dad's lighter out at Logan's birthday party, and my heart just about broke all over again.

"Especially since Bill was MIA. Four days it took, for his body to turn up downriver. Fishermen saw it caught in a tangle of branches. Stones in his pockets. Then Scotty Nash was free to go."

I flicked the switch and the microfilm screen faded to black. I didn't need to see any more. "Go where?" I asked quietly.

"Well, now. Isn't that the million-dollar question?" Sindy said. "He's at Belmont."

With a father in the psychology profession, I had a passing knowledge on mental institutions within the tri-state area. No wonder Nash didn't feel he had a home to come back to.

"Stuart—your Nash—he headed west soon after. He needed a good, clean slate, that boy. I had no doubt he would go far. It was Bear I worried about. He was in a real bad way. Pretty much catatonic, until he adjusted to his happy pills. I don't know how he and Quinn could stand it, going back to that house so soon. The two of them, rambling around in the quiet. I think they both stopped talking altogether, actually. Just signed. It was what they always did with their mother, bless her, and maybe it brought them some peace? I just don't know. But Logan was born into that silence. That boy was a shining light and a godsend to Quinn. But ain't that a kick in the rear? Testing his hearing was an afterthought."

I sat, absorbing all that information. Sindy pulled out a lipstick and compact and made the rounds, puckering up her lips before turning to me.

"Honey, have you and Nash gone over to the Orphans' Court to apply for your marriage license yet?"

"Oh, uh . . . no. I was going to research where to go." *Orphans' Court?* That sounded like the last place you'd need to check off on your wedding to-do list. "Why Orphans?"

"Oh, that's just how things are done here in this county, dating back to the 1600s. From births and adoptions to wills and deaths! Marriage is somewhere in there, if you're lucky." She winked at me.

"Sindy, can I ask . . . ?"

"Yes, honey." The way she answered so firmly spread warmth through me, like I could ask her just about anything. And something in her eyes gave me the feeling she knew the topic was her nephew.

"Was Mick . . . an orphan? He mentioned his mom once, and never knowing his dad, but—"

Sindy pushed the rewind button on the microfilm machine, and the reel began its trek backward. We watched it go. Slow at first, but then it picked up speed. Sort of like the older woman's answer.

"Sofia was my sister's youngest. And she was just a baby herself when she had Mick. Fifteen. She was a good kid, a little on the wild side. Just so young, and scared out of her wits. Lots of religion in our family upbringing, so that baby was being born, so help us God. Not sure who the father was. A boyfriend?" Sindy gave a shake of her bangle bracelets to show her doubt. "Maybe. Sofia wouldn't give up the farm. Took that knowledge with her. And she wouldn't give up little Mick for adoption when she laid eyes on him, no way no how. Especially since he was born smack-dab on her birthday!"

The film slowed as it reached the end, and flapped off the spindle with a loud clack. The librarian gave us his best death stare, but Sindy just eyeballed him right back. "Don't blame me," she said to everyone around us. "Blame the technology." She stuffed June 1, 2002– December 31, 2002 back into its little gray box.

"Anyhoo," Sindy continued, as she gathered her purse and bags and signaled toward the exit door. "She tried her best. Really, she did. And I always looked after them both. Walt and me, we never had kids of our own. And my sister, she had enough kids, and enough problems. When Sofia left, my sister couldn't go through raising a kid again. So Mick came to us."

I pulled down my sunglasses, perched on the crown of my head, to combat the noonday sun's glare, and to hide my tears. My heart ached for the boy who had become the man I was getting to know. "How old?" I asked, my voice barely a croak.

"He was five. Almost six." Sindy kept her chin up and squinted down the sun like she was up for a challenge. "Sofia was turning twenty-one. It didn't take a crystal ball to see what the future held, had she stayed here. Money and men were waiting in the bars. We didn't discourage her from leaving. But it caused a rift between my sister and me that was never mended. The two sides of the family were never close again. It's just me and Walt and Mick."

"And Sofia? Do you ever hear from her?" *Or does Mick?* I wanted to add, but couldn't bring myself to.

"No." Sindy marched across the street, and I had to scurry to keep up. "What's done is done," she said quietly, finally donning a pair of cat's-eye sunglasses. "No regrets. We support those we love. When it came time for Mick to go to school and to train, off he went."

But Mick had come back. Did he feel bound by that duty, perhaps to make up for the sins of his mother? Maybe that was the reason behind his anger toward Nash as well. Nash, like Sofia, had left their little town and never looked back.

I thought about Nash comparing love to a soldier. Wounded at war. *Even if it comes back, it's never the same.*

"Now those Bradley kids." She clicked her tongue. "It was love they needed after that tragedy, not money. And luckily, I got that in spades." She twirled, skirts ballooning and pocketbook swinging out, and grinned like a starlet in those vintage glasses. Only Sindy could pull off pale yellow Bakelite without looking kitsch in the twenty-first century. "And I think you have that charm, too, honey." She tweaked my cheek with a white-gloved hand. "Lots of love in you."

"Thanks, Sindy. It was a nice afternoon." And I meant it, too. Even after all the heartbreak that had been revealed today. "You heading back to the Night Kitchen?"

"You go on. I believe I'll do some antiquing therapy across the bridge." She hustled across River Road while the light was in her favor, then turned and blew me a kiss before journeying on.

Yes. Even after all the heartbreak, Sindy was a strong testament to the staying power of love.

Mick was bent over a beautiful wooden boat replica sculpted in cake, his steady hands in food-service gloves carefully affixing a set of zebras crafted from fondant. A mixture of surprise and pleasure crossed his expression as I walked in. "Hey!" His brow, however, wrinkled in alarm. "Did I forget we had another consult?"

"No." I suddenly felt shy. "Just wanted to come say hi. Is that Noah's ark?" Mick had already added a menagerie of fondant animals, two by two, up the chocolate gangplank. "That is magnificent."

"Thanks," Mick said, leaning this way and that to inspect his handiwork. "It's for a little boy named Noah, would you believe? His sixth birthday."

"Lucky kid. That's a pretty extravagant cake."

"Yeah," Mick said absently, tilting his head and using a toothpick to run a realistic-looking groove through the "wood" made of modeling chocolate. "It's all about the parents these days, usually. And what they want."

I couldn't help but think of the conversation I had just had with his aunt. Of Mick's mom leaving when he was that age, and of them sharing a birthday. Was it painful, to create such beautiful reminders of your own painful memories?

"I just ran into Sindy outside," I said softly. "A while ago, actually. We went to the library."

Mick twirled the toothpick between his fingers and didn't meet my eyes. "Quite a history there on the Half Acre, huh?"

"I'm still processing it."

"Nash should've told you before you got here, just what you were up against."

I nodded; in many ways, that was true. He had come to set some things to rights, and had wanted my help. But I couldn't really help with so many secrets and unanswered questions. Sort of like massage; if you didn't tell me what hurt, I had a hard time figuring out how to fix it.

"Family histories are complicated," I agreed.

I thought about Jax and Dex. They had been living under the shadow of a deathbed confession for fifteen years, made by their grandfather. A religious man, the family patriarch had felt the need to absolve himself of any sin, by confessing a secret he'd promised his wife he would never reveal: she had been pregnant with another man's child, and he had raised that son as his own. And now that son's children, twin boys, were the only ones left to carry on the Davenport name . . . except they weren't really Davenports by blood. The news had split the family at the funeral that day, pitting relative against relative, as the elder Davenport knew it would. He had borne no ill will against his wife for her past transgression, but he wanted to make sure her soul was clear so she could join him in heaven. He changed his will and tied up the fate of the boys' inheritance until the day she passed, and her own will would decide the outcome. Jax, of course, loved unconditionally. But Dex had turned resentful and distrustful of women. My mother likened the cruel family dynamics to Harlow's monkey experiment. Jax tended to cling to women, longing for contact comfort, whereas Dex? He was more like the severely disturbed monkey kept in the isolation chamber too long.

It hurt too much to think about Jax. And unconditional love.

"Yes. Even when you barely have any family, it's complicated," Mick said, bringing me back to the here and now. "Sindy telling tales out of school about me?"

"I learned a little about your history, too," I admitted.

Mick pressed his lips into a hard line, nodding. He moved to pick up a tiny blue bird he had fashioned out of fondant off the wax paper in front of him. With a little bit of gummy glue, he adhered it to a toothpick. The bird made me think of his tattoo, and what it meant to him. Reassurance that solid ground—home—couldn't be too far away. It must've been what he was trying to reassure himself about since his mother left.

"She wasn't a bad person," he said softly, running his finger over the top of the thatched roof to decide where to place such a small, but significant, creature. "She was just a scared kid. You know, we shared a birthday."

I nodded.

"But every year she made a cake and it was for me. The flavors I

wanted, the decorations I asked for. The candles . . . and the wishes . . .
She always thought of me first."

He perched the bird on the exact middle point of the ark's roof,
gently pushing the toothpick in so the bird was flush to the shingles.
"Someday I might try to find her again," he said softly. "When I've got
my act together." He smiled and placed something in my palm.

It was a second little blue bird. A helpmate.

I carefully held it as Mick attached a toothpick to the underside.

"Will you do the honors?" he asked.

"Where should she go?"

"Anywhere you want her to go."

I nestled the bird next to its mate. What had Bear said about swallows? That they mated for life.

"I had great role models in my aunt and uncle." Mick ducked down
to examine the birds at eye level, smiling with satisfaction. "My mom
did right by me, leaving them in charge."

"Sindy told me about how she raised you like her own. And took
care of Nash, too."

Mick pinched a thin chocolate snake and dropped it on the deck
of the boat. Then he shot me a pointed look. "Did she tell you what
he did in return? How she and my uncle took out a second mortgage
on the bakery to help get him to California, to help set him up for his
so-called sure thing? He blew through their money out there faster
than you can say Ponzi scheme. Girls, clothes, drugs . . . oh yeah, and
his 'Jumpstart My Heart' demo. Don't even get me started on that.
Everything Nash has in this life was begged, borrowed, or stolen."

He didn't add it, but I knew what he was thinking. *Even you.*

I gulped a mouthful of the sweet bakery air. "I . . . I had no idea."

"My aunt is too much of a class act to talk about it. The day my
uncle crashed through the window? He wasn't coming to work that
day. The bakery had been foreclosed on. Shuttered. Waiting for a short
sale. But we bakers . . ." He took the snake's mate and slung it through

the slats on the boat's railing. "We are creatures of habit. And we're ever hopeful that things are going to work out in the end. He was doing his daily drive-by. Hoping for some miracle."

"Well, in a way, he got it." I touched his gloved hand lightly. "You came home, right?"

Mick

BUSTED

It was hard to see Dani's eyes when she used that waterfall of hair to hide behind, those sun-drenched kinks veiling her delicate features. But I heard all the warmth and understanding in her voice that I had been longing for, since having had to leave New Orleans before I could find her. I gently placed my other hand over hers, and we stood there for a long moment, amid the industrial baking racks and under the bright fluorescent lighting as my workers buzzed by us. Even through the annoying barrier of my stupid poly gloves, it felt intimate and exciting.

"You know so much about me. Isn't it time you let a little slip about you?" I asked.

Dani smiled and gave a modest little shrug. "I'm used to being everyone's rock. Sometimes it's hard to let others chip away at the stone. Maybe someday, Mick."

Despite all the ordinary chaos going on around us, it felt like we had climbed up a steep incline, just the two of us, and had been transported to somewhere wholly new.

"Thanks again for coming to the rescue with my sister's cake. She said they loved it."

"Thank *you*," I said. And her smile confirmed what I had suspected; asking me to "re-bake" Posy's cake was her way of saying that all misunderstandings down in New Orleans were behind us.

"I'd better get back," she finally said, and moved away, a wave of regret in her breezy tone.

"I'll walk you up," I said, peeling off the gloves. I wished my hands could touch hers now, and I felt an undercurrent of lust surge as we made our way to the front of the shop.

"Uh-oh, don't look now!" Tom hissed a warning. "I told you she would catch on to you."

I caught a glimpse of the customer clanging past the bells on the door, and ducked behind the big glass counter like a soldier jumping into a foxhole, dragging Dani with me.

"I demand to see Mick Spencer!"

"Is that your mother of the bride?" Dani whispered, peeping between the desserts on doilies in the case, taking in what I was seeing: the marshmallow orthopedic shoes, the knee-high stockings that didn't quite make it up to her knees, and the clutch on a cheap pocketbook that would no doubt come to bop me on the head, if given the chance.

"Please. Give me a little credit, will you?" I replied. "That's Mrs. Vega. Angie's mother." She had to have a good ten years on Mandy Davis, and her no-nonsense, old-world ways made her seem even older.

"If he is not here," she trilled to Tom in the South of the Border–meets–Southern belle accent she had cultivated after moving here from Mexico in her teens, "I will wait. I've got all day."

I squeezed my eyes shut, took a deep breath, and slid open the case on the pretense of grabbing a cheesecake. "Oh, hey, Mrs. Vega. What can I—"

"The jig is up, Mick Spencer." She slapped her hands on the top of the glass to show she meant business. "You think I don't know what you and my Angie are doing?"

I heard Dani's sharp intake of breath. Great. I know how that must've sounded to her. Rolling my eyes heavenward, I said a silent prayer. If I kept my mouth shut, Mrs. Vega would absolve me all by herself. Sure enough . . .

"How dare you let my baby girl fool that boy into thinking your *polvorones* are Palomar's *polvorones*? I see her sneaking your white boxes"—she wagged a finger at a stack on the counter, all with the telltale Night Kitchen label—"into the Dumpster at our restaurant after she empties them into one of our takeout boxes. And then off she goes"—Mrs. Vega arced her arm through the air as if she were conducting an angry orchestra—"to Jenkins Auto Body, sweet as pie. Six months now, Mick!"

"People do crazy things when they're in love, Mrs. Vega." I couldn't stop the smile from spreading over my face. Dani was watching with interested amusement.

"That's the problem! That boy is going to fall in love with her, and what's going to happen when he realizes his bride cannot bake a decent Mexican wedding cookie to save her life, eh? This is a crazy scheme!"

Other customers in the shop, who had paused with guarded looks, began to ease back into their shopping, some laughing quietly behind their hands.

"You need to do right by my *niña*, young man! Promise me, that? You need to bring her in here, and you need to teach her how to make a *polvoron* she can be proud of." She hung her head, shaking it sadly. "Because the Lord knows, I cannot. The day I can make mine taste like yours will be the day I die happy."

"Okay, Mrs. Vega," I laughed. "I promise. Only problem is, Bear's already in love with her."

"Then you'd better hurry up." She clicked her tongue. "*En nombre del amor*, Mick. And give me a half dozen to go, please. In a bag."

"For you? They're on the house."

Dani shook her head slowly as I bagged the cookies and sent Angie's mom on her way.

"What?" I asked innocently.

"You never told Bear?"

"What would I say? 'It's my cookies that have been giving you a hard-on every week for the last six months'? I'm just the baker. Angie's gotta be the lovemaker. And the risk taker."

Angie had broken his heart back in the day. Now it was her job to jumpstart it again.

"She's courting him with Mexican wedding cakes." Dani sighed happily. "That is so sweet!"

"Oh? But not when I do it?" I asked, palms out.

Dani slid a fresh pair of poly gloves onto my hands and dropped a kiss on my cheek. "Get back to your baking, baker."

"Maybe you should come back when Angie does," I called after her. "You might learn a thing or two!"

Mick

SI NOS DEJAN

Bear bounded down the stairs in a huge, wide-brimmed sombrero and high, tight black embroidered pants.

"Oh, hell no." Quinn did a double take.

"Hell to the yes." Bear tugged on the short jacket. "The guy who usually plays *guitarrón* has shingles. The gig, she is mine!" He raised a fist triumphantly. I'm pretty sure that was code language for the fact that he was finally going to score with Angie, who got out of waiting tables on the nights when she played violin in the mariachi band. "Who's coming down to Palomar for dinner tonight?"

Quinn looked at Nash, and Nash looked at Quinn. Something had broken open over the last week, and I couldn't quite put my finger on it. Maybe it had something to do with guests in the house. Nash's celebrity status kept the reservation book full, which, in turn, kept Quinn busy. Warmth and energy reverberated through the Half Acre. Proprietor and star attraction were on their best behavior, but it wasn't their usual wary circling: sizing each other up like caged animals. They seemed to be looking at each other in a new light. The vacant look had left Nash's eyes, especially when he gazed at his son.

"Logan is cooking for us at home," Quinn said.

"Breakfast for dinner," Nash supplied. "I taught him how to cook an egg in the nest. Remember those?"

"Do I ever." I could practically smell the butter in the pan, browning before Nash's dad could get the bagel in fast enough. *Why use bread when the bagel has the hole already built in?* His dad would shrug over his logic, tilting back a beer and supervising us as we cracked eggs into the center. *Stand back, you little fuckers,* he'd say, when it was time to do the flipping. *I've never broken a yolk yet. This is Scott's Special.* He'd serve them up on paper plates and we'd sit on the floor of the trailer, dipping pieces of the bagel into the delicate center. The crispy, fried whites were never runny, and the yolk was always liquid-gold perfection. Every damn time. Nash's dad was a sad drunk, and unpredictable when sober, but when he cooked those Scott's Specials for us, we ate like kings.

"Logan's Special." Nash smiled at the renaming, and I was glad he had been able to pass a good memory down to his son. "I still can't get him to eat one, though."

"I'm free. How 'bout it, Dani?" I asked. "Mariachi Monday?"

She laughed. "This I gotta see."

"Well, it's about frickin' time!" Bear drawled. "I've been trying to get you out to see one of my tributes for weeks."

Logan bounded into the room, his eyes lighting up at the sight of Bear's Charro costume. He made the taco sign and gave us all an angelic grin.

"Why, you little schemer!" It was good to see Quinn laughing. "You're going to cook us dinner and then cut out on us?"

Logan threw out the name sign he'd given his uncle, two swipes of his hands like bear claws, followed by the universal *I love you* sign, which he zoomed up into the air.

Dani laughed. "I believe he just said he's Bear's wingman."

"I guess we've got ourselves a chaperone," I murmured to Dani.

Palomar wasn't kitschy Mexican. It was a cozy refuge, with amber lights that hinted at subtropical warmth and subdued terra-cotta walls. But it came alive with Mariachi Monday, and when the band stopped at your table, you were on the spot to sing along with your requested song.

We settled in with sangria and ordered a root beer for Logan, which he held exactly like his father, encircling the top of the bottle with his thumb and index finger before turning it up to his lips, cocky and confident. Hangman was the name of the game using the paper placemats on the top of the table, but underneath was a different story. Her knee had brushed mine the minute we slid into the booth, and I did my damnedest to keep it there, anchoring my foot firmly along the side of her sandal.

"Camelburp?" I protested, as Logan gleefully hung me from his crayon-hewn noose and filled in all the letters I had missed before my time, and available limbs, ran low. "Should've been two words, buddy." I flashed him the number two with my hand. "I totally would've had that, otherwise," I said to Dani, whose pretty lips were pressed into a smile behind her fruity sangria glass. "How do you sign 'cheater'?" I asked her.

"I don't know the sign for it, but you can finger spell it," she said, demonstrating. Logan put his hands on his hips, and Dani mock-discreetly gestured that it was really me who was the cheater, not him.

"Nuh-uh." I shook my head, and worked my fingers through the letters, aiming them at him.

Logan just laughed, shook his head, and began to draw another gallows pole.

"Picking on a ten-year-old," Dani ribbed me. "Nice. Although maybe he turned eleven, given the time it took you to sign that word."

"Har har. So I'm a slow learner. You up for schoolin' me?" I nudged her bare ankle, and she in turn tipped her toe and dragged it across the top of my laces.

Tilting her head, she regarded me. "All that time growing up near the Half Acre, and you didn't learn any signs?" To Logan, she signed the letter *P* and earned a nice round head in the noose for her trouble.

My libido tensed and took a nosedive at her question. "I grew up in the shadow of the Half Acre," I said slowly. "My mom worked there, cleaning rooms. Under the table. But I wasn't really allowed inside."

Our food arrived, and we dug into the homemade, spicy fare. Logan was wholly immersed in a burrito, bigger than the size of his head, and between bites, I felt it safe to confide in Dani. "When Mr. and Mrs. Bradley weren't around, she would bring me to work with her. I'd sit in that turreted nook, you know, the one in the front room? And she'd read me books, and we'd pretend we lived there."

Dani touched my hand that was fidgeting with the stem of my sangria glass.

"She got fired. And then . . . well, Sindy told you. But there's one detail you won't find in the papers . . . I went and confronted Bill Bradley. Demanded to know if he was my father. He denied it. That was . . . the day of the fire."

"Oh, Mick." Dani's brow creased with concern.

"I carried that guilt with me for long after, telling myself I must've been the reason Bear and Quinn lost their parents." I shook my head. "Silly, right? He obviously had a lot of other problems, and I would've been the least of them."

"Did you ever tell Bear or Quinn?" Dani wanted to know. "I mean, there are ways—"

I shook my head and managed a smile. "It doesn't matter. I've . . . made peace with it all."

But had I, really? I had split town soon after. First, in pursuit of my mother, who I last heard was in Florida. Then up the coast, raising hell till Sindy and Walt threw me into culinary school. Then down to New Orleans, a good a place to get lost in as any.

The exuberant blare of a trumpet cut my words to a clip. The mariachi band had made it to our table, consisting of a beaming Angie serenading us with a careen of her violin bow, Bear grinning at us behind the big-ass wooden Mexican guitar, her mustachioed grandfather on a regular acoustic, and Angie's stern-looking father, red in the face as he blew his trumpet and placed himself between the two lovebirds, who kept making eyes at each other as they sang.

"Any requests?" Bear bellowed to us. He quickly signed something to Logan.

"What did you tell him?" I asked.

"I told him nobody better request 'La Bamba' or I'd kick their ass," Bear said.

"Bear!" Dani admonished the shaggy-haired *guitarrón* player. "We should wash your hands off with soap for swearing."

"How about that song you were singing in the shower today?" I joked.

"You heard that?" Bear asked.

"Dude, the whole B and B heard it."

"'*Si Nos Dejan*,' everyone." Bear grinned at Angie's extended family and began to count off. Angie's wide brown eyes grew even larger and sparkled with tears, but she grinned and busied herself with positioning the violin under her chin. Meanwhile, Mr. Vega looked like he was going to bust a vein as he glared at Bear and began to play.

Bear sang along easily, meeting Angie's grandfather's baritone with a mellow harmony that could only come from having melded his voice for a myriad of tributes over the years. Whatever the words were that were spilling from his mouth, he seemed to be nailing them to a T. Angie's mother bustled out from behind the hostess station, happily shaking maracas and trying to catch her husband's eye, but he just squeezed them shut and continued to play. As the song dwindled down, she handed the maracas to Logan, who gladly set down his executioner's crayon and joined the band as they began to drift to the next table.

"*Gracias*," Bear said, as I slid a twenty into the hole of his instrument where he collected tips. With a wink at Dani, he strolled off in those tight pants and that ridiculous hat to join the rest of the Vega family, and Logan, who was shaking his moneymaker with glee.

Dani leaned across the table, eyes wide and shining. "What do you think that was all about?" she asked, her smile wanting in on the joke.

"I haven't a clue," I said truthfully. "But whatever that song was that he dished out, had Angie and Mrs. Vega eating it up with a spoon."

Dani laughed. "Wow. I can't believe he can play and sing like that."

"Yeah," I said, pouring more sangria for the two of us. "Bear can play circles around Nash."

Dani grew quiet at the mention of his name. I wondered if she had noticed the closeness growing between him and Quinn, and how she felt about it. *Careful what you wish for, Mickey*, I could hear my mother say. Logan returned, and we ate the rest of our meal in silence.

Driving past the Night Kitchen on the way home, I glimpsed Nash's Porsche out front. It looked like he and Quinn had decided to have dessert out. Whether Dani noticed or not, she didn't say anything.

"Bedtime, buddy." I made a sleeping motion with my hands under my tilted head. He held out his hand and made a motion with his fingers for our shared notepad.

Can I play you my song first?

I showed Dani what he had written. "How can we deny that?" she asked, amused.

Logan raced upstairs and returned with his guitar, and a journal.

He propped the book up, pulled a sheet of lined paper from it, and arranged the guitar carefully on his knees. With a bit of fanfare, he stroked the pick slowly down the strings before carefully forming his first bar chord.

I could see Nash's diagrams and lettering littered over the note-paper, but the lyrics were written separately, in the journal.

Without warning
Dawn slices through the night
I said I'd stay
Till the morning
You know I tried with all my might
Don't blame me for leaving
Blame the time, the place, the night
How was I to know
Without warning
Something would start to feel so right

Logan took turns strumming, signing the words, and smiling at us. The crazy thing was, it sounded like a song. And even crazier, the lyrics weren't written in Nash's handwriting. They were written in Quinn's.

My mind raced. It was always my first instinct to blame Nash for everything, and not trust him as far as I could kick him. But Quinn? Was she sneaking off with him on the sly? And here I had pushed them together, during that stupid double date and after, begging her to spend as much time as possible with her son's father so I could have more time with Dani.

I tapped the cover of the journal questioningly. Logan gave me an innocent shrug. Every room had a journal, even those occupied by the inn's regular residents. I rarely used mine, only to jot down a design idea or dessert recipe. Bear probably used his to keep track of his tribute itinerary. Logan's, of course, had become our secret commu-nication handbook. I had no doubt that Quinn normally kept her journal under lock and key, probably under the mattress of her Teen Dream canopy bed. I handed the book to Logan and pointed up the stairs, indicating he should put it back where he found it. He began his trudge up the stairs.

Dani was at the computer for guests' use that sat in the nook under the spiral stairs. Corn silk curls fell before her eyes as she leaned over the keyboard. I tucked a lock behind her ear, watching as the screen lit up her eyes. Her hand flew to her mouth.

"What's up?"

"'*Si Nos Dejan*' . . . Bear's song tonight? It's a traditional proposal song." Now the screen was reflected in her tear-filled eyes. A smile slipped out from behind her hand. "It's known to have the most romantic lyrics and melody you will ever hear in a song . . . according to Wikipedia."

"Well now, gotta trust the divine oracle of Wikipedia," I joked. "*Si Nos Dejan* . . . What's that translate to?" The height of my Spanish language exposure was circa tenth grade and pretty rusty.

"If They Allow Us," Dani said softly, clicking the Internet browser closed. The words, on her lips, sounded like the most beautiful and forlorn thing. Her eyes were shaded a melancholy blue as I wrapped my arms around her.

"It kills me to listen to you and Nash make love, night after night, knowing what I know," I blurted.

Dani's angelic eyebrows rose. "And what's that?"

"That Nash has no intention of marrying you."

"And?" She didn't bat an eye.

"And that the evening you spent with me in New Orleans meant way more than you're letting on."

"Ah." Dani stood up and moved toward the stairs. "Follow me, I want to show you something." There was no flirtation in her voice. "Well?"

I followed her up the spiraling staircase. She raised her brows at me as she pushed open the door to her room.

"Olive!" The Half Acre's most elusive resident was perched in the middle of the bed, not a care in the world. When she saw me, she gave a mew and rolled over on her back, one paw up in the air like she wanted a high five. "You furry little traitor!"

Dani smirked. "She's been sleeping with me every night."

"Lucky cat."

I'd been in room number twelve before, but not since she and Nash began . . . occupying it. Still, it looked the same as I remembered. King bed. Old couch. And a great view of the river and orchard. Dani slowly eased the engagement ring off her finger and set it on the nightstand. I moved to the window and peered out at the view illuminated by the moon, my memory conjuring up the voices of children as they wove between the trees.

Mick the Spic!

Stewie Nash is trailer trash!

Nash, Bear, and I would scurry up the slats nailed to the big maple and hunker down on the wooden platform wedged between the branches. We'd throw rotten apples from our arsenal, pelting Queen Quinn and her friends, to drive them out of the orchard. *Get out! No girls allowed!*

And in later years, when Bear would pin his sister to the garden gate and let us kiss her through the scrollwork. Punishment for some wrong she had inflicted upon him at the time. *Cooties!* she'd yell, kicking at our shins under the gate with all she had.

It was easier when it had simply been boys against girls. Now things were far more complicated.

Dani's hand slipped under my shirt, and I felt her lips brush the back of my neck. "Come to the bed," she hushed into my ear, sending ripples of pleasure through me. She broke away and walked to the edge of it. I followed, picking up the ring between my thumb and forefinger.

"Did you know that, traditionally, a bride used to pass tiny, fortune-blessed morsels of cake to guests through her own wedding ring?" I held it close between us as I inspected it, matching her stare through the small platinum band.

Her lips parted as her gaze dropped to my mouth. "No more stories," she whispered, pulling the ring from my hand and setting it down again. I reached for her. She shook her head, stepping behind me. "Shirt off. Facedown, please."

I slowly peeled my shirt off, and lowered myself down.

"This," she said softly, straddling the backs of my thighs, "is what I do with Nash, up here in this room."

I felt an elbow dig deep into a knot between my shoulder blades, eliciting a moan from me that vibrated through my skull. Sweet pain and agonizing pleasure buzzed through every nerve ending.

"What do you think of that?" Humor laced her tone, followed by a satisfied click of her tongue as the knot in my muscle dissolved under her touch and she attacked another one.

"I think those elbows are lethal weapons," I managed.

"Yep. Registered weapons in ten different states." She cooed close to my ear as she moved firm, warm hands over my shoulders. "How's the old baker's arm?"

I laughed. "You tell me." Hours spent lifting, kneading, whisking, folding, and cake decorating were murder on the shoulders.

"Ice is your friend, especially with repetitive motion strain. And so is a good massage therapist." Her fingers gently kneaded the past twelve hours of work out of my joints and my mind.

"Oh yeah, right there. Don't stop." I groaned loud enough to shake the apples from the trees outside. I realized how it sounded, but I didn't care. "Nash is a lucky bastard."

"Nash is a friend," she began slowly, "who happened to need a good massage therapist. And an unusual favor." Pressure eased as she raised herself slightly, giving me the advantage to rotate quickly, still beneath her. God, she was gorgeous. My thumb grazed the bottom of her lip, tracing its troubled path.

"I don't mix business with pleasure, Spencer."

It was the first time she had called me that, since the day Nash introduced us. Not that we had needed an introduction. Her body, her voice, her laughter had been etched deep below the smooth, shallow surface she and I had been skating on since she arrived in New Hope. Grooves with no end, constantly spinning through my thoughts and emotions. Like a beautiful song that I couldn't quite put my finger on, yet I couldn't stop humming its tune.

"I don't understand."

There was a shimmer in the satin ice of her eyes as she blinked to stave off the tears. "I know. And I'm sorry I can't tell you more. I never would've agreed . . . never would've even come here if I had known you—"

"Shhh, no. Don't say that." My fingertips brushed the feathery curls falling over her cheeks as she slowly shook her head. "Dani."

Her hands braced my shoulders, and just as I rose to her touch, she pushed off the bed and stood. My shirt was handed to me at the door.

"I can't mix business with pleasure."

Dani

POLVORONE PALS

A repentant Angie blew into the bakery in a cloud of perfume and a clack of high heels. "God. My mother." She covered her eyes with her hands, those long red nails mingling with her wavy black bangs. "I'm so embarrassed, Mick. I'm sorry."

"Don't be sorry. I'm happy to show you. You remember Dani, right? From mariachi night? She's here to learn, too."

Angie flashed me a bright smile. "Of course."

Within minutes, Mick had us in aprons and up to our elbows in confectioner's sugar and ground pecans.

"So you're staying with my Bear, then?" she asked. I liked that she was so fondly and unabashedly possessive. "At the Half Acre?"

"Yes, for a little while longer. Just until Nash gets his award," I explained. I wasn't sure how much Bear spoke about family dynamics in mixed company, but I figured basic was better.

Angie's smile hardened. "Hasn't Nash taken enough from this town?"

I winced; there really weren't a lot of members in the Nash Drama fan club.

"Here." Mick interrupted us, placing a huge bowl of flour in front of us. "Dani, cut the butter and add it to the flour in chunks. Angie, get in there with your hands and mix it. Don't break a nail."

Angie smirked and flipped a plastic-gloved middle finger in his direction. We got back to work, no choice but to make nice in such forced proximity.

"So, you've known Bear a long time, then?" I ventured.

Angie's long lashes fanned against the tops of her cheeks as she smiled down into the bowl. "Since the ninth grade. He was always so sweet to me. But my dad was pretty strict." She sighed, plunging her hands in the flaky, crumbly dough. "Bear didn't give up, though. He always held that candle for me. And the feeling was very, very mutual."

I smiled, thinking of Bear telling me back at the garage about swallows mating for life, as he had nibbled thoughtfully on one of "Angie's" cookies.

"We even went to prom together. Finally, my father gave just that little bit." She emphasized with her sticky thumb and her index finger. "Bear was so excited. He even got Old Man Jenkins to loan him his antique Rolls-Royce for the night."

Her words played out like a movie in my head, and I pictured a young Bear and Angie, dressed to the nines, sliding into the fanciest car. Nostalgia washed over me as I remembered heading to prom with Jax in that sleek, sexy white Lotus on loan from his family. It was followed by a wave of sadness so profound, I had to stop what I was doing.

I missed my beautiful friend.

Jax hadn't deserved the horrible treatment I had given him.

"Here. You have a turn squishing the dough." Angie offered up her spot in front of the large bowl. "It feels so good under your fingers."

She was right; diving into the butter and flour mixture was very therapeutic.

"Of course, the crazy car was so old, it broke down on the way home. Bear tried everything to get it started, but we were out on this deserted road and couldn't get a jump"—her laugh turned sultry at the memory—"so we just passed the time, if you know what I mean."

"Wow, go Bear!" I giggled, and she jostled me like Laney would've, had we been kissing and telling back in high school.

"He even wrote me a song that night . . ." She sighed at the memory. "The sweetest song. It broke my heart to have to walk away. But at the time? Family." She knocked her fist sadly to her heart. "I was late coming home, and my dad threw a holy fit. I was forbidden to see Bear after that, or any of the Bradleys."

She turned toward the walk-in to make sure Mick wasn't in earshot. "You know, my mom and Mick's mom were neighbors. The Latina girls in this town, they all stuck up for each other back then. Didn't matter if they were Mexican, Puerto Rican, younger, older . . . my mom was like a big sister to her. She always said . . ."

Angie drifted off as Mick came back for the next step. He stood at my side, guiding me as I sifted the powdery pecan sugar mixture into the dough. I loved watching his strong, tan arms strain, and the way the dark hair curled at his wrists. I was so distracted, I almost lost half the mixture to the floor.

"Can't take you ladies anywhere, can I?" His teasing was affectionate, but the sexy arch of his brow was directed solely at me. My hands might've been covered in Mexican wedding cake dough, but my belly felt full of Mexican jumping beans.

"Nope," Angie said. "Just leave us be in the kitchen, Mick. Shoo."

He gave us scooping instructions and did indeed leave us alone, and with just the rest of the kitchen staff bustling behind us, Angie continued her story.

"My mother always said the Bradleys had too many skeletons in their closet. And after the fire, well . . . too many ghosts in their river."

I rolled a ball of dough in quiet contemplation, thinking about Mick confronting Quinn and Bear's dad. The guilt that must've followed him, after mustering up such courage, was a heartbreaking thought.

Together, Angie and I placed ball after ball of the dough on cookie sheets Mick had provided, giving each a gentle tap, and into the oven they went.

"Well, Boss," Angie demanded, as Mick pulled one of our golden brown baked goods from a cooling tray and nipped it with gusto.

Lucky cookie.

"Airy, buttery . . . slight crunch," he noted, dropping the rest onto his tongue. "Mmm. You ladies must've had a great teacher."

Angie gave him a one-two punch while sneaking a cookie sample to try. "Want one, Dani?"

"Not so fast," Mick said. He had shakers of confectioner's sugar in his hands. "Go ahead, go wild," he advised, as we showered them with an extra dusting of powdered sugar. "These cookies can take it. Now, try."

Angie and I paused, cookies held poised at our respective mouths, and both bit down at the same time. The customers up front must've assumed a three-way was in progress, given the groans of satisfaction.

"Tastes better when you make it yourself, eh, Angie?"

"And easier than I thought," she agreed. "I wonder why my mother's always fall flat, then?"

"Too much butter. And I'm pretty sure she overworks the dough," Mick ventured a guess.

Angie smirked. "My mother? Overworking, and fussing too much over something? You don't say."

We boxed up some of our handiwork, and Mick had his staff plate the rest for today's offerings behind the glass displays. "I think I'm going to bring mine to Bear," Angie said, twirling her white box by its candy cane bakery twine. "I'll give you a ride, Dani. But first . . ." She blinked confectioner's sugar off the mascara lengthening her lashes and laughed, "I think a trip to the powder room to de-powder myself is in order."

I turned to Mick. "Thanks for the baking lesson."

"Don't think this gets you off the hook, you know. We still have a tasting to do."

I pressed my lips into a sheepish smirk, and he pushed his flat, black bakers' toque back a bit with his hand. "You know what I think?" he added.

"What?"

"I think you're dragging your heels picking out a cake because you don't really want to marry Nash."

"Really. Well maybe I haven't picked out a cake yet because I want to keep spending time with you."

"Same thing."

"Not really."

"So . . . you *want* to marry Nash then, *and* spend time with me?" He grabbed an order form from the counter next to him.

"I didn't say that."

"My point proven," he said smugly, placing pencil to paper.

I laughed. "Your point is broken."

He mock frowned at the pencil. "Okay, so you're right about one thing." He tossed it, and the order form, onto the counter. "But this charm you pulled from your sister's cake?"

I held my breath; his fingers had found an excuse to fondle the bit of silver gracing my neck. "What about it?"

"I don't think it means you'll be the next to marry."

"No?"

"No. There's usually—and there probably was—a ring charm. I think pulling the cake charm meant you were destined to meet a baker."

I paused outside the door of room number twelve. I could hear the chords of the song Nash had been working on with Logan. Taking a deep breath, I turned the knob.

Nash was by himself, a pair of noise-canceling headphones on. He was strumming with his eyes closed, his lips moving slight but silent.

I wondered if he could, like Bear had said, "feel" the music. He began singing louder, adding a new verse to the song I hadn't heard before.

Faking your way
Leading me along
Dying each day
As I sing you my song

He seemed to feel my presence, as he soon opened his eyes and stopped playing. Slowly, he pulled off the headphones.

"'Jumpstart My Heart' . . . that wasn't your biggest hit, was it? It was Bear's song."

Nash set his guitar into its velvet-lined case with the gentleness of a lover, snapped it shut, and turned to me. "So what if it was?"

"So?" I sputtered at his inability to grasp the significance of the situation. "You took a song that some guy poured his heart and soul into, and passed it off as your own? And made thousands . . . I don't know, maybe millions of dollars on it?"

"Go on." He pulled his shirt over his head, and shucked off his pants. "I'm listening."

I watched, incredulous, as he climbed right up between the sheets on the massage table and lay down on his belly. Reaching back, he yanked the top sheet over his glutes and a moment later, his boxers fell to the floor.

Something caught my eye and I stepped closer. He had added a second blue swallow to his opposite shoulder, just like he had said he wanted to, early on.

Nash did whatever he wanted.

The new tattoo was still raw and red. I had half a mind to rake my fingernails over its fresh ink to show him what I thought of it. But I couldn't.

Dependability, respect, and the utmost professionalism while you work with the artists.

"I can't do this any longer."

"Dani, he gave it to me."

"What do you mean?"

"Bear gave me the song. He didn't want it after Angie Vega up and married some cholo to please her father. He vowed to never play it again, and told me to do with it what I pleased."

I heard Angie's bitter query in my head: *Hasn't Nash taken enough from this town?*

"So you spun it into radio gold, and now he has to hear it every day of his life? How do you think that makes him feel? Or Angie, for that matter?"

Now I wanted very badly to lay my hands on him. But I wanted to hurt him, not heal him. He was the faker. Just like the words he'd just sung. But the pain he had left in his wake was real.

"I changed my mind. I want you to work on my front, not on my back today."

When I didn't move, he made a motion to. My mind went into automatic work mode then. *The comfort level and privacy of your client must be kept in mind at all times.* I pressed my body against the top sheet, keeping it secure against the table. "You can turn over now," I instructed. "Away from me." The top sheet remained taut as he shifted, coming to rest on his back, and I saw tears glistening in his eyes.

"I know," he said quietly. "It doesn't matter how many miles I log, or how many damn birds I tattoo on me." He squeezed his eyes shut, and let the tears roll in hot rivulets to his ears. "There's no going around it. I know what I put them through. And Quinn, too. I'm going to make it right, Dani."

"Well, that would be a bridge or two mended." I took his hands in mine and smiled. "What about Quinn?"

"Quinn's a superhero mixed with a saint, wrapped up in a friend, inside a total MILF." His description made me laugh. He sighed. "I need to tell her. Everything. But I'm scared I'll lose her."

I didn't know what to tell him. That was a chance he was going to have to take.

Dani

CAKE COURTSHIP

The night of my tasting had arrived.

Closed for Private Party, read a new sign on the Night Kitchen door in those curvy, eclectic letters, yet the heavy blue-black door yielded under my push. The only lights on were the night stars, twinkling on the sky of the ceiling.

Mick was behind the counter, waiting. Leaning forward on locked arms.

Bracing himself, for me.

I think we both knew we were so far beyond the pretense of a bridal cake consult.

"James, party of one?" His voice echoed richly through the empty, tall-ceilinged space.

"Lead the way."

Two of the high-topped tables were pushed together, displaying an assortment of small square plates. Petit four–sized bites of unfrosted cake sat on the plates in neat little rows, arranged by color. Judging from their subtle hues, I guessed there had to be at least a dozen flavor possibilities. Tiny silver forks impaled each sample. Accompanying them were shot glasses filled with frostings, each with their own little demitasse spoon.

It was after eight o'clock. And my sweet tooth was in trouble.

Mick pulled out a chair for me like a waiter at a fancy restaurant. I felt his thumb tangle in one lone curl along the ridge of my collarbone and linger there, as he guided the chair in place.

"Shall we start with the tame and move over to the more exotic?"

"I'll follow your lead."

"Who am I kidding? There's nothing tame about my cakes." Smiling that wicked smile, he sat down next to me and slowly rolled up the sleeves of his white button-down shirt.

"Yellow butter cake." He picked up the first fork and swirled it with rich, velvety frosting. "With chocolate buttercream."

The fork was cold but his gaze was hot as he watched me devour the fresh, firm tidbit.

"Simple. Classic . . . ," I praised.

"It's missionary position with the lights out. Tired. Boring. Here, try."

He slathered the next cube of snow-white cake with a deep blushing cream, and pushed it past my lips. "White chocolate with raspberry," he announced, as I gasped.

The sweet richness of the white chocolate combined with the tart fruitiness seemed like a perfect choice for celebrating a union that touted "in sickness and in health, for richer for poorer" and all that jazz. Until he held up a deceptively ordinary-looking white-on-white sample.

"Any guesses?"

"Um . . . vanilla on vanilla?"

Mick pretended to be highly offended. "Just for that, I don't think you deserve to try this one." He lifted the fork to his own mouth, then made a stealth U-turn and toppled it right onto my tongue as I laughed. Creamy coconut and tangy lime shocked my taste buds.

"Did I just hear you moan?" he asked, incredulous . . . and looking incredibly pleased with himself.

"Whatever happened to just plain, underrated vanilla?" I asked helplessly.

He rested his elbows on the table and steepled his fingers to his lips. One rogue brow arched playfully. "You don't strike me as a classic vanilla." I felt his knee brush mine. "You don't kiss like you're classic vanilla," he added.

"Like you'd remember how I kiss," I challenged. "You've had a lot of . . . *tastings* since then, I'm sure."

"I'm pretty sure I remember everything about that night." He manipulated a few strokes across the keyboard of his computer and the gentle jangle of guitars and tambourine began to play. "But refresh my memory."

I took his outstretched hand, and we began to move to Mazzy Star's "Fade Into You," under the starry Night Kitchen sky.

"You're chocolate-bourbon cake with praline buttercream," he murmured, as my forearms came to rest on his broad shoulders for the first time since leaving him in New Orleans. We danced with no masks, no disguises to hide behind.

"You're a tower of whisper-thin French crepes . . ." I shivered with delight as his fingertips ran lightly up the delicate undersides of my arms ". . . three hundred layers, filled with lavender-infused cream. You're naked almond, with just a dusting of powdered sugar." He breathed me in, nuzzling my neck.

"Mick, you're the only taste I've been craving."

Mick

BUSINESS AND PLEASURE

Her lips were the sweetest flavor, sweeping across mine. There was no way of duplicating that complex and heady mixture I'd first sampled in New Orleans with any recipe I knew of, but time had tested it. Enhanced it. Heightened my appreciation for it.

"Girl, you've got some sweet voodoo, you know that?"

"You bring it out in me." She bit her lip. "What?" she wanted to know, as I just shook my head, in awe.

"Your eyes."

"Yeah, they're blue." She gave an embarrassed laugh.

"Nah, I'd say they're a two-to-one ratio of royal with sky." I was a serial color mixer; I had been for the better part of my life. I used to think there were more hues of color out there in the world than there were moods. But all the ways Dani made me feel . . .

"I forgot how amazing they were at close range," I whispered. She kept her eyes open as our noses gently bumped and I caught hold of her bottom lip in a soft tug-o'-war between both of my own. I felt her surrender, body blending to mine, and watched her face change in a hundred ways as she fell into my kiss.

I had wished with my eyes open for once, and it finally had come true.

Headlights swept high across the rear wall of the Night Kitchen, and a car door slammed. Julia Morris's husband hulked past the front windows toward the door, something large in his meaty hand.

"Oh, shit. Dani. Baby, listen to me. Get in the back, behind the counter."

"Not Mrs. Vega again?" She fiddled with my collar, thinking I was playing.

"I'm serious. Now."

She blinked as if coming out of a daze, and her eyes darted over mine, searching out the reason. As my hands dropped from her, she backed up. I cursed myself for not locking the door behind us, and considered making a run for the dead bolt now. Jimmy Morris had a short fuse and an assault record, and if he was lit up on Yuengling and Jäger shots, there was no reasoning with him.

"Spencer." His hulking form filled the doorway. It sounded like he had left his car running, which I couldn't decide was a good or a bad sign. The bag he carried was a brown-handled Night Kitchen bag, heavy from the looks of it.

"Hey, Jimmy. It's a little late for making a return."

People say your life passes before your eyes at such dire and critical moments, but the only thing I saw was the number of times Julia came on to me, the obvious and wanton lust just there for the taking. But I never once did take her up on it. She fucked me with her eyes over the countertop of Wolkoff's as we discussed serving sizes for her daughter's First Communion cake before I had even left for New Orleans, and had all but propositioned me the night before her wedding to Jimmy, a second marriage for both of them roughly a year ago. And the offers had stacked up, layer upon layer, during the time since.

"Yeah, I got a return for you, all right. You cocksucker." Drink had definitely roughed up his voice, and he looked like he had been choosing booze instead of showering the past few days.

"My loving wife told me she can't fuck me without thinking about you. How's that for a first anniversary gift? Huh?" With every word, his voice took on a manic curve, as he sidestepped closer to me. "And now, when I think about our wedding night, the happiest day of my goddamn life, how we took that cake of yours and fed it to each other? All I see is your goddamn jizz all over her face," he hollered, "and she's loving it!"

"I never touched her, man. I swear on my life."

I knew Dani had heard every word in the back room, and I hoped to God she had called 911. Jimmy was a frequent flier with the local police, and surely they knew how to talk him down. Defuse the situation. The hell if I knew. I eyed the bag, trying to remember if he had a license to carry a concealed firearm. There was a shooting range just up the road and I had no doubt half the townies in Bucks County rode by my shop in their pickup trucks, locked and loaded.

Jimmy laughed in a way that made my blood run cold. "You think it fucking matters, man?" He had tears trailing down into his grin turned grimace. "I can't be with her, knowing that she is fantasizing about you." His opposite hand swept into the bag, and it dropped away to the floor.

In that split second, I recognized the top tier of his wedding cake. Unlike his vows, it had survived the elements, nestled next to the Hot Pockets and unidentifiable foil-wrapped leftovers in the family freezer for the last year. And I even remembered the flavor, too.

With a roar, he lobbed the freezer-burnt cake at my head like a fondant rock. I ducked, and felt shards against my back as the entire glass display case to my right exploded.

My only thought was Dani, whom I had sent back there for safety.

The low moan of faraway sirens turned into a plaintive wail as two cruisers squealed to a stop in the middle of the street. I heard the shouts and the scuffle as Jimmy was subdued and restrained, but I focused every effort on finding Dani in the darkened back room. Shouted her name, blindly stumbling through the place I knew like the back of my hand, lost without her.

"Mick."

She was crouched low behind two rolling racks. The utility lights above the back exit door accentuated the tears streaking her cheeks as she turned her face up to meet my gaze.

"It's okay, baby. Everything's all right." She held out a shaking hand, and I helped her up. "Nothing happened with Julia. You have to believe me."

"I know. Take me back to the Half Acre, please," she said quietly. "I want to go home."

Dani

HELP ON THE WAY

It didn't matter that Mick was telling the truth. He was still mixing business with pleasure and I just couldn't. After all the chase and all the wanting . . . if I gave myself to him, I opened myself up to the danger that he may find the "having" not so pleasing as the "wanting." I kept my distance, and didn't visit him down at the bakery anymore.

My wanderlust had started to dig at me once again. Especially since Bear had got Mean Mistress Mustard street-ready. And since Nash was doing so well.

After testing the waters with Open School Night, Nash plunged headfirst into involving himself at Logan's school. While Riggs's list had suggested he donate some new equipment to the school's computer lab, I had convinced him that the kids would remember an in-school music performance for far longer. It wasn't long before Nash was performing at elementary and middle schools around the county, and talking to kids about caring for their communities. He seemed to genuinely enjoy it, and it didn't appear that he had just pulled the short straw in the draw.

With my help, he had also taken Quinn's honey-do list of crap that needed to be done and spun it up to a whole new level. It extended far past running Logan to his various activities. Staying active was helping keep Nash's AS flare-ups at bay, and it turned out, he had taken after his father when it came to home improvements.

"The place is looking good," Mick said one day, as he joined me for a jog through the orchard. "I didn't know the old girl—or Nash— had it in 'em. I guess you guys want the place to look as nice as possible for the wedding, huh?"

"That's the plan," I replied. But my mind hadn't been on Nash's and my nuptials for a while.

My phone, tucked into the waistband of my running pants, jangled a text.

WWDD if everyone in the world (and their mothers) was trying to plan her wedding for her?

Poor Laney. She and her mother had come to a tentative truce back in Hawaii, and had been closer than they ever had before. But knowing Vera Hudson, there was no way she was able to keep her nose out or her mouth shut when it came to her daughter's Big Day. Unless someone were to bind and gag her.

I'd do something romantic as hell. I texted back.

"What's up?" Mick asked.

"I'm channeling my inner Aunt Sindy, and giving wedding advice to my best friend." I smiled as my fingers flew across the keypad. Lord knows I had learned enough from her about the self-uniting Quaker licenses that were unique to this part of the country.

Got three days and two witnesses?

I hate everyone. Except Noah. And you and Jax. Will you be my witness?

The mention of Jax's name flooded me with guilt, but I pressed on. This was about Laney. This was her day.

Gladly. Just get your butt down here.

"Everything okay?" Mick asked.

"Yeah. If my friends come down here to get married next week, will you save a wedge o' wedding cake for them?"

"What are friends for? If not to help their friends," Mick made a point of saying. I smiled gratefully.

A VW bug rolled past the driveway, then backed up and tentatively crept up the gravel toward us.

Mick leaned down and addressed the two giggling girls through their lowered car window. "You lost, ladies?"

"Can you tell us how to get to the Half Acre Bed-and-Breakfast?"

"You're looking at it."

"Oh my God!" The passenger had spotted Nash, shirtless and up on the ladder again. "Is that Nash Drama?"

"Nope." I smiled. "That's the handyman. You can go see Quinn at the front desk to check in. I am sure Nash will make an appearance later."

By the beginning of October, the entire inn was occupied. The oracle of Bear had spoken the truth, apparently. Mick even moved out, despite everyone's protests, to the loft apartment above the Night Kitchen. "No excuses to be late for work," he joked, but I couldn't help wonder if it had something to do with me. He had even hired Angie, who had an interior design background, to help fix up the place. "But I promise to still make breakfast."

Bear continued to give tours of both the orchard, and all the childhood haunts of their favorite singer, although Quinn threatened him with bodily harm if he so much as walked them by the darkroom trailer.

Nash, surprisingly enough, was not opposed to making conversation . . . as long as it didn't take away from his quality time with Logan. The two got up early and shared a silent breakfast together, often forgoing Mick's elaborate fare in favor of just PB&Js, before heading up to Logan's room to work on scales. And that was on the weekdays, before the school bus even came.

One morning, I noticed something was different the moment I got downstairs, and it wasn't the fact that the entire dining room was buzzing with people. Logan was polishing off his customary PB&J for breakfast, but he was shirtless, and he had gel spiking up his normally tamed blond hair. Mick and Bear were bumping into each other and swearing in the kitchen.

"What the fuck is that?" Bear asked. He towered over the kitchen island, wearing platform heels that added four inches to his already six-plus lanky frame. His hair appeared to have been ironed flat and looked two shades darker. He had more make-up on than a hooker, and he was frowning over a brown-bag lunch.

"Logan loves chocolate pot de crème." Mick tried peering into the bag, but Bear was hogging it.

"Dude. I'm not sending my nephew to school with a foo-foo dessert in a fuckin' ramekin. He's gonna get beat up."

"You're gonna get beat up if he misses the bus because his lunch isn't ready." Mick gave Bear a dark glare as he slam-dunked a baggie full of celery and carrot sticks into the paper sack.

"Guys, what's going on here?" I asked. "Where's Quinn?"

"Oh, you want a piece of me?" Bear stood to full height, hands on hips. He wore his usual leather pants, but his top looked like some sort of leather bondage contraption. "Just because I'm wearing lipstick don't mean I can't kick your ass."

"Guys!" I hissed. "Stop. Now. And tell me what the hell is going on."

They both looked up at me. "It's Quinn," Mick finally said. "She won't get out of bed."

"What?" Quinn normally rivaled me for earliest early bird. "Is she sick?"

Bear pulled a Sharpie from his back pocket and wrote Logan's name on the bag, complete with a skull and crossbones to represent the O.

"It's okay. I've got this covered. I can get Logan off to school." Bear's last word was drowned out by the roaring of the school bus as it blew past the house. "Motherfucker!"

"She's . . . depressed," Mick said, voice low and through closed lips, with a concerned glance at Logan, who was draining a glass of milk and seemingly unaware.

I signed good morning to him, before turning back to the two Mr. Mom rejects at the kitchen island. "Why is he shirtless? And who put all that product in his hair?"

"Apparently it's school spirit day, and the only orange shirt he owned was in the wash. I'm trying to dry it now. Nikki Sixx over here went a little crazy with the hair gel." Mick wagged an accusatory thumb toward his friend.

"I'm the guitarist, dude. Mick Mars. Same first name as you. Get a clue!" Bear glanced down at me. "Mötley Crüe tribute. We're called Toast of the Town."

"At eight in the morning?" I sputtered, pulling Logan's damp shirt from the dryer housed in the old scullery room.

"We got hired by Shaded Glen nursing home for a lunchtime performance," Bear explained. "Ladies of all ages love the Crüe."

I inspected Logan's lunch, wondering what was more disturbing: Bear's last comment or his lunch bag artwork. At least the skull had a cheerful smile.

"Okay," I said, taking charge. "Mick, swap out the pot de crème for something a little more portable. Like a Pop-Tart. Bear, throw a jacket over your bondage gear, a different shirt on Logan, and drive him to school. Just hold the orange tee out the window; it will be dry before you get there and he can swap it out." I poured hot water into a mug and slapped a tea bag in. "I'm going to check on Quinn."

Mick threw me a grateful smile before grabbing a coffeepot to provide refills for the guests.

"Send up reinforcements if I'm not back in an hour," I murmured as he passed.

"Go away." A small voice responded to my gentle knock and inquiry, but the doorknob gave way under my hand.

"Not until I make sure you're okay," I said softly, setting the tea on her bedside table and taking in Quinn's quarters.

The twin canopy bed was a little unnerving, and the rest of the room looked like a shrine to her teenage years. Photos of prepubescent friends were jabbed into the corners of the vanity mirror, and school achievement ribbons were pinned to the wall next to it. A faded, dried rose corsage rested on the dresser next to a framed picture of Quinn in her prom gown, held by a stone-faced teenage boy posing formally behind her. A dusty set of candles flanked another gilt frame, this one containing a picture of her parents on their wedding day. The glass was broken, cracks spiderwebbing out from one corner.

The frilly curtains, with their balloon valance matching the eyelet on the canopy and bedspread, were drawn shut tight against walls covered with rosebud floral wallpaper. Certainly no testosterone party was happening in here. The room smelled like the half-used bottle of Clinique Happy on the shelf, combined with despair.

"Can we talk, sweetie?" I sat down at the edge of her bed, like Posy used to do for me when I was having a bad day.

Quinn rolled over and displayed a tear-stained face. "Nash always wins, he always lands on his feet, while I'm left to fall on my face! He comes back to town, captures the full attention, and the heart, of my child, and brings a full house of business to my inn. He basically accomplished what I've been struggling to do for ten years in one freakin' month."

"Logan loves you so much, Quinn. There's enough to go around." I pushed a hank of her hair back behind her ear. "And Nash hasn't done it alone. Well, the fans coming are totally his fault. But I helped him fix the wall, and it was Bear who sanded the rust off the gate. And Lord knows, Nash can't even butter his own toast. Where would we be without Mick's amazing breakfasts?"

This seemed to upset her even more. "See? I'm not even needed. No one would even miss me."

"Bullshit." Her pity act didn't fly with me. "I knew something was wrong the minute my foot hit the first floor. You're the glue in this family, and yes . . . it's a weird, patched-together little family, but you're its glue, babe. Without you, this place would come unhinged."

She gave a small snort through her tears, and rolled back over.

"Sometimes I wish this whole place burned to the ground," she whispered. "So I could've walked away."

"Oh, Quinn."

She fingered her high school graduation tassel that hung from her bedside lamp. Above it was a black and orange Princeton Tigers team poster. "You know I got pregnant my last year at Princeton, right? Never finished." She sat up in bed, drawing her knees to her chest and hugging them with her arms. "The little girls in those pictures?" She nodded toward her vanity mirror. "They don't even recognize me when I pass them in town. Or maybe they do but they don't remember ever being friends, or playing with me. All those ribbons, all the awards . . . they were all to please my dad. I studied so much, I didn't even miss having a social life. Until the prom. I had to go with my own brother, since no one else had bothered to ask."

"That's Bear?" I asked, incredulous. I hadn't even recognized the clean-cut, straight-faced kid in the picture.

"My dad was a fan of the crew cut. And of kids being seen but not heard."

No wonder Quinn was depressed. She was living in limbo between a missed childhood and her reality now. What she really probably could've used was a break from this place. Starting with leaving this room. I glanced around. A vacation might not be in the cards, but a mini-escape might do the trick.

"Throw on your robe and meet me in my room in ten minutes," I said, grabbing the candles from the dresser. "And I want you to drink at least half your tea."

She stared at me, but didn't protest. I took that as a good sign.

Down in my room, I positioned the massage table far from the bed and the door, angling it near the corner of windows. After years of practice in whipping up a serene space out of chaos and on the fly, I knew I could do this. I pulled a fresh sheet from the closet and draped the table, then slid Nash's heating pad in between. I set the ceiling fan on low, drew the curtains, and lit the candles. Then I ran the tub till steaming, and let several hand towels soak. Nash had nothing but noise on his iPod, except for the Shonnie Phillips album I had down-loaded to annoy him when we first met. Perfect. I set it in the dock on a low volume.

"You're kidding me, right?"

Quinn was in the doorway, watching me ready my oils. She was in her robe, and carrying her tea.

"Do you have a preference?" I asked, gesturing to the array of bottles like a game show model. I removed Nash's ring and slipped it into my pocket.

"What is this, Baskin-Robbins?" she asked flatly. "I'm going back to bed."

"Oh, no you don't." I caught her by the shoulders of her robe and directed her toward the massage table. She plucked two of the tiny vials of essential oil without so much as looking at them and thrust them at me. "I'm going to step out of the room. *You're* going to climb on the table and lie on your stomach, face in the cradle." I was going to get her to relax, even if I had to tackle her.

She gave pause. "Do I . . ." She bit her lip and touched the belt of her bathrobe.

"Wear as much or as little as you're comfortable with."

"I don't have pretty underwear," she blurted.

"That's the least of my worries," I assured her.

I had never been a fan of the cucumbers-on-the-eyes, dripping-waterfall, rub-a-dub school of massage, but being able to offer it to someone as tightly wound as Quinn made me appreciate it a little more. She tensed as I slowly lowered another sheet on her bare back, and tucked it gently into her waistband of her panties. "It's okay, it's just to prevent the oil from staining them."

"Like I said, they're nothing special," she mumbled.

I made a mental note to get out to the mall alone with her one of these days. Maybe dainty lingerie was superficial, but it was a start. "Believe me, they're a world better than what some of these musicians climb up on the table with. Pretty sure the jeans Nash was wearing could've walked off on their own."

I cringed as the words left my mouth, realizing the N word probably wouldn't go far in relaxing her, but she chuckled. "How did you get into massaging rock stars, anyway?"

"Well," I started, rolling the lotion between my palms and moving to stand behind her head. "I'm cursed with the people-pleaser gene." Leaning over her, I laid my hands at her tailbone, and began to slide my way up toward her shoulders in long, sweeping strokes.

"Me, too." She sighed as I feathered my way down her right side, fingers and palms in constant motion, warming the tissue. "That feels amazing. I've never had a massage before."

"Never?"

"Not ever. Not even with . . . you know, with a guy, unprofessionally." Her skin was pale and soft, and I had a feeling she didn't display it often, to anyone. "The closest I've come to a day spa is visiting the Curl Up and Dye."

We both got a laugh out of that. "Hardly counts. We should go to one together someday, and get facials. I love them even more than massages. The cleansing, the toning, the hot towels." I felt warmth wash over me, just thinking about it. "I love the luxurious ritual of it."

"I love rituals, too," she breathed. "Like here, at the inn. I love the look of all the rooms when I've freshly made them up. Everything presented and in its place. People sleep, people eat, they go on their way and then it all gets a fresh start, all over again."

I supposed we all had our rituals. I thought of Mick, in the bakery, and even Nash. The way he started and ended each show was sacred to him, no matter how unconventional of a ritual it was. I thought of how far out of his comfort zone he had traveled to be here.

Going through it. Not around it.

I warmed lotion between my palms and worked it into her dry, cracked hands. Bear was a laundry speed demon, but Quinn did the majority of the work at the Half Acre. "Have you ever had any help here?"

"When I was little, we did. But then my dad sent them away."

I remembered Mick's story about his mother, leaving town. And I pictured Quinn at his age, learning to help her own mother with the chores. My heart ached for all of them.

"You know, I like you, Dani," Quinn said, the words traveling up and washing over me like a fluttering effleurage. "I didn't want to at first. But I do."

"I know," I said, and left it at that. I was glad to hear it, but I wanted her to forget that it was me, Dani, above her. I just wanted her to enjoy the sensation of someone caring for her. I worked her left side in circulatory strokes, never breaking contact, then back up to her center, thumbs and knuckles applying friction. Using a petrissage sequence, I kneaded her upper trapezius muscles, reducing tension in her neck and shoulder muscles.

She began to really relax under my hands, and I worked in silence, save for the soft guitar tones and silky voice of my idol. I'd collected many maternal figures in my life, starting with Nana, moving to Bree and now, I even counted Sindy among them. But Shonnie was the constant force, before and after meeting her in real life, which had nurtured and empowered me. I hoped I could do that for people someday. Could I do that, if I kept running from town to town, breaking down and loading out with bands, night after night?

I shifted position and checked my own alignment, careful to employ good body mechanics. Spreading more oil with my palms, I then transitioned to the back of my hands, stretching out the extensors in my forearms and giving my flexors some needed rest. Massaging others was hard on the masseuse, too. Would there come a time where I couldn't keep doing it, couldn't keep running?

And then what? I heard Nash's lone howl on the mountain. *Then what?*

And then Jax's voice, close to my ear. *Listen to that little voice inside your own head for once, will ya? WWDD?*

What Would Dani Do?

I glanced at the bedside table. When you worked in blocks of time sessions, you got used to watching the clock. I wondered what it would be like to forget about time. Suspend it, like in Bear's auto body shop. I pictured having my own spa, with real beds, and towel warmers. I could practically feel the hot, smooth massage stones under my hands. And could see Logan's drawings hanging on the walls.

I reached for the other bottle of essential oil Quinn had selected and cracked it without even so much as a glance at the label.

The smell of cedar hit me, making my eyes water. But that wasn't what stopped me in my tracks. It was a knock at the bedroom door.

"Hang on a second," I said to Quinn. Opening the door a crack, I found Mick waiting, two plates in his hands.

"I figured Quinn was with you. And you two might be hungry," he whispered, holding up what appeared to be quiche and fruit from breakfast. "Spa lunch?"

He smiled, and my heart swelled at the thought of this lovely, lovely man taking the time to consider such a thing. Sindy had indeed raised him well. His aunt had given him love in spades, and had taught him to share it as well.

"Thank you." I gave his cheek a kiss, and relieved him of the plates. "We'll be down soon."

I resumed the massage after he left, but even the amazing food waiting for us couldn't stop the aroma of cedar from invading my thoughts, nagging at me. It reminded me of the Montauk house, the day of the Davenport funeral. And how I had wanted to be there for a beautiful stranger like Jax. And how I had continued to be his rock.

Someday, Mick, I had said, but I wondered if I could ever let anyone chip away my stone and reveal all that was lurking so deep under there.

"Is that quiche I smell?" Quinn murmured. The proprietor had forgone the most important meal of the day; I heard her stomach growl.

"Spa lunch, courtesy of Mick Spencer," I replied.

"He's the best. I can see why . . . why you fell for him," Quinn said. My hands froze along her shoulders.

"How—," I stammered.

"I've known since the morning after you arrived. When I developed pictures from Logan's party. Your eyes were locked on him in almost every shot, and the way he looked at you was like, well . . . like how Nash sometimes looks at me, when he thinks I'm not noticing," she said shyly.

And here Nash thought Quinn would only warm up to him with me around, as a buffer. Turned out she knew more about him, and me, all along.

"It's okay, Dani. Your secret is safe with me."

Before I could reply, Nash burst into the room.

"What the fuck is going on in here?"

Quinn gasped, clutching the sheet to her body. "Get out!" she hollered. "You have no right—"

Nash cut her off with a bitter laugh. "Just the way you planned it, huh? No fucking rights at all. I know, Quinn. I *know*!"

Quinn grabbed her robe, frantically covering herself as Nash stormed closer. But he strode past her, straight toward the closet and began throwing items into a suitcase. "We're leaving, Dani. Now."

"Nash . . . calm down," I pleaded, grabbing his arm.

"Don't tell me what to do! You're not my fucking savior, Dani!" His elbow jerked, shaking me off. "You're no better than a groupie in the end, minus the sexual favors."

I reeled back into the massage table, knocking over the bottle of essential oil. Cedar permeated the air and I could barely breathe.

"You left me off the birth certificate!" The entire inn must've heard him holler. "Just a fucking John Doe, isn't that right, Quinn?"

Quinn gave a wounded cry and made for the door. Nash pursued her.

"Get out of here," he yelled at the gawkers who had assembled. "Fucking vultures, all of you! Leave! Now!"

I raced down the stairs after him, but Mick was already out the door and tackling Nash.

Mick

MOMENTS OF TRUTH

We hit the lawn hard, rolling, pushing, and swearing.

"What the fuck, Spencer! This isn't your fight!"

"The hell it isn't!" I was done taking his shit. And he was done taking from the people I cared about. "You want custody of Logan. That's why you came back." Dani had called hers an "unusual favor," and I got that now. "And you needed Dani to do it. You used her. Like you used Quinn." I had heard his shouts from the bedroom, telling Dani to pack, and about the birth certificate. "I won't let you do this!"

"Mick! No!" Dani rushed to Nash's side, as he clutched his hip. "Stop!"

"Give me one reason why I shouldn't kick his ass!" I pulled a fist back, watching him wince beneath me. "And give me one reason, Dani, why you care what happens to this scumbag."

She pushed between us. "Please," she pleaded.

My entire body felt like it had been doused in an ice bath. She was choosing him. Him over me.

"I get it," I said, pulling myself off him.

I thought I finally had a fighting chance with her. But in the end . . . story of my life.

"No, Mick. You don't get it," Dani whispered, as Nash waved her away and limped toward the trailer. "Let him go to her." She laid her hand on my arm. "They need to deal with this."

"Quinn!" he hollered. "You can't keep shutting me out!"

She swung the door open and nearly knocked Nash off his feet.

"I want you to leave, Nash. Now."

"It's always what *you* want, isn't it Quinn? And then you get to play the fucking martyr."

She moved to pull the door shut again, but he heaved himself up the top step and into the small space. I broke away from Dani. "I'm not leaving her alone with him."

I had made a promise to Logan, written in black and white in our shared notebook. That I wouldn't let Quinn get hurt. Not by me, not by anyone.

Nash's voice was hoarse from hollering. "You knew exactly what you were doing that night, didn't you, Quinn? Coming here to me, in this trailer?"

I raced up the steps. Nash was at the window with one long stride, yanking back the blackout curtains, and ripping back the red film that covered the glass, allowing light to pour in.

"Stop!" she shrieked, throwing herself toward him. She clawed at his shirt. "We both got what we wanted that night!" I froze at her words.

"That's right. You came in here that night because you knew two things. You knew I wouldn't stop you if you came on to me. And you knew I could get you pregnant."

"They were gone! Gone!" She beat at his chest with her fist, but the fight had left her. "I didn't want to be alone," she sobbed.

"Well, neither did I!" Nash shouted. "You came in here with your tears, and your whispers, and you wrapped yourself around me. You let me hold you, you let me inside you. You knew how long I had wanted you. God, how many times had you led me to that garden gate, Quinn? Leading me on. And then rejected me . . . never giving me a chance to prove myself? Until that night. And I gave you my everything that night, Quinn. I gave you my all. I gave in to every desire, every fantasy. The idea that you could love somebody like me. That I could belong . . . finally belong here, with you. And trade all that pain we shared, for happiness. Only to wake up at dawn and find you gone. I'd raced across the yard, but you'd already locked yourself back into that goddamn fortress, Quinn. You shut me out!" His hands locked into her hair, forcing her to look him in the eye.

I lunged forward, ready to throw myself into their fight. Ready to take Nash down again if he so much as laid a finger on Quinn to harm her.

But Quinn made the first move.

Nash fell to his knees before her as she deepened her kiss, and his fingers found the tears on her cheeks and wiped them away. It was such an intimate embrace, I had to turn away, stumbling down the trailer steps and back out onto the lawn.

Dani was gone.

Dani

TIME TRAVEL

The smell of cedar was everywhere.

I pushed my face into the crook of my arm, eyes streaming, as I threw my essentials into my backpack. Avoiding the glass shards from the bottle as I moved as swiftly as I could.

"You're running. Again."

Mick filled the doorway. Trapping me between the lie that had brought me here, and the truth that was spurring me to move on. The look on his face told me he had gleaned much more insight into the reasons why Nash came home from having stuck around out there by the trailer. Sometimes actions spoke louder than words. And I knew Quinn and Nash had broken through the barrier of their gentle sins; the healing had begun.

Like the essential oil, my own sins had been stowed in the dark, in their own fragile vessel. I had assumed if I stored them properly, they—like the cedar oil—could've stayed indefinitely, preserved untouched. Forgotten.

But my feelings for Mick had shattered me.

He had permeated my entire being.

"I can't let you go." Within seconds, he met me in the center of the room. Just like he had in the ballroom of Posy's reception. No masks to hide behind this time. "I don't want to lose you again. Dani . . ." He reached for me, pressing me into his strong arms. Like dancing with him under the whisper dome, even the quietest of words carried. "I love you."

I inhaled what I could of him, that comforting sweetness. I needed it to linger; I needed it to last with me.

There was something I had been skirting around that I needed to go through.

"Then you need to trust that I will come back." I stroked my promises into his hair, down his back, and kissed his temple as he bowed to me. "I love you, Mick. Oh, God. I love you. But I've got my own denial, my own darkroom to deal with."

Those eyes of his were still powerful truth serum. I knew—I hoped—I'd be able to tell him everything, someday. But first I had to be honest with myself.

He squeezed them tight, and gave the smallest nod before releasing me.

I didn't turn to see if he had opened them, I couldn't.

I just had to have faith and go.

"China Doll."

Nash stepped out from behind my van. Reaching it had been my prize; I had promised I wouldn't break down until I reached it. But hearing Nash call me by that nickname he had given me just shattered me.

"I'm sorry," I said, shaking my head and trembling in his arms. "I can't help you anymore, Nash. Not until I help myself." I pulled his ring from my pocket and pushed it into his hand.

"Shhh." He touched my hair gently, and leaned down until I looked him in the eye. "It's okay. You have helped tremendously. I just told Quinn everything. About my illness. About why I needed Logan's birth certificate. She's agreed to the genetic testing for this marker. She . . ." He smiled the most humble smile I had ever seen him crack. "She wants the Tin Man after all."

He kissed my forehead.

"You and Spencer, huh?" He gestured back to the darkroom trailer. "I saw Quinn's photographic evidence. I don't know how I missed the chemistry myself. I guess I was too busy, and too afraid to admit it. Funny, China Doll. I thought you were the only thing in my life that I didn't have to beg, borrow, or steal." He brought my hands to his lips. "But really, you were only mine to keep for a short time. I've got Logan now. I've got . . . real family. I'm not afraid to let you go now."

And with that, he set me free.

Mick

GOING WITHOUT

Dani was gone. But not forgotten.

My time spent with her was a powerful memory that kept pushing me forward.

Quinn came into the bakery with a bombshell redhead. I hadn't been over to the Half Acre in a while, but I knew this must be Laney. In town for three days to get her marriage license. I had promised to save her a wedge o' wedding cake.

"Oh my God," she breathed. "It is the Night Kitchen. Just like the book! And you. You're Mick." Her eyes channeled warmth and sympathy. I couldn't find my voice just yet. I couldn't bring myself to ask.

"I remember that book," Quinn blurted. "My God, Mick. I don't know why I never made that connection. The nanny used to read it to me."

"No," I told her. "That was my mom. She was a maid there and she would read it to both of us. It's okay to remember, Quinn."

Sindy bustled out from the back, wiping her hands. "Quinn's mother gave you that book when you were born, Mick. I remember that, clear as day." She smiled a faraway smile at the both of us. "Sofia would bring it to work and read it to the children. Laney darling, let me show you some of Mick's amazing cake samples."

Quinn turned, looking at me as if it were the first time she laid eyes on me. "My dad fired her. But my mother didn't want her to leave. Do you think—?"

"I honestly don't know," I admitted. "At one time I thought maybe your dad . . ." I shook my head. "Maybe it had been wishful thinking." Just like those rare moments when Nash's dad would make us Scott's Special. Even a once-in-a-while dad was better than no dad at all.

Let's play a game, Mickey. Let's pretend we live in the Night Kitchen. Time to get to sleep so you can get baking.

My mother had turned my favorite book into my favorite game. But the game always ended too soon, when I would fall asleep. I remembered waking once, in the middle of the night. The moon was full and friendly, and I crept down to the kitchen in my footie pajamas. Maybe there was magic in the world, and maybe I really did live in the Night Kitchen. Wouldn't that be great?

An eerie light like no other had lured me into our tiny galley kitchen. There, standing in front of the open refrigerator door, was a man. Tall and dark-haired, naked except for a pair of boxers, he chugged from the jug of milk I used for my cereal in the morning. He must've caught sight of me from the corner of his eye, because it widened, but he didn't lower the jug until he took two or three more fluid swallows. I watched, in a trance, as his Adam's apple bobbed up and down.

"Sorry, kid. You caught me in the act." The jug went back into the fridge, and the fantastical light disappeared as he let the fridge door shut. With a tousle to my hair, he padded back to my mother's bedroom without looking back.

They fought, and he left. I never got to ask him—or her—if he was my father. Or if he was just one in the long string of men my mother loved and made leave by the morning. Trying to shield me from whatever loneliness she was trying to chase away. I hadn't understood any of it until much later, after she was gone.

I didn't understand myself, until after Dani came along—and after she left.

My own string of conquests—all the women, all the impossible situations—came from my fear and unwillingness to be hurt further. I had to love 'em and leave 'em . . . before they could leave—or tell me to leave—first.

Except for Dani. When she had asked me to stay the night, to be with her, I had refused. I had refused because I couldn't bear running the risk of being kicked out in the morning, as another regret. Being asked to take the back service stairs.

I don't know who you are, or where you came from, but you'd better know exactly what you want, and what it's worth to you, okay?

Dani's sister's words continued to echo through me, throughout the entire time. As did the memory of the girl who got away.

I knew who I was now, and where I came from. And Dani was all I wanted. And she was worth the wait.

Dani's friends fit right in at the Half Acre. Laney would go round for round with Bear and Nash in music trivia by the light of the fire pit, and she and Logan created strips of kooky comics over the breakfasts I continued to serve. Noah helped Quinn create new websites for both the inn and for her photography business, and he pimped the entire place to the gills with high-powered Wi-Fi.

When their three-day waiting period had passed, they shyly approached Quinn and me and asked us to be their witnesses. They wanted no fanfare, no guests. Just a quick union . . . and a wedge of wedding cake after.

Dani wasn't coming to be their witness after all.

Dani

DREDGING THE PAST

Jax was standing on the porch of his grandparents' Montauk estate, watching as I pulled up the steep drive. God only knows how long he'd been there, waiting under the weathered shingles. He'd traded in his car salesmen khakis for a pair of worn blue jeans, and a Central Bluff High School T-shirt that had clearly seen better years. I was out of the van in an instant and zigzagging up the maze of stairs, fingers barely skimming the white railings, on my way to him. The frayed collar of his shirt was soft against my lips as he hugged me to him and whispered his thanks.

"I'm so sorry, Jax. I should've been here sooner . . . I should've been here for you."

"Shhh, you are now. You are."

"Where is everyone?" The house had a sort of relieved silence to it, the beach-worn boards of its porch sagging slightly like an exhausted hostess who finally had a chance to sit down after all the party guests had gone home. There had been no other cars in the driveway, save for Mean Mistress Mustard.

"Nice ride. Dani James behind the wheel. Watch out!" Just the feeble attempt at a joke seemed to exhaust Jax. His fingers clutched at the back of my shirt as he used my embrace as a buoy to keep himself upright. "They're reading the will today, in the city. I didn't want to be there."

He broke away from me and went to lean on the railing, focusing on the ocean. I understood why he had stayed behind. No matter what verdict those papers contained, this was the real view his grandmother had, the beauty of and love for the ocean—and her family—that had surrounded her, all these years. Worst-case scenario, at least he would have this serene and unspoiled moment, and memory. A calm before whatever storms threatened to come this way.

"She'll always love you, Jax."

"I know," he replied quietly. His shoulders rose and fell in a sigh that he sent out to sea. Turning to me, he gave a slight smile. "Come inside with me?"

It was a question, but one I couldn't bring myself to say yes or no to. Actions had to speak louder than the words.

I had been avoiding it my entire adult life. It was time to go through it, not around it.

Cedar was known to reduce stress and anxiety for some people, but the sharp smell hit my nose and placed my system on high alert before it even hit my memory triggers. There was no escaping it again as I led Jax through the hidden door behind the bookcase.

"Right there"—I gestured, where the ceiling slanted to its lowest point in the windowless room. I shivered, noting the cashmere blankets perfectly folded on the cedar shelves above. I remembered slowly shucking off my dress and waiting. He'd kicked off his pants but had left his tie and dress shirt on, buttons scraping my bare belly as he pushed me to the floor and climbed on top of me. "He'd laid a bunch of blankets down. I was . . . I was buzzing on the rum and Coke and smitten by the boy with the rosy cheeks and the blue tie." I laid my hand on Jax's chest, feeling his rapidly beating heart and conjuring up the vision of him that day for the both of us.

"But . . ." His strong, dark brow wrinkled. ". . . but I had already taken off my tie. Earlier."

"I know," I said quietly. Realization had dawned on me when my young lover had gazed down with cold, heavy-lidded eyes as he brought me to my gasping peak. But my raging teenage hormones continued to rule and betray me; I had been powerless to respond with anything but a quivering moan, bucking under his touch before my oversight and orgasm flooded me with guilt and regret.

"You didn't choose the wrong brother! You were tricked."

I'd let my mind float up to the tiny point where the walls met the ceiling, had let Dex finish, rough and quick. No sound but his panting. His breath and hatred for me searing hot against my turned cheek.

"He raped you, Dani."

I had taken the memory and the emotions, squeezed them up as small as I could, and pushed them through that pinhole in the wood where the walls met. And I had run away, and hadn't stopped running from them since. Refusing to let any lover get too close, lest he sand down the surface and allow those memories to permeate and repel him . . . just like pungent cedar itself.

But as I stood there, being held in the comforting arms of my friend, I realized that time had mellowed the rigid wood and its scent had diminished. The planks above us had shrunk with age and separated from each other; their cracks were now too wide to contain what I had hidden all these years.

And I knew I no longer wanted those secrets hanging over my head.

I pulled a cashmere blanket down off the shelf and contemplated it. "Dani, we don't—"

"Yes. I want to."

Jax took the blanket from me with shaking hands, smoothed it across the floor and we settled in, talking our way out of the haze of that day. Finishing each other's sentences, filling in the blanks when the other fell short on courage and memory. Holding nothing back.

"Dex had been sneaking alcohol for years, while I had been the pious holdout. His tolerance level must've been much higher than mine by that day. Although God only knows what the ratio of rum to Coke had been in the glass he mixed for me, and maybe for you. But he knew exactly what he was doing. He'd told me to down it, 'for courage,' he'd said, before leaving me alone with you. And I did, remember?"

I nodded, recalling the loopy, tingling feeling in my stomach when Jax had set down the empty glass and took my hand, rubbing his thumb across my palm. "I remember you looked like you were going to kiss me, but then you mumbled something and stumbled out of the room."

"My head was spinning and all the events of the day were catching up with me. And I had this, this . . . God, this gorgeous creature." He pushed a wayward curl from falling against my tear-stained cheek. "As if sent to me from above, you'd wound your way in between the gravestones to be with me and . . . and then suddenly I had you all to myself. And I was too drunk. I was going to blow it. I remember, I made it to the bathroom just in time and threw up."

"While Dex must've gone into the room you shared, swapped his red tie for your blue one, and made his way back to me." I recalled how he'd dimmed the lights on the way back into the attic rec room. He'd told me to follow him, there was a secret room where we could keep drinking and not get busted by the adults.

"I woke up with groove marks on my face from where I had passed out cold on the ceramic tile. And you were gone."

I'd hitched a ride to the train, made the concert, and hadn't breathed a word about what had happened. I had no more reason to revisit the event than summer folks had reason to visit our deserted beach town come fall. The Davenport boys had been an anomaly. Until they became townies themselves, enrolling at our high school after their parents' exodus from the city.

"You never told anyone? Not even Laney, or Posy? What about your parents?"

I shook my head. "And become one of their textbook case studies? Hell, no." I snorted. "I was so ashamed, Jax. We were so well-adjusted, we bordered on dysfunctional."

Shame for what had happened led to secrets, which led to more shame, and my feelings of unworthiness. And so I had used reason and rationalization to rob myself of any hope of romantic feelings for Jax. I wove my way into his life as an indispensible, platonic friend instead, because I couldn't bear—or dare—to consider any alternative. He had a steady string of dates at the ready, anyway, from the first day of school onward. I wasn't his type. He was too good for me. And I made sure I was too wild for him.

But I wasn't wild. Latching myself onto a wild spirit like Nash— trying to make myself indispensible once again—had shown me my real properties. Grounded. Steady. And allowing myself to fall for Mick had let me take that a step further—I was worthy. I was capable of loving, and of being loved. Of committing myself to the very possibility.

Not such an insane coincidence after all.

And I had dreamed of it—of him—the night he placed that silly slice of cake under my pillow. It had scared the hell out of me, but I was no longer scared anymore.

"This house was built by Stanford White; do you know about him?" Jax asked. I shook my head. "He was a genius architect. Famous for building homes for the area's most elite clients. But most of his professional accomplishments were overshadowed by his sensational murder. Shot in the face by a jealous husband. White had apparently ravaged the man's showgirl wife years back, when she was just sixteen." His fist balled, his face a changing tempest of fury and anguish. "I could kill Dex for what he did to you."

I felt faint. "No. It's over, Jax. Forget it."

"It's never over, Dani. You will always be the tear that hangs inside me. On my soul. Forever." Jax was a wordsmith, but I knew the words were not original to him; they came from the soundtrack of that day, from the album we'd been listening to as he had been on the cusp of kissing me.

I leaned in now and placed my mouth ever so sweetly on his waiting lips. A sob rose deep within me but tamped itself down into a relieved sigh as his tongue found mine in a gentle stroke. I felt him shudder under my touch, my fingertips playing lightly down his temple and wiping away the tears mingling on both of our cheeks. He broke the kiss with a nip at my bottom lip, reluctantly pulling away as the shake of his head mirrored my own.

Maybe there had been a moment in time when and where we could've been right for each other. But the moment was gone.

"I wouldn't trade our friendship, or your happiness, for anything," he breathed.

He walked me to my van. "I told you this old girl would get you to where you needed to go."

He had been right, of course. It had brought me to Nash.

Who had brought me home to Mick.

Home. I was ready to go back.

"Are you sure? What about the will? I don't want you to be alone."

He smiled and squeezed my hand. "I'm not. I've got a blank doc on my computer waiting. And when I write 'the end' to this one, I'm going to finally cash in my rain check on that massage from you."

"You'd better."

Quinn

**THE HALF ACRE BED-AND-BREAKFAST
ROOM JOURNAL #10**

It isn't the same around here, without Dani. I miss her. And there's so much I want to tell her.

Nash, of all people, is telling me to give her the gift of time.

She left an entry in room number twelve's journal. I came across it while I was cleaning the room after she left. And after Nash had vacated it. We're in room number ten together. Next to Logan's. No more view of the river, no more view of the trailer. I get to look out at the garden gate where we first kissed, the open-air chapel standing patiently beyond it.

No more canopy bed, either.

She hadn't dated or signed the page—perhaps she had hoped to add more to it at some point. There were just two sentences in her straight, round handwriting:

Quinn,

I wanted to thank your family for opening your home to me. I had a wonderful stay.

Dani

As I sit here now, writing, I realize she is right. This is more than just a house; it is a home. It's filled with sound now, where once upon a time, there was only silence.

I can hear my amazing son practicing his bar chords. And Bear and Mick, trash-talking as well as any best friends and brothers could. Sindy's down there, spouting advice while Walt cracks his bad jokes. And Nash's beautiful voice can be heard over them all. He's singing. I no longer want to shut doors, I want to fling them open, I want join the party. To hear my laughter mingling with theirs. It feels so good.

We were one big happy family after all. And I had warned Dani about that when I first met her, as if it were a bad thing.

She did so much to bring us together. I'd like to thank her properly someday.

And let her know that Nash is doing well in his treatment. And that Logan tested negative: he doesn't have the HLA-B27 gene Nash was worried about. That's not to say that he will never develop his father's condition, but he is certainly less susceptible. But no sense in worrying or blaming—just accepting. Nash and I are learning to cross bridges when we come to them, not burn them.

Gotta run. Nash's key ceremony is today!

Mick

KEY NOTE

The borough's second-oldest citizen died on a sunny October day. The mums Nash had planted for him were still heartily blooming in his yard. Woolhouse's last request was to have no funeral, no memorial service, just the key ceremony the following weekend. A celebration, he instructed. With meringues to be served at the reception.

Sindy and I baked them in silence together.

We gathered in the town park.

Nash was the sole recipient to receive a key, but Woolhouse's other request had been for the local guitar hero to read the speech the old man had prepared. Nash stood up there, Quinn and Logan at his side, as his heavily ringed fingers fumbled with the paper.

"Check. Check one, two." He tapped the mic as the bystanders laughed, then settled in to listen. Bear sat in the front row between me and Angie, and interpreted for Logan.

"I'll keep this short," Nash began. "Because I'm an old, cranky bastard." He looked up at the crowd. "His words, not mine." That broke the ice, releasing relieved laughter all around.

"As town historian, I made it my business to know this town better than anyone. Yes, even you, Sindy Wolkoff." Next to me, my aunt pushed her handkerchief to her eyes and laughed a little. "When I nominated Stewart Nash—" Nash paused, just as surprised as everyone else at the fact, before recovering and speaking up, over the murmurs. "When I nominated Stewart Nash to receive this award along with me, it was because I knew it was finally time to let the past rest. Now . . . take it away, Drama. Because this is your show."

Nash stood for a moment in silence. It looked like he was wishing the paper had more instructions on it, more words to use. But as he looked up, I realized he was determined to use his own words. Words he didn't have to borrow. No begging. No stealing.

"It's too late for me to look old Mr. Woolhouse in the eye and thank him, but it's not too late . . ." He broke off, scanning the audience and standing tall. "It's not too late to thank all of you. And to tell you I can't accept this key."

The collective gasp whirled like fallen autumn leaves, somersaulting across the New Hope–Lambertville Bridge.

"I can't accept this key," he continued, "because I didn't earn it on my own. But I can share it. With my former bandmate and my best friend, Bartholomew Bradley." He motioned for a stunned Bear to join him at the podium. "Bear wrote the song you all love to sing. Yeah, even you, Walt. Sindy says you sing it in the shower." My uncle gave my aunt an embarrassed elbow in the ribs, but he had a grin on his face. "I owe you so much, dude." Nash dropped something small into Bear's hand and I saw the glint of the diamond from the ring Dani used to wear. "Starting with some retroactive royalties. But all songs aside, I never could've gone as far as I had, or come back around, without the love and support of my son, and my family. All of you." He met my eye, and then gave a subtle brow raise and nod to the row across from mine.

I turned to see Dani. Even sitting, she was a standout in the crowd. Just like that day I spotted her, dancing the second line on Royal.

The mayor approached and did the honors of bestowing both men with a plaque bearing a shiny key. They raised it together in the air.

"Key to the borough!" Bear crowed triumphantly, throwing the horns. Angie stood up and clapped, beaming at him.

Nash pulled Quinn to his side, and she situated Logan in front of them, so father could plant a kiss square on top of his son's tawny head.

"Thatta boy, Nash!" hollered Walt, from his chair. "It's about damn time."

"It's a start," I said. "What about the money he owes you?"

"Mick Spencer!" my aunt scolded me. "Do you think I tell you every blessed thing? Nash has been sending checks to me and your uncle every month since he left. Who do you think built that wheelchair ramp? Well, he would've built it, had he been here. That is a generous boy up there. And a handy one, too. As handy as the day is long."

"The days are getting shorter, Aunt Sindy." It was going to take me a while to see Nash in a new light, but it was dawning on me.

"Yes, dear. But they'll get long again. And this time, he's sticking around to see it."

I glanced over at Dani. She had been watching the exchange, a small smile playing on her lips. She may have known more about Nash than I gave her credit for. Or at least was able to see the shred of good in him when I couldn't. She dropped her eyes when mine met them.

I wished there was a way to get her to stick around.

Dani

MASKS OFF

It was wonderful to see Nash receive his award. And for him to share the limelight with Bear. Even better was to see Quinn by his side. But the best part of the ceremony was Logan, making his musical debut. He grinned as he stood at the podium and played a simple, but beautiful melody for all to hear. And even though he himself couldn't, and never would, he could feel the music, as Bear always said. And he could feel the love from all of us, smiling proud.

"I never got to ask, how did your Mötley Crüe tribute go at the nursing home?" I addressed Bear, whose arm was slung over Angie's shoulder. She held on to his hand, eyes shining.

"Oh," Bear mumbled. "Not so well. Turns out, there was a slight misunderstanding. The director thought they were booking an *Ed Sullivan Show* tribute called Toast of the Town. Needless to say, they were a bit shocked when we broke into 'Shout at the Devil.'"

I laughed. "You clearly need to label your tributes better."

"Taking a break from the tributes for a while. Nash and me . . ."

Bear glanced over at the crowd surrounding the man of the hour. "We're gonna jam. See where it takes us."

"Hey, Dani." Quinn approached, Logan and Nash in tow. "Welcome back." She gave me a hug and whispered a thank-you in my ear.

"No thanks necessary. I kind of always knew he wanted to come back and win your heart." Along with Logan's, and the rest of the town's. "I just came to help him get the key."

A hand tugged at my sleeve, and Logan was there, offering me a meringue.

"It's like a kiss," he signed.

"From who?" I asked. "You?"

Logan shook his head and gave me a smile. Then he signed a name sign I had never seen before. Starting with a *U* close to his right temple, for *Uncle*. And ending with a V-shaped slicing movement over his less-dominant hand, using an open-fingered letter *M*.

"He thinks you're . . ." Logan's next motion was the sign for *sweet* but it was also the sign for *cute*.

"Oh, he does, does he?"

No more finger spelling Mick's name. Logan had bestowed a name upon the cute, sweet baker who'd crashed my sister's wedding and the gates of my heart. I searched the crowd for him, but didn't see him anywhere.

I pulled Mean Mistress Mustard up to the curb in front of the Night Kitchen. She gave a gentle sigh as I cut the motor, as if to say, *It's about damn time, girlfriend.*

The handwritten sign hanging on the Night Kitchen's window read *Closed* in curvy, eclectic letters, and sure enough, the heavy blue-black door was locked. The entire town of New Hope was down at the reception.

Save for one.

Smiling, I made my way around to the back door. I, too, was a lover, not a fighter. I had struggled with my past, and fought my feelings for Mick, since arriving in town. Hiding behind Nash and the ring he had placed on my finger. Running away, when I should have been running to. No more.

Upstairs, Mick's door yielded under my touch. A sign commanding MASKS OFF ushered me past a red velvet curtain. The sexy, soft undertones of a saxophone drifted through the studio apartment, mixing with the beat of the ceiling fans above. Above the bed, tranquil emerald silk and cream tulle billowed in the half-light down from the loft's high industrial ceiling. Angie had done a good job of bringing a cozy and intimate vibe to such a cavernous space.

A small wrought iron table sat beside the bed, and the hot, luscious smell of beignets hit my memory triggers. Suddenly, I realized the canopy overhead resembled the famous awning of the café of our missed connection.

Mick had brought New Orleans to us.

My waiter was shirtless and barefoot as he set down cups of milky-rich, chicory-laced coffee. There were no chairs at the table, so I perched on the bed and he joined me there.

Without a word, he picked up one of the sugar-kissed pastries and offered it up to my lips. I took a bite, relishing the light, crisp taste. It couldn't have been fresher had it come served steaming from the kitchen of Café Du Monde.

"I cheated a bit," Mick admitted. "Had my staff proof the dough for me. But I cut and fried them myself." He took a firm bite, leaving a trail of powdered sugar across his stubble. "Kind of a messy first-date food."

"It's perfect," I whispered, nibbling the warm sugar from his chin before moving up to his mouth. "But totally not necessary." I took it from his hand.

"Are you kidding me?" His expression fell. "I've been wanting to make that morning up to you ever since."

"You've made me breakfast *every* morning," I said, pushing the last bite of beignet into his mouth. "Waking up in the B and B to find you . . ." I gave a small gasp as his tongue lingered, licking the glaze of sugar from my thumb.

"Not the same," he insisted, picking another beignet up from the warm stack and feeding it to me. "This is breakfast . . . and then bed."

"Are you trying to ply the single woman with sweets?" I asked, as he eased me back on the bed. The striped swathes above canopied our romantic playground.

"Who are you calling single?" Mick murmured, his breath hot as he worked his way down my neck to the first button on my dress. My hand was resting there, and he kissed my naked ring finger. "And no, I'm just giving the café au lait time to cool."

He was right; I was so, so taken . . . ever since Posy's reception, where the air had felt electric. And it crackled when he had walked into the room.

WWDD?

My fingers trembled as I helped him unbutton me out of the silk sheath, wondering how he would react when he saw what I had done.

"Are you mine?" he whispered, against the soft curve of my hip, his mouth on the wide, lace band of my red panties. They were my prettiest pair, with lace woven through the hem, and small rosettes dotting the border.

"For the asking," I whispered back. Like his red velvet cake in reverse, he pushed away the fancy decoration to reveal my creamy skin and best intentions.

Fingers fell on the tiny, new tattoo gracing my hip.

The small swallow was in flight, its feathers shaded with the blues of his eyes, and mine. A symbol of home . . . and of hope and renewal.

Mick smiled up at me, with that bashful half smirk I was totally addicted to. His forearm came to rest across my navel, our birds meeting for the first time as he laced his fingers with mine and gently tongued his way down, savoring and tasting my skin. He circled in on my sweetest spot and lingered there, sending me out of my mind with pleasure. My free hand snaked through his hair, as he moved his talented one down my thigh and his fingers joined the party. I gasped and bucked against the solid stroke of his knuckle while the soft probe of his tongue coaxed me into a shattering climax.

"Mick . . . lover," I sighed. My breathy words were lost to the heavens as he gave a long, pleasured growl. His lips and fingertips were registered weapons, quickly rendering me quivering and useless a second time.

His cheek grazed my blue bird. "Home," he mouthed against my belly as he slid toward me, rolling us in his strong arms.

My lips communed with the salty sweetness of his skin, memorizing his nicks and scars, tracing the black outline of my bird's mate. My hands ghosted over his as he nimbly worked down his button fly and shucked the denim down. He sucked a sharp breath as my curls brushed over his thighs on my way to claim him.

Mick

FROM HOPE TO HOME

Nash's long-held theory of love had been somewhat right. When it did come back to you, it wasn't the same. It was stronger, sweeter, and swifter than anything I had ever known.

Dani had me so far gone, yet anchored to her as we moved as one. Fading into each other, forgetting where one of us ended and the other began. I rose to meet her, watching her eyes as their ratios changed, sky blue darkening to the most royal hue of blue velvet along with her desire. She rode my hard length, taking me above and beyond with each satisfying sigh and moan.

"Baby, you've got this. You got me. Now." I grasped at the curls spilling down her back, losing myself as I filled her. Her eyelids fluttered and trapped my gaze, as we stared in wide wonder and rode out the hard wave before crashing together.

"I know you're not a fan of mixing business with pleasure," I murmured into her hair afterward, as we waited for our pulse rates to steady themselves. "But there is a vacancy in the building right next door."

She played with her curls, smoothing them out over my chest.

"They're connected, actually." Dani laced her fingers through mine, her head warm on my heart.

"Business and pleasure?" I asked.

"I was talking about the buildings," she said, giving me a nip and a nudge. "I know because I've already talked to the landlord about a day spa. Although"—she teased her curl around my collarbone—"when you love what you do . . ."

"And do who you love?" I joked, kissing her forehead.

"Yeah, that, too." She laughed. "So, should we mix business with pleasure here, above the Night Kitchen . . . and Cravings Day Spa?"

I could already feel a stirring in my groin, craving her sweetness. Setting a course for satisfying her every wish. "Between here and the Half Acre? I think we've got a built-in clientele."

Dani snuggled close in agreement. "I love this music," she whispered.

"This?" I pulled her even closer. "This is my friend Derek. Remember the old guy whose arm you grabbed and danced with, in the second line? I was right there that day. That's when I saw you. And that's when I knew."

Fate had grabbed me that day as well, and had taken me for a whirl, full circle.

From New Hope to New Orleans and back again. When I spotted Dani that day, I had known home wouldn't ever be too far away.

Epilogue

DANI

"Sindy was right; this place is so perfect for a wedding."

I leaned over and clasped Nash's hand in mine. The grounds of the Half Acre were truly heavenly once again. Behind us, the new paint on the wrought iron gate gleamed. Below us, dewy fresh rose petals were abundantly strewn along the flagstone path.

And ahead of us, the open-air chapel stood majestically, rightfully at home among the trees in the orchard.

I think we both finally felt we were home as well.

Nash squeezed my hand and smiled. Thanks to the right cocktail of treatment, his grip was strong and he hadn't had a flare-up in the past year. He looked dashing in his light gray suit, his blond locks carefully groomed for the occasion.

"The scenery ain't got nothing on you, China Doll."

I blushed. For once, I was wearing a dress that I had chosen myself, and this one wouldn't be handed over to Bree at the end of the day.

Little fingers tugged at the chiffon of my dress. Logan stood there, handsome as all get-out in a miniature version of Nash's suit and giving us a pointed look. Instead of a traditional ring bearer pillow, a small bird's nest handcrafted from twigs and moss nestled in his palm. Small paper flowers in a dusty rose color were twined artfully around the edges, and it was topped with a bow tied from a long slice of matte silver ribbon. With his free hand, Logan signed "Do you mind?" by placing his index finger on the tip of his nose, and then moving it out to point at the both of us, his eyebrows raised in question.

"I think he's trying to tell us were holding up the procession," I stage-whispered.

Nash bit back a bashful smile at his son. He dropped my hand from across the aisle, clutched his fist to his chest and rolled it emphatically.

Sorry was one word in sign language he was really good at, but he was learning loads more as well.

Logan grinned, gave a nod in thanks, and continued down the path toward the open-air chapel. Quinn followed behind him, beautiful in a strapless gown of dusty rose that hugged her petite curves. She clutched a small bouquet inspired by the foliage all around us, and made her way down the aisle as the string quartet played. Nash's eyes danced over her as she slid into the seat next to him. I caught her wink from across the aisle as she settled into the crook of his arm, and turned her head expectantly down the path.

The quartet finished their classical piece, and began a beautiful rendition of "Jumpstart My Heart."

"Seriously?" Mick murmured against the shell of my ear. "Who uses their own biggest hit as their wedding song?"

"Bear, of course."

Our gaze followed Angie as she flowed down the stone path, her gown gathering the rose petals at its hem on her way to Bear, beaming under the arches of the open-air chapel in his smart, charcoal gray suit.

I tilted my head back against Mick's shoulder. "He totally deserves to, don't you think?"

"I think," Mick said softly, running his finger around the creamy ribbon at my neck until he came to the tiny silver cake charm resting at my throat's hollow, "it's about damn time we all got what we deserve."

Mick

"You'll be next, you two!" Sindy gushed in a stage whisper from her seat behind us, dabbing at her heavily made-up eyes with one of her vintage handkerchiefs.

"Will you make like a door and shut up already?" my uncle scolded. "We're trying to have a wedding here." But my aunt was right.

Dani and I would be next. She'd walk down the aisle to meet me in that dress she kept hanging in the closet of the Half Acre, layered with Chantilly and esprit lace like the finest cake.

Oh, and there would be one of those, too.

We didn't know which flavor yet. But we knew we'd be next.

And not because Dani had pulled a tiny, silver three-tiered wedding cake as her charm.

Or because she had dreamed about me the night I tucked that slice of groom's cake under her pillow.

It was because we had found home in each other, together. A place we never wanted to leave. And it was because she loved me just as much as I loved her.

All the rest was just cake.

Keep reading for a special excerpt from the first book

in the *Much "I Do" About Nothing* series

Dictatorship of the Dress

Available now from Berkley Sensation

Terminal C Departures

Really, LaGuardia? One of the busiest airports in the country, and you couldn't come up with a better name? You could've skipped *C* altogether, like some hotels do when they omit the unlucky thirteenth floor. You know, Terminals A, B, D, E . . .

I'm sure there would still be some clueless tourists in life, scratching their heads, consulting their maps. Pointing and asking, *Whatever happened to Terminal C? Where's Terminal C?*

"It's in my bones, Laney Jane." I could still hear Allen's throaty whisper and feel his long, strong drummer's fingers tangle through my hair. "It's not going away this time."

If I were an airport architect, I would've come up with something better. Because only 25 percent of people make it five years through Allen's type of Terminal C.

I pushed on, eager to check my luggage: the crappy soft-sided Samsonite I'd had since college, and the invisible, matched "his and hers" mental baggage I had solely inherited two years back. Perhaps Hawaii would be good for something.

The lame heel on my favorite pair of boots finally gave out, sending me sprawling right foot over left. The heavy garment bag I carried twirled with me as I pirouetted like a demented ballerina across the concourse to the closest bench.

Freakin' A, talk about adding insult to injury. I rubbed my ankle in quick consolation before yanking the boot zipper down the length of my entire calf. They were cheap 8th Street boots, not even worth the fix if it could be made. But they had been my first Big-Girl Paycheck purchase when I moved to the city, and their soles had carried not only me, but also miles of memories. Va-va-voom boots, Allen had christened them upon first sight.

There was no time to mourn them; into the trash they went. I plucked my flip-flops from my carry-on and slipped my freshly pedicured feet into them. Onward.

"Hi, one bag to check, two carry-on items."

The Windwest Airways desk attendant threw a skeptical glance at the bulky garment bag as she reached for my license and boarding pass. "Are you sure you don't want to check that now?"

I could hear my mother's words echoing in my head louder than the PA speakers booming last call for Flight 105 to Miami. *Whatever you do, do not let them check it, Laney. Do* not *hand it off.*

"No, thanks."

Rebel on the outside, mouse on the inside, Allen always used to say. *Do you always do what your mother tells you to do, Laney Jane?* Only Allen Burnside had the cojones to call me out on that.

"We can't guarantee there will be room in the overhead. You may have to gate-check it anyway." The attendant slapped a tag onto my Samsonite and sent it hurling onto the rolling belt, where it was quickly swallowed by two rubber flaps in the wall. She fixed a stare on me that made me wonder whether she got paid a commission per checked bag.

I contemplated the huge midnight blue bag with *Bichonné Bridal Couture* emblazoned across the front in frosty silver lettering. The metal hook of the hanger was cutting into the skin between my thumb and index finger. It would be so easy just to let it go. I imagined it getting chewed up through the luggage shoot, mangled in the greasy, mechanical gears. Stepped on by the handlers' dirty boots. Run over on the tarmac by a baggage cart. Left behind in the dust.

I smiled.

"My mother called ahead. The airline told her a wedding dress could be carried on if the bag was under fifty-one inches."

I watched as the attendant's demeanor did a complete one-eighty; I'm talking ollie-on-the-half-pipe-at-the skate-park one-eighty. "Oh, true!" Her left hand fluttered up near her name tag—April R.—and a lone carat of promise on her ring finger glittered in solidarity. Apparently I had said the two magic words. "I would die if anything happened to my dress. I'm June."

"I'm Laney," I said slowly. "But your name tag says April."

She laughed. "I mean my wedding! I'm a June bride."

And you're an oversharer, but that's okay. "Cool, congrats." I hefted the bag's bulk to my shoulder and used my free, noncrippled hand to grab my carry-on. Out of available limbs, I had no choice but to pop my boarding pass between my lips. April the June bride was still smiling at me expectantly, so I offered my raised brow as valediction and lumbered on.

People talk about a monkey on your back; well, mine was eggshell white silk and taffeta, beaded and sequined and weighing in around ten pounds. About as heavy as my regret, but nowhere near as heavy as my grief.

And it belonged to my mother, the blushing bride.

Third time's the charm, or so they say.

"Shoes in a separate bin, handbags, too. Any metal, loose change . . . take laptops out of their carrying cases," droned the TSA worker. "Separate bins for everything, keep moving."

Strangers around me in various stages of undress—belts whipped off, shoes untied and loosened—shuffled toward security. Oh, crap. I instantly regretted my sock and boot toss as I was forced to kick my flip-flops off. *Think happy thoughts. Clean thoughts. Sanitary thoughts.* My toes curled as my bare feet touched the cold airport floor. In less than twelve hours, I could buff my feet in Kauai sand and let the Pacific wash away the East Coast grime. *Happy thoughts, happy thoughts . . .*

"Is that yours?"

"Yep, that's one of my two allowed personal items." *Personally, though, I wouldn't be caught dead in it.*

"Ain't no bin big enough for that, girl." TSA and I both watched as the garment bag went down the conveyor belt, followed by my bag and my cell phone, chirping happily. It was probably Danica texting, loopy on the time change. I wasn't going to need an alarm clock in Hawaii, not when I had a best friend who was an extreme morning person under normal circumstances. I couldn't imagine Dani on Hawaii-Aleutian Standard Time. I was going to have to slip an Ambien into her mai tai.

Although as heavy as chain mail, the dress made it through the X-ray and metal detector with flying colors. Me, on the other hand . . .

"Anything in your pockets, miss? Belt on?" I shook my head. "Jewelry?"

Allen's class ring.

I hadn't removed the chunky platinum band with its peridot stone since the weekend of our ten-year high school reunion, except to replace the string knotted on the back keeping it snug.

"But it's so small." And LaGuardia Airport was so, so big.

My heart vibrated in my chest like Allen's sticks on the snare drum when he sound-checked to an empty room.

Mr. TSA wasn't backing down. And there was a pileup of travelers in their stocking feet, holding up their trousers and grumbling, behind me. "All right, all right." I plunked the ring into the little gray dog dish, held my breath, and crossed over to the other side.

East Concourse, Gate C15

Nothing a grande latte and a lemon poppy seed muffin wouldn't fix. Ring? *Check*. Dress? *Check*. Phone? Useless, but I had time to power up before boarding. Boarding pass: nowhere to be found.

Are you kidding me?

I could practically hear my mother's voice as I retraced my steps, back through Starbucks and over to the newsstand. "I swear, Laney, you'd lose your *tuchus* if it wasn't stamped on the back of you!" No boarding pass tucked between the trashy novels I had contemplated buying for a beach read. I checked the perfume counter where I had impulse-purchased Aquolina Pink Sugar because no one was around to judge me . . . no sign of it. Nor was it in the restroom, first stall on the right.

I was a ticketed passenger without a ticket.

"Not a problem, we can certainly print a new one up for you, Ms. Hudson." The attendant at the gate clacked manically at her keyboard. "I may even have an upgrade for you. That way you'll be closer to your gown if there's room for it in the first-class closet."

"It's my—" I paused. If I had to be the dress bearer while my mother globe-trotted around with her sugar daddy fiancé, shouldn't I at least milk it for all it was worth? I had lost a boot heel and a boarding pass, but gaining a first-class seat would more than make up for it. "It's my first time on a plane," I finished, flashing pearly whites to go along with my little white lie. "That would be terrific, thank you."

"Oh, then you definitely deserve a bumping up, Miss Bride-to-Be!" she enthused. "I won't know until boarding time, so I'll call you to the desk then, okay?"

"Sounds good."

I made a beeline into the waiting area, in search of my favorite comfy seat and a power source. Between touring on the road with Allen's band and escorting him down to that medical trial in Philadelphia, I was actually a frequent traveler through this particular waiting lounge.

The airline had pairs of great square chairs near the windows, in padded black leather with electrical outlets built right into the armrests. Unfortunately, the only free one was next to a guy in a matchymatch gray suit, draining half the tristate's electric grid. Not only was he hogging both armrest outlets, with his fancy phone and his tablet charging, he was also typing one-handed on a laptop balanced on his knee, its power cord like a tightrope that I had to maneuver past just to get close to the empty seat. At close range, his cologne was a force field I had to skirt around. A hands-free device winked from behind a lock of his thick jet-black hair like a glowing blue locust. This guy was wired to the gills and completely self-absorbed within his sensory-overload bubble.

I made a production of carefully draping the garment bag across the chair before plopping myself down on the floor near the one wall outlet he wasn't zapping power from. New text messages from Danica lit up the minute I plugged in.

Where are you!?!?! TEXT ME.

Sorry, needed to find a plug. Evil supervillain is harnessing all airport energy at his superbase to fuel his death ray.

Tech-Boy had stopped typing. I stole a glance. Maybe that was no ordinary Bluetooth device in his ear: could it read my thoughts? *Or my texts?*

English, please?

Dude totally hogging the outlets at my gate. And now he is staring at me.

Oh. :-) Is he cute?

I flicked my eyes up nonchalantly. He now had his cell phone in his hand and was frowning at the screen as he loosened his tie.

A little like Keanu.

Pre-Matrix or post-Matrix?

Pre-Matrix. But with more technology. And more hair.

LOL. Take a pic!

Are you THAT bored in Hawaii already? What time is it there, anyway?

Laney! Come on. Pic or I don't believe you.

The stuff I do to amuse you, Dani.

I nonchalantly angled my phone and pretended to admire my toes, freshly shellacked in a blue the color of sea glass, and stealthily captured him still in frowning mode. Three button pushes later, his picture was in Hawaii, in my best friend's waiting hand. Gotta love technology.

Pretty hot. I like the scruff.

I snuck another peek. I liked it, too. It was a nice contrast to his high cheekbones.

Maybe I should go buy him an electric razor so he can have one more thing to plug in.

Ha! Maybe he'll be sitting next to you.

Just what I don't need. Thanks.

Come on. Live a little. Think WWDD.

What Would Dani Do? You'd probably be joining the Mile-High Club with some sexy pilot.

LOVE a man in uniform! LOL. But no, not exactly . . . I would keep my eyes open, tho. And you should, too. You're one bad sweater away from becoming a crazy cat lady, you know.

I frowned, glancing down at the long, gray, belted cardigan I had picked for my traveling ensemble. After a day of criminal-butt-whooping badassery, I could totally picture Wonder Woman or Super-girl kicking back to relax in such a thing. It was comfy and hip when paired with my black leggings and high black leather boots . . . although my boots were no more. True, I had picked the sweater's neutral color with the thought in mind that it wouldn't show cat hair as much as black would.

One cat does not a crazy cat lady make, Dan.

Wait, I thought you had three cats.

No, Sister Frances Tappan Zee Got Milk just has a really long name.

LOL. Whatevs. You're about to board a jet for a grand adventure, Laney. At least take off Allen's stupid ring.

I bit the raised stone on the ring guiltily. Even from the middle of the Pacific Ocean, my best friend knew me all too well. The peridot was warm against my lips, but the metal was cold. It was a subject I really didn't feel like talking—or texting—about. I deleted her last comment and changed topics.

They want to upgrade me AND the dress to first class. Isn't that a scream?

Cool. Will it get you here any faster? Cuz your mom is already driving me crazy! Tell me again why she didn't just have her wedding on Long Island. There's a perfectly good beach, like, a mile from your house.

You know my mom . . . she was worried people would get stuck in traffic on the L.I.E.

I sent the last text and smiled, picturing Danica laughing at the absurdity of Hawaii being an easier commute than the Long Island Expressway.

A half hour till boarding time. Reaching into my bag, I pulled out my sketchpad, a fresh Faber-Castell 2B, and my earbuds. Music was essential when I worked, especially with Tech-Boy keeping up his staccato one-hand typing trick just inches away from my eardrums. Using my legging-clad knees as my easel, I began to flesh out an elaborate throne. Coils of wire and tubing emanated from every crack and crevice; if I had my colors handy, I would ink them in neon yellow or toxic green, perfect for the supervillain siphoning all the world's energy for his death ray.

I bit my lip into a smile as I sketched, my lines becoming looser and freer with every stroke of the pencil. Tech-Boy was sprawled spineless in his airport lounge chair now, barking short responses at someone on the other end of his Bluetooth. Funny how one tiny piece of technology was the fine line between socially acceptable and looking like a crazy person ranting into thin air.

In my drawing, he was rod straight in the chair, long fingers gripping the armrests in evil victory. A large *T* was emblazoned across his muscled chest in classic superhero style. I added Bluetooth devices to both ears—why not?—and, for added effect, a metal band around his head like a crown, connecting with bolts to all the tubes. May as well wire his brainpan. With simple wavy lines and a few bursts, I achieved a glow effect in a halo around him.

I was totally lost in my process now, not even aware that I was staring as I studied his facial features. Those cheekbones could cut glass, they were so sharp. His dark eyes were almond shaped, but I could see the curling fan of perfect, lush lashes. I had eyelashes like that, too, but mine came out of a mascara tube. His brow was thick and straight. He was actually a dream to draw. I smudged in his five o'clock shadow with the tip of my pinky, softening his strong jawline.

Allowing myself one last look to make sure I had captured the

2 1982 02861 1287

length and wave of his hair, I was met with a stony, irritated stare. I quickly dropped my eyes and slammed my sketchbook shut. Since leaving my job at Marvel, drawing was a guilty luxury, an escape.

Since losing Allen, I had a hard time being on board with the whole justice-prevailing-over-evil thing. Turns out, the good guys don't always win.